THE COST OF LOVE

THE COST OF LOVE

DRUE ALLEN

FIVE STAR
A part of Gale, Cengage Learning

GALE
CENGAGE Learning

Detroit • New York • San Francisco • New Haven, Conn • Waterville, Maine • London

GALE
CENGAGE Learning

Copyright © 2010 by Vannetta Chapman.
Five Star Publishing, a part of Gale, Cengage Learning.

Set in 11 pt. Plantin.
Printed on permanent paper.

LIBRARY OF CONGRESS CATALOGING-IN-PUBLICATION DATA

Allen, Drue.
  The cost of love / Drue Allen. — 1st ed.
    p. cm.
  ISBN-13: 978-1-59414-867-5 (hardcover : alk. paper)
  ISBN-10: 1-59414-867-8 (hardcover : alk. paper)
  1. Women molecular biologists—Fiction. 2. Terrorists—Fiction. 3. Domestic terrorism—Fiction. 4. Bioterrorism—Prevention—Fiction. 5. New Mexico—Fiction. I. Title.
  PS3601.L418C67 2010
  813'.6—dc22   2009046844

First Edition. First Printing: March 2010.
Published in 2010 in conjunction with Tekno Books.

Printed in the United States of America
1 2 3 4 5 6 7 14 13 12 11 10

This book is dedicated to MOTHER and DADDY. Thank you for giving me everything I needed—and more.

ACKNOWLEDGEMENTS

I would be remiss if I did not acknowledge my first draft readers—Bobby, Donna and mother. Without your critical eye, we wouldn't be in print today.

I appreciate my family's patience during all those days and nights I locked myself away in the study. Bobby, you are my inspiration. Cody, I apologize for spending so much of your growing-up years at my laptop. I hope one day you'll understand why. Kylie, Yale, and Jordyn—you're lucky you weren't there for that part, but I appreciate your encouragement. Yale, thank you for turning me on to SK. He changed my writing in more ways than you can imagine. To friends and family I wouldn't answer phone calls from while I was writing (you know who you are), I apologize. I'd like to say it won't happen again, but we know it will. Thanks for putting up with me and loving me still. Maw, every New Year's, you whispered encouragement to me. Paw, you are such a sweetheart.

Mother, you have always been, and continue to be, my biggest fan. I am lucky to have you.

A special thanks to Mary Sue Seymour for taking a chance on me, Roz Greenberg for acquiring this book, and Jerri Corgiat for being a pleasure to work with during its production.

CHAPTER ONE

Dean Dreiser did not want to start his day viewing a biologically hot, still decomposing body. He preferred stiffs with bullet holes.

He shuffled out of the central command trailer, convinced the biohazard suit he wore had been designed to amplify the desert's heat. It occurred to him he should have taken his dad's offer to help with the family's Brazos River guide business. Why the hell did he think he needed to be a government agent?

If he weren't an agent, he wouldn't be working for U.S. Citizenship and Immigration Services. If he didn't work for US-CIS, he wouldn't be in New Mexico at White Sands Missile Range. At forty miles wide and one hundred miles long, God had forsaken this land long before the U.S. government arrived.

"This way, Agent Dreiser." The lab doctor took off on a southeast heading, assuming Dean would follow.

The man had to be at least seventy and looked as if he'd been in the desert most of those years. His skin had wrinkled up so that he resembled a prune more than a person. By Dean's calculations, the old guy didn't weigh enough to keep his biohazard suit from floating off the desert floor.

Ten yards away, the good doctor noticed Dean had stopped. He turned with the impatient expression of someone who had important lab experiments to run and demanded, "Is there a problem, Agent?"

They could communicate through a universal intercom

system within their suits, a fact that had Dean at a distinct disadvantage. He knew the doc's security clearance, but he did not know the clearance level of every man on this frequency. He'd learned last year what a single security breach could do, and he wouldn't risk it again.

That security breach had come in the form of an agent Dean had met only once—Keith Servensky. A mole inside USCIS, the bastard had nearly killed Dean's best friend and one of their best agents. If someone had checked Servensky's security clearance at every point in the mission, he would have been stopped before he'd done any harm. Instead, he'd pushed his way into operational maneuvers above his level. In the confusion of the moment no one had stopped him. As a result, he was complicit in Operation Dambusters and the killing of thousands in Bath County, Virginia.

Dean wanted his weapon, and he didn't want to state why on an open frequency.

Doctor Kowlson—Dean could see his name sewn on his BHZ suit now that he'd stomped back to join him—raised his left hand, pointed at the blue intercom button, and pushed it. "This opens a direct channel between the two of us. Now, is there a problem, Agent?"

"The problem is my weapon is still in the trailer, and even if I had it, I couldn't very well use it while I'm in this suit."

Doc Kowlson held his gaze for a count of five, then glanced toward heaven as if to pray for mercy. Finally he held up his hands, as if in surrender. He looked to Dean like the Pillsbury Doughboy, hands waving in the morning heat.

Kowlson used his white gloved fingers to enumerate each point, as if the visual would lend credence. "One. You're surrounded by armed military personnel, so one less weapon shouldn't concern you. Two. The threat we face is biological and therefore microscopic. You can't shoot it. Three. It's a fucking ninety-eight degrees and rising, and I'd like to finish before it reaches one-hundred-and-ten. If you don't mind."

Without waiting for an answer, the good doctor shuffled off. Dean had never been put in his place by a Doughboy, and he still wanted his Glock on his person where it belonged. But ten years in active operations had taught him some battles cost more than their net worth. The New Mexico sun combined with the two dozen guards holding a ready military stance—and no biohazard suit—confirmed this would be one of them.

Dean took off after the doc. For a little old guy he moved with amazing speed.

They reached the front of the site in ten minutes. The biohazard dome stretched roughly the size of half a professional football stadium and rose out of the desert like some freakish giant jelly fish. All to cover the location of one deceased?

Another twenty military personnel surrounded the side they approached from, including guards posted at the single entrance. Anyone going in passed through an ocular scan first. Dean started to remove his helmet, but the guard stopped him. The lieutenant, a young man who couldn't have seen thirty, placed the scanner over Dean's helmet and waited for the light to blink green.

The site resembled a NASA moon outpost he'd seen in some old science fiction movie. It was easy to forget Albuquerque lay just seventy-five miles to the northwest. Once the scanner confirmed his identity, the guard allowed him to pass. Dean stepped inside the dome, thinking the inside could not be more surprising than the outside. He was wrong. The facility glowed with enough computer and satellite equipment to run a very large, very advanced op.

As if in answer to his unspoken question, Doc Kowlson said, "All computers respond to voice prompts, since typing in these suits is quite cumbersome. Of course, each computer has to be synced to the operator's voice nuances. The victim's body is over here."

A smaller tent, approximately twenty feet by twenty feet, sat off to one side. A separate air supply ran from this structure into a filtration system and out of the bigger dome to an area Dean couldn't see.

"Still a hot zone?" Dean asked.

"Yes, and it will remain contaminated for some time. Possibly years."

They stopped outside the smaller tent's entrance, where yet another armed guard stood at attention. This one recognized Kowlson and stepped aside when he approached. Instead of entering, the doctor turned to Dean, held out a hand to prevent him from going any further.

"Do you have any firsthand experience with victims of biological attacks, Agent Dreiser?"

"I've seen plenty of vics, Doc."

Kowlson paused, then nodded. "I'm sure you have. Biological weapons have a way of degrading the body, as you've been taught. It can be disorienting when you witness this. The body has a natural reaction, wants to reject what it sees—often by vomiting. You must fight this response since you're in a biohazard suit. Under no circumstance should you attempt to pull off your hood, or one of the men inside will shoot you with a tranquilizer."

"I appreciate the lecture." Dean shifted in his suit, but never broke eye contact with the doc. "I have a terrorist to catch, so can we get on with this?"

He saw something less cynical appear in Kowlson's eyes, then it vanished like a fleeing shadow. It wasn't a look of doubt—regret maybe. Before he could figure out why the man might have misgivings, they entered the hot zone.

"Push your yellow com button. All communication within

this zone must be recorded."

Dean pushed the button. Let the shirts in Langley review his every word from their safe distance. If he did his job well, they'd have that luxury. If he didn't, no doubt Virginia would be on the target list.

Four additional guards stood watch over the victim inside the tent. They stood at rigid attention—their weapons at the ready. Their eyes never met Dean's. They reminded him of the sentries posted at the unknown soldier's grave in Washington D.C.

Even through his suit, he noticed a marked drop in the temperature.

"The colder temperature maintains the integrity of the body," Dr. Kowlson said.

The young woman, if she could still be called that, lay on the floor in the middle of the area. She wore hiking clothes—khaki shorts, a t-shirt, and sturdy boots. The shirt had been sheared up the middle for the preliminary autopsy.

Dean's first sight of the victim told him why Kowlson had felt the need to issue his warning. He'd seen many victims in various stages of dismemberment, but he'd never seen one with most of their skin dissolved.

He swallowed the bile that rose in his throat, kept his hands still at his side. Some lab technician outside would be reading his heart rate. Fuck them. Anyone who could look at this poor girl and not register an increased heart rate wasn't human.

"Estimated time of death?" Dean forced his voice to sound normal.

"Less than twelve hours ago."

"How is that possible?"

"This agent works quickly, as weaponized forms usually do. I would like to say her death was painless, but my medical opinion is, it was not."

Dean glanced up as new guards replaced the men who had

been standing there.

"We rotate guards every seven minutes. We're fully protected in our suits, of course, but it makes everyone feel better—psychologically—if we rotate the personnel."

"Who found her?"

"Two hikers who were, let's say, lost."

"What will happen to them?"

"That is not my problem, or yours."

Dean willed his feet to step closer to the girl. His skin began to tingle and burn, but he recognized it as a psychosomatic response to what he was seeing. He wanted the expression of horror on her face engraved on his memory. The more he understood of what she had endured, the better chance he had of catching these bastards. And he would catch them.

"Why is only the hair from the front half of her scalp gone?"

"A good question. When she inhaled the bio-agent, it went to work immediately, dissolving the skin around her face. The hair at the front of her scalp lost purchase and fell out. The agent then travelled down the bronchial tube toward her lungs, which is why you see the burn marks down her throat."

"She didn't grab her neck?" Dean squatted beside the body.

"She didn't have time. That would have been a natural reaction to a tickle along the throat. But at the same time her esophagus began to burn, the bio-agent paralyzed all the neurons in her brain. Although she wanted to grasp her neck, her fingers had forgotten how."

"She would have collapsed then."

"Yes, but she wouldn't have been able to crawl or move." The doctor now spoke in a clinical, detached tone.

"She would have been conscious?"

"So our preliminary results indicate."

"For how long?"

"Perhaps ten minutes. No longer. Much of her skin dissolved

causing her to sustain a great amount of blood loss. She bled out. That, technically, would be the cause of death. It would have been a very agonizing ten minutes."

Dean had all the information he came for, but he stayed a moment longer, stared into pale blue eyes that would never again see a New Mexico sunrise.

"Approximate age?" he asked softly.

"Early twenties."

Dean stood and made eye contact with Kowlson who nodded toward the opposite end of the tent.

They exited out a different door, where they passed through three different showers. Dean would have stood through a dozen had he been ordered to—anything to mitigate the burning and itching that had begun in his throat but now had spread to every inch of his body. Then he stripped and stood under two additional showers, dressed, and again submitted to the ocular scan. Stepping into the desert sun, he took a deep, steadying gulp of fresh air.

As an afterthought, he turned back to the guard. "We're being extra careful that the same folks who go in, come out."

The lieutenant—this one a woman and no older than the one at the entrance—didn't bother to reply.

Dr. Kowlson joined him, and they made their way back toward Dean's once-red Jeep. A layer of dirt made it nearly indistinguishable from the surrounding desert. Anyone watching would be hard pressed to name the color, or year, for that matter. The Jeep had seen better days, as had Dean.

He could have been imagining it, but the old guy seemed less pissy.

"You handled yourself well in there," Kowlson said.

"It's my job, sir." Dean held out his hand, shook the doc's, then climbed into his Jeep. "What kind of bastards create something able to do that?"

"The worst kind. Ones we haven't had on our soil before."

Dean stared out through his windshield, but made no move to drive away.

"We're sending you the best person we have in bioterrorism," Kowlson said. "She's a genius in the area of bioweaponized agents, and she completed field ops training last month. Her name is Dr. Lucinda Brown. She's better than whoever did this."

"She'll have to be."

Kowlson nodded and stepped back. They both recognized the task facing them was daunting, had both received the same encrypted message from headquarters three hours earlier:

Terror alert critical. Attack imminent. Message received and confirmed—
What you will find in the desert is only a taste. You cannot stop the justice you deserve. We will strike where you will suffer the most. We will strike swiftly. We will strike soon.

While the terrorists hadn't made any demands, they had made themselves clear. According to their analysts, the attack would occur in ten to fourteen days, and the weapon would be dispersed over a minimum of six major metropolitan areas. No why. No terms of negotiation. Only the threat and the proof they could do what they claimed.

Dean started the engine and drove through the makeshift military facility that had been set up around the victim's body—a body found in the middle of a government base. As he drove the sun continued its daily climb, oblivious to the plans of men.

Why New Mexico, why now, and why on his shift? Why had the terrorists even bothered sending the message? It had told them nothing, but had managed to put them on alert. Why would they want to do that? Commander Martin had relayed nothing else. More data would come from the body of the girl. Bodies always gave up their secrets—eventually.

Dean pulled to the side of the road in time to vomit up the little he'd eaten for breakfast. He grabbed a bottle of water from behind his seat to wash the taste of sour coffee out of his mouth. They'd never shown him corpses with no skin in ops training. He'd battled many terrorists in his ten years, but he'd never dealt with one his trusty Glock couldn't kill.

Leaning against the door, he gazed out over the barren landscape.

Dr. Brown better be as good as her reputation. USCIS had staked all their lives on it.

CHAPTER TWO

Dean drove the Jeep north out of White Sands, turned east on 380, then north again, toward Corona. On a direct route he would hit Roswell in two hours, but his job rarely allowed for doing things directly.

The temperature had topped one hundred when he pulled into the run-down Texaco station. He was relieved to see his old Ford truck waiting for him. Commander Martin sat in a black SUV with another agent. When he spotted Dean, he stepped out. The other agent stayed inside, staring straight ahead.

Dean set the brake, unfolded himself from the Jeep, and shook his boss's hand. Martin's handshake was firm, the grip of a man who didn't need to prove a thing.

"New kid?" Dean nodded toward the SUV.

"Rookie," Martin explained in a low voice. "We have him moving cars."

"Rookies have to start somewhere—moving cars is a good, safe place." Dean glanced back at the young agent. "Are you sure he has his license?"

Martin laughed. "We're aging, Dean. I feel it on mornings like this."

The no-nonsense confidence of his boss and the calm way he had of looking you straight in the eye caused Dean to think of his father. He should call home more.

Martin was nearly Dean's height at five foot ten, with no sign of a middle-age spread. His hair was grayer now than it had been six months ago, but at sixty-five he had the physical bearing of a man half his age. Standing next to his boss in the desert sun, Dean realized he *was* half his age. After ten years, they knew each other well. Dean recognized when a silence stretched long enough to indicate there might be more information than his commander could officially share.

The shadows around Martin's eyes had deepened since they'd last met. Had there been more than the single body at White Sands?

Martin nodded once. "You made good time."

"Yes, sir. Not much to slow you down between the Missile Range and here."

"It's a wasteland. That's the truth." Martin walked away from their vehicles.

Dean followed. They stood watching the occasional car pass. Even at the height of tourist season, Corona didn't see much of summer crowds. Most drivers stuck to the interstates, and locals were otherwise occupied at two in the afternoon.

Dean had learned patience and normally took information as his boss saw fit to dole it out. But the girl's image still haunted him. "Any idea who these bastards are?"

"No."

"Foreign or domestic?"

"God help us if they're domestic. Honestly we don't know. We can't rule anyone out."

Dean considered the top ten terrorist groups on the list. He knew the foreign groups were capable—they had openly declared war against them again and again. But could Americans do something like this to Americans? He didn't think so.

"We've narrowed their operation down to forty possible locations," Martin said. "All in the lower half of the state. I ranked Roswell in the top six."

"Because—"

"Several reasons. It's midsize, so activity is less likely to be noticed. Roswell's notoriety could be an advantage. The occasional odd story will be dismissed as another nut's attempt to be in the spotlight. Then there's its proximity to the military base. These bastards are arrogant."

"Do you think that's the reason they dumped the body I saw at White Sands?" Dean didn't move as he waited for Martin's answer. His shirt had begun to stick to his back, and the cap he wore did little to fend off the heat pouring down.

"I don't think they dumped her there. I think they killed her there. Make no mistake, Dean. So far, they have orchestrated every step. They're shitting in our backyard and then sitting back and laughing as we try to figure out how they got in."

"We will catch them, sir."

"Hell yes, we'll catch them. But we have to do it before what you saw this morning is released on the general population."

A mini-SUV pulled into the station, a Navajo mother and three children spilled out as soon as the wheels stopped. Dean thought of how many families would be in danger should the terrorists succeed. His mind flashed back on the bodies he had zipped into bags in Virginia last year, but he pushed the memory away.

The middle child, probably two years old, squatted beside the SUV and played with a small dump truck, rolling it back and forth in the dirt. He either didn't hear his mother calling or couldn't be interrupted. His playing was serious work. The mother switched her baby to her other hip, circled impatiently back, reached down, and plucked his collar. As the mom urged him toward the station, the boy ran the truck back-and-forth across his pants leg.

Dean watched the scene play out, one hardly worth noticing, one of thousands that day in hundreds of desert towns. Families unaware of the danger lurking in their midst. He watched, remembered Virginia, and swore it wouldn't happen again. Not if he could stop it.

When the family had gone into the store, Martin clapped Dean on the back, and they walked back toward their vehicles. The rookie agent slid behind the wheel of the red Jeep. Without a word to either of them, he started it, then pulled onto the four-lane highway back in the direction Dean had come.

"My gut tells me something will occur in Roswell," Martin said. "That's why I put you undercover at E.T.'s. How's that going?"

"Great. I'm a natural bartender." Dean stood straighter, tried not to look as exhausted as he felt.

"Pull your full shift at the bar tonight, then pick up Agent Brown in Albuquerque tomorrow. You've arranged her cover?"

"Yes, sir."

"Good. I've sent the details of her arrival to your PDA."

"Not a problem, boss."

Dean unlocked the old truck and cranked the window down. It would be a long day and a longer night. He might steal three hours sleep after his shift at E.T.'s.

He gave his boss the easy smile everyone expected. The last time they spoke, Martin had teased him about his handle—Falcon. It was a sign of his age that he'd been around long enough to have one. Dean would bet his old friend Aiden Lewis had started the Falcon label. It would be just like the wiseass to name him after a bird.

"I'll try to insert another agent in Roswell," Martin said. "For now, assume you and Brown are on your own. We don't want to tip our hand. There's too much riding on this."

"I understand."

"I think you do. I know I don't have to say this, Dean. You've served on more than your share of missions. After what we went through together in Glacier and Virginia, I wish I could say you've seen the worst there is to see."

Martin's gaze met his. For a moment, the man's tiredness was replaced by something Dean couldn't have imagined the day before—vulnerability. It slipped away as quickly as it appeared, but Dean realized the only man he'd ever worked for at USCIS wouldn't live forever. The thought unnerved him as much as the body he'd viewed a few hours ago.

"Be careful."

"Always, sir."

Dean had no trouble finding a parking space at Albuquerque International Sunport.

The place was characteristically uncrowded at six in the morning. Why Agent Brown had opted to take the red eye was beyond him, but then he had a lot to learn about his new partner. They had a three hour trip back to Roswell—plenty of time for him to brief her. He'd also be able to get a basic feel for how she operated. Although, if Lucinda Brown was similar to the other women Dean had known in ops, she'd be like one of the guys—which meant she'd spend the two hundred mile drive sleeping, not yapping. Good thing too. Dean's head still pounded in spite of the four Tylenol tablets he'd popped before leaving Roswell.

Undercover bartender was his dream cover job only eight years ago in Chicago. Not anymore. Had he aged so much? The late hours were kicking his ass, and the smoke irritated the hell out of his allergies. Add in a few nightmares complete with skinless victims crawling across the desert begging for help, and Dean did not feel his sunny best. Walking into the terminal, he knew he resembled a falcon less than he did a bad-tempered crow.

As he scanned baggage claim, Dean tried to push down his temper. Where the hell was Lucinda Brown? The area remained empty except for a mother dragging two kids behind her and a very young, skinny woman talking on a cell phone. Maybe he had the wrong gate. Hell, considering how little he'd slept, he could have the wrong airport. Damn zombies and terrorists had chased him all night long.

Maybe her plane had been delayed. Dean pulled out his BlackBerry and searched for the email with her flight information. He was so busy paging through emails and ignoring the throbbing in his head, he barely realized the woman with kids had left. Some part of his brain did notice the skinny lady crossing the room.

"Agent Dreiser?"

Dean's head snapped up.

"I'm Lucy Brown. Nice to meet you." She held out a slim, brown hand, tilted her head like a terrier, and waited.

"Uh, yeah. I'm Dean Dreiser." Dean shook her hand, hastily, and let go of it. Then he glanced around the baggage area as if he might find another Lucinda Brown. "You're Agent Brown?"

"I am. I only have my backpack and this one bag. So if you're ready . . ."

She seemed to be waiting, although Dean couldn't imagine for what. "Ready?" he asked.

"To go to Roswell."

Dean shook his head as if it would clarify what she was talking about. "You are not my new partner."

"Yes, I am. Is there a problem? Do you need to see my identification?"

Dean stood staring and tried to remember how old you had to be to go through field ops training. He was a field agent not a babysitter. She reminded him of his little sister—a hundred and twenty pounds of naivety that had probably never stood in the line of fire.

The pounding in Dean's head increased and the weight of

his responsibilities caused his stomach to clench. Your partner covered your ass. How old was she? He couldn't do it. He couldn't watch over her. He backed away, realizing she was looking at him warily, as if something was wrong with him.

Then he heard Kowlson's voice. "She completed field ops a month ago."

"You all right, Agent Dreiser?" She stepped closer, peered up at him.

Dean watched her lips move, but remembered himself asking, "Approximate age?"

"Early twenties." The doc had said.

But that was the age of the victim. The faces and numbers collided in Dean's mind. He drew a deep breath. Had he read Agent Brown was twenty-eight? Brand spanking new to USCIS, and her file so glowing with recommendations, he'd overlooked the fact that she had no experience. And how did he know? That look on her face said it all—rookie. Might as well give her a t-shirt that proclaimed it. She should be moving cars, not going undercover in a hot spot.

She was all of five feet, five inches, with black hair cascading down her back. Large eyes gazed at him from an oval face. Without question she was Spanish, as her first name suggested, and something else as well. Cop eyes—that's what stared at him now. He'd read it in her file. Her dad worked as a Boston cop, and her mom had once been a semi-famous dancer.

She was beautiful, but in Dean's mind that counted as another point against her.

And damn sure not experienced enough to be assigned to a covert operation of this magnitude.

"Well, shit," Dean said. Thinking that summed things up, he turned and strode out of the airport, hoping she wouldn't follow. Knowing she would.

At the Ford, he held the door open for her because it was

second nature. She climbed in and tucked the backpack near her feet. It was a damn good thing she didn't comment on the old truck, or he would have taken her back inside, orders or no orders.

Stowing her single bag in the truck's bed, he slammed the tailgate hard enough to vent some of his frustration. Backing out of the parking space, he glanced her way. She sat there watching him with the same expectant, patient gaze she'd worn in the airport.

Tugging on his ball cap, he accelerated on to Interstate Forty East.

Lucy Brown studied Agent Dean Dreiser as he drove. There might have been a day when he wasn't bad looking, but that day had come and gone. The man needed a shave and a vacation. In fact, he looked like he needed a retirement pension.

She'd grown up around men like him all her life—washed-up cops. Dean Dreiser could be the poster child for burned-out, in-need-of-retirement cops.

At five-foot-eleven, he couldn't have weighed more than one-eighty. Scrawny. The man looked scrawny. He sported a three-day growth of beard. His hair curled past his collar, a good two inches past regulation length. Both mirrored the color of the desert sand outside their window. Crow's feet lined deep blue eyes. Before he'd shoved the sunglasses on, she'd noted the eyes—blue as the sea back home in Boston, and bloodshot if she wasn't mistaken. She didn't have to be a detective to deduce that bartending might be too perfect a cover for the man.

His file listed his age as thirty-five, but watching him in the New Mexico morning light, Lucy would have guessed him to be closer to forty-five. She'd heard and read about his ops— more ops than an agent should have in ten years—highlighted by jobs in Barcelona, Mexico, Glacier, and Virginia. The man

25

was notorious for working in the background, catching the perp, and slipping away like a shadow before the sun.

Lucy had a hard time reconciling the file with the person sitting beside her.

"You're a man of few words," she said, once he had maneuvered the pickup onto the interstate. "Two if we count *well* and *shit*."

"Look Agent Brown, we might as well get this out of the way up front."

"Please. Let's do."

"Obviously they've rushed your training."

"Is that so?" Lucy leaned against the door so she could study him. Dean Dreiser wasn't the first man to try to set her straight. She always enjoyed watching them squirm as they dispensed their friendly advice.

"Hell yes, and I would be irresponsible to let you go galloping into harm's way at this early stage in your career."

"Don't hold back, Agent Dreiser. Please, go on and explain to me how you can tell in less than an hour that I have been under-trained."

Dean glanced her way, apparently trying to judge if she was kidding. She watched him mentally calculate the odds she'd slug him. It was like staring at the gears of an old clock. He grimaced. Set the old truck on cruise. Draped his hand over the wheel, and adjusted the visor. She'd seen the same patronizing look before. No doubt, he was trying to think of how to break it to her easy. It wasn't so much their chauvinistic attitudes as their protective tendencies that made her want to laugh. Or gag.

"Glad you're willing to listen," Dean said. "Some agents aren't. What with your higher level of education—I read your file—I hope you'll consider the logic in what I'm saying."

Lucy took off her sunglasses and encouraged him with a smile, doling out her charm like a nice section of rope. Hopefully he'd take all that was necessary to hang himself.

"Field ops is dirty business," he explained. "And don't think I'm saying this because you're a woman. We have women. Hell yeah, we do. 'Course most of them are big. Someone small, like yourself, well, I don't suppose that matters."

"It doesn't take a large person to aim a weapon."

"True."

"And I am an expert marksman."

Dean hesitated, then continued. "I read your qualifications, but expert marksman on a range is one thing. Expert in the field can be another. Have you ever killed someone?"

"Well, no."

"Ever shot anyone?"

"No."

"Ever had a weapon aimed at you?"

"This is ridiculous."

"Have you been undercover before?"

"Of course not, but—"

Lucy could sense Dean gaining confidence with each question. Suddenly she wasn't so sure who was holding the rope anymore, or who was being tripped up by it. She couldn't hold the false smile in place any longer. It melted at the exact moment Dean hit lecture mode.

"Every agent has to be trained some time. I realize that. But undercover with me is not the place or the time. I won't be responsible for putting you in a dangerous situation. This thing we're dealing with in Roswell is the worst I've seen in ten years. It's a helluva thing to begin on, and I'll have the assigning agent's head on a platter when I find out who put you in the middle of this."

"That agent would be Commander Martin. He called me personally and said I was being assigned to you."

He stared at her for one heartbeat, then two. The truck drifted into the next lane. Dean jerked it back. Silence filled the truck for several seconds. "Where was I?"

"You were explaining how my training hasn't been adequate."

"Right. I know you graduated top in your class, but this is no ordinary mission. Rookies start out moving cars, practicing covert procedures, tailing an experienced field agent. They're steps every agent needs to take in real field work—"

"Unless there's a national emergency," Lucy said softly.

"That's my point. We're in the midst of a national emergency. We don't know how many terrorists are involved."

"Plus there's the weapon to find," Lucy reminded him.

"Correct."

"Which I'm sure you know how to disarm."

Dean shook his head. "Nope. I'm a field rat. I don't know any of the molecular shit. Once I find it, I'll call in and talk to the lab coats."

"And what if you can't reach the lab coats, Agent Dreiser?" Lucy put on her sunglasses. "What will you do then? Risk your life or the lives of all those in a hundred- or perhaps a thousand-mile radius? Some biological weapons carry that far."

Dean switched driving hands, wiping his left on his jeans. "We're not talking about me right now. I'll figure out what to do when the time comes."

"But it is *my* job, isn't it, Dreiser? My little old doctorate in molecular biology from MIT that American taxpayers paid for should be used for something, shouldn't it? And what if you can't reach me on a cell phone? Then what?"

"Now look Agent Brown—"

"*Doctor* Brown. You can call me *Doctor* Brown."

"Fine, *Doc* Brown. This isn't a classroom or laboratory. These terrorists would kill you, or that school bus full of kids we just passed, without a second thought. They might pause to torture you first. You're not ready—"

"Cut the crap, Dreiser." Lucy's Spanish temper flared, even as she heard her mama's voice warn her to keep a handle on it, even as she thought of her brother and how much stopping these bastards meant to her and to him. "You don't know if I'm ready. Maybe it does scare the shit out of me, but I'm here to do a job. I'll stay until it's done. Let's get *this* out of the way up front: I'm your partner whether you like it or not."

"We'll see about that." Dean punched the accelerator. They sped past a group of teens on motorcycles.

"I guess we will."

"We're meeting with Commander Martin tomorrow night. We'll let him decide."

"We could assume he already has since he sent me here."

"I happen to think he made a mistake."

Lucy knew she should shut up, could still hear her mama's voice ringing in her ears. Like every time before, she chose to ignore it. "When he sees your bloodshot eyes, he might agree."

Dean didn't answer. He kept the truck in the left lane and glared out at the desert landscape.

Dean had expected her to talk the entire way. Hell. He expected her to yell at him the entire way. So he was surprised when, ten minutes outside of Albuquerque, she fell asleep. He shrugged. At least one of them would be rested when they reached Roswell, which, at the rate he was driving, they would do in record time.

Ninety minutes later, he pulled into a station in Vaughn, got out and slammed the door. After a pit stop, he picked up a donut and coffee. He practically collided with Lucy when she exited the ladies' room.

"For me?" She eyed him warily.

"Actually, it is."

"Peace offering?"

"Nope. It's breakfast. You're driving." He thrust it into her hands and vanished. By the time she climbed into the truck, he'd sunk into his seat and pulled his cap low enough to block out most of the sun and all of her.

"If you weren't hungover, you wouldn't be so cranky."

"I don't recall asking you, Doc."

"A medical observation," Lucy said. Gravel flew as she floored the accelerator.

"This truck is an eighty-two. It has to last us two weeks. You might go easy on her."

"Her? Why do men insist on calling trucks her? Trucks, ships, planes. They're all female. Why?"

"Because we like the illusion of control over something feminine. Did you need to hear me say that?" Dean scowled at her and tried not to envy her energy.

"Yeah. I did. Thank you." Lucy smiled as she took a big bite of the chocolate donut.

"Can I sleep now?"

"Absolutely. Sleep away." She reached for the radio, set the volume low. George Strait whispered through the cab.

But violin and a steel guitar weren't the last things Dean heard before sleep claimed him. The sound following him into his dreams was the light, somewhat off-key singing of Lucinda Brown.

CHAPTER THREE

Lucy had planned on waking Dean when they reached Roswell, but she didn't have to. Twenty minutes outside of town he sat up, rubbed his hands over the stubble on his face, and started briefing her. The man must have a damn GPS in his head.

"The place we work, E.T.'s Bar, is on the southwest side of town, near the Hondo River. You're a friend of my sister's who needs a job. Sally, the lady who owns the place, happens to be a hand short on waitresses—"

"Tell me we didn't kill someone."

Dean gave her a wolfish grin. "You're confusing us with the FBI. We work for Immigration Services. We don't kill citizens. We relocate them."

"We deported her?"

"Jill is fine. She'd been talking about moving to the west coast for months. Winning a mid-range lottery prize last week was all the push she needed."

"The statistical odds of someone winning the lottery at the exact moment we need them to would be approximately . . ."

Dean reached into the back seat and pulled a short-sleeved, button-up shirt off a hanger. "Save the brain energy, Doc. We planted the winning ticket, and don't let the ethics worry you. It cost the good taxpayers a hell of a lot less than your average relocation deal."

Lucy was worrying all right, but not about the ethics of relocating innocents. Dean had begun to undress in the truck,

31

and Lucy thought she might drive off the blacktop.

He had pulled off his jacket, revealing a white undershirt and an antique shoulder holster—the kind even her father didn't wear anymore. At the moment it held no weapon.

The holster she could ignore. The biceps she couldn't. Damn. He was sculpted better than the plastic model in med school that the students had called Mr. T.

Dean reached across her to pull down her visor. Clipped to the visor was a holster holding his weapon, which he removed and placed on the seat between them after ejecting the clip. When he brushed against her, goosebumps danced down Lucy's arms. Ridiculous. She was a doctor, and she was a government agent. She would not be aroused by this burned-out has-been.

He'd struck her as scrawny earlier, but now that she'd seen him without his clothes, she needed to revise her medical opinion. The man had more muscles than someone so old and burned-out should have. "You're staring, Doc."

Holding a dare, blue eyes paused inches from brown ones. Lucy jammed her sunglasses back on and shifted her attention to the road. "If I'm staring, it's at that ancient Glock. Why not carry around a rock to whack people with instead?"

He gave her a genuine grin—one without sarcasm or weariness—startling her. Double damn. She must be exhausted. Maybe she could blame the desert heat. Possibly he'd drugged her coffee.

Or perhaps she'd misjudged him.

That was a disturbing thought. She continued to steal glances at him as he checked and holstered his weapon. No, he might not be as homely as an ugly pup, but, grin or not, the man was still completely devoid of personality. Lucky for her this op would only last ten days. She could tolerate him that long—she'd had colds last longer.

She'd have to think of him like the old stray dog her family had taken in the summer she'd turned fifteen. The mutt had shown up the first day of summer break, looking like he hadn't had a meal in weeks. Stayed around long enough to get some meat on his bones and steal their hearts. By the time the leaves changed to gold and drifted to the ground, Jake had shoved on. There was a lesson in that.

"You look like you're chewing on something, Doc. I worry when you stop talking." Dean took off the holster, put on the shirt and buttoned it. As he unzipped his jeans, he sent Lucy another smile—and, damn, her heart skipped a beat. Tucking the shirt in, he re-zipped the jeans.

Lucy thought about offering to help, but bit it back. Dean slid the old holster rig back on, then slipped the clip into the Glock and the Glock into the holster. The brown bomber jacket sat like icing on his rough-assed cake.

"You're going to wear a jacket?" Her voice actually cracked. Sweat trickled down the small of her back, and she tried to convince herself the air conditioner needed service. She'd always been a sucker for old leather jackets. "It's obvious you're carrying. No one would wear a jacket in this heat."

"A/C is freezing at E.T.'s. Besides, most folks in Roswell carry a firearm. It's not a problem with the sheriff so long as they have a permit." He settled back into the corner and studied her. "Tell me you declared and brought your weapon on the plane."

"Of course."

"Let me see it."

"No."

"Let me see your weapon, Agent Brown."

"Now you're being nosy and personal." Lucy felt decidedly cranky. What she could use was a glass of ice water.

"Are you always so damn stubborn?"

She changed the subject. "Tell me more about my job."

Dean tugged on his cap, a sure sign she'd irritated him. It instantly improved her mood.

"I told you about Sally."

"And that Jill won the lottery."

"Right. So Sally's walking around, spitting nails and whining about how hard a time she has finding good help," Dean continued. "I mention my little sister's college roommate might be looking for a summer job. I let her beg a little, then tell her you might be willing to come through this way since you've always been fascinated with UFOs."

"I what?" Lucy's voice went up a full octave.

"You know everything there is to know about UFOs, Doc. Which is why you're willing to come to Roswell for a waitressing job paying minimum wage. The low pay also explains why you're bunking in what used to be the town's whorehouse. Now it's a motel, if you define motel loosely enough. The good news is it looks out across the alley behind the bar."

"Back up to the whorehouse part."

"Don't worry. The sheets are clean. Josephine's been out of the business—at least officially—for years. The more important point is, we can watch that back alley from our rooms."

"Great. A whorehouse and a back alley view."

"Commander Martin thinks E.T.'s might somehow be involved. That's why he set up our cover there. It's a central hub of the town. Either someone who works there, or someone who frequents the establishment is involved or knows information we need to attain."

They drove past the Roswell city limit sign, complete with a little alien symbol. Lucy paused at the first stop sign long enough to roll down her window and pour out the remains of her coffee. The hot, fresh air revived her, so she left the window down, proceeding through town without asking directions. She had punched E.T.'s into her handheld GPS unit while Dean talked. She did love new gadgets; this technological marvel had debuted only last month. Smaller than the average cell phone, it fit in her palm.

"Do I have time to unpack before my first shift?" She thumbed through the display with one hand and drove with the other, noting his look of aggravation.

"What the hell are you doing?"

Why did it bring her such satisfaction to irritate this man? "Playing with my GPS."

"Well turn it the fuck off."

"What?"

"You heard me. Give it to me."

Dean slid to the middle of the truck and tried to grab the unit, but Lucy switched it to her left hand and held it out the window.

"Are you crazy, Dreiser? What the hell is wrong with you?"

"Don't you know they can track you with those things?"

"Right. By *they* do you mean the bad guys or the aliens?"

"Turn it the fuck off."

"Because I have to tell you, at the moment, I'm more freaked out by you than I am by terrorists or little green men."

As they argued, Dean continued trying to grab the GPS, but Lucy refused to give it up. Every time Dean reached for her hand, Lucy jerked the wheel. A few locals stopped and stared as the truck lurched down Main Street, jumping back-and-forth across the median line.

Dean finally settled back to his side and lowered his voice, tugging so hard on his cap, Lucy feared for his head.

"Look, Doc. As we established, you're new. Maybe the instructors didn't get around to mentioning you can't carry around every new gadget on the commercial market. If you can find your position via satellites then you can be tracked the same way. Now turn the damn thing off."

Lucy spied E.T.'s Bar out the front window of the truck, thumbed off her GPS unit. "We'll talk about this later," she said sweetly as she parked the truck a few doors down.

Dean got out and slammed the door. "Damn straight we will."

"When's my shift?" Lucy grabbed her backpack and met him at the front of the truck. She placed the keys in his hands.

"You're on at three, beautiful."

Lucy refused to respond to the compliment, though her heart did jump. A purely physiological reaction. Her brain knew he only meant to bait her. "Then I have plenty of time to unpack. Where's my room?"

"Don't worry your pretty little brain about unpacking. I imagine once we talk to Commander Martin and get this thing cleared up you'll only be here one night. Why don't you go shopping or something?"

Instead of answering, Lucy stepped up to the wooden boardwalk. They'd undoubtedly been added to give the place an authentic feel, but they didn't. Something wrong lurked here. When she glanced toward the door of E.T.'s, she thought of the old western movies she watched as a girl.

Sunlight from the summer morning spilled across the planks, but a part of her mind saw blood splashed across the boards. Cold crept down her spine, and she shivered in spite of the heat. Her mother would say someone had walked over her grave. Lucy pushed the premonition away, denied again the gift her family insisted she had.

She made her way back to where Dean waited beside the truck. She stopped where she could look him straight in the eyes. Damn cowboy with his old weapon and his outdated attitudes. She would not be run off her first assignment by a relic.

"You don't decide when I leave. Okay, Dean? You promised me a job for the summer, and you know how college girls need summer money." She stepped closer, into his personal space, didn't bother to move when her breasts brushed up against him.

Show no weakness. Never back down.

"I'll go meet Miss Sally now. Then I'll be back for my suitcase. I'll rest and unpack. Everything. Even my lacey lingerie."

She gave him her best smile, but didn't allow it to carry to her eyes. Then, she stomped down the boardwalk toward E.T.'s.

Dean watched Lucy storm into E.T.'s, then sagged onto an old bench in front of a closed antique store.

He could handle the concept that Lucy Brown was the smartest agent on the boardwalk—possibly smart enough to save a lot of lives. Lives lost if it were left up to him. Yes, he did realize what was at risk.

What he struggled with sitting in the August morning was the dead girl's image he'd seen yesterday morning superimposed over Lucy's features. Lucy had no idea how fucking vulnerable she might be. Why the hell did he have to draw her for a partner? What had Martin been thinking?

Brains should come in a bigger, tougher package.

Had he ever been so young? Hell, he was only thirty-five. But at Lucy's age, he'd been an agent for three years. Been in Barcelona, picking up pieces of a plane, bagging bodies. Since then he'd taken two hits in the leg in Mexico. Recovered hundreds of bodies in Virginia.

Hell. How could he train her, watch her back, catch the terrorists and be on guard against a weapon he couldn't see?

Both Doctor Kowlson and Commander Martin claimed Lucy was the best. He needed to trust them. In spite of what he'd said to her, he really had no choice. Truth was he needed her. God it hurt to admit that. He didn't mind needing his partner, but he did mind getting an erection sitting beside her in the truck.

The woman had no idea how damn sexy she was.

Dean stood, started toward the truck and found himself yearning for the good old days—a sure sign this job had aged him. What he'd give to have Aiden Lewis for his partner again. And wouldn't his friend be laughing at him now.

No. He wouldn't laugh about what waited in the desert. More importantly, he would be in Roswell on the first flight if Dean placed the call—with or without Martin's orders. Their friendship went deeper than USCIS. Aiden remained Dean's ace in the hole, and he hoped he wouldn't have to play it. Aiden was home, safe with his wife and baby. Dean didn't want to bring him here, not considering what he'd seen at White Sands.

But what to do about Lucy?

Maybe he had underestimated her. If he could talk the GPS out of her hands. If he could see what kind of pussy gun she packed. If he could convince her there was a difference between a disease in her lab and a biological weapon that ravaged the body of a young girl. A young girl and how many others? For Dean suspected there had been other victims already.

He needed answers, but he realized he would find none standing next to the old truck.

The country rapping of Big & Rich interrupted his heavy thoughts. Three of Sally's regulars, Bubba, Billy, and Colton, pulled up to the curb in a Dodge truck that belonged in a commercial instead of on Roswell's Main Street. Spot lights were fitted over the cab, guards protected the front lights, and of course it sported oversized tires. Bubba and Billy opened the door and nearly fell out before the noise from the diesel engine had died down.

A month on the job had been long enough to learn Sally's regulars—especially these three.

"Why ain't you working, Dreiser?"

"Yeah. It's way past drinking time, and we're ready to drink!"

Dean resisted the urge to point out most of E.T.'s patrons were eating breakfast. As he watched, Bubba threw a Coors can into the back of the truck. He and Billy lumbered up the stairs, laughing and weaving toward E.T.'s. Colton trailed behind and stopped outside the door to answer his cell phone. A look of cold anger passed over his features before he disconnected, crammed the phone back in his pocket, and entered the bar.

Dean would bet every dollar in his wallet that not one of those boys had celebrated his twenty-second birthday yet. Hopefully, they'd have a few brain cells left on the day they finally decided to grow up.

With a shake of his head, he trudged to the back of his truck and pulled out Lucy's suitcase, then made sure the cab was locked up.

He'd just secured the toolbox which spanned the length of the back when he heard gunshots.

They'd come from E.T.'s.

CHAPTER FOUR

Dean inched through the door, hand on his weapon though he hadn't drawn it. One look inside told him he wouldn't need to.

Sally stood behind the bar, sawed-off shotgun resting against her slim hip, cigarette dangling from her lips.

Lucy lay on the floor, pinned by Billy who was yelling, "Don't fire, Sally."

The boy was hopeless.

Lucy began to inch her hand toward her ankle holster. Dean paused long enough to make eye contact, shake his head once. Then he stormed across the saloon, trusting Sally wouldn't shoot him. "Move the hell off her, Billy. You could have broken every bone in her body."

"It's not my fault, Dean. Sally's the one who brought out the shotgun. I didn't even do anything."

"The hell you didn't." Sally said. "Dean, get those boys the fuck out of my bar. I told them not to show up here again drunk and waving their weapons around. I won't have it. Next time, I won't pull out a shotgun with blanks."

Dean wanted to laugh, or slip behind the bar and pour himself a shot of Maker's Mark. Instead he pulled Billy to his feet and pushed him toward the door, then reached down for Lucy. "You all right?"

The expression in her eyes changed from alarm to anger to laughter in a matter of seconds. They reminded him of the one time he'd watched the Northern Lights play across the sky—

only this was within his arm's reach. As he helped her up, Dean realized in the space of a breath he could fall for this woman. Suddenly he found himself considering more than a shot of bourbon, he could probably befriend the entire bottle.

She nodded and brushed off her pants.

"Bubba, Colton. You're out of here too." Dean retrieved the two guns from the table near where the boys had dropped to the floor. "I'll walk you to Joe's Coffee Shop. Colton, hand over the keys to your truck. You can pick everything up from Sheriff Eaton later this afternoon."

Colton appeared ready to argue as Dean held out his hand and waited. Dean had him by three inches and twenty pounds. Sally still held the shotgun. Colton was stubborn, but not stupid. He shrugged and dropped the keys in Dean's palm.

Dean focused on the last of the stooges.

"I only wanted to show how I could shoot the can off the top of Billy's head," Bubba whined, but he handed over the last of the pistols. He added as an afterthought, "I've done it before."

"Yeah. We even practiced before we got here." Billy chimed in.

"I bet you did." Dean nudged the three boys out the door. Behind him, the customers in E.T.'s resumed their breakfast.

"You sure you're all right?" Sally asked.

"Of course. I have a brother." Lucy extended her hand. "I'm Lucy. Dean's friend."

Sally shook her hand, then stepped behind the counter to store the shotgun. "Not the best way to see the place you're going to spend the summer. Those boys are about the worst we have though. In general, people here are harmless."

Lucy looked out across the room. Tables remained full. Televisions played softly, running morning shows. No mad rush for the door in spite of the ruckus. "We run a good daytime crowd. Nights stay even busier. Not a lot to do in Roswell. As temperatures rise, folks get restless, come in for a drink or a game of pool." Sally motioned to a bar stool, shook a cigarette from her pack, and lit a fresh one.

Of average height, she looked to be between fifty and sixty. Gray hair cut in a no nonsense shag. Thin and wiry. Something told Lucy she'd have a struggle taking her in a fight. The woman had the demeanor of a lone wolf. Or maybe she'd gotten the wrong impression since her first image of her new boss had been with a Remington in her hand.

"Haven't had to pull out my shotgun in months. Hell. Most of the time, putting it on the counter would be enough, but those boys have skulls thicker than the boardwalk out there."

"Will the sheriff have to file a report?"

"For shooting blanks over their heads?" Sally inhaled the nicotine as if it were sustenance. She blew out the smoke with great reluctance. "If Sheriff Eaton had to investigate every time someone discharged a weapon in Roswell, he wouldn't have much time left to do his job, now, would he?"

Sally stopped a young waitress headed out with an order. She sent her back to the kitchen to retrieve an extra round of drinks for the table she was tending.

"Does Roswell have a lot of crime?" Lucy asked.

"Hell no. We have a good town here. Roswell's small with a small police force. Folks don't want to fork over more money for a larger one either. But what with the tourists claiming they've been abducted by aliens, hikers getting themselves stuck in spots they have no place going to begin with, and the people who honestly need help—well, Roswell's finest stay busy enough." Sally inhaled one last time, then crushed out the cigarette. "No, I don't suspect Sheriff Eaton will be by here unless it's for dinner. Go and unpack. Your shift doesn't start until three."

Lucy nodded, slid off the barstool, slipped her backpack over her shoulder.

"Why Roswell?" Sally asked.

"Pardon?"

"Why would a young gal like you want to spend the summer in the middle of the desert?"

Lucy peered into those steel gray eyes and knew Sally had seen and heard it all. She'd spot a phony a mile away. Hell, for all Lucy knew, Sally could be one of the perps she had come here to apprehend—one of those intent on ruthlessly killing thousands. She had trouble imagining the woman in front of her consorting with terrorists, but what had Dean said? Commander Martin suspected E.T.'s.

The sounds and smells around her crystallized—bacon frying, babies crying, someone laughing at a joke. Lucy realized she'd jumped into her first covert operation with both feet, and she could hear her mama's voice whispering, "In for a penny, in for a pound."

She pulled her long hair behind her shoulders, then glanced around as if to assure herself Dean was still outside with the three musketeers. She stepped closer to Sally so her low voice could be heard over the noise of the morning crowd, close enough to smell the cigarette smoke in the woman's hair.

"Dean thinks I'm here because I'm interested in UFOs." She paused, let Sally consider and discard the notion. "The truth? I've listened to my roommate Laurie talk about her brother Dean for three years now. I decided he might be worth checking out."

Sally's eyes squinted. "Little thing like you, shouldn't have to come to the middle of nowhere looking for a date."

Lucy cinched the backpack up on her shoulder, stuck her bottom lip out in a pout she knew made her look five years younger. "College boys. I'm sick of college boys. I figured I'm old enough for a man and a little adventure."

"Well, hell. I've got enough girls already staring at the man's ass. Lord knows, I don't need one more." Sally reached for her pack of Marlboros, lit one, then pointed the smoldering end at Lucy. "I don't approve of the help sniffing around each other, but what you do on your own time isn't my business. Be sure, while you're on the clock, you keep your mind off Dean Dreiser and your eyes on your work."

"I can do that."

Lucy turned to leave and bumped into Dean. "Miss Sally told me I should go unpack."

"I'll carry your things." His grasp was firmer than necessary.

As they left the bar, Lucy thought she heard Sally say, "Trouble. All I ever get these days is more trouble."

Dean let go of her arm as soon as they stepped out on to the boardwalk.

"You want to explain why Sally mentioned my ass?" Dean stepped to the wooden railing, surveyed the street.

Lucy stayed at the door as if considering her answer, then pushed on her sunglasses and stepped up beside him. "She did?"

"You know good and well she did."

"Maybe she likes your ass, Dean."

"Don't play stupid with me, Lucy."

"I'm not playing stupid. Lots of older women fantasize about middle-aged men." She lowered her sunglasses and smiled.

"I leave you alone for five minutes. You manage to get flattened by one of the biggest goons in Roswell and piss off our boss."

"I don't think I pissed Sally off. I think she likes me."

"She was smoking."

"So?"

"She's trying to quit." Dean grabbed the suitcase he'd left beside the front door and strode down the boardwalk. He didn't look back to see whether Lucy followed.

"She smoked the entire time we talked."

"Exactly."

"Oh."

E.T.'s sat half a block from the corner of Main Street and West Mountain View Road. Dean turned left at the corner, realized Lucy's footsteps weren't echoing behind his, and doubled back.

She stood at the railing, gazing out over the wide open vista that lay ahead. "That's quite a view, Dean."

"Yeah. I suppose it is."

He tried to see it through her eyes—Guadalupe Mountains and Texas in the distance, Hondo River directly below, the desert rising up to meet The Roswell Industrial Air Center to their left. It all shimmered with heat and seemed to promise him death and danger. But he supposed Lucy saw adventure in the view.

He glanced down when she reached out and casually touched him. Willed himself not to jerk away from the exquisite, brown hand on his arm. Tried to pretend it didn't faze him.

"It's beautiful, Dean. Roswell looks so plain, but that is magnificent." Brown eyes found his, smiling, causing him to forget for a moment why they had come to this place.

"Maybe the view will make up for your room." Dean led the way the last half block to Josephine's Guest House.

Josephine's was a three-story, frame structure with a first floor wraparound porch, second floor balconies, and, on the third, a widow's walk. It had seen its heyday fifty years ago. Paint struggled to hang on in some places and had given up in others. Attached to the building's west side, a one-story addition of individual rooms ambled for as far as they could see.

"Josephine could use a carpenter," Lucy said.

"Josephine likely had plenty. But none of them came here to work. Our rooms are toward the back."

They bypassed the main house via a side parking lot where every slot was empty. Anyone staying at Josephine's tended to work during the day—another major benefit in addition to the back alley view.

"When prostitution became illegal, Josephine began adding on rooms and renting them out. She tended to forget things like building permits."

He led Lucy through a small breezeway and back out the other side to the very end of the building.

"Our rooms are the last ones?" Lucy asked.

"We don't want to be cornered in."

Dean stopped in front of room twenty-seven.

"You're twenty-seven?"

"Right."

Lucy cinched up her backpack. "Where am I?"

Dean unlocked his door. They stepped into an interior hallway. An arched entrance to the left led to his room. He nodded toward four stairs to the right.

"My room is down there?"

"Room twenty-seven B."

"I don't even get my own number?"

"Your room isn't big enough to need its own number."

Lucy held out her hand, and Dean handed over the key. Before he could explain further, she'd stomped ahead of him down the four stairs. Already having glimpsed her Spanish temper, Dean decided to give her a minute. He waited until he heard her unlock the door, let her clomp around the room which took less than a minute, then carried her bag down.

She stood in the middle of the ten-by-ten room, hands on hips, glaring at him. Slowly she pivoted, taking in the twin bed, single dresser, small closet and bathroom. A poorly-covered armchair and stool were positioned next to the bed. A battered desk and straight-backed chair completed the room's furniture. The only light came from a two-foot window which ran along the top of the south wall. "You have to be kidding."

"I'm afraid not, beautiful."

"How big is your room?"

"Bigger than yours."

"I can't even enter mine without going through yours."

"Exactly."

"It's like I have a damn gate keeper."

"You have a problem with the way I'm doing things, Agent Brown?"

"Hell, yes. I don't need a chaperone."

"It so happens I think you do."

"So we have to do everything your way?"

"Yeah, we do. Get used to it. If you don't like it, then take your skinny doctor's ass back to Albuquerque International. There are plenty of jets headed east."

Dean held his ground. Lucy didn't. She crossed the room and didn't stop until she was in his face, an intimidation technique she'd tried earlier in front of E.T.'s. It was almost comical, given that she stood a good half a foot shorter. He didn't fall for it then, and he wouldn't fall for it now, in spite of the scent of her perfume—powder and spring flowers.

How long could she hold that scowl? Neither flinched. Dean wondered if they'd stand there all day. Him, he'd rather end up on the bed where he could tame her faster.

His phone rang so he moved first, pulling the damn thing out of his back pocket.

"Dreiser," he snapped, turning to stare out the tiny window. "Yes, sir. She's here."

He squinted at Lucy, then sank into the armchair in the

room. "How many?" He listened for another minute, then terminated the call with a curt, "Copy that." After removing his ball cap, he put the phone back in his pocket.

"Lock the outside door," he said softly.

Lucy flew back up the short flight of stairs.

Returning to the room, she crossed to where Dean still sat.

"Commander Martin said they've found two more bodies. He's sending pictures to your email now." He held her gaze, saw again in her eyes the quick movement through emotions—this time from sadness to a stubborn resolve. "You need to pull them up and try to identify the bio-weapon based on the preliminary information Dr. Kowlson is attaching. We're meeting at one-thirty—A.M."

Lucy sank onto the bed, her eyes widening.

"You have secured wireless in this room. The router is located in the closet in my room. I've forwarded the access code to your email."

She rose slowly, picked up the backpack she'd placed beside the bed. Unzipping it, she removed her laptop and placed it on the small table.

Dean stood too, feeling so much older than he had when he'd crawled out of bed eight hours earlier. He walked over to her and stopped. Knowing he shouldn't, he reached out and pulled her hair back behind her shoulders, studied the deep brown eyes searching his. "You should eat. I'll go buy you something and bring it back."

She didn't pull away. Her eyes locked on his, and something passed between them. Then she nodded and re-focused on her monitor, on the answers they needed.

They were in this together, though Dean still questioned the wisdom of allowing an agent with no field experience on such a mission. Ten days, fourteen at the most, then Dean would get as far away from those eyes threatening to drown him as he could.

Until then, he'd watch her back. This was a hell of a mission to pull for your first.

Two more fucking bodies in the desert. Someone had sent a message, and it had come through loud and clear. What worried Dean the most was the bastards still hadn't breathed a word about what they wanted. He knew from experience that no demands equaled the worst possible scenario.

CHAPTER FIVE

The suite of offices looked like any other place of business in Roswell. The occupants went to extreme measures to assure legitimate business was conducted there on a daily basis. No one could tie it to the terrorist organization it housed, because no evidence of any kind was allowed within its walls.

The woman entered the outer room with her passkey. It was empty of personnel, as he'd promised. Always, they met alone. If other section leaders existed, and logic dictated they did, she would never meet them. It was enough to know she was allowed to be part of this mission. Of course, she had men and women working under her, but even then she preferred not to know their names.

She knocked on the door to the executive office, waited for his command.

"Enter."

She opened the door but didn't step over the threshold. Instead she waited for him to look up. When he did, her heart nearly stopped. The longing deep inside her threatened to consume her. Only he could awaken this passion—it was a desire unlike any she had known before. She had considered such feelings dead.

Her existence had become consumed by their mission and her need for him. She would—she had—given her life for both. She didn't regret her decision. She did marvel that she could feel excited and alive again.

"All four bodies have been found and transported to secure locations," she said.

"How can you be sure?"

"We injected tracers in each one. These tell us the exact location for up to twenty-four hours."

He approached the window, gazed out over the flat, desert scene, then pivoted and pierced her with his cold stare. "Dr. Kowlson's team will find these tracers."

"No. They must follow a very strict protocol, which begins by photographing the body. Then they will catalogue the damage. By the time they begin the autopsy, the isotopes within the tracers will have dissolved."

"Nothing will remain?"

"Nothing at all."

He searched her eyes for any hesitation. She knew he would find none.

"We are watching flight manifests at both the military and local airports?"

"As you ordered. There has been a fifteen percent increase in activity—nearly all military and government personnel."

"They are reacting as we predicted." He sat back down at the desk, opened a laptop.

"And according to our time frame."

"Then we proceed to Phase Two."

CHAPTER SIX

Laden down with BLT, fries, and a coke, Dean walked into the apartment and stopped short at the sight of Dr. Lucinda Brown.

She had twisted her long hair and clipped it to the top of her head. Why did women do that? If their hair bothered them, why not cut it off? Truth was, he didn't understand women anymore at thirty-five than he had at eighteen. She'd kicked her shoes off, and tucked her feet up underneath her, though a perfectly good stool was right in front of the wingback chair she sat in. She had her bottom lip stuck out in a pout, and all teasing was gone from her face. She looked for all the world like a woman trying to solve a puzzle.

As Dean crossed the room, he realized it wasn't a bad analogy—except this puzzle had already cost three lives and could cost thousands more. From the look on Lucy's face, she was well aware of the fact.

He rattled the bag. "Honey, I'm home."

"Come and look at this, Dean. Tell me what you think."

Dean snagged the straight-backed chair and plopped it next to where she sat. "Eat," he said, pulling the laptop from her hands.

"I will, but let me show you this." Her hands followed the computer across her chair, across his lap.

Dean told himself to ignore her perfume. Again. "I know how to work a laptop, woman. Your shift starts in forty-five minutes. You need to eat and change your clothes."

He shifted the laptop to his right so she would back away, but she didn't. She leaned over him to reach the keyboard. In fact, she had practically crawled into his lap—a real problem given the tightness in his jeans that she nearly bumped into as she reached for the tiny mouse pad.

"Here's a picture of the first vic you saw yesterday."

All thoughts of rolling Lucy onto the bed fled as Dean studied the image. "Yes, she's the girl at White Sands."

"And here are the other two."

"Shit." Dean's stomach tightened at the photographs.

Lucy's fingers flew over the keyboard as she maximized windows, lining them up beside each other so they could compare the images. "The other two victims were male. Approximately twenty-five and forty-five years of age. In the first two—the girl and the twenty-five year old male—death occurred in much the same way. Inhalation of the bio-agent, paralysis, dissolving of facial tissues, and then death due to massive hemorrhaging."

"You learned all of that without seeing the bodies in person?"

Lucy sat back in her chair, and Dean felt suddenly—unexplainably—lonely.

Lucy rummaged in the bag, pulled out the BLT, and ate. "Yeah. The third vic died differently, though. The question is, why."

Dean eyed Lucy as she bit into the sandwich, then stared back at the picture, then back at Lucy.

"What?" She paused mid-bite. "You told me to eat."

Dean turned back to the images, tried to put on his agent brain. The guy appeared dead, and he wouldn't be having an open casket funeral. In fact, his family would never see this body. What happened to the good old days when you eyeballed a vic and figured out what kind of gun he had been whacked with?

"He doesn't have much skin. Looks the same to me."

"You can do better, Agent Dreiser."

Lucy finished her half sandwich, stood and stretched, then began rummaging through her bag for a change of clothes. When she removed her t-shirt, Dean saw she wore one of those strappy camisole things underneath.

Dean drew a shaky breath, had a sudden need for a cigarette though he'd quit three years ago.

Lucy smiled. She reached across him for her drink, long hair brushing his cheek, perfume lingering after she shifted away. "You're staring, Dean."

"You have a bathroom, Lucy."

"I remember someone performing a little striptease in the truck."

Lucy pulled her belt out of her jeans, gave him the sexy smile he was learning to like. Dean groaned. He was man enough to admit when he was in over his head, and at this moment Lucy Brown had him by the balls.

"What's different about the pictures, Dean?"

Focusing again on the images, he ignored the fact that she was walking back toward him, behind his chair, leaning over him. Then her brown arms draped around him, hands working the keyboard, rearranging files.

"This is victim number one. Compare her to vic two. What difference do you see?"

Dean knew she'd already figured it out. Knew it must be right in front of him.

He stared at the pictures, forced himself to look past the horrific scene on the screen.

Seeing the answer to her question, he snapped the laptop shut, placed it on Lucy's chair. He ran his hand down her arm, pulled her around to sit on the stool in front of him. He needed to look in her eyes. "The woman has burn marks on her throat.

54

The man doesn't."

She nodded. "Very good, Dreiser."

Some hair had escaped the clip. He tucked it behind her ear, but didn't let go of the hand he held. Didn't stop rubbing his thumb over her palm. "What does it mean?"

"It means they're experimenting with the dosage. The man died before the bio-agent entered his respiratory system. In vic one, we estimated the total time from contact with the weapon until death to be fourteen minutes. In the second, they sped up the process to approximately three minutes."

"Three minutes?"

"Right. He died almost instantly. One massive hemorrhage. The facial skin dissolved, but as you saw, it left no marks on the throat."

Dean glanced down at her hand, nails filed to a practical length. He knew he should let go, realized this couldn't be personal. It was an op. Soon, they would both be off on different assignments. They'd probably be in different parts of the globe. But today, it seemed important they hold on.

"What about the third?"

"The third seems to be in the middle. Burn marks exist around the throat, but they are less intense. Estimated time, nine minutes."

"I don't understand what difference it makes. If their goal is to kill massive amounts of people, and with this weapon they can, what difference does it make whether it takes three minutes or nine or fourteen?"

"I have a theory."

Lucy's eyes had become impossibly round, and Dean again thought of those Northern Lights. Suddenly he wanted to go there, to leave today, walk away from this place. He'd never gone AWOL, and he wouldn't start now. Yet, a veil of evil surrounded everything about this mission. It made him want to take Lucy as far from here as he could. Alaska seemed a safe distance. "Go ahead."

"They don't want it to be quick—three minutes is much too fast. If their goal was to kill quickly and efficiently, they could do so with a bomb."

"Agreed."

"They also don't want it to be too slow. Fourteen minutes would allow emergency medical personnel to arrive on scene."

"But they couldn't help."

"True and irrelevant. The point is terror, Dean. Emergency response time averages thirteen minutes. It's not a coincidence the third vic died in nine minutes. They're refining their technique. I would expect to find one or two more before they move on to a wider release. They'll probably settle at ten or eleven minutes."

"Sweet heaven." Dean dropped his head between his arms, felt Lucy run her hands through his hair.

"Either way, people are going to die," she said. "But whoever has designed this knows our systems. They want people to realize no one can get to them in time. They want them to die alone and afraid."

CHAPTER SEVEN

It all came back more quickly than Lucy would have believed. Greet the customer, smile and leave some menus, check on your previous tables. Go back to take their order, slap it on the cook's ring, and give it a spin. Pick up drinks and rolls while tossing a smile to the single guys at table three—a big tip couldn't hurt. Above all, keep turning the tables.

She found her old rhythm in the first hour. By the time Dean showed for his shift at six, Sally had stopped watching her like a hawk.

"Hey, Dean." Lucy slipped behind the counter, clipped table seven's order on Jerry's ring, and picked up three iced teas. "I need two Mooseheads and a house Chablis."

"How's she doing, Sally?" Dean poured the wine and pulled the drafts in a fluid motion, smiling as Lucy's hands brushed his when she picked up her tray.

"Not so good since you walked in." Sally sat at the end of the bar, well away from the food prep, but still close enough to keep her eye on things. She reached in her pocket for the Marlboros, scowled at the label, then shook one from the pack and lit up.

Lucy stuck out her bottom lip and leaned against the bar. "You said I was doing great ten minutes ago."

"You were." Sally studied her through the smoke for a moment, then waved her away. "Take those drinks and get back to work."

"I thought you told me to take a break."

"I changed my mind."

Lucy settled the tray on the flat of her palm, rolled her eyes, and turned to go.

"Problem, boss?" Dean asked.

"The problem is trying to keep the help away from your ass."

"I heard that," Lucy said as she walked off toward her table.

"I hoped you would," Sally called after her.

"I thought you gave up smoking." Dean wiped off the counter as he studied Sally.

"I took it up again."

Dean nodded and reached under the bar top for an ashtray. Finding one, he pushed it her way.

"Here comes another member of your fan club," Sally said, as she tapped ash. They both shifted to watch Angela.

The girl was twenty-two and built like a brick house, literally. Five-foot-eight, one-hundred-thirty pounds, tiny waist, long legs, and double-D bazookas. Blond hair cut in a bob made her look too young to serve the drinks she carried. The right touch of rose-glittered blush and pink lipstick pulled the picture together. She knew how to use it all. At the end of the night, her tips always tallied highest.

For Angie the game stopped at the barroom door. It was all in a good night's fun. The girl had a heart as innocent as a morning's sunrise. She saw no harm in shaking and showing what God had given her.

Walking up to the counter, she leaned over and gave Dean a double-barreled view. "Table twelve wants four Buds on tap."

"Sure thing, Angie. How's it going tonight?"

"Better now with you here."

"I'm sure Paul has taken care of you all afternoon. He runs a good bar too."

"Paul's all right, but he's like eighty-five. We like when your shift starts."

Sally coughed, then inhaled more deeply.

"A bunch of us are going out to George's Bar after we close tonight." Angie picked up her tray, adjusted her posture to make the best of her assets. "Wanna go with us?"

"George's Bar? Where is it? What is it?" Lucy was back. She set her tray on the bar top. "Two margaritas for the ladies in the corner."

"You'd love it, Lucy." Angie wiggled her size six bottom and grinned. "They even have a little dance floor. You should see Dean dance."

Sally rolled her eyes and chain lit a cigarette. "Speaking of floors, get back to ours and tend your tables."

"We're waiting for our bar drinks, Sally." Angie took the mugs of beer, gave Dean a once over, and winked at Lucy. "He goes with us most nights."

Angie turned back to Jerry, who stared at her through the pass-through. "Remember the time you were arrested for starting that fight at George's?"

Jerry grinned at her, "You mean after you locked your keys in the car in Grand Junction?"

"Yeah. I didn't want to call you, so I hitched back."

"Which was fine until the trucker from Central Freight thought he could cop a feel."

"This isn't Memory Fucking Lane," Sally mumbled. "Could someone go back to work?"

"I've loved George's Bar ever since that night." Angie hustled off toward her table before Sally banned her from the bar area.

"You go most nights?" Lucy gave Dean her best smile. "Spanish girls love the flamenco, but I never would have guessed you to be a dancing cowboy."

Dean refused the bait, shook his head, and began uncrating the longneck beers sitting next to the cooler.

While he bent over, Lucy whispered to Sally in a voice she

hoped would carry, "He is so hot."

She heard, more than saw, him hit his head on the bar counter.

Lucy pivoted toward her tables, followed by Sally's familiar refrain of "Trouble. I might as well put it on the menu—special tonight: trouble."

Since it was a weeknight, E.T.'s closed at eleven. Dean wasn't sure how Lucy talked him into joining the regular night crew—Angie, Nadine, even Jerry. They'd agreed to meet at George's Bar which stayed opened until two.

He felt wrung out. The last thing he wanted to do was bop around a dance floor like some fucking twenty-year-old.

"Dean, we're supposed to act like one of the locals. Plus, I'm a college student, remember? College students do not go to bed at eleven. Trust me. This, I know."

"Fine. We stay for one drink, and then we go. Remember, we're meeting Martin at one-thirty."

"So what is the point of going to bed beforehand? We can do some reconnaissance. Find out if anyone at E.T.'s knows anything."

"New agents are so damn eager."

"You're grumpy because I flirted with you all night."

They were in the truck again, driving down Main Street, and he was actually pissed because he'd had one hell of a hard-on most of the night. He didn't plan on sharing that with his partner though.

"It's part of my cover, Dean. Sally wasn't going to believe your UFO story. I already explained that to you." Lucy had her feet propped up on the dashboard. Streetlights shone through the front windshield on bright pink toenails complete with two silver rings—nothing practical about that. The woman was an enigma.

Why did women paint their toes? Where did they buy rings small enough to fit on their toes? When did she get a Seventy-fifth Ranger Regiment tattoo on her ankle? His mind started wondering what other tattoos she might have, and he made a sharper left than he intended. The screeching tires relieved at least a portion of his frustration.

They were government agents for God's sake.

His partner did not fit into his previous experience. Dean's head hurt. In fact, it throbbed along with a few other places. He needed some sleep before tonight's meeting. He did not need to go drink and dance with Lucinda Brown for two hours.

"One drink. One dance. Then we're out of here." He pulled the truck into George's, shut it off, and rammed his baseball cap down on his head.

Lucy slid her sandals back on. "Okay, Dean."

They both got out of the truck and walked toward George's. Music poured from the bar. Classic rock so loud it made the vein in Dean's head pulse as his blood jumped with every strum of the electric guitar.

She slid her eyes up and down his body. The look left him tense and bristly—as if he had fur, and it had been rubbed the wrong way. Then she smiled. Her expression said she understood he was calling the shots, but this part they would do her way. He tugged his baseball cap down further, and opened the door to George's.

The bar reminded Lucy of every other bar she'd been in. She found comfort in the familiarity. Whether you were in New Mexico or Massachusetts, the dance floor was always small and at the front of the room, the juke box old and to the side, and the tables scarred and dimly lit.

If there had been waitresses, they'd gone home. Dean walked up to the bar and ordered them both a beer while Lucy joined the rest of the group from E.T.'s.

"Lucy, Jerry says he's too tired." Angie was at least one drink in the lead, maybe more. "You come dance with me. I love this song."

"Girlfriend, I can never refuse an offer to dance."

With a shriek, Angie pulled her to the hardwood floor. As they began to move to the blaring sounds of Los Lonely Boys, Lucy couldn't help but envy the younger girl. More than Angie's age, Lucy envied her innocence. Angie's biggest problem was finding a dance partner for the current song. She seemed blissfully unencumbered by the weight and responsibilities pulling at Lucy, threatening to push her under.

Lucy had felt so free once, so lighthearted. Had it been only a few years ago? Before her brother had come home from overseas. Before she'd seen what war could do, up close and personal. Lucy pushed the images away. She couldn't deal with them tonight.

Instead she focused on dancing with Angie. They lost themselves in the rhythm. They danced with abandon, allowing themselves to forget the group at the table, the dusty desert around them, everything except the sounds of *How Far is Heaven.*

When the last of the melody died, they made their way back to the table. Lucy's mood was better. How could it not be? Laughing, she fell onto the stool beside Dean, but Angie had no intention of sitting back down.

"Come on, Jerry. I know you'll dance to George Strait." Angie pulled the big guy off his bar stool and out onto the floor. At over two hundred pounds, he still managed to two-step quite gracefully.

Lucy took the beer from Dean and smiled. The drink felt cold and soothing as it went down her throat. She told herself not to notice the way his hand brushed against hers when he handed the bottle to her.

"You're sweating," he said.

"Yeah. Get out there, Dreiser. You'll work up a sweat yourself." She shrugged out of her jacket. Knew her t-shirt clung to her breasts. Felt Dean's stare on her and waited until he raised his gaze.

"Lucy—"

"Dean." Nadine leaned across the table, locked eyes with him. Dared him to deny her. "I didn't get to come out last time, but I heard about you. Dance with me?"

Barely old enough to be at George's, she had just celebrated her twenty-first birthday. Tiny and tired, she didn't look as if she'd have the energy to make it around the dance floor. Lucy could tell from one night at E.T.'s that Nadine was the group's favorite. Her older brother had walked away from his family a year ago, leaving a wife and two small children. Climbed into his sixty-five Mustang and driven out of town—never looked back. Nadine had given up a college scholarship to stay and help with her niece and nephew.

"You promised if I came the next time you would spin me around the floor. Remember?"

"Yeah, Nadine. Of course I remember. Come on."

Before Lucy knew it she was dancing with Angie again, then with Jerry. Thirty minutes turned into an hour, and it was midnight when she checked her watch. Suddenly Dean cut in, as Alan Jackson sang about the love of a woman. Lucy had drunk two, maybe three, beers, and somehow the image of three victims in the desert had begun to hurt a little less.

"You're beautiful. Though I doubt I'm the first man to tell you so tonight." Dean's voice in her ear caused every inch of her skin to come alive. He held her close, his arm easily encircling her, his hand barely touching the side of her breast.

She wanted to melt into him, wanted to believe he wouldn't

disappear in the night like her old dog Jake. More than anything, she wanted to rest, even if it was only for this moment. Instead she said, "You do have a nice ass, Dreiser."

His laughter made her heart feel good. She could almost believe things would be all right.

"We need to go, Doc."

"Right."

And then they were gone, speeding through the desert night. They rode with the windows down, and Lucy must have slept for part of the drive. When she woke they were bumping down a gravel road, and the lights of the old truck were off.

CHAPTER EIGHT

"Geez, Dreiser. How the hell can you see where you're going?" She scooted next to him in the truck, needing to feel his warmth.

"Compass."

"How do you see it?"

"It's in my head."

She felt more than saw his wolfish grin. Had she really known this man less than twenty-four hours?

He slowed, then stopped, the truck. Opened the door, and pulled her out on his side. She tried not to jump when Commander Martin stepped out of the darkness.

"Dreiser. Brown."

"Commander." Their response came in stereo.

"I received your report, Dr. Brown. Dr. Kowlson agrees with your analysis. Good work."

"Thank you, sir," Lucy said.

"Dean, we're working through the list of names you sent us. So far, there have been no hits. What we can assume is these are not your traditional terrorists, so we need to broaden the field."

"Meaning what, exactly?" Dean asked.

"Meaning anyone is to be considered suspect—man or woman, any age."

As she listened, Lucy was reminded again of the history these two shared—they had worked together on many missions. She thought back over what she'd read in Dean's file, about Barcelona and Glacier and Virginia. Dean had seen evil before and stopped it. She knew he would again.

She trusted him. The realization calmed her somehow.

"I called this meeting to inform you that we suspect someone on the inside is handing information to this group."

Even in the darkness, Lucy felt Dean stiffen.

"You have confirmation?" Dean asked.

"We found a fourth body in the desert."

"I didn't receive photos of a fourth victim," Lucy said.

After a brief, almost imperceptible hesitation, Martin said, "He was an agent."

"Son of a bitch." Dean didn't bother to lower his voice.

"We didn't release the information to you or anyone else. The information was kept highly classified, and yet we have reason to believe someone leaked it."

"I don't understand." Dean jammed his fists into the pockets of the old bomber jacket.

"Neither do I, Dean. All I know is there's a terrorist group, and they have an informant somewhere within our organization—either on the military side or within USCIS."

"How is that possible, sir?"

"It happened in Glacier. We court-martialed one man and dismissed three others, because our intelligence division found suspicious activity in their accounts, but we never confirmed they were the source of the activity. We hoped they were. Now it looks as if there might have been someone above them."

Lucy remained silent, trying to understand what she was hearing, and what it meant to her and Dean.

"Each team will work independently," Martin continued.

"We're going dark?" Dean asked.

"You're only to make contact in a critical situation. Any information you have, send directly to me. Under no circumstance do you send it to anyone else. If something happens to me, you send it directly to the head of Homeland Security.

Delete all previous addresses I've given you. In fact, don't even use your systems. Trash them. Assume they've been compromised."

Martin doubled back to his SUV, a dark shadow in an even darker night. He returned and handed a BlackBerry to Dean. He gave Lucy a small laptop.

"These systems are clean. I checked them myself. No one else has touched them."

In the starlight, Lucy saw him reach out, shake Dean's hand, then turn toward her. She placed her hand in his.

"I won't insult either of you by emphasizing how critical this mission is. I know you'll do your job. You're both the best we have, which is why I chose you to be here. Now all I can say is be careful and Godspeed."

He slipped into the SUV and drove off into the night.

Dean opened the door to his truck. Lucy climbed in on the driver's side. She had a hundred questions, but didn't ask any of them. At this point, she knew she didn't want to hear the answers.

The dashboard clock flashed four A.M. when they reached Josephine's. Dean somehow resisted the urge to kiss Lucy's upturned face as they hesitated between their rooms. He told himself to maintain a professional distance, though he recognized he was probably too far gone for that.

He was also exhausted and fucking furious. Someone had infiltrated their op and killed an agent.

"You want to stay in my room?" Dean asked. He softly pushed her hair back from her face, let his hand trail down her back. He wanted more than anything to take her to his bed, hold her close to him, assure himself she remained safe as she slept.

"I'm fine, Agent Dreiser." Her voice was teasing, but as tired as his. He watched her walk down the four stairs, unlock her door, and enter her room.

When he'd entered his own room he couldn't resist calling her on the room-to-room phones. "You okay in there, Lucy?"

"You could have tapped a Morse code on the wall, Dean."

"Yeah, guess I could have."

"I'm fine."

"All right. Just checking."

"Get some sleep, Dean."

And he had no trouble falling into a deep sleep, so deep that the pounding on his door made no sense.

He checked his clock, noted the morning light pouring through the window, heard the pounding again, and rechecked the clock. Someone had the wrong room. Lucy would use her key or shout at him to get up. So, who the hell kept knocking?

With a sigh, he stood up, pulled on his jeans, and looked through the peephole.

"Hang on, Jerry."

Darting across the room, he transferred his Glock from the bedside table to the bathroom, then shut the bathroom door. Jerry continued banging on the door. If someone hadn't died, Dean might be tempted to punch the big old guy.

He jerked the door open.

"Where's Angie?" Jerry demanded.

"It's ten in the morning, Jerry. What the hell are you talking about?"

Jerry stormed into his room, and Dean let him. He had nothing to hide—other than the Glock. He sure wasn't going to find Angie. Besides, Dean wanted to get back to sleep as soon as possible. The fastest way would be to let Jerry have a look around.

"She's not here, Jerry. Have you checked her house?"

Jerry stood in the middle of the room, having already checked under the bed and in the closet. He'd spied the bathroom and was moving toward the closed door when Lucy walked in.

She stood in the doorway, hair mussed, nightshirt barely covering her ass, and suddenly Dean didn't feel so tired.

"What's wrong?" Lucy asked.

"Jerry lost Angie."

"Didn't she have a nine o'clock shift?" Lucy asked.

"Yeah, and Angie doesn't show up late for her shift—ever." Jerry's eyes shifted from Dean to Lucy, then back to the bathroom door.

"Well, hell. Maybe she slept in." Dean was still watching Lucy, watching the nightshirt ride up and down as she made her way across the room.

"Sit down, Jerry," Lucy said. "We'll help you look for her. Let me get you a glass of water."

"She's never late, Dean. I'm telling you something's wrong. I called her house, and she never came home last night."

Lucy retrieved the glass of water, nearly dropped it when Jerry's cell phone buzzed. They all stared at each other.

"It might be Angie," Dean said. "Better answer it."

"Hello. Yeah, this is Jerry Caswell." The big guy sat down on Dean's bed. "That's impossible. No. You must have the wrong Angie."

Jerry slid off the bed onto the floor, still gripping the phone. "Angie Brewer? Are you sure? But, no, that can't be right."

Jerry let the phone slide to the floor. He didn't seem to notice the tears rolling down his cheeks. Covering his face with his hands, he began rocking back and forth.

The person on the other end of the phone was still speaking.

Lucy went to Jerry, placed a hand on his back, and murmured to him.

Dean picked up the phone. "Dreiser speaking. Who is this?" He listened for a few minutes, his eyes never leaving Lucy's face. "Okay. Yeah. We'll bring him over."

When he disconnected, he held the phone a few seconds, then reached out and placed a hand on Jerry's shoulder. "What happened?"

Finally Jerry glanced up. "I don't know. Eaton didn't say, but she can't be dead, Dean. We were dancing a few hours ago, remember?"

"Yeah. I remember."

Dean crossed the space to his closet in three strides, yanked a clean shirt off a hanger. "I'll drive Jerry to the police station in his car." He sat down and tugged on his boots.

Jerry continued to stare at the floor. He never saw Dean slip into the bathroom, didn't hear the door click. Even if he'd been sitting on the bathroom counter, he wouldn't have noticed when Dean placed his weapon in his holster, his holster over his shirt, and his jacket over everything.

When Dean returned to the room, Lucy's eyes met his. He could read the question she longed to ask—the same one he'd been chewing on since Jerry had collapsed on his floor. But the only person with answers would be Martin. Their orders had been clear, and this was not critical. They'd file a report later and wait for a response.

Asking wouldn't change the grim fact of Jerry's anguish. So the question hung between them. Was Angie's death connected to the other victims in the desert?

"Get dressed." Dean tossed her the truck keys. "Meet us at the police station. It's on the corner of Main and First."

"Jerry." Lucy rose from the floor. "You need to go with Dean now."

Jerry stumbled to his feet, peered around the room as if seeing it for the first time. "Yeah, okay. It's probably a mistake. We'll go straighten it out." He staggered to the hallway. Pausing in a shaft of morning sunshine, he gazed out like a man hoping to find himself waking from a dream.

Dean followed, glancing back at Lucy only once. He sensed the mission had branched in a different direction, and he hoped six hours sleep would be enough for him to follow it.

CHAPTER NINE

Lucy surveyed Dean's room, assured herself everything looked as it should. She'd watched him pocket the BlackBerry. She switched off the bathroom light, paused at the open closet. Seven shirts hung buttoned at the top, facing the same direction. It reminded her so much of her brother, her breath caught in her chest and she found herself standing not in a motel room in Roswell, but in an Army barracks in Fort Benning, Georgia.

Marcos had graduated Basic Training and was scheduled to begin the Ranger Indoctrination Program. Family had been allowed to tour the barracks, and Lucy had ribbed Marcos about how he once left his clothes strewn around his room. Lucy reached out and placed two fingertips between the hangers holding Dean's shirts and smiled, but it didn't come from a place of happiness. It came from a place deep inside, a place she tried to keep buried. Then she would see something—like Dean's shirts—and the pain would rise like tulips in the spring. Her heart would split like the soil. She smiled because the feeling remained familiar, although the hurt never lessened.

She had always worshipped her older brother, never more than the weekend at his graduation as he had pledged his life to Uncle Sam. Had they all stood and applauded as he crossed the stage? She'd baked him a bag of raisin-chocolate chip cookies to take with him to Airborne School. They'd all been so fucking optimistic.

Lucy closed the closet door, leaned her head against it. The

72

images of the bodies in the desert, Jerry sobbing on the floor, and Marcos in the military hospital all swam together and collided. The weight of peoples' pain threatened to pin her there. She felt so damn hopeless.

The sound of a bird pulled her back. It perched on the windowsill over Dean's desk. It was a ridiculous window, similar to the one in her room though not as long—like what they put in prisons. The size of a small microwave and too high in the wall, but the bird didn't seem to mind. It set up a chatter, and Lucy smiled when she recognized the mockingbird's song. *Figures.* She needed guidance and what did she get? Mocked.

As she locked the door behind her, her mind settled on another old movie she'd watched with her dad—*To Kill a Mockingbird*. Gregory Peck had proclaimed it a sin to kill a mockingbird—because they only make music for us to enjoy. Lucy thought of Angie dancing the night before, and felt her resolve return.

She would find out who had killed her. When she did, she wouldn't have any problem using her Sig P229 to even the score. She made her way back to her room, changed, and was driving down Main fifteen minutes later.

The police station was located on the opposite side of town from E.T.'s. Two cruisers were parked in the back, several cars to the side. Nothing indicated any great emergency had taken place.

Inside, Lucy went directly to the dispatch officer manning the desk.

Fortyish, shoulder-length red hair and unreadable eyes, the woman had a no-nonsense demeanor. "Can I help you?"

"I'm here to meet Dean Dreiser and Jerry Caswell. I work with them at E.T.'s."

"They're with Sheriff Eaton now. I'll let them know you're here."

"Please don't interrupt them. I'll wait."

Lucy sat down in a plastic chair. Why had Angie died? What happened to her?

"I want to see her body, Sheriff. She was my girl, and you can't stop me." Jerry burst from a back room, barreled down the hall, and stopped short when he saw Lucy.

Dean and the sheriff followed him into the room. Sheriff Eaton looked to be about fifty-five, a gaunt man just under six feet tall. He was balding, with a salt and pepper mustache. He glanced at Lucy, then focused on Jerry.

"I'll do what I can, Jerry. At this point though, I can't promise anything. I'm not going to lie to you, son. I know this is a shock."

"It's not a fucking shock. It's a fucking crime, and I'm going to see her. You can't stop me. She was my girl. You know she was my girl." Jerry stormed out of the room, letting the door slam behind him. Never looking at his car, he took off walking down Main.

Eaton took a deep breath, stared out the window, then shook his head. "I've known Jerry since he started elementary school. Hate to see him go through this." He turned and studied Dean. "You have his car keys?"

"Yeah. I'll drive his car to E.T.'s and leave the keys with Sally."

"Fair enough." Eaton concentrated on Lucy for the first time.

Lucy had lived with a cop long enough to know he was sizing her up. She held the man's gaze, waited for him to speak first.

"This is Lucy Brown, Sheriff." Dean motioned for Lucy to join them. "Lucy went out with us last night. She's attending MIT with my little sister and came to Roswell for a summer job."

"Sally mentioned you," Eaton said.

Lucy cringed, thinking what such a discussion might have included. "Nice to meet you, Sheriff." She shook the man's hand, noticed he didn't shy away from shaking hands with a woman the way some men did, gave him points for it.

"I'd rather have met you over a piece of pie at Sally's. Hell of a thing, this is. I'll send an officer down to take statements later today."

"So it really was Angie? She's really dead?" Lucy's voice shook slightly.

"Yeah, we have a positive i.d." Eaton ran a hand over his bald head.

"Sheriff." The dispatcher held a phone in one hand and a patrol radio in the other. "You have a call on line two. It's the state. And Preston has a four-car pile-up on the loop. He needs backup."

"Alice, send Truss out to Preston."

"Truss is with—"

"I know where Truss is. Pull him off it and send him to Preston. I'll take line two in my office." Turning back to Dean and Lucy he shook both their hands again. "Tell Sally I'll need to see everyone who worked the same shift with Angie last night. If she could call them all in, I'd appreciate it. I want them at E.T.'s by four."

Dean and Lucy both nodded.

After Sheriff Eaton had left, Dean led them back outside to the boardwalk. Lucy remembered her first premonition of those old westerns—of blood and death. She again pushed the image away.

"Follow me to E.T.'s," Dean said. "No telling where Jerry went, but we'll leave his car there and deliver the Sheriff's message." Dean held open her door, and she slid behind the wheel.

"What happened, Dean?" Lucy fumbled with her sunglasses, pushed them on so he couldn't see her tears.

He reached out and touched her face. Lucy had the feeling he could look straight through the reflective tint of her glasses.

Straight into her soul to the fears and doubts threatening to overwhelm her on this sunny summer morning.

"Eaton either doesn't know what happened, or he isn't saying. She is dead though. He had some of her items to show Jerry—clothes and stuff. The strangest part was he didn't want Jerry to identify the body. In fact, he won't even let Jerry *see* the body."

"Why?"

"I don't know, but I can think of one good reason. If this is a homicide investigation, maybe Sheriff Eaton isn't ready to let anyone know the cause of death."

Lucy set her tray down on the bar and sank onto one of the stools. Emily and Nadine tumbled into seats beside her.

"I didn't think our last customer would ever leave," Nadine said.

She looked perpetually exhausted. Tonight was no exception. Dark circles had crept beneath her blue eyes, and curly blond hair escaped in every direction from the ponytail trying to hold it back. Angie had said Nadine took over the care for her niece and nephew when her brother left. Being a full-time mom was taking its toll on the young girl. Lucy remembered Nadine mentioning that last night's outing had been her first in ages.

"You three girls look like you could use a drink," Dean said. "What's it going to be? This one is on the house."

Emily's hazel eyes were red and puffy. Her hands shook as she reached in her apron pocket for a pack of cigarettes.

"Let me get that, sweetheart." Dean took the lighter and helped her. Emily was the oldest of Sally's waitresses—the mother hen of the brood. Wafer thin with hair cut in a stylish brunette bob, tonight she looked her full fifty years.

"Only one though," Dean said softly. "Angie told me you two

quit together. The last thing she'd want is for you to start again. Right?"

Emily nodded, then couldn't seem to figure what to do with her hands. She settled for shredding the wrapper.

When nobody took Dean up on his offer for a drink, he pulled a bottle of whiskey from the shelf, set out four glasses, and filled each a quarter full.

"What time did Sheriff Eaton leave?" Lucy asked.

"About nine o'clock." Emily picked up a glass, swallowed the shot in one gulp, and pushed the glass back toward Dean.

"You driving?" he asked.

"Nope. Joe's picking me up in thirty."

Dean nodded and poured her another. "Drink this one slower, baby. Or Joe will come in here and kick my ass."

That earned him a smile from all three women. A computer geek, Joe might weigh in at one-hundred-and-forty-five pounds dripping wet.

"Sally still here?" Nadine asked.

"Nah. She left with Eaton." Emily drew heavily on the cigarette.

"They still have a thing going?" Nadine tasted her whiskey, made a face, then sipped some more.

"I think so." Dean leaned against the counter. "I walked in on him bending her over the beverage cart one night in the supply room."

"Eww. Not a pretty image." Nadine declared, but she smiled and drank more of the Maker's Mark.

Emily couldn't be distracted though. "Eaton kept asking me the same questions. I don't understand. He wanted to know what time we left, and if Angie was mad at anyone. I never knew Angie to harbor a grudge. As far as anyone being angry with her—"

"No way. Angie was always the life of the group," Nadine agreed.

"I only met her yesterday, but she seemed like a very gentle soul," Lucy said.

Emily's phone rang. She answered it, listened, then snapped it shut. "Joe's here, so I'm gone."

"I'm walking you out," Dean said.

All three women turned to stare at him as he stepped out from behind the bar.

"Better careful than dead, ladies. It's our policy from now on." He escorted Emily to the door and unlocked it.

They stepped out into the night. Without letting go of her arm, Dean re-locked the door behind them. Their footsteps rang out on the boardwalk as they moved toward Joe's car, parked a mere ten feet away.

Nadine and Lucy stared at each other.

"Did he say he was walking her to the car?" Nadine asked.

They both hopped off their stools to peer out the window. Emily's husband had parked directly in front of E.T.'s. Dean was talking to Joe, gesturing toward the bar, while Emily stood beside them—arms crossed, face grim. The two men shook hands, and Joe led Emily around to her side of the car.

Dean stood watching the car drive away. Lucy thought she could see the weight of all their lives resting on his shoulders. She found herself longing to reach out and help him. Didn't partners lean on each other?

Dean finally made his way back into the bar.

"You ladies like staring at my sorry ass?" His tone was teasing, though the expression on his face remained dog tired.

"Why sure, Dean. You know we do." Lucy winked at Nadine.

Nadine had managed to finish her whiskey. She gathered her

things. "Don't lock that door, Dean. You have one more maiden to deliver."

With a laugh, he put his arm through hers and walked her out—again careful to lock the door behind them. Lucy shook her head and took one more swallow from a second shot he'd poured. At least he had found a way to ease their tension and keep them safe. The man made a damn good agent.

She couldn't resist resting her head on the counter. Whiskey's fault. It made her feel all warm and soft inside. She allowed her thoughts to unwind for a minute.

Dean could see Lucy through the front glass window. He re-entered without making any sound. When she didn't move, he closed up around her. She might end up with a crick in her neck, but she needed the sleep.

He would have liked to let her sleep longer, but he knew he needed to wake her. Instead of using one of several more professional ways, he paused behind her, lifted her hair, and brushed his lips against the back of her neck.

"Lucy."

"Hmm?"

"We have to go now."

He slid his arms around her waist. Nuzzled her neck. Allowed himself a moment of enjoying the smell of her.

"Go where?"

"I was hoping you wouldn't ask."

She tilted her head back, and he found himself following the curve of her throat. God, she was beautiful. Her skin tasted of sugar and lemons.

"Lucy."

"Yes?"

"If we don't go soon, I'm going to fuck you on this bar."

She spun around on the bar stool, slowly, stretching like a

cat. Her arms came up and wrapped around his neck. "Did they teach you to sweet talk a girl like that in agent school?"

"I've refined my technique over the years." He kissed her on the lips then, finally kissed her like he'd been thinking about for forty-eight hours. Or was it years?

She was like holding on to a Spanish firecracker. He could feel her burning his fingertips, feel the heat racing through his veins. She slid one knee between his legs and pressed it gently, firmly against his erection. He slipped his hands under her shirt and caressed her breasts. When he began to rub his thumbs over her nipples, they immediately became taut—every bit as hard as he was.

With something like a purr, she pulled back. "Where did you want to go?"

"Huh?" He dropped his head to her breasts, began suckling her through the cotton of her blouse.

"You said, we had to go somewhere."

"Shit."

"What?" She put her hands in his hair and pulled his head up. When his eyes focused on hers, she kissed him thoroughly, then placed her forehead against his.

"Fuck," he said.

"I know you want to fuck, Dean. Where were we going?"

"God, Lucy. You're making me crazy." Dean pulled away, paced to the other end of the bar. He put his hands against the bar top, as if he planned to perform pushups, and took a few deep breaths. When he trusted himself to look at her again, he couldn't help laughing at her teasing smile.

"Where are we going, Dean?"

"To the morgue."

"The morgue?" Lucy stood, stretched. "Wow. I've fucked in a lot of places, Dean. Never in a morgue though." She reached down, pulled her nine millimeter compact P229 out of her ankle holster, checked and reholstered it.

Dean shook his head, pulled his own weapon out of his shoulder holster and did the same.

"Are you expecting trouble, Dreiser?"

"I have trouble, Agent Brown. I have you." He pulled his car keys from the pocket of the leather jacket he'd been wearing since his escort service had started.

Lucy grabbed her own jacket and bag. Before they stepped into the night, she reached up, touched Dean's face. "Let's kick some terrorist ass, Dean."

"Yeah. Let's do that, Lucy."

As they made their way toward his old truck, their footsteps echoed on the boardwalk and rang out across the deserted streets of Roswell. They didn't know what they were walking into, but they knew they had each other's back. It was all an agent could hope for.

Then they were back in the truck, driving through the night, driving toward death, and maybe toward a few answers.

CHAPTER TEN

The morgue lay tucked into the far west corner of town, conveniently located next to the hospital. Lucy had done her share of rotations in morgues, but never in one so unapproachable. The plain brick building was surrounded on two sides by clumps of trees. Harsh fluorescent lights cast circles on the pavement and building. They looked for all the world like alien ships come to claim their own. No doubt some architect's sense of humor. Everyone in Roswell wanted the last laugh. Or perhaps she had been abducted, and the past twenty-four hours had been an alien-induced dream.

The morgue appeared closed for the night. Dean parked at the hospital's visitor center, next to a row of hedges separating the two parking lots.

"Wouldn't want a late shift nurse noticing our truck at the morgue." Dean motioned her out on his side, pulled a duffle bag from behind his seat, then shut the door without a sound.

"I'm assuming we don't have an appointment."

"You're a quick study, kid."

They kept to the shadows as they approached the back entrance. Dean stopped her a hundred yards from the door, when they reached the top of the hill between the two buildings. He reached into the bag, and pulled out two pairs of night vision goggles. They watched the play of shadow and light, reality and unreality, for several seconds.

"I see no security cameras or guards," he said.

"Apparently there's not a big problem with people stealing stiffs."

Dean pushed his goggles back into his bag. "Not yet."

"No twenty-four hour morgue service?" Lucy asked.

"Fortunately for us, no." Dean pulled out a small bag of picks and two earpieces. He handed an earpiece to Lucy and showed her how to wear it.

She ignored the feel of his hand in her hair, the touch of his fingers on her neck. Goosebumps shimmered down her arms, like so many stars falling from the sky. Then an owl hooted in the woods, and she spied Dean's grin—the grin of the wolf. They would make it through the morgue. Heaven alone knew what they'd find, but his wolf grin told her they'd make it.

"Tap it once to turn it on," Dean whispered. "This provides a secure channel between the two of us and works for up to twenty miles."

Lucy smiled. "I won't be going twenty miles."

"Good. Scan the building, parking area, and surrounding road continuously until I tell you to follow me to the back entrance. If you see anyone approach, stay here. I'll have a cover story, but I need you to hold your position. Understand?"

She nodded. They had covered similar scenarios in Virginia when she'd been in ops training, but it felt different with the stars above her, Dean's eyes staring into hers, and Angie's body on a slab in the building below them.

"It should take me three minutes to get down there and another two or three to move in. I'm going to disengage any interior security before I clear you to join me."

"Okay."

"Questions?"

"No."

He turned to go, but Lucy reached out to stop him.

"Dean?"

"Yeah?"

"Be careful."

"Yeah."

Then he evaporated into the black night. She watched for him through the goggles, listening to his steady breathing in her earpiece. He appeared at the back door in no time. She wanted to stare at him, as if doing so could will him through the locks more easily. But she forced her eyes away, back to the road, to the front entrance, constantly scanning. Everything remained quiet, ominously deserted.

"How you doing, Doc?"

"I think there's a coyote breathing down my neck back here, and a snake closing in from the east."

"That's my city girl."

She heard a soft click, jerked her attention from the road to Dean in time to see him open the door and step inside.

"I'm going in. Hold those wild animals off a few more minutes."

"Copy that."

As soon as the door shut behind Dean, she heard the crunch of tires on gravel. A Jeep pulled off the side road, passed the morgue, and pulled into the adjoining hospital lot. Lucy held her breath until it stopped at the emergency entrance. A pregnant woman and young man stepped out and disappeared through the doors.

Much calmer and cooler than she felt, Dean's voice sounded in her ear. "I've disengaged the cameras. You're clear to come down. Remember to stick to the shadows, in case anyone happens to look out a hospital window."

Lucy removed her goggles, placed them in her bag, and headed for the morgue. She'd just reached the back door, when Dean pulled her in. He locked the door behind them.

The lights of electronic appliances dimly lit the inside corridor. A microwave showed the time as one-twenty-three. A monitor scrolled through a screen saver with pictures of aliens. A few overhead lights glowed on lab tables. A refrigerator hummed.

Dean tapped his earpiece to turn it off and motioned for her to do the same. "Any idea where they keep the bodies?"

"Most morgues are laid out the same. There's a refrigeration section toward the middle of the building, where the bodies are stored until the autopsies can be performed. Once they're completed, bodies are transported to funeral homes." Lucy led the way down a hall.

She stopped at a pair of doors. A sign posted outside reminded personnel the importance of maintaining safe decontamination procedures. They pushed through and found themselves in an outer room with sinks, gowns and gloves. Biohazard containers stood along the walls, and boxes with biohazard masks lined the shelves overhead.

Dean pushed at the doors to the interior room. Lucy reached out a hand and pulled him back.

"What is it?"

"I don't know." Lucy scanned the room. She'd spent part of her residency in forensics. There was something different about this lab though, about this morgue. More than the night sounds had wormed their way into her soul. Something other than Angie's body in the next room had her every nerve on alert.

Dean watched and waited as she paced around the outer room. She remembered again her mother's admonition, "You have your *abuela's* second sight, Lucy. It doesn't matter whether you want your grandmother's gift. The question is what you will do with it."

Looking around the scrub room in the dim reflection, she sensed the danger that lurked. She knew with a deep certainty what they had come to Roswell to unearth waited within these walls. It felt like a predator in the grass. She chose in that moment to trust what she couldn't see.

"Dean, we need to gown up."

"Huh?"

Lucy strode over to the boxes—grabbed gloves, gowns, and a mask. "Put these on."

"Lucy, we don't have time for this."

"Then, you'd better hurry."

In the dim glow of the suite's night lights, she saw his confusion.

"Dean, I can't explain how I know, but there's something in there pertaining to the bioweapon we saw in the photos Martin sent us. We need to scrub up and put on these suits. They aren't biohazard suits, but maybe they will be enough."

Dean nodded, let her put the gown over his clothes, help him snap the gloves on.

She selected the best filter she could find, stood on her tiptoes to place it over his face. "Don't take this off. For any reason."

Dean watched her put her own scrubs on as naturally as he'd get dressed in the morning, and he realized she'd done this many times before. She was, after all, a doctor—wasn't she? He shook his head, wondering at how different her life was from his.

"Ready?" Brown eyes were all he could see, peeking between the cap she'd placed over her hair and the mask around her face.

He nodded. The damn mask itched, and the gloves felt, well they felt like wearing a condom—another one of life's irritating necessities he'd rather dispense with but didn't, given the risks.

Lucy entered the main morgue with no hesitation. She began opening refrigeration doors and pulling out slabs. He crossed to the other side of the room and did the same.

Most were empty. Dean had found two bodies when he heard Lucy's sharp intake of breath from the far corner of the room.

"I'm going to need some light, Dean."

He joined her, looked down, and saw Angie—a twenty-two year old girl who'd had no enemies. First glance told him she'd died from a twenty-two caliber bullet hole in the middle of her forehead. Correction. Two bullet holes. He didn't need to read an autopsy report. He'd killed a few men that way himself with the same caliber gun.

"Double tap to the head. Looks like the mob." Dean left to find a portable light. By the time he'd returned, Lucy had pulled the drawer out all the way and removed the sheet covering Angie.

Twenty-two was young. Too damn young to be on a slab.

"Hold the light as I work up her body, please." Lucy spoke softly, but Dean knew she was struggling to remain detached. "Does it make sense to you the mob would want to kill Angie?"

"Vegas isn't so far from here. It's possible she could have stumbled into something, seen a deal she shouldn't have."

Lucy raised her eyes to meet his.

"Possible, but it doesn't seem to fit," he admitted.

Lucy had reached Angie's thighs. She parted her legs. "Dean, move the light so I can see better."

"What are we looking for, Lucy? This can't be the same as the previous vics. Look at her face. Her skin is completely intact. There are no burn marks on her throat."

Lucy didn't stop, merely kept working her way methodically up Angie's body. "You're right, but there's something here we haven't found yet."

"I know this is upsetting, but maybe it's what it looks like. Or maybe it's something else entirely. It could have nothing to do with our operation."

Lucy had reached Angie's chest. She stopped, looking at a

butterfly tattoo on Angie's right breast. She took a step back, cocked her head, then bent closer again.

"What do you think of her tattoo, Dean?"

"Looks fairly new." Dean grimaced and leaned closer. "I'd say someone botched it."

Lucy glanced up. "You have a tattoo, don't you?"

"Yeah. So do you, Doc. Seventy-fifth Ranger Regiment?"

Lucy smiled, but it didn't reach her eyes. "Mine's on my ankle. There's not much subcutaneous fat there." She tapped Angie's breast lightly, then bent closer to examine it again. "Unlike the chest area."

"I don't have fat on my chest."

Lucy stopped examining Angie's tattoo long enough to give him a thoughtful stare. "Breasts, whether on a man or woman, are composed of glands, muscles, and connective tissue—including subcutaneous fat. It's one reason they're a popular place for tattoos—more fat, less distortion of the tattoo. I remember seeing your tattoo as you changed shirts in the truck, and, again this morning."

Dean's eyes narrowed. "So we know you like to stare at my chest. What's your point?"

"How long have you had the tattoo?"

"Three years."

"It's not irritated, swollen, or red."

"Not since the first week or so."

Lucy nodded, peered more closely at the butterfly tattoo.

"And how old was Angie?"

"Twenty-two. Jerry told Eaton she'd turned twenty-two last month."

"Right." Lucy pulled up a rolling stool, sat on it, and took the light from Dean, shining it on the butterfly tattoo. "Bring me the magnifying lamp from the corner, please."

He rolled it to her side. She focused its beam on the butterfly, adjusting until she had the exact image and magnification she wanted, then motioned him toward it. He hesitated, but with a sigh bent and peered through the lens.

"Jerry also said Angie had this tattoo done on her eighteenth birthday. I heard him teasing her about her wild days. He asked her when she'd get a matching one on the other side."

"But I see needle marks, as if she'd had this done recently," Dean said.

"Exactly. It's also irritated, indicating she had it inked in the last few weeks."

Dean stepped back and began pacing.

Lucy clicked off the lamp and pushed it away. "Have you ever watched an autopsy, Dean?"

"No."

"To begin, a J incision is made under the rib cage on each side. It's a very messy procedure, with bits and pieces of bone mass spraying about." As he watched she traced a pattern on Angie's chest, beginning at the base of her throat, and working down and under her breast. "You cut into the lungs with shears and a saw. Particles become airborne. It's very difficult to perform an autopsy in a hot zone. The precautions you have to take are cumbersome and make it difficult to maintain a clean site. That's assuming you've been trained in biohazards, *and* you know the body has been infected." She waited for him to put the pieces together.

"You think the terrorists injected Angie's tattoo with the bio-weapon?"

Lucy nodded.

"Why?"

"An autopsy would cause the bio-agent to become airborne."

"Which would kill everyone in the room." Dean studied Angie's still form. "But it would only kill everyone in the room. We're talking at the most one or two people."

"Who was scheduled to perform this autopsy, Dean?"

They shifted to the end of Angie's slab, picked up the clipboard fastened there. The orders were written on the top sheet.

Angela Brewer to be picked up by military personnel and transferred to White Sands Military Base at eight A.M. *Autopsy to be performed by Dr. Benjamin Kowlson.*

"It would kill Dr. Kowlson," Lucy said.

"And anyone else with him." Dean shoved the paperwork back.

"Why make it look like a mob hit?" Lucy asked.

"Throw off Eaton? Hell, maybe Eaton's in on it. Who knows? The point is, when there's two bullet holes in the head, people don't usually look for a cause of death."

"So how could they be sure we'd even do an autopsy?"

Dean slammed a fist against a metal table, causing Lucy's taut nerves to sing like strings on a guitar.

"Eaton let slip they found Angie's body outside of town, in the desert. How the hell did she get out there? This has been a setup from the word go. The bullet holes were to get her in this morgue to begin with—keep the body cold but without an autopsy. The desert location assured she'd end up at White Sands eventually, same as the other vics."

"Dean, there's something else. I still believe these have been trials. We should expect them to accelerate things. There's a possibility they may merge the bio-agent with another virus—a communicable virus."

"What are you talking about?"

"Take the common cold, for instance. They could merge what we saw in the former victims with something that can be passed through casual contact. If they injected that into Angie, and released it—"

"Dr. Kowlson wouldn't even know he'd been infected."

"Not before he had infected hundreds of others."

"God help us." Dean's face blanched even whiter above the surgical mask. For the first time since Lucy had met him, he seemed unable to move—the restlessness drained out of him by the sheer enormity of what they faced.

Lucy wheeled the lamp across the room. After she'd slid the stool under the lab station, she turned back to Dean. "What are we going to do?"

Dean proceeded slowly but deliberately to the end of the morgue table, zipped up the body bag around Angie. "We're stealing this body, and we're taking it to Commander Martin."

CHAPTER ELEVEN

"We need to double bag the body," Lucy insisted.

"Whatever you say, Doc." Dean pulled out drawers, looking for an extra body bag.

"Check the outer room," Lucy suggested. "Sometimes they have, uh, accidents during the autopsy and need an extra bag."

Dean stood straight up so suddenly, he cracked his head on an overhead cabinet door. "Do not say another word. If I mess up on the job, a terrorist gets two bullets instead of one. You mess up, some poor bloke's family needs a coffin with a hatbox. I don't want any details, Doc."

"Got it." Lucy located packing swabs and placed them around Angie's torso, taking special care to pad the area around the butterfly tattoo, then zipped the bag shut.

"I hope they shot her first," Dean said as he pushed the image from his mind, carried the extra body bag across the room. He set it on the ground and unzipped it.

Together, they picked up Angie in her original bag and tucked her into the second one.

"There's no sign the bio-agent traveled from the site of injection. My preliminary analysis indicates they did kill her first, then injected her. It's fair to assume Angie never knew what she stumbled into."

Carrying the body into the outer room, they both ripped off their gloves, masks, and caps.

"It still seems small-time to me. The clock's ticking. With less than two weeks, why mess with a girl and a few people on a military base?"

"Think of it as the perfect field test for an airborne weapon."

"Not quite a bomb," he said.

"But the next step."

"A sort of Phase Two."

"Exactly." Lucy dropped her suit inside the biohazard bin.

"Stop. We take it with us."

"Right. Old habits die hard."

"We might have a few hours before they find the missing body." He unzipped his black bag, handed her his night goggles and picks. "Put these in your pack. I'll carry the biohazard stuff. Give me the entire trash liner with all our garb."

"What else do you have in there?" she asked.

"Cover story. Don't worry about it." He quickly zipped it shut, motioned for her to put her earpiece in. "Go move the truck. Hurry, but be careful. I'll bring Angie to the back door, then reconnect the cameras."

"I thought you didn't find any security."

"No exterior security, but they had a hidden camera system for the interior—maybe they watch the docs. Don't worry. I took care of it. Walk back the way you came, in case anyone drives past, then drive over with your lights off."

Lucy made it to the door, but didn't open it. "Dean, we can trust Commander Martin with this, right?"

Dean had been wiping down surfaces. He stopped and looked her directly in the eye. "Lucy, I've trusted Martin with my life before, and now I'm trusting him with yours."

She thought about it a minute, nodded, and stepped out into the night.

The hospital parking lot was still deserted when Lucy reached the truck. She left the lights off, drove back to the morgue, and pulled up to the back door, talking to Dean the entire time.

"We need to cover her body, Dean. We can't just throw it in the bed of this truck."

When she pulled up, Dean told her to stay in the cab, keep watching out the front window. She heard him rummaging around in the toolbox, pulling out items, and finally securing a tarp with bungee cords.

She watched him work in the rearview mirror, near darkness cloaking his movements, only the light of a quarter moon occasionally revealing his silhouette.

"That should do it."

Lucy stared at Dean, struck by how casually he spoke. "Tell me you've never done this before."

"Why do you think I have a truck?" he asked.

"I was hoping you liked to fish or take women to make-out points."

"A good backup use." His wolfish grin flashed in the moonlight. "Let's go, Doc."

He climbed into the driver's seat, but when she started to scoot over to the passenger side he stopped her, snugged her in close to his side.

"People don't do it this way in Boston," she admitted.

"I imagine not."

She searched his eyes for any sign of worry, found none.

He whispered, "Stay close."

He put the truck in gear, and drove to the edge of the parking lot. The dashboard clock said four ten. Roswell slept in peaceful ignorance.

Dean switched on the lights, pulled out, and accelerated to the speed limit. He'd gone approximately three miles, and Lucy had drawn her first easy breath, when red lights flashed behind them. Dean sighed and pulled over.

Lucy watched Sheriff Eaton approach Dean's window.

94

Dean opened it, keeping his hands in view. "Sheriff."

"Dreiser. You're out late tonight."

"Yes, sir."

"Saw you pull out from the morgue's parking lot. License and registration, please."

"License is in my back pocket." Dean pulled it out. "Lucy, look in the glove compartment for the registration."

"Is it all right if I do that, Sheriff?"

Sheriff Eaton shone his flashlight in the car, settling on her for the first time. "Yes, ma'am."

Lucy found the papers, and handed them over to Dean.

Eaton took his time looking them over.

"Step out of the vehicle please, Dreiser."

Lucy and Dean exchanged glances, but she resisted the urge to look in the rearview mirror.

"Sure thing, Sheriff."

"Have you been drinking, son?"

"Had some whiskey about four hours ago."

"Nothing since?"

"No, sir."

"Are you willing to do a sobriety test?"

"You want me to count backwards or walk a line?"

"I didn't ask you to do anything, yet, Dreiser." Eaton continued to look at the two of them, frowning.

Lucy could practically see him trying to add the numbers together and come up with the correct equation.

"You carrying?"

"Yes, sir. I have a nine millimeter Glock in a shoulder holster. Would you like me to remove it?"

"Put your hands in the air for me, and turn and face the truck."

Dean did so, and Eaton removed his weapon. "Nice piece."

"Thank you, sir. I'm partial to it."

"I assume you have a license."

"Yes, sir. Lucy, my chl is in the glove box."

Lucy retrieved the license and used it as an excuse to jump out of the truck.

"Ms. Brown, do I need to ask if you're carrying?" Lucy thought Eaton looked older than he had only a few hours ago, but she followed Dean's example.

"Yes, sir. I have a Sig P229."

"You don't appear to be wearing a shoulder holster. You want to tell me where you keep this pistol?"

"Ankle holster, sir. My daddy insisted I have a handgun permit from the time I was old enough to legally carry."

"Understandable, since he's a Boston cop."

Lucy met the man's eyes, appreciated that he'd done his homework.

"Why don't you remove your piece real slow, set it on the ground here, then back up next to Dreiser."

Lucy took out the Sig, placed it on the ground.

"You can turn around, Dreiser."

With Lucy, Eaton had remained relatively calm, but one glance at Dean seemed to set him off. Lucy feared the sheriff might burst a blood vessel in his bald head. "You want to tell me what the fuck you were doing in the morgue's parking lot, armed, with your lights off?"

"Lucy's hobby is UFOs, and there are woods behind the morgue where UFOs have been sighted twice before."

"Don't bullshit me."

"I wouldn't, sir. I researched it on the internet for her."

"And you needed to be armed for UFOs?"

"Yes, sir. You never want to underestimate a situation."

Lucy tried to look innocent, then remembered she needed to appear capable of believing in UFOs. What did a person who believed in aliens look like? No telling. She aimed for clueless.

Sheriff Eaton continued his efforts to stare Dean down. No doubt, it worked with most of Roswell's boys. Dean, on the other hand, acted like he was having the time of his life. Lucy's chest tightened, and she didn't need her doctorate to recognize the beginnings of a panic attack. They stood on the side of the road at four-thirty in the morning, waiting for the real questions to begin. In minutes, Sheriff Eaton would discover Angie's body.

"What's in the bag?"

"Pardon?" Dean asked.

"What's in the black bag on the floorboard of your truck?"

"Personal items."

"Don't fuck with me, Dreiser. I'm very tired."

"Personal items, sir."

"Brown, bring me the bag."

"Yes, sir." Lucy retrieved the bag and set it on the ground. Back beside Dean, she put her hands in the air, mimicking his stance.

"You can lower your hands, Ms. Brown. Unzip the bag, please."

Lucy tried to breathe evenly while she unzipped the bag. She worked to push away images of the Roswell jail cells, but something told her she would soon be offered a tour.

"Take out the items, please."

Lucy removed wine, a blanket, a flashlight, a string of condoms, and the trash sack liner full of surgical scrubs.

Sheriff Eaton looked like he needed a drink.

"Can you explain what you have there, Dreiser?"

"Which part, sir?"

"All of it. Any of it."

"Well I had hoped to score, sir."

Lucy knew it was past time for her to jump in. Call it her second sight. "Don't you ever play games, Sheriff?"

"Excuse me?"

"You know, games. At college we play games, and I talked Dean into bringing those things. I wanted to play doctor."

Dean lowered one hand to encircle Lucy's waist. "Maybe you and Sally should try it sometime, Sheriff. Give you a change of pace from showing her your pistol."

Eaton placed his hand on his pistol, and Lucy closed her eyes. But instead of shooting him, the Sheriff began walking around the truck. "What's in the bed?"

"Tools."

"I didn't ask what's in the box. I asked what's in the bed. What's under the tarp?"

"I was hauling some things for Lucy."

"Take the tarp off."

Lucy and Dean exchanged a quick look. The gig was up. They had no choice but to reveal they worked for USCIS. If Eaton was in with the terrorists, it would come down to who could shoot the fastest. Unfortunately, their guns lay on the ground.

Dean nudged Lucy in the direction of their weapons. He moved toward the corner of the tarp, stepping between Eaton and Lucy. She might have enough time to hit the ground, grab the gun, and roll.

Or she could fall back on the law.

"Don't you need probable cause, Sheriff?"

He turned on her like a hurricane changing paths. "I'll tell you what the hell I need—answers."

"I know I'm new to the South," Lucy offered her best smile. "Daddy's always complaining about due process in Boston. How he can't so much as go through a perp's car without having drug dogs alert on it first, and another officer stand by as a witness. Course it could be different here."

Dean stepped closer, slid his arm around Lucy's waist. "The girl has a point, Sheriff. We can all sit out here waiting for your dogs and backup officers to arrive, or you can let me and Luce get on home."

Eaton chewed on his mustache, but didn't move away from the tarp.

"A girl has to protect her reputation, Sheriff." Lucy practically purred.

When Eaton still didn't answer, Dean nudged Lucy toward the cab. "Get in, Luce. Let me and the Sheriff talk for a minute."

She sat facing the front, but could hear them murmuring.

At one point, Eaton's voice outshouted Dean's. Then she heard Dean say, "Fine. But make it quick."

She thought it was over, but Dean picked up their weapons and climbed into the cab beside her.

"Don't say a thing," he whispered.

Eaton drove off, and she collapsed into his arms.

She needed him to hold her until her trembling stopped. She felt like a hypothermia patient, coming in out of the cold.

"It's the adrenaline, Lucy." His voice was a caress, like the breeze in her hair. She needed the warmth his hand brought to her back. When his lips brushed against hers, she wanted to wrap herself around him. His hands cupped her face, and he forced her to meet his gaze. "You did great."

"But I almost went for the gun."

"Good. It's what I wanted you to do."

"But he looked—"

"He only saw a tent, some sleeping bags. He only saw what I wanted him to see."

She wanted to feel his heart, to lean against him for a moment and forget the threats closing in from all sides.

But they couldn't wait there long. They had a body to deliver.

CHAPTER TWELVE

Dean wanted Sheriff Eaton in his rearview mirror. Since Eaton had driven toward the southwest, Dean headed out of Roswell in the opposite direction. "Call Martin. Tell him to meet us at PS5. Tell him we have a package."

He had to give her credit. Lucy pulled the phone from the pack without asking a single question. Two minutes later, she'd delivered the message and repacked the phone. "Answered on the first ring. Does he ever sleep?"

"The man's a ghost. I've never known him to sleep or eat for that matter." Dean rolled his window down halfway, needing the fresh air to revive him. The clock crept toward five. The eastern sky showed faint signs of lightening. He pushed the truck's speed over eighty.

"I'm sure someone mentioned a PS5 in training, but it's slipped my mind." Lucy stifled a yawn.

Dean slipped an arm around her, pulled her close, and ignored the tug in his gut when she rested her head against him.

"Predesignated Site Five."

"Predesignated by whom?"

"Yours truly."

"So you scoped out a few places."

"When I first arrived. You go in undercover, you need a fall-back position. An exit corridor if the heat comes on. You also need places you can meet."

"Or deliver things," she said softly.

"But you can't always be sure you'll have a clear frequency when you need one to set up the meetings."

"So you predesignate the places and use the code."

"Exactly."

"PS5 is—"

"Bitter Lake—twelve thousand acres and not very crowded at five in the morning."

Dean didn't wake her until he pulled off the blacktop into the Wildlife Refuge parking area. Though the lot appeared empty, Dean cut his lights and pulled to the far corner, backing into the last slot.

"Did you see that bobcat?" Lucy stared into a field to the west. The cat returned her gaze, then padded into the tall grass.

"He won't hurt you, sweetheart. Come on out."

Dean was already removing the tarp, folding it and storing it in the tool bin. "The Pecos River runs north through the Salt Creek Wilderness. The Oxbow Trail is four miles and follows it northeast to the curve in the plateaus. Martin should be there by the time we are, so we need to move."

Lucy inched her way out of the truck, but she continued to stare at Dean uncertainly. "You're going to carry Angie? Four miles?"

Instead of answering, Dean pulled a backpack from the bin. "You'll need to carry this. It has water, food, rations, and a few other supplies." He also pulled out two flak jackets.

They strapped them on in the predawn light, then he helped her with the pack. Satisfied they were ready, he shouldered the body bag, and they started down the trail. His watch said five-thirty. The comforting cloak of night was receding as quickly as the bobcat had fled.

Lucy considered herself to be in shape—less than eighteen

percent body fat, one-hundred-and twenty-two pounds, and she could run a mile in under twelve minutes. So why did she have to push to keep up with Dean when he was carrying a dead body?

"Watch the sinkhole," Dean called back.

Lucy jogged around a hole big enough to hold all of her dirty laundry. "What the hell are those things?"

"Sinkholes created by groundwater erosion."

Damn cowboy. He wasn't even breathing hard. She vowed to check under his bed next time he had an early shift. He probably had a workout bench hidden there.

"I think I saw something in that one." Lucy resisted the urge to look back.

"Probably did. Sinkholes are marvels of nature, Doc."

"How so?"

"They provide habitat for things."

"Things?"

"Fish, amphibians, other wildlife."

"Back up to amphibians. I hate frogs. They sound harmless, and everyone sells them as knickknacks with smiling faces. But those suckers can jump." Bobcats she could handle—they, at least, resembled her Aunt Daisy's cat. Amphibians creeped her out. What if there were hundreds of them? She'd seen a movie once where frogs took over the world—large, evil frogs.

Lucy jogged faster to close the gap between her and Dean. "You never know where frogs will land. Can we shoot one if it provokes us?"

"You wouldn't shoot a lowland leopard frog, would you Doc?" Dean laughed, then gave her the grin which bewildered and melted her at the same time.

How could she have both reactions at once?

They rounded the trail and came to the place where the Pecos made a turn through the red-rimmed plateaus. Lucy stopped to soak in the landscape that had unfolded before her. Her mind tried to untangle the fact such beauty could exist even as they carried the results of pure evil.

"Good place for a water break." Dean placed his burden on the ground with care, as if the bag contained more than Angie's flesh and bones. He crossed to Lucy, put his hands on her shoulders.

She thought for one moment he would kiss her again, like he had only a few hours before in the bar. Instead, he spun her around and grabbed a bottle of water from the pack before pulling her back snugly against him. His arms around her, he pointed toward the Pecos, where a flock of birds rose against the lightening sky.

"Ducks?" she asked.

"Yes. Canvasbacks. They migrate here by the thousands."

As they took wing, the sun broke the horizon and washed the plateaus in a dazzling array of red, orange, and copper. The colors played before her eyes, and Lucy remembered her vision as she'd first stepped onto the boardwalk outside E.T.'s. Looking at the desert sunrise, she knew more blood would be spilled before this mission ended. She closed her eyes, pushed the thought away, and grew aware only of Dean's warmth, his hands on her arms. They would survive this together. As surely as the sun would rise over the plateaus, and the canvasbacks would return again next year. She found comfort in that certainty. Comfort and strength.

Dean kissed her cheek and stepped away. "One more mile." He shouldered Angie's weight once more.

This time when Lucy followed she had no trouble keeping up. She'd found her pace. They were partners now. She had his back, and she felt confident Dean knew where he was going.

Dean stopped Lucy before they made the final turn into the

clearing he'd chosen for PS5. He set Angie down, this time placing her beneath some scrub where she couldn't be easily seen from the ground or the sky. Lucy shrugged out of the pack. It felt like she'd shed a hundred pounds.

"Around this corner, there's a small clearing. I'll circle around and take up position on the far side. I want you to stay here, where you have a clear view of both the field and Angie's body." As he spoke, he pulled out two semi-automatic rifles from the pack she had placed beside Angie's body, fastened on their scopes, and handed one to her.

"But, you trust Commander Martin, and no one else knows about this location." Lucy checked the weapon, then took up the position he had pointed out. The clearing was empty, as he'd promised.

"Better safe than dead. Always assume you've been compromised, until you're certain you're not. If anyone comes into this clearing other than Martin—if anyone else steps out of the 'copter—you start shooting." He reached back into the pack for two helmets. "Wear this, gorgeous."

"I wondered why that pack felt so damn heavy." She donned the helmet, unhappy about wearing it in the heat.

"It'll protect your beautiful head."

"Are you expecting an air attack, Dreiser?"

He smiled as he donned his own helmet, then tapped the comm unit and tested it. Satisfied with the signal, he gave her one last canine grin and jogged away, leaving Angie's body beside her. She focused through the scope and saw only the clearing, red plateaus in the distance, and, once, Dean's silhouette before a rising sun.

Ten minutes later, she heard the helicopter's approach. Heart racing, she glanced at Angela's form, then back at the sky. The helicopter was unmarked—which could indicate Martin had reason to take extreme measures. Or it could mean Dean's spooks had arrived.

"Hold your position, until he steps out." Dean's voice in her head was a calming breeze. She sighted in the 'copter and waited.

"Skies remain clear."

The helicopter landed with a soft thump. A man stepped out in a black jacket, USCIS printed across the back.

"Wait until I make confirmation."

Martin ran in a crouch from beneath the whirling 'copter blades as dust from the Chihuahuan Desert swirled up and around. When he had cleared the 'copter, he straightened and waited.

"That's him. I'm coming down. Do not move from your position. Keep him in your sight."

Lucy kept her weapon focused on Martin, though she couldn't imagine why. She felt more than heard Dean beside her. Then she watched them both through her scope as Dean carried Angie out, loaded her in the helicopter. She could hear him talking to Martin, but she couldn't make out his words over the noise.

Martin boarded the 'copter, and Dean hustled out from under its blades. He had covered half the distance between the 'copter and her when she caught the smallest glint of sun off metal from the northwest corner.

The plane had risen no more than twenty feet when the shooting began.

Dean dove to the ground and rolled.

The helicopter tilted. She heard the ping of shots against metal and thought maybe it was beginning to fall.

Lucy sighted in the camouflaged form, adjusted for distance and the slight morning breeze, took one steadying breath and fired.

She fired again as he fell backwards.

She waited, counted, watched to see if he would move.

Through the scope, she saw the blood seep out around the hostile, confirmed the kill.

Only then did she allow herself to lift her eye from the scope. The helicopter was again gaining altitude, pulling away from the clearing.

Lucy whirled to search for Dean and rock exploded behind her.

Heart pounding, she brought up her rifle and whipped around in time to see the second hostile fly backwards, a bullet tearing through his neck.

Dropping to the ground behind a rock, she searched the ridgeline for more attackers but saw none. The morning grew eerily quiet. Martin's helicopter disappeared. At first, only the sound of her pulse pounded in her ears, then Dean's heavy breathing joined hers.

"Is the north side clear?" he asked.

"Affirmative."

"South is clear."

"I don't have a good visual of the east and west."

Dean threw himself against the front of the rock she hid behind. "Bastards came in on a north-south heading. I don't think you'll see any others."

"Other than the two dead ones?"

"Other than those."

"Great. Dead bastards are the kind I prefer." Her breathing remained fast, and her voice shook, but her adrenaline helped her hold herself together. One part of her mind was wrestling with the fact that she'd just killed for the first time. She pushed the thought away. Right now she needed to continue to scan the rocks around them. Nothing stirred, but then they wouldn't move now. They would wait.

"Looks clear," she admitted.

Lucy finally dared to peer over her position at Dean. Blood ran down his arm.

CHAPTER THIRTEEN

The look on Lucy's face hurt nearly as much as the wound in his arm.

"Sweet Jesus. Dean." She knelt on the ground beside him, tearing off her helmet then gently removing his. "You need to lie down."

"We don't have time. It's six-twenty now. The headquarters office at the wildlife refuge opens at seven-thirty. We need to be gone before anyone else arrives."

"Not going to happen." Brown eyes snapped, and behind the anger something else simmered, something Dean hadn't seen in a woman's eyes in a long time—perhaps ever.

She began cursing him in Spanish. He wasn't fluent enough to understand all the words, but he caught the general gist as she tried to look at the wound.

"Apply a pressure bandage and stop the bleeding," he said.

"Did you earn a fucking medical degree in the last hour? No? I didn't think so. Then lie the hell down before I knock you out and make you lie down."

Her fingers probed the bullet wound, and he wondered how her lab mice had survived her bedside manner.

"No arterial bleeding. There's an entry and an exit wound. You're very lucky, Dean. Other than the blood loss—"

"You are starting to take on an angelic glow," Dean muttered, but he didn't argue when she retrieved the pack, pulled out a cotton shirt and pressed it against the wound.

"I need to call Martin."

"No. Martin's delivering Angie. We do this alone."

"Bad idea. This isn't exactly a sterile area."

"There's an emergency med kit in the pack."

"Dean, let's get you to the hospital then—"

"Lucy, we can't do that. You know we can't." He clamped his jaw against the pain. He'd been shot before. It felt every bit as bad as the last time.

"Stay with me, Dreiser."

"Keep your weapon close," he mumbled.

"Right. I'll perform surgery in the desert with my right hand and shoot the bastards with my left." But she pulled her rifle closer and searched the horizon one last time before she opened the field kit. He watched as she positioned a tourniquet above the wound, but she had to release the pressure bandage in order to tie off the tourniquet. When she did, the bleeding began again in earnest.

"If it didn't hit an artery—"

"You still have a hole in your arm, Dean."

He thought he should feel something at the sight of so much blood. Given that it was his own, he should feel panic. He didn't, though. What he felt was tired. She tried packing gauze into the wound to staunch the flow of blood, but it, too, became saturated.

"I need your help. Dean? Damn it."

He could hear her, barely. But his eyes felt impossibly heavy, heavier than Angie had been.

The next thing he knew the unmistakable odor of ammonia pulled him back, causing his eyes to water. The pain in his arm had doubled, which he wouldn't have thought possible.

"You need some new perfume, Doc."

"What I need is your help. If I'm going to do this, you have to stay awake. Got it? Stay awake, or I'm calling Martin and you can argue with me about it later. As it is, I'm getting pretty tired of doing everything your way. Don't know what made me wake you up."

She took his good hand, placed it firmly against the wound and pushed. "I suppose I feel indebted because you saved my life, and I like the way you kiss. You don't have to start grinning like a wolf. Save that energy. You're going to need it if you really expect to walk out of here."

Her eyes appeared in front of his—Spanish eyes, a beautiful chocolate brown, soulful eyes. Promising him the world. There, and then gone. They were replaced by a clear blue New Mexico sky, one well into daybreak. And that didn't seem right. How could it be right?

The mission came back to him like an arrow piercing his core. They should be walking. They had to be back. He had to take care of Lucy now, get her to the truck, get her out of the desert before anyone else showed up.

"Shit."

"Sounds like you're back."

"Yeah. I'm here."

He heard her ripping open supplies, laying out a makeshift triage.

"How am I doing, Doc?"

"You're still losing blood."

She removed the soaked bandages and applied new ones, then pushed his palm back over the top. "I need you to hold this compress. Steady pressure. Two minutes, Dean."

His world shrank into a blur of sounds and images. The snap of rubber gloves. The glint of sun on a scalpel. The wetness of blood soaking through the bandages, pulsing into his good hand. Lucy's eyes peering into his.

"The kit contained a small amount of morphine. I saved it for now, but I'm not sure how much it will help."

"No."

"Dean, you are not in charge right now. Damn it, do what you're told for once."

"Lucinda—" He had never used her full name. He'd been saving it, but not for this moment. The thought surprised him, though it shouldn't have. "You can't carry me out of here. I'm walking. No morphine. Now let's do this."

She nodded, leaned forward and kissed him quickly and gently. When she pulled back a calmness and change had come over her. He wasn't looking at Lucy Brown the agent anymore, but at Dr. Lucinda Brown. In the instant before he passed out, he realized he'd pull through with her caring for him.

Lucy knew arguing with him was a complete waste of their time. Studies showed the use of morphine on the battlefield was largely for psychological reasons. She for one had no desire to test the theory—on herself or anyone else. Yet here she was, and Dean's argument made some sense. She'd never be able to carry him out.

The point was a moot one, as she knew it would be.

He slipped into unconsciousness as soon as the scalpel probed the wound. While the bullet had exited, small pieces of residue remained—his shirt, dirt, even pieces of rock where he'd fallen on the ground. She removed the pieces she could see with the scalpel, then irrigated the wound to clean the rest.

Dean remained blissfully unaware. The human body had its own way of dealing with pain. With unconsciousness, his heart took on a slower and steadier rhythm. She should have knocked him out earlier. She'd have to remember that next time. God forbid they ever share a next time quite like this one.

She resisted the urge to look around and assure herself no one had a firearm pointed at her head. If they did, she couldn't do anything about it at the moment. Her hands flew, doing what they had been trained to do—healing. As she sutured the wound closed and applied a clean dressing she became aware again of her surroundings, of the sweat pouring down her face, of the fact they still had four miles to hike back out.

As gunshot wounds go, it was actually somewhat minor. Now that she had him sewn up. Of course, he'd need antibiotics, but she had some of those packed in her things at Josephine's—just in case.

His pulse remained steady and strong. He continued to amaze her. Had she actually considered him old and decrepit on that ride from Albuquerque? Pouring water over a bandana, she wiped his brow, then his face, let her fingers brush through his hair. She pulled a jacket from their pack. It still smelled of him and she buried her face in it, allowing the terror of the last hour to claim her—only for a moment though. Dean needed her. She rolled it up and placed it under his head. He still didn't stir.

Knowing she couldn't postpone the inevitable any longer, she took a long drink from the bottle, recapped it, and stood. After repacking all their supplies, she did the one thing left to do. She approached the dead guy lying twenty feet behind them.

Dean woke to a vision of true loveliness—Lucy sitting three feet away, staring straight at him, holding the rifle. She still wore her flak jacket, and she had dirt and some of his blood smeared across the bridge of her nose. He'd never seen a more beautiful woman.

"Don't shoot." He struggled to sit up and the desert began to spin. "Son of a bitch."

"Slower," Lucy cautioned. She helped him to a sitting position and handed him the bottle of water. "No morphine, remember?"

"Yeah, I remember. How long have I been out?"

"Forty minutes. It's seven fifteen."

Dean tried to stand. The fact that Lucy stopped him by pressing her hands on his shoulders pretty much summed up how fucked they were.

"We're not making the seven-thirty opening, cowboy. You might as well slow down and think of a plan B."

Dean leaned back against the rock and let the weariness wash over him. She was right of course. Too bad he didn't have a plan B.

"Have more water. Maybe you can think up one."

"Are there cartoon bubbles above my head again?" But he accepted the water and drank deeply. His eyes never left hers as he finished it off. "How you holding up, Lucy?"

"Better than the dead guy in the bushes." Lucy handed their phone to Dean, which showed a picture of the shooter. "I also took DNA samples and fingerprints. Then I dragged his body a little further off the trail. He had no identification on him. I did find this."

She handed Dean a small satellite phone.

"You've been busy, Doc. Nice work. You took his weapon?"

She nodded. "Broke it down and stowed it in our pack."

Dean shifted to pull his ball cap down, then realized he wasn't wearing one.

Lucy smiled at the gesture.

"All right. The phone will probably be a dead end. They will have realized something's wrong when he didn't make contact. By now all records have been wiped clean, but we'll get it to Martin anyway."

"So what do we do?"

"We walk out of here like we've been enjoying an early morning hike."

"What about the bodies?"

"I scoped this preserve out two weeks ago. Trails were empty on weekday mornings. No one will stumble across the guy on the ridge, and the one you pulled off the trail won't be a problem for a few hours."

"Someone will find them eventually though."

Dean struggled to stand, leaning against Lucy until he found his equilibrium. "I'd bet good money that whoever sent these two here had tracers injected in them. Someone will be after their bodies tonight. Or they won't."

"They would leave them?"

"We'll alert Martin. If the bad guys don't pick them up, we will. It wouldn't be the first time a man or woman has been left behind. If no one picks them up they can count on animals to take care of any evidence." Dean zipped out of his flak jacket. He couldn't help smiling as Lucy did the same. "Have I ever mentioned how swell you look in a bulletproof vest?"

"Do you hit on all your doctors, Agent Dreiser?"

"Only the sexy ones."

They stuffed the flak jackets into the pack. With the added weapon, Lucy had trouble picking it up. Dean made a motion to carry it, but one look from his doctor had him backing off.

"Maybe I should go and check the other guy," she said. "He could have some identification, some clue as to who these people are."

"Don't count on it. These people were professionals. You found no i.d. on this one, there won't be any on the other one either." He entwined his good hand in hers. "We need to get out of here and back to Roswell. Our priority stays the same— alert Martin and maintain our cover."

"You also need to start on antibiotics as soon as we get back."

"Uh huh."

"You scared the hell out of me. You know that, right?"

"It was a test of sorts."

"Is that so?"

He stopped on the trail and pulled her to him. Reaching up

he touched her face, allowed his hand to follow her hair down her back. The thick braid disappeared beneath the pack that was too heavy for her. This mission, the weight of it threatened to crush them. It would take the two of them to carry the burden of it. Standing there in the morning light with the bodies behind them and more questions in front of them, they both realized the odds of their winning slid further away each moment.

She cocked her head and gazed up into his eyes. "What kind of test?"

"A check out the new doc under pressure test."

She pierced him with eyes capable of melting the toughest old heart. In fact, they had.

"Are you going to tell me if I passed?"

"Sure. It'll depend on if I survive your doctoring or not."

They ambled down the trail, their pace slow at first, but gradually increasing until it resembled something approaching normal. For all the world, it began to take on the feel of an average summer day—a guy and a girl out on a morning hike. Forgetting the two dead guys behind them, the hole in Dean's arm, the bioweapon in the desert, and the thousands of lives at stake. All that aside, they could have been any other man and woman in the midst of falling in love.

CHAPTER FOURTEEN

Lucy drove the truck back to Roswell. Dean didn't complain about her driving, maybe because he had once again passed out. He woke up when she shouted their order into the fast food drive-through speaker.

"Breakfast of champions?"

"I'm lowering my standard for you, Dreiser."

He smiled, sat up in the seat and dove into the bag she passed him. They had devoured the egg sandwiches, hashbrowns, and orange juice, before she'd driven the remaining six blocks to Josephine's.

"Explain to me, again, why we don't have any damn coffee," he mumbled.

Instead of answering, she set the brake and gathered up their trash. She wanted to ask how he felt, but a few stragglers were walking to their cars, leaving for work. They did not need to overhear her questioning him about his vitals. So she stayed a few steps in front of him, scoping out the bushes for terrorists.

Once in Dean's room, they removed their weapons—placing them within easy reach of the bed. Dean sank onto the mattress, not bothering to turn down the covers. Lucy started the water in the shower.

Laying out a towel and soap, she returned to find Dean nearly asleep.

He opened one eye. "I know you got the small room, but if you'll search it, I think you'll find your own shower."

She perched on the bed's edge and touched the face that had become as familiar as her own. "Your biggest risk is infection. You have to take a shower and cleanse the wound."

He answered with a groan.

"I'll help you undress."

"You're saying that, so I'll think I'll get lucky." But he sat up, and he didn't resist when she unbuttoned his shirt and tugged it off his shoulders.

"I need to cut off this t-shirt, Dean." She rested her forehead against his, kissed his lips, let her fingers run down the length of his chest.

"You're not cutting off my shirt." He bit her lip. His bluster was all gone though, and they both knew it.

"It's covered in blood. You can't raise that arm over your head, anyway." She trailed a path down his neck with her lips, enjoying the salty taste, then captured his face between both of her hands. "You can argue and the shower will run out of hot water, or you can let me cut it off."

"Damn it, woman. Scissors are in the desk drawer."

She stopped running her hands over his chest long enough to cut away the fabric, peel the blood-soaked material from his arm. When he stood, and she helped him pull off his jeans, the last of her professional demeanor slipped away faster than the denim.

"Hell, Lucy. I think I've got it from here."

"Right. Of course." She stepped away, but he pulled her back, kissed her once.

"I'm going to my room to get more medical supplies. Cleanse the wound with the new bar of soap, then rinse it with the rag. Don't hold it directly under the water."

"You did a good job, Doc."

She nodded, wanted to believe him.

Once in her room, she kept thinking of other things he might need. Then it occurred to her Martin might have sent a message. She gathered all the medical supplies and the laptop and hurried back into Dean's room.

He was sprawled across the bed, only the bed sheet covering him, and he was sound asleep.

She worked her shift, and told Sally that Dean might have the flu.

Every time the door to E.T.'s opened, she jumped. Hopefully he'd have the sense to stay in bed at least twenty-four hours, but she doubted it.

At the end of her shift, she bagged up some food, and headed back to his room.

He was still out, so she ate and watched him sleep.

It reminded her of the long nights she'd spent as a resident.

When she didn't think she could keep her eyes open any longer, when she'd monitored him all night, and he still showed no signs of fever, she stood, stretched, and admitted to herself he'd be fine.

Knowing only a hot shower would revive her, but still not willing to leave him, she went into his bathroom, but left the door cracked. She'd hear him if he called.

The hot steam had begun to work away the knots in her shoulders when Dean stepped into the shower.

"No, you don't." She put a hand on his chest and attempted to push him back out.

"Tell me you don't want me in here." He lowered his head and nuzzled her neck where the water streamed down.

"Dean, you can't. You're not ready."

He guided her hand down, until she held the full length of him. "I'd say, I'm ready, Lucy."

"That's not what I meant." She tried to pull away, but only succeeded in arching her neck. Her hair fell back and he kissed behind her ear. Nothing had ever felt so delicious.

"I know what you meant. My arm is fine. I have this great doctor."

She stood on the very tip of her toes, pressed her body fully against his, and kissed him—her lips barely caressing his. Tasting him. Teasing him and reveling in the familiarity and the strangeness of him. "We need to be gentle."

She pulled him more completely into the shower, under the steaming water.

Picking up the bar of soap, she whispered, "You still have your bandage on."

"I cleaned it before. Like you told me."

"Then keep your left arm out the door, keep it dry."

"Right." His voice was ragged.

His lips found and claimed hers.

She lost herself, for a minute, for two. Pulling away, she lathered the soap in her hands. When she rubbed it over his shoulders and down his chest, his breathing quickened. Always aware of his stiffness between them and her ache, her need for him. The water fell like a cleansing rain, washing away the death and fear that had surrounded them since they'd arrived in Roswell.

With his good hand, he pulled her closer. Pushing her against the back wall, he bent and nuzzled her breasts. His hand caressed between her legs, and he would have sent her over, but she stopped him.

"Not yet."

She raised his mouth to hers, then kneeled in front of him. She washed his length. Barely aware of his hands in her hair, his voice calling her name. She forgot they were in New Mexico, neck-deep in danger. She let herself go. Allowed herself to claim him, pulling him into her mouth, until his groans pierced her reverie.

"Lucy, come here. Please, sweetheart."

One-handed, he pulled her to her feet. When he kissed her this time, she yielded to him completely. The shower had renewed him. With his good arm, he helped her maneuver until he was inside her. She wrapped her legs around his waist, let her hands claim his face, his hair, his shoulders. Explored him with her lips and her tongue, without restraint, even as he drove deeper.

Then he pressed her back against the shower wall, and sensations threatened to overwhelm her: the tiles' chill, Dean's heat. The water cascading—an endless stream of rain.

"Lucinda, sweet, sweet, Lucinda. Come with me, darling." He nipped at her neck, and she gave herself over to the rightness of being in his arms. The last bit of her control crumbled away. She joined him in that place she had gone to with so few people and never in this way. Never with such complete abandon.

He had taken a bullet for her. The thought rang through her mind, her body.

She orgasmed and her every muscle went slack. He had risked his life for her, and he would again. Her mind and heart cleared.

She cradled his face, ran her thumb along his jaw line. He held her gaze for a heartbeat, then buried his face in her hair and murmured her name. She understood the solace they sought went beyond what a man and woman normally offered one another. No doubt, partners had been caught up in love affairs before, but had they faced a terror of the scope that now lurked beyond these walls?

The truth struck her even as they stepped out of the shower and toweled each other dry. They had little chance of survival. The doctor in her accepted the fact as calmly as it would look at Ebola under a microscope. Between the bioweapon they faced, and the terrorists who knew no limits and didn't play by the rules, their odds of survival shrank with each tick of the clock. It reminded her of Marcos' stories of sniper patrol during his first few weeks in Iraq. She finally understood what her brother had endured.

And she recognized the value of the bond she shared with Dean. Even as she administered the injection of antibiotics she had brought and re-bandaged his arm. Even as he tumbled off to sleep, and she curled up beside him. The truth stared at her with the same clarity as the hands on their bedside clock.

They had each other—and they only had each other.

Dean woke to a blaring alarm and a note on the bedside table.

Your shift starts in an hour. I left coffee and food in the microwave. Lucy.

He ran his hands through his hair, stumbled to the bathroom, and found himself staring at the shower. "Damn."

Turning the thing on full blast, he wrapped his arm in the plastic wrap she'd left beside the shower, and stepped into it, not bothering to wait for it to heat up. The cold did little to clear his mind or improve his mood. Had he really had sex with Lucy here six hours ago? What had he been thinking? He'd been an agent for ten years, and he'd done a lot of damned foolish things, but he'd never been stupid enough to sleep with his partner while on an active op. Of course he'd never had a partner like Lucy before either.

Stepping out of the shower, he winced when he bumped his left arm against the bathroom door. Stripping off the plastic, he gripped a corner of the tape and yanked off the bandage. He stared at the stitches Lucy had neatly sewn.

"She's one damn fine doctor." He argued with the man in the mirror. Unsure how else to justify his behavior, he bandaged the arm with a fresh dressing. Within thirty minutes, he devoured the coffee and sandwich he found in the microwave, dressed for work, and drove the old truck around the block to E.T.'s.

Walking into the bar, the first thing he noticed was Sally behind the grill. "You running the grill tonight?"

"No, Dreiser. I'm standing back here, because the view's better. How's your flu?"

Dean never missed a beat. "Not as bad as I thought."

Nadine set her tray on the bar top, "Three Buds please, Paul."

The older man started to pull out the Buds, but Dean stopped him. "I'll take care of it. You've been on all day. Go ahead and clock out."

"Don't have to tell me twice."

"You have a hot date, Paul?" Dean smiled at Nadine as he placed the bottles of beer on her tray.

"Nope, going to the desert. Haven't you heard about the sightings?"

Nadine rolled her eyes and turned to go.

"Guess I missed that memo. Someone see something?"

Emily rested on a barstool, "Two Coors, Dean. Every customer in here tonight keeps yapping about those damn sightings."

"The only sighting I care about is your ass sitting on a bar stool when it's not break time," Sally barked from the kitchen.

As they all stared at her, she grabbed the latest order off the cook's ring and stormed back to the grill.

"Please bring Jerry back soon," Emily groaned as Dean placed the Coors on her tray.

Dean started to ask Paul what sightings he meant, but the man had left. He turned back around to ask Emily, but she'd been replaced by Lucy.

"Oh, hi. I thought you were Emily."

"Sorry to disappoint you, Dreiser." Lucy grinned and slid onto a bar stool. "I need three Coors and a single shot of bourbon with a side of ice."

"Coming up," he said. But he didn't move. He couldn't. He stood there mesmerized by the sight of her. Damn, but she looked as good in a waitressing uniform as she did in a flak jacket.

"Something wrong? Do I have ranch on my uniform or something?" Lucy started patting down her clothes, looking for an offending spot.

Unfortunately she started near her breasts, and Dean felt the heat creep up his face and spread down his groin. He hadn't felt this confused since he'd been caught feeling up Jeina Potts in fourth grade. Pulling the beers from the cooler he changed the subject.

"What sightings?"

Lucy checked the grill window to be sure Sally couldn't hear, then leaned across the bar. "According to half of Roswell, the little green men are back."

"Huh?" Dean poured a double shot of the bourbon instead of a single, but placed it on Lucy's tray anyway.

"Yeah, it's pretty strange. The reports vary a bit, but they all agree the lights appear in the desert near the Mescalero Indian Reservation. The Indians say it's the old ones, coming back to fulfill the prophecy to rise up against the white man. Whatever it is, the sightings started sometime after midnight and ended before four this morning. Flying saucers, strange lights, the whole bit."

Lucy picked up her tray to go, but paused to give him one of her soul-searching looks.

Dean nodded to convey he felt fine.

She had stepped away, maneuvering through the crowded bar, which Dean realized was busier than normal, when the door opened again.

Sheriff Eaton didn't pause as he crossed the room. He took

one look at Lucy, then headed straight for the bar. His hand remained on his sidearm.

In a low, but clear voice, he said, "Dreiser, you're under arrest."

CHAPTER FIFTEEN

Lucy's pulse kicked up to double-time as she watched the way Eaton walked over to Dean and squared off. She couldn't hear what he said over Bubba and Billy, but she could tell from the set of Dean's jaw whatever it was didn't make him happy.

When Dean grabbed Emily to cover the bar and stepped out the back door, Eaton remained close behind him. Too close.

"I'll be right back with your drinks, boys."

"Don't go yet, Lucy. This is the interesting part. See, the UFO hovered in the sky above where we parked. Damn thing was bigger than a Volkswagen Beetle."

Lucy had stepped away from the table when Colton grabbed her wrist. His hand was big and muscular and hairy, there was nothing boyish about it. "Bubba hasn't finished yet, Lucy. It's rude to walk away when someone's talking."

Instead of trying to twist away, Lucy stepped closer. Close enough to smell his sweat and the odor underneath, an odor she could only describe as meanness. Something she recognized from walking with her father on the streets of Boston. Some things smelled the same no matter where you encountered them.

"You might want to let go of my wrist. Unless you want your balls closer to your throat than they were when you rolled out of bed this morning."

Bubba and Billy stopped midsentence, deciding it was safer to pick up their beers and concentrate on emptying them. Colton did what came natural. He stood up and loomed over her, giving Lucy the exact vantage point she had hoped for. She rammed her knee into his testicles, and, at the same time twisted her arm back and away.

The big guy released her wrist and hit the floor, holding his crotch. "Holy shit, Lucy. What the hell did you do that for?"

"Do we have a problem, boys?" Sally was standing beside the table, before Lucy even realized she had left the kitchen.

"No problem," Lucy said. "Colton fell. I'd like to take my break now."

Colton dragged himself back onto his chair, refusing to meet either woman's eyes.

"Hang on a minute, Lucy. Do you have a problem with the service here, Colton?" Sally's voice dared him to give her a reason to show him the door.

"Damn straight. This damn beer isn't even cold."

"You're welcome to go somewhere else." Sally leaned on the baseball bat she had brought with her, studying them as if she could figure out what had transpired between them. Finally, she nodded at Lucy. "Go on and take your break. Make it short though. We've got a full house tonight."

"Yes, ma'am." Lucy fled out the back door, before Sally could change her mind. She stepped out into the night. Even in the alley's near-darkness, she had no trouble finding Dean and Eaton.

The sheriff had Dean down on the ground with his hands cuffed behind his back and was reading him his rights.

"What the hell are you doing?"

Dean shot her a warning look. "Stay out of this, Lucy."

"The hell I will. Why are you arresting Dean?"

"I don't see how that's any of your business, young lady. Unless you want to be hauled in, too, I suggest you get yourself back inside." Eaton jerked Dean to his feet and hauled him toward the end of the alley, blocked with his patrol car.

"I'm making it my business. I happen to be his counsel, and I want to know the charges."

Eaton stopped in his tracks, jerked Dean around, and said, in a voice that sounded as if he hadn't slept in weeks, "You're Dean Dreiser's *counsel?*"

"That's right." Lucy closed the gap between them and drew herself up to her full height. "I demand to know what you have on my client."

"So now you're a lawyer."

"There is no requirement to be a lawyer in order to represent a plaintiff in this state. Now, why are you arresting him?"

"Well, hell." Eaton still grasped Dean's left arm—his injured arm. Lucy guessed he hadn't figured that out yet. His other hand reached for his weapon. "I'm arresting Dreiser for burglary."

"Of?"

"Of the morgue. You know what the hell of, and you're damned lucky I'm not arresting you, too. Stop playing because this isn't a game, young lady. I do not have time for you."

"Oh, so you don't have time for me—" Lucy felt what little restraint she possessed snap.

"Lucy, let the sheriff do his job," Dean said.

"I'll tell you what you don't have time for. You don't have time for reporters on your front doorstep, which is where they'll be in three hours. You also don't have time for an ACLU lawsuit, which will be filed within twelve hours."

"Just because you're a cop's daughter who thinks she knows the law—"

"You'll find out how much law I know. For all you know, I'm majoring in law. So, unless you have evidence, probable cause, motive, and some damned good witnesses, I suggest you uncuff my client right now."

She watched Eaton calculate the odds. She suspected he

didn't have the time or energy to call her bluff, and he knew she'd follow through to get Dean out of his jail. With a curse, he reached into his pocket, found the keys to the cuffs and released Dean.

The three stood there looking at each other as Eaton removed his hat and cleaned some imaginary dirt from the rim.

"Someone stole Angie's body from the morgue last night. You two are my primary suspects."

"Why would we want Angie's body?" Dean moved to Lucy's side, placed his hand on her back.

"You tell me."

Lucy pushed her bottom lip out in a pout. "Dean hasn't done anything. There's no reason to arrest him. The morgue really lost her?"

"The body should have been transferred to—" Eaton placed the Stetson back on his head. "Well, let's just say it wasn't, and no one knows why."

"Strange. Poor Jerry. He must be crazy. Is he pressing charges?"

"No. And neither are—" Eaton stopped, as if he'd said too much. From the light of the lone street lamp, she could see the lines and miles the man had travelled. She could also see he hadn't given up. "Bodies do not disappear on my shift in my town. I will find out what's going on, and I don't care who I have to arrest to do it."

"A bartender hears a lot of things. I'll keep my ears open and call you if I hear anything."

Eaton considered the offer, then nodded. Turning to Lucy he said, "I guess you learned that shit from your father."

"Actually, my mother is the hard ass."

"You two watch yourself. Because you're walking tonight, doesn't mean I won't have you behind bars tomorrow." With that, he slammed the door to his cruiser, fired the engine, and drove off, flipping the siren once.

"Maybe we should tell him, Dean. It wouldn't hurt to have someone on our side."

By way of an answer, Dean pushed her against the wall, kissed her until she thought he would take all the breath she had.

When he finished, he pulled away, but he didn't let go of her hand. "We trust each other, Lucy. No one else."

She nodded in the darkness.

"How's your arm?" she whispered.

"Good as new."

"You're sure?"

"I've been slinging cases of beer all night."

"You'll pull the stitches."

"I won't. You either gave me a miracle drug or you have some special kind of doctoring."

His laughter quieted her worries. She reached up, kissed him once more, then stepped out of the comfort of his arms and made her way back inside.

When they entered the bar, all eyes were on them. Dean squeezed Lucy's ass one final time. Lucy swatted his hand and picked up her order pad. Sally squinted and grumbled, no doubt ready to kill him with her chef's knife. But he'd achieved the effect he'd wanted. Customers forgot about Sheriff Eaton and started gossiping about whether Dean had gotten any in the alley. A few of his regulars even gave him the old thumbs-up as he made his way to the register.

Fishing five bucks out of his wallet, he handed it to Nadine and gave her a wink as he picked up a map of Chaves County. "Keep the change, sweetheart."

"Thanks, Dean."

He pulled the office keys out of his pocket. The bartender's job included locking up every room before he left. Unlocking the office, he went to Sally's desk and pulled open the right-hand drawer. After grabbing a brand new box of pushpins, he relocked the office, and hurried back to the bar. The crowd had grown. He caught snippets of conversations about the sightings. As Lucy had said, everyone seemed to be talking about it.

On the way to the billiard tables, Sally croaked. "You thinking about working tonight, Dreiser?"

He didn't slow, but did wink at Emily, who continued to pull drinks behind his bar. When he reached the two dart boards, the area was empty except for Bubba, Billy, and Colton.

"Guys, want to give me a hand?"

Colton ignored the request and continued throwing darts, but Bubba and Billy set down their beers and ambled over. "What ya' need a map of Roswell for Dean? You still getting lost?" Bubba laughed at his own joke, but it was a good natured laugh.

The boy didn't have much sense, but he didn't have any malice in him either.

"Hold that corner a little higher, Bubba." Dean positioned the map between the two dart boards, centering it high where people could see it from across the room, but not so high they couldn't reach it.

"Looks nice, Dean. I sort of forget how big Chaves County is." Billy took a big gulp of his beer and leaned back against the pool table.

"Now where did you boys go last night when you saw those lights?" Dean didn't look at Colton straight on, but he felt him stop midway in the throw of his dart, then lower it to his side.

Turning to look at Dean, he crossed over to where the three stood in front of the map. Bubba and Billy were scratching their head. They'd been more caught up in *what* they'd seen than *where* they'd seen it. Colton picked up one of the push pins from the container and, without hesitating, pushed it in at Bluewater Creek, southwest of town.

"You're sure?"

"Yeah." Colton held his gaze, daring him to question what they'd seen.

Dean shrugged. "We might never know what you all saw, but we can at least figure out if the bastards return to the same spot." With that he placed the box of pushpins on top of the jukebox and went to the bar.

"Thanks for covering, Emily. I owe you."

"Not a problem, Dean."

Bubba had called more friends over to the map.

Dean was soon too busy filling orders to stop and watch, but every time he glanced that way, one or two people stood beside the map, pushing in a pin.

Eight hours later, Sally dropped onto a bar stool, as did the small crew that had remained to close. She didn't need to ask for an ashtray. Dean had one out before she could light up.

"Why the hell did you put a map on my wall, Dreiser?"

Dean shrugged, then set some ice water in front of her. When her eyebrow shot up, he added a shot of whiskey beside it.

"Wherever you get your ideas, they're good. We didn't slow down all night, what with everyone coming in to see The Map."

"And, of course, everyone who saw The Map ordered a drink or two," Emily added.

"I didn't think Billy and Bubba would ever leave." Lucy groaned.

"Though, I did notice Colton didn't give you any more trouble." Sally studied her through the smoke.

"What happened with Colton?" Dean sat down on another stool and pulled a Corona from the cooler.

"Nothing," Lucy said.

"Nothing, except Lucy tried to feed him his balls for dessert."

Sally crushed out her cigarette, considered lighting another, but pushed the pack back into her apron pocket. "Damn things will kill me one day."

"So, why did you put the map up, Dean?" Nadine held the glass of ice water to her forehead. The circles under her eyes were darker than usual.

Dean realized no one had probably slept much since Angie's killing. They continued going through the motions of their days, but with no body, there had been no funeral, and therefore no closure. Jerry remained MIA, and the aura hanging over the rest was one anyone in the military would have recognized— SNAFU. Their collective ache hovered beneath the surface.

Or could the pain in Nadine's eyes be from something else? Had she betrayed her friend? Had something caused her to cross to the other side? What about Sally? Or Emily? Could he even afford to trust Paul?

"You girls noticed what was going on first," Dean said. "Everyone seemed to be talking about spaceships. I thought if we gave them something to do with their sightings, it might help them relax."

Sally snorted. "And you happened to hang it ten feet from the bar, which didn't hurt your tips."

Dean smiled and took a long pull from the Corona he was nursing. He didn't defend himself, but he didn't bother denying what she said, either.

Emily saw the look that passed between Lucy and Dean. "It doesn't hurt that your girlfriend is fascinated by UFOs."

Lucy slugged her in the arm.

"Did you two make out in the alley?" Emily asked.

"Eww. I've heard rats back there, Lucy. Both the four-legged and two-legged kind," Nadine said. "You wouldn't catch me back there. Not even to cop a feel of Dean's ass."

That sent all three girls into peals of laughter. Sally seemed to decide dying of nicotine poisoning would beat suffering through their conversation without a buzz and lit up.

Dean noticed Emily's husband flashing his lights in front of the bar. He was grateful to be saved from further female interrogation.

"Let's go, sweetheart." Dean walked around the counter and put his hand on Emily's arm.

Sally squinted through the smoke, staring after Dean and Emily. "What the hell is he doing?"

Nadine and Lucy exchanged looks. Already the routine had become, well, routine.

"Dean thinks he needs to walk us out," Nadine said. "After what happened to Angie."

Sally's eyes hardened and her mouth, which never quite formed a smile, set in an even firmer line. Dean had barely made it back inside when she attacked.

"If you think this bar had something to do with Angie's death you can pack your shit and leave now, Dreiser."

"What?" Dean whirled around as Sally jumped off her stool.

"You heard me. We don't need you, and we don't need your macho man attitude," Sally snarled.

He looked to Lucy and Nadine for a clue. Both shook their heads, indicating they had no idea why she was reacting like this. He didn't have much time to watch them. Sally hissed like a cat that had been dumped in a pan of water.

"Or maybe you want to accuse someone here. Is that what your little conversation with Eaton was about?" Now she had her finger poking in his chest, her smoky breath in his face. Dean didn't usually back up from an attacker, but it was either back up or slug her. And since the minute he cold cocked his boss, he'd lose his cover, he backed up.

"Why don't you calm down, Sally?"

"Don't fucking tell me to calm down."

Dean realized her eyes weren't focused on anything in this room. He was grateful there wasn't a weapon within reach—at least not one she knew about. As long as he kept himself between her and the bar, between her and the shotgun.

"You think someone here had something to do with Angie's death? You come out and say it. Or maybe you're too fucking smart. Maybe you don't think I can protect my girls, because of what happened to her. Well she was like a daughter to me, okay? And I can protect my girls. I can, and I will."

The change was instantaneous. One second, Sally was on the attack. The next she deflated like a punctured balloon. Dean caught her, but barely. She sank to the floor, sobbing incoherently. The one word he could make out was Angie's name.

"Lucy, bring me some water. Nadine, call Eaton. See if he can get over here."

They stayed with her until the sheriff arrived. She remained inconsolable. The grief she'd held in poured out of her in a fountain of despair.

"I'll see her home safe. Thanks for calling me." Eaton nodded to Nadine.

Sally sat in the police cruiser's front seat, staring straight ahead. Nadine pulled away ahead of them. Dean and Lucy closed up, then climbed into the truck. They sat there a few minutes, staring at E.T.'s.

"I didn't expect that from her." Lucy drew in a deep breath. "She always seemed so strong and so remote."

Dean didn't answer. He did pull her closer, needing to feel her by his side.

"I guess she was closer to Angie than I realized."

"I'm not sure what we saw tonight was real, Lucy."

She tilted her head back, stared up at him in the moonlight. "Are you doubting she would have scratched your eyes out? I had my hand on my weapon. I was ready to back you up, Drei-ser."

He reached out, held her face in both hands. Traced her profile with his thumbs. "Her anger seemed real. There was a moment there where her eyes . . ." He stared out into the night, tried to put into words what his instinct was telling him.

"Hey. Talk to me, partner."

"I don't know. It was like she was looking at someone else. She was angry all right. I don't know about what, though. You can't believe everything you see is what you see."

Lucy studied the boardwalk. "My *abuela* said that I have the gift of second sight."

Dean waited, sensing she was about to trust him with something important.

"The first day we drove into town, I parked the truck and walked up those steps. The sun was spilling across the board-walk. That isn't what I saw, though." Lucy pulled her eyes from the night, gazed into his. "I saw blood splashed across them, as clearly as I'm seeing you right now."

Dean didn't question her. Didn't point out the absurdity of such visions. He pulled her closer into the protection of his arm. Then, he put the truck into reverse and drove them home.

CHAPTER SIXTEEN

The woman had been picked up by his driver on one other occasion. It was both the best and worst moment of her life—the point at which she had willingly stepped into the well from which she would never emerge. Yet, she found comfort in the darkness of her circumstances. Even now, she longed for the death which her choice would eventually bring. She found solace in reminding herself some of *them* would die with her. It was a small consolation for the loss of her son, but she would accept it.

She knew the driver by sight, if not by name. He'd acted as courier several times. Tonight, apparently she would be the package.

"I've been instructed to blindfold and restrain you." He waited for her to turn around.

"Bind them in front, or I won't be able to work tomorrow. Damn shoulder won't tolerate being pulled back. Last thing he wants is to raise more questions in Roswell. Unless I'm never going back to work, then hell—bind them in the back."

He showed no pity, but doubt flickered in his eyes.

Finally he nodded, bound her hands in front, and affixed the blindfold.

Reaching into her jacket, he removed her weapon. "That he wants you blindfolded is good."

"You mean, I might come back alive."

"I do not pretend to know the mind of our leader. The ones I do not blindfold, he always kills. The ones I blindfold . . ." The sentence hung between them as he helped her into the back of the SUV and shut the door.

The night sounds closed in around them, reminding her of that other evening so long ago. The one she'd never forget. The similarities weren't lost on her—the hoot of an owl far off, the late hour, even the time of year were the same. Perhaps it was a sign. Or it could be her fate to be cursed with the same scene again and again. Surely this would be the last time though. Either their plan would work or she would die trying. She worked her hand into her pocket, though it cut against the tie to do so. Thumbing on the GPS unit, she kept her head up and faced the driver. As they turned off the blacktop, she pressed the button once.

The driver sped up, and the car fishtailed on the road. Pushing her feet against the floorboard, she struggled to right herself in the seat.

"How long will it take to get there?"

He didn't answer. She hadn't expected him to.

The Land Rover bumped along into the night. She counted seven turns, clicked the unit each time. Then they stopped.

When he helped her from the back seat, the desert night surrounded her. The smell of creosote and sagebrush came to her along with the unmistakable tang of hot white sand. She sensed it without her vision. After all, she'd been born and raised in Roswell. She would have known if they'd returned to town. They hadn't.

It was like waking from a dream to find yourself in another part of your home. You might not remember how you got there, but you knew where you were all the same.

The howl of a coyote pierced the night.

He jerked her to a sudden stop. She heard the tiny beep of a card scan, then felt a rush of air conditioning. He nudged her forward. A door, heavy steel from the sound of it, shut behind them with the finality of the closing of a coffin.

All the desert sounds and smells immediately disappeared. Only an airtight seal could erase all traces of the desert instantly. She became aware of the low hum of machinery as they made their way through a maze of hallways. When her escort hesitated, she knew they had reached him.

"Enter," he said.

They stepped into a room that was colder than the corridor behind them.

"Remove the blindfold and unbind her."

Her eyes resisted the fluorescent lights' brightness, which was, of course, what he wanted. He, no doubt, had a vast amount of experience in disorienting prisoners. Is that what she had become? She fought the shudder rising from her soul—fought it and failed.

The smile never reached his lips, but she saw it in his eyes. She held on to enough sanity to be disgusted by the fact. As before, the desk he sat behind was immaculate, though this time they were in a state-of-the-art lab.

"Leave us."

The driver scurried away.

"Do you know why I brought you here?"

Shaking her head, she rubbed the circulation back into her wrists. She resisted the urge to look around for clues as to where *here* might be.

"Errors have been made. Errors that cannot be corrected. Someone must pay for them." He steepled his fingers, leaned forward. "Tell me what you know. Say no more or less than you need to in order to be accurate. You must not try to protect yourself or anyone else. In return, if I find you at fault, I can promise your death will be quick."

He sat back and waited for her to begin.

Her legs started to tremble. She considered sitting in one of the chairs in front of her, but knew she wouldn't dare. You did not sit in his presence unless he offered, and he never offered.

She opened her mouth to speak, but nothing came out. A pitcher with water and ice, condensation forming on the glass, sat on his desk. He met her eyes, glanced at the pitcher, then leaned forward and poured a glass. Never taking his eyes from hers, he took a long drink, set the glass down, and leaned back again.

"Begin," he said.

"At five yesterday morning, I received word Martin had requisitioned a helicopter. He didn't file a flight plan until he arrived at White Sands. Once the pilot had recorded the flight plan, we intercepted the coordinates. I sent two men to intercept the girl's body, before the helicopter arrived if possible. If not, they were instructed to engage the helicopter. We never heard back from them." She resisted the urge to defend her team. They both knew their qualifications. She didn't know what had happened at Bitter Lake, but she knew they hadn't screwed up. They'd been outplayed.

Silence filled the space between them. If she cared one ounce for her life, she might have thought to defend it. Since she didn't, she waited.

"The two men you sent are dead. USCIS picked up their bodies at nine-twenty yesterday morning. You should have sent more than two. That was your first mistake."

She didn't contradict him.

"Explain to me how the body could have been stolen."

"We injected it with RSF30, then dumped it close to town and called in an anonymous tip."

"The call could have been traced."

"No. We used the payphone at the corner of Third and Main."

"Continue."

"The police transferred the body to the morgue. Per our procedural plans for Phrase Three, we staged this to look like a mob hit, but left the body within the zone. This guaranteed the Roswell ME would not conduct an autopsy. Instead, Dr. Kowlson would have to see it and sign off."

She stopped, because she didn't know what else to say. She'd followed their procedural plan to the letter. When she'd received the text message indicating the body had been stolen, there had been no time to ask questions. Then again, in this organization, one did not ask questions. She'd taken the necessary steps to handle the situation.

"How was the body stolen?"

She'd agonized over this very question for the past twenty-four hours. She did not doubt her answer could, and probably would, cost her life. Even as she formed the words, she felt herself slide further into the darkness of the well.

"I don't know."

He leaned forward, steepled his fingers again. "Why do we have no recording of the theft?"

"Whoever broke into the morgue disconnected the security and replaced the tapes with clean ones."

"Why weren't backup monitor devices in place?"

"I don't know."

"Who was in charge?"

For the first time since she had committed her life to their cause, she didn't answer a question.

His steps were slow and deliberate as he came around the desk. He stopped when he was behind her. He didn't surprise her when he placed his hands around her neck, caressed the skin with his fingers. He didn't surprise her, and yet she jumped at his touch. She knew the strength of his hands, remembered well watching him choke the life out of a man.

"Do not think to protect one of your men. Your loyalties lie with me and me alone."

She closed her eyes against the feel of his breath on her skin.

"Johnson was in charge of the lab, but I should have told him to set up additional perimeter security."

"Of course, you should have." He let his hand slide down her throat as if considering, then rejecting, the idea. "Which is why you will be the one to kill him."

He stepped behind his desk, picked up the phone. "Bring Johnson here."

Opening the right hand drawer, he pulled out a nine inch knife. "Use this."

"I won't."

He sat back, ever the patient teacher. "Of course you will. Mistakes resemble cancer. Allowed to remain, they will grow. They must be cut out. Our mission is bigger than any one person. Bigger than you or me. Now you must prove your dedication. Are you willing to spill the blood of any man or woman in your unit? Will you stain your own hands in order to achieve our goals?"

The knock on the door ended her time of mercy.

"I can't," she said, tears catching in her throat.

"You can, and you will—here and now. Or I will do it for you. If I do it, the price will be higher to cover your cowardice. I will find his family and kill them as well. Two daughters and a *son.*" His eyes met hers. He smiled. "Enter."

Johnson entered the room, and she picked up the knife.

CHAPTER SEVENTEEN

Lucy woke to banging on the door and Dean's hand cupped around her breast.

"Shit. Dean, wake up."

"I'm awake. Can't you tell?" He pulled her closer to his morning erection to prove his point.

"I'll slip into the bathroom. Answer your door." She attempted to pry his hand away from her breast, but the man had a death grip. When he started nibbling on her neck she eyeballed her weapon on the nightstand and considered threatening him with it. If she could reach it. And if he believed she would shoot him, which of course she wouldn't since they'd had sex before, during, and after falling asleep. "We're government agents. We can't play hooky. Answer your door."

"Newbies are so fucking eager." He eased up on her breast, but only so he could turn her toward him, slide his hand down her body. "It's housekeeping. They'll go away if we're quiet." Then, he ducked beneath the sheets, and she forgot about the gun and the person at the door. She forgot about everything except him and the way he made every inch of her skin vibrate.

"Dean, it's Jerry. Open up. I need to talk to you."

"Shit," they said simultaneously. Both rolled out of the bed and hit the floor on opposite sides in a bizarre synchronized dance.

"Hang on, Jerry." Dean pulled on his pants, tucking his weapon into the back and snatching his shirt off the ceiling fan where it had landed earlier in the night.

Lucy scooped most of her clothes into her pack, along with her weapon, and left if unzipped. She yanked on a pair of jeans, but couldn't find her blouse. Dean snagged a t-shirt from his closet and tossed it at her. After pulling it over her head, she nodded. Dean jerked the door open.

Jerry no longer resembled the man who had gone AWOL seventy-two hours before. His tears had been replaced by a hard, cold resolution. But more than the change in demeanor, Lucy noticed the physical wounds.

He had deep cuts over much of his face and arms, as if he had crawled through a cactus patch with no heed for himself. His right eye was nearly swollen shut. The skin around it had purpled. Instead of defeated, the man who stood before them had been emboldened. Like he'd been through hell and had emerged ready for battle.

Dean pulled him into the room and checked the corridor before he slammed the door.

"Jerry, what happened to you?" Lucy forgot the story she had concocted to explain her presence in Dean's room. Jerry wouldn't have noticed if she had been wearing a clown's suit complete with a bright red nose.

"I found the bastards is what happened." He paced between the bed and the bathroom, glancing occasionally toward the high window. "Thought they had me. Well the bastards didn't reckon who they were up against. Shouldn't have messed with a former artillery man. Should have fucked with somebody else and somebody else's woman. I'll kill every fucking one of them even if I have to go back and do it one at a time."

"Slow down, Jerry. Sit and tell us what happened." Dean nodded toward the chair.

Jerry ignored him and kept pacing. "Soon as I slow down, they'll be here. I have less than a twenty-minute lead. I came to ask for your help." He reached in his pocket and unfolded a sheet of paper.

Lucy leaned forward to take it, but Dean got their first. "What are these numbers, Jerry?"

"You know what they are—you've been in the military."

Dean didn't confirm what Jerry said. He didn't deny it, either.

"What are those, Jerry? What's happened to you?" Lucy tried to take a closer look at Jerry's eye, but he pushed her away.

"Dean knows what they are. They're the coordinates for where it went down."

"How did you get these?" Dean asked.

"I had LoJack installed on Angie's car a few years ago. Remember the story about her hitching back from Grand Junction? That sort of shit happened all the time. She'd be content with Roswell one day and gone the next—and lost."

Jerry kept moving the entire time he talked. Lucy also noticed he'd glance at the window every few seconds. She wondered if he'd slept at all since they'd last seen him. How much caffeine had he consumed? What else had he taken? His eyes were dilated, and he was breathing too fast. Studying him, she realized his face was flushed and not because of what he was telling them. She estimated his blood pressure at over one-eighty.

A man of his size couldn't sustain that level for long. Adrenaline put every biological system under enormous amounts of stress, and the body could only endure it for a finite amount of time before crashing. In Lucy's medical opinion, Jerry wouldn't last another twenty-four hours. She tried to catch Dean's eye, but he remained focused on Jerry.

"So you accessed her LoJack logs." Dean pulled a couple bottles of water from the mini-fridge, put one in Jerry's hand.

"Yes." Jerry took a long drink, then set the bottle on the table. "I went to where she'd been that night. I knew they'd come back. The bastards. So, I set me up a blind, and I waited."

"Why didn't you call Sheriff Eaton, Jerry?" Lucy wanted to make physical contact, wanted to settle him down, before he stroked out. But every time she shifted closer, he started pacing again.

"You saw how Eaton acted, Lucy. He wouldn't even let me see her body. I wouldn't be surprised if he's on their side."

"You can't believe that." Lucy kept her voice calm.

"I don't know what to believe. I think you and Dean are clean. I did some checking and according to the neighbors you got back here at four that morning."

Lucy noticed Dean's eyes narrow, but he still didn't speak.

"Angie and I didn't even leave George's parking lot until four. I don't see how you could have killed her while you were here screwing like bunnies."

Lucy blushed. She again glanced at Dean, but he never took his eyes off Jerry.

"What did you do next?" Dean asked. "What did you do when they came?"

"I planned to pick them off one-by-one. It would have worked too, until the UAVs showed up."

"What's a UAV?" Staring at the men, Lucy realized she was the only one in the room lost.

"Dean knows. We had them in Bosnia, Kosovo, Afghanistan, even Iraq."

"You saw one?"

"Saw one? The damned thing chased me for the last thirty-six hours."

"That's impossible."

"It's not impossible. It happened. I guess I know what happened." Jerry stumbled to a halt and ran a hand over his face. He noticed the cuts and scars as though seeing them for the first time and fell silent.

He slumped down on the bed, ran his hand over the comforter.

Lucy knew he'd gotten lost in a memory. The comforter was the same one he'd sat on when Eaton had called, when he'd first heard of Angie's death. Tracing the geometric pattern, he closed his eyes and took a deep breath. When he glanced up, the caged animal expression had retreated.

"I crawled underneath some rocks, like we did in Iraq. A man can lie in the desert for days if he sets up his blind right. I had. I saw them drive up in a military Jeep." Jerry paused and let his words sink in. "That's right—a *military* Jeep. But they weren't military unless the U.S. Government had a reason to kill Angie. Plus these guys weren't in uniform, and they didn't act military. You know what I mean." He threw Dean a pointed look. "Something was off about them. No real chain of command. It's hard to explain. As for the Jeep, maybe they stole it. I don't know. You have the coordinates on the sheet I gave you, so I'll let you draw your own conclusions. It was oh-two-hundred hours."

Jerry closed his eye, probed the wound with his fingers. "Three men stepped out. I didn't have a clear line on them. They were pulling something. Bastard number one walked toward me to take a leak. I had him in my night scope, and I had a silencer. I was confident I could take the other two out, before they knew I was there. I took the shot, and he went down. As luck would have it, he was the operator."

"The what?" Lucy sat down beside Jerry, not too close, but close enough to put her hand on his arm.

"An operator is the remote pilot to a UAV—an Unmanned Aerial Vehicle. Britain has developed a spybot that can fit in the palm of your hand. The Predator that crashed in Arizona in 2006 weighed ten thousand pounds. I don't know what model they had, since this one mostly chased my ass. I would guess mid-range."

Jerry rose and went to the window. "After I'd taken him out, the other two started offloading the UAV. I didn't have a clear shot, so I waited. They finally came looking for their operator— with their weapons drawn and readied."

"And you opened fire." Dean interrupted, more comment than question.

But Jerry took to it like a bull to a red flag. "Hell, yeah, I opened fire. What was I supposed to do? It was a matter of minutes before they found the first body. I used what I had, the element of surprise and my gun. If you tell me these jerk-offs stole a military Jeep, I might believe you, but I'm not buying that they stole a UAV, too. If they bought it, they're extremely well financed. The only other possibility I can think of is someone on the inside is dirty and checked it out on supposed maneuvers. I'm telling you, they didn't just steal it."

"Someone would have reported it missing," Dean admitted.

"Hell, yeah. Equipment that expensive—"

"How much are we talking, Jerry?" Lucy felt as if she were trying to catch up fast.

"Last I heard, the mid-range bots ran close to a quarter of a million dollars. What chased me sure as hell belongs in that middle range."

"I think I did see something about them on the news," Lucy said. "We considered using them for border security."

"We have been, for years," Jerry said. "Along the north and the west borders, anyway. Not here. So, what the hell was one doing in Chaves County? Let me tell you these babies can light up the night, and it did. They immediately saw the body."

"And the rest was history."

"I fired two more shots, so they'd take cover, which they did. Their backup operator knew his stuff, though. Bastard chased me halfway across the desert. I've been running since then."

"How did you get away?" Lucy asked.

"A robot may be smart, but it can't think." Jerry's panther-like grin startled her, and she realized what a formidable enemy he would be. He stood, finished the water, and set the bottle on the table, glancing again at the window. "I can't stay here, and I don't know what to do with that information, but I have a feeling you do."

Dean shook his head, handed the paper back. "I don't know why you'd think that."

"A man has a lot of time to think while he's running. Things become clear when your life is about to end and the woman you love is lying on a slab." Jerry stepped into Dean's space. His hands remained at his side, but his arms were shaking as he clenched his hands into fists. "Seems odd to me that you showed up a month before this happened. You're either in on it, or you're not. If you're not, you'll help me."

"Sorry, man. I can't help you. I'm a bartender. You need to take this to Eaton."

Jerry stared at him in disbelief. "Haven't you been listening?"

"I did, and I still think you should go to Eaton."

Lucy stared at Dean, unsure she had heard him correctly. She had her hand on the backpack, ready to pull out the secure phone. Dean's hand closed tightly over hers.

"We'll go with you," Dean said.

"That's the best you can do?"

"What else did you expect? Let's take this to Eaton."

Jerry stopped at the door, when his hand touched the knob. "You know I can't do that, Dean. You do what you need to do. I'm going after the other two men who were operating the UAV. They were at the site where Angie was killed. Either they had a hand in her death, or they know who did."

His voice was soft for one so big, so battered. His meaning left no room for doubt—it never wavered, so surely bent on murder. Lucy felt pierced by the contrast of the tone and the meaning of his voice.

With that, the big guy was gone.

Lucy turned on Dean with the fury of a tornado, but he was ready for her. He caught her, his hand over her mouth, his eyes inches from hers. Shaking his head in warning, he pulled his weapon out, flipped off the safety, and motioned for her to do the same.

CHAPTER EIGHTEEN

Dean hit the breezeway seconds after Jerry. He would never have believed a man's military training could come back that quickly, but maybe Jerry had never put it behind him. He stood looking up-and-down the street, but saw nothing. Like a ghost, Jerry had vanished.

Motioning Lucy toward the building's south side, he took the north, whispering, "I want to know if he's alone. Meet me back by the river. If you see anything suspicious, do not engage."

Then he took off. His weapon drawn, his senses alert, he hoped he wouldn't run into a housekeeper. The north side was clear, as was the parking area. Sweeping around to the river, he saw Lucy had arrived ahead of him. The maneuver hadn't eased her temper, but then he figured few things did.

"Do you mind telling me what the hell we're doing?" Her dark eyes were livid, and he found himself grateful she'd holstered her weapon.

"I needed to know if he was alone."

"Of course, he was alone. Who do you expect would be with him? Did you see how many wounds he had? How exhausted he was? If he hadn't been in shock I would have said he was terrified."

"Did he seem terrified to you, Lucy? Did he really?" Dean reached up for his cap, found he hadn't put it on. "He seemed pretty calm to me for a man who supposedly hadn't slept in forty-eight hours. If you had been chased by the most advanced technological device in the western arsenal would you have been able to waltz into Josephine's and give that spiel?"

She continued to stare at him, then sank onto the burnt brown grass beside the river. "Damn. You are a piece of work, Dreiser. You don't trust anyone. Do you?"

"Listen to me. Maybe he was telling the truth. Maybe he wasn't. It's not our problem."

The look she gave him could have frozen the Hondo River lazily slipping by in front of them. It pissed him off. Damn newbies. They fell for every pitiful story, which was why they needed to start with parking cars. Martin should have left her in a lab somewhere.

"The man lost his girlfriend," she said. "Then he nearly gets killed, and you say it's not our problem?"

"It isn't our problem, Agent. And you'd better learn not to trust every story that comes your way." He wouldn't have thought it possible, but her eyes grew even colder.

"Why did you give the coordinates back? Why didn't you at least pass them on to Martin?"

"I memorized the numbers on the sheet, Lucy. But I will not pass them on to Commander Martin. If Jerry's a mole—"

"You cannot believe Jerry had Angie killed."

"Listen to me. If Jerry's a mole then the terrorists are trying to flush out who the undercover people are. They'll plant different information or different coordinates. As the coordinates come in—and we know our communications are being intercepted, how else did they find us at Bitter Lake—they will know who turned them in." He crouched in front of her, forcing her to look at him. "Lucy, it's like a game of battleship. Plug in the numbers, and sink the ships."

She continued to stare at him as if he had no heart, and, in fact, some days he wondered if he did. This was turning into one of those days.

"And what is the upside?" Dean sat beside her on the dry grass. "If the numbers are good, there's little-to-no chance they'll go back to the same place. So they have UAVs. With all the sightings, Martin has that information by now. We have a fucking wall full of pins marking the sightings. I took a picture of them last night before we closed and sent it to him. I'm pretty sure he can figure out what to do with it."

Lucy stared out at the river. "I don't believe he's one of them."

"It doesn't matter what you believe. What matters is that you do your job."

She didn't look at him, but he knew his words hit home by the way her body stiffened.

"I don't get any say in what that is?"

"No, you don't. I'm the agent in charge."

Her head dropped for a few seconds, but then her chin came up. When she stood, he knew that he'd hurt her, but he also knew she'd stick. He stood as well, forcing himself not to reach out.

"I didn't think you'd pull rank on me, Dreiser."

"Think again. Our job is to find the terrorists, find the weapon, and disarm it. You need to do your job."

"And is fucking you part of my job?"

"Lucy—"

Apparently satisfied she'd had the last word, she stormed back toward their rooms. He followed behind her, giving her a little space. She didn't pause when she passed through his room.

Lucy arrived on-time for her shift at E.T.'s. Hopefully she looked the same, but she felt as if she'd aged a good ten years in the last three hours. She didn't consider herself a naïve person when she'd started this job, but suddenly she felt ancient.

So why had she signed on with USCIS? As she mindlessly filled orders, the question ricocheted through her mind. She considered and discarded several possibilities before she settled on the truth. It had been a knee-jerk reaction to what had happened at home. Until the summer she'd turned twenty-one, life had been a breeze. She was attending Yale on an academic scholarship. She'd always been the brains of the family—a fact her brother Marcos loved to tease her about.

She wished she could talk to Marcos now. She needed to hear his laugh, see his easy smile. He had always been the one genuine person she knew, and she needed someone genuine right now. Someone who *was* what they appeared to be.

"You all right?" Dean set the Heinekens on her tray and gave her a once over.

She nodded, not bothering to answer as she moved off to deliver the drinks. She wasn't punishing him, but her mind lingered on Marcos. Somehow, he held the key to all of this, because it had all started with him. The decisions she had made, the path that had led to this bar on a hot Tuesday night in August, had begun the summer between her junior and senior year in college.

Marcos had gone off to serve, laughingly declaring Lucy could earn the bucks, and he'd provide the brawn for the family. He wasn't scheduled to come home that summer. His tour wouldn't end until December. So when they got the call in June, everyone knew it meant he'd been injured. It wasn't a bullet or a grenade that had sent him home, it was a fucking germ.

Germ warfare—the one adversary you couldn't see to fight.

Ironically, they'd sent him into a village to rescue some nuns and children who were holed up in an orphanage. Somehow he'd landed in the middle of someone else's battle. Marcos and his unit had liberated all of the people in the orphanage from the artillery attack. The bastards had retreated as soon as someone started firing back.

The medics didn't realize until forty-eight hours later that a bio-agent had been used. Apparently, the orphanage was filled with undesirables. If they couldn't be captured or killed with gunfire, the attacking unit had been instructed to use the experimental germ.

The American soldiers had paid a high price, along with the sisters and children.

The summer had been excruciating as Lucy had watched her parents sit beside Marcos' bed, watched Marcos drop from one-hundred-and-eighty-five pounds to one-hundred-and-forty. Watched the life literally seep out of him as the doctors tried one treatment after another.

In the end, a combination of new drugs had slowly brought his body back, but his spirit seemed hollowed out.

Lucy thought she'd lost every thread of naivety that summer Marcos had come home. Since that day, she'd been well-aware life wasn't fair. Her brother was the reason she'd chosen to pursue a doctorate in molecular biology. He was also why she chose to work for Uncle Sam instead of corporate America, even when big business would mean big bucks. She wanted to help the good guys win. She'd promised Marcos, sitting by his bed that stormy night they thought he'd die. She'd vowed to fight for him.

Watching Dean across the busy bar, she fought the urge to put her head down and weep.

She'd learned watching the doctors' work on Marcos the value of working as a team. Her doctoral studies had confirmed that only by corroborating could progress be made. Now Dean insisted they had to do this alone. They couldn't help Jerry, though her heart told her they should.

Perhaps Dean had been undercover too long. She didn't doubt his loyalty or dedication. Her heart confirmed the depth of both. But, damn. If it turned you into ice, what good was it?

"Lucy, you going to hand me that cold one or drink it?" Billy asked politely. He and Bubba had been careful not to offend since the incident three nights before with Colton. As for Colton, he hadn't shown at E.T.'s again.

"Sorry, Billy. Guess my mind isn't on my job."

"Maybe you should get out more." Bubba cleared his throat.

"Oh, I should? And where would I get out to?"

"Ow!" Bubba stared at Billy. "What the fuck did you kick me for?"

Billy rolled his eyes and gave up prompting his partner in crime, or whatever they had up their collective sleeves. "Bubba and I wanted to know if you'd like to go and watch the UFOs with us."

"Hmm. That actually does sound fun." She set her tray down on their table. "I haven't been away from E.T.'s in ages. Not since the night I went dancing with Angie."

Billy played with his beer, and Bubba cleared his throat again. Lucy glanced over at Sally who was waving at her to get back to work. She did need a few hours away from the job. She hadn't made any progress on the files Commander Martin had sent her. Maybe if she got out, she'd think of something new.

"Tell you what. I'm off in another hour. Why don't you boys swing by and pick me up?"

"Seriously?" Billy's mouth fell open as if Lucy had said she'd take him home to meet Mama.

Bubba recovered first. "Great. We'll go ahead and fill up the truck. That way we don't have to waste any time. It takes a while to get out to Bluewater Creek. That's where the bulk of the sightings have been according to Dean's map."

Lucy couldn't help the grimace that came over her face at the mention of Dean's name.

"Uh, Lucy. Dean won't kick our ass because you're going out with us, will he?" Billy glanced in the direction of the bar, then angled his chair so his back faced it. "Not that I'm afraid of Dreiser or anything."

Lucy tossed back her hair and snatched up her tray. "Anything give you two the impression Dean owns me?"

"No. Absolutely not." Bubba pulled out his wallet and started counting out enough money to pay their bill.

"You boys think I need his permission to go somewhere?"

"We're going to fill the truck up now." Billy finished the beer and pushed back his chair. "We'll meet you out front at nine."

Lucy turned away from the table in time to catch Dean glaring at her. She stared right back. She hadn't deeded her life over to him when she'd signed on. He might be the damn agent in charge, but that didn't mean he owned her twenty-four hours a day. It was a damn truck ride.

She stormed through the last hour of her shift. As she clocked out, Dean came up behind her.

"Where are you going?"

"None of your damn business."

"Tell me where you're going, Lucy."

Lucy threw her apron into the laundry bin, and spun on him like a lion on its prey. "I'm going for a ride with Billy and Bubba. Is that okay with you, Dean? They wanted to show me the UFOs, and you know how I'm interested in flying objects."

Emily pushed past them to enter the storeroom. "I needed more cigarettes for the front register. Sorry. I won't listen. You two can keep fighting."

Dean backed Lucy up until her shoulders pressed into the time clock. He hadn't touched her since their talk by the river. They'd been polite and professional, nothing more. He'd given her space, but apparently that was coming to an end.

Lucy wasn't intimidated by men, and she damn sure wasn't about to let Dean Dreiser make her squirm. She could maintain a professional distance even when he stood an inch from her, his eyes gazing into hers, his arms positioned on both sides of her body.

Damn he made her furious. Why did her hormones respond to him this way? Why did she care about him?

"This isn't over Lucy. We'll talk tonight." He hissed the words into her ear, sending a shiver down her spine, and then he left.

She collected what she could find of her pride, and strode out of the storeroom, out of E.T.'s and into the night. She had UFOs to locate. With any luck, she wouldn't have to bust Billy and Bubba's balls in the process.

CHAPTER NINETEEN

Dean thought about following them. Hell, he considered shooting them, but then he'd have to account for two more bodies. In all fairness, Bubba and Billy didn't strike him as terrorists—though he refused to count anyone out at this point. Which was how he pissed off Lucy to begin with. He would never understand women. Until this point in his life, he'd managed to avoid trying. So why did it matter so much that she understand?

If he were honest, it wasn't so much that he worried she would get herself killed. He knew she had her shiny new Sig P229—she'd finally shown him the damn thing. Given the marksmanship she'd demonstrated with the rifle, he had no doubt she could handle the Sig just fine. He didn't doubt for a minute she knew how to use it either. Lucy could handle Bubba and Billy. He wasn't even concerned she'd actually see a UAV.

No, he wasn't worried about her safety tonight, and that realization hit him harder than the bullet in his arm had.

His fears weren't professional. They were personal. He couldn't afford a personal entanglement right now. He needed to stay focused.

He'd spent the last two nights driving around trying to locate and photograph one of the birds himself, without any luck. Chaves County spread large, and the likelihood of spotting one wasn't particularly good—though looking at the fucking map filled with pins it would seem like everyone else had.

He had ridden around each of those nights until dawn, after

his full shift at E.T.'s. And he had done it alone. Lucy had opted to stay home and study the data Commander Martin had sent. She obviously did not relish a late night ride with him. Looking at his sorry ass face in the mirror over the bar, he realized there was the rub.

"Throw those bottles into that cooler any harder, you're going to bust one. Then I'll have to dock your pay." Sally stood looking at him, hands on her hips. Fortunately, no cigarette hung from her lips, so at least she hadn't passed an eight on her ten-point irritation scale.

"Guess I might be slinging them a bit hard."

"A woman can rile a man like that." Sally climbed on a stool, pulled out her pack of cigarettes, and began twirling it. When Dean pushed an ashtray toward her, she waved it away. "Don't tempt me. So far, I'm happy playing with them."

"Just like a bitch." The words slipped out before Dean could call them back, while he was still puzzling over the ways a woman could make an otherwise content man crazy.

Sally put her head back and laughed. It was the first time Dean had heard anything joyful come out of her mouth. The purity of it surprised them both.

"Dreiser, you're the only one who would ever say that to me. You and my old man, Travis. That may be what I miss most. He would stand up to me."

"I wish I had met him."

"Travis was a health nut." Sally's voice had dropped some, but the smile hadn't left as the memory of her husband brightened.

Dean waited, began wiping the glasses.

"Played golf every day, even worked out at the fucking gym." She ran a finger down the cover of the cigarette pack until she reached the Surgeon General's warning. "Wouldn't be caught smoking one of these."

"What happened?"

"Colon cancer. He started shitting blood one day, died six weeks later."

Sally stared past him, beyond the map with the pins marking the UFO sightings. Her fingers started twirling the pack of smokes once again.

"We had our plans—worked all those years and had our plans. He'd retired ahead of me. I intended to train someone to take over the bar six months a year so we could travel. I was waiting for the right person to come along."

She twirled the pack once, twice, three more times.

"Guess I waited too long."

Dean waited for her to break again. Waited for the cat to leap out of the bag and attack him like before. Instead she shrugged. "It happened three years ago. Some days it seems like yesterday."

Dean nodded, placed a glass of ice water in front of her.

"Lucy's young—too young for your old ass, if you want my opinion. Which I realize you haven't asked for. I'm guessing she's the first one you've ever thought about this way."

Dean's head snapped up. He had worked undercover for ten years. How had she been able to see through him? And what else had she seen?

"It's written on your face every time she walks by. You might as well purchase a t-shirt that says I Love Lucy."

Dean dropped the rag he'd been using to wipe the bar. By the time he'd picked it up and resumed cleaning, he'd found some of his equilibrium.

"You going to deny it?"

"Well, fuck. She's hard-headed. She's stubborn. She won't listen to reason."

Sally held up a hand to stop him. "Here's the thing. You won't be happy with anyone you can control. Travis used to say loving me reminded him of living in the middle of a hurricane.

You never knew if each day would turn into a Category Five or not. But he also said once you'd lived with a hurricane, you couldn't live without it. Life without it resembled a black and white collage—more like *watching* life than *living* it."

At some point, while she was talking, Dean had stopped wiping glasses. He stood staring at his boss. Her words melded into the background as he noticed for the first time how pale and lifeless her skin seemed. Was she a phantom from some future of his—a ghost of what he might become if he let enough lifetimes slip through his hands? Her eyes met his, then she picked up her pack of cigarettes, slipped it in her pocket, and left. She didn't wait for Dean to walk her out. The last time he'd tried, she'd threatened him with the shotgun.

Dean locked up the bar and got into his old truck. Drove to Josephine's and let himself into their still, dark rooms. More than once in the last month it had occurred to Dean that Sally could be involved in all of this. She had the perfect position, and she had the anger.

But she had been right about Lucy, and that scared the hell out of him. When this op ended, when he'd been assigned to the next mission without her, would he find his days had somehow slipped into the realm of black and white?

He pulled a chair from his room and set it outside their entry where he'd still have a view of the parking lot. Lucy wouldn't want him to watch out for her, but that was too damn bad. Lucy didn't have to know everything. Checking his weapon, he made sure he had a full clip. Then he reholstered it and waited.

Lucy had memorized the map of Chaves County at Dean's insistence, not a difficult task given her near-photographic memory. She knew it shouldn't take over an hour to get to Bluewater Creek.

"You boys aren't lost, are you?"

"Hell no. We grew up here." Bubba drove with one arm out the window and the other thrown casually over the steering wheel. Every now and then, he tossed a grin at Lucy, as if still surprised to find her sitting in his truck. Billy had been on the phone since they'd left, setting up a rendezvous with their group of friends. Lucy didn't know what worried her the most—being alone with these two or finding herself in the middle of a litter of more just like them.

She had been prepared to worry about their drinking, but neither had touched the cooler behind the seats. Apparently, the thrill of extraterrestrial encounters provided enough of a rush for the moment.

She peered through the windshield, but she saw only the caliche path stretching into darkness and a million stars overhead. "Are you even on the road?"

"Yeah. Sure I am."

Billy flipped his phone shut. "Brandon said to meet him at the top of Long Canyon. They saw something headed that way last night, but couldn't get there in time."

"Shit. We'll have to go around. This road don't go up to Long Canyon."

Lucy could hear their brains simultaneously seize on the thought at the same moment their mouths found the word.

"Off-road," they said together, high-fiving over Lucy's head.

"This isn't a Chevy commercial, guys."

"No, but this is a Chevy truck." Bubba geared down.

"Hell, yeah," Bubba shouted.

"Hang on, Lucy girl."

"This won't be like a college town ride."

It was lucky for the two of them she did have to hold on. Otherwise, she would have pulled out her Sig, and regulations or no regulations, she might have shot them. Instead, she clutched the dash until her fingers ached, planted her feet against the floorboard, and still slid first into Bubba and then into Billy. She didn't have to worry about them noticing her bumping against them. Any sexual thoughts they might have entertained had fled. The boys had focused on the joy of the ride, and what a ride it was.

Her last trip home, Lucy's cousins had talked her into riding the Superman Ride of Steel in Boston. She had walked away green and trembling. That ride paled in comparison to this one. The mad dash to the top of Long Canyon ran steeper, bumpier, and inherently fraught with danger. A drop over the side would be worse than the two hundred and twenty-one foot drop off the roller coaster. The lap buckle provided by Chevrolet didn't inspire near the confidence the harness had—even if she had been strapped into a railroad car. Glancing at the speedometer, she thought the speed might be about the same, give or take a few—fifty-seven miles per hour.

Maybe she should let go of the dash and reach for her gun. If she could shoot Bubba in the foot, he'd have to take it off the accelerator. The thought had barely formed when the Chevy gained the top of the rise, and the boys let out a victory cry that would have made Chief Seattle proud.

Before Lucy could regain her composure over how they'd arrived, she peered out the window and had her second shock of the evening—at least twenty Jeeps and trucks lining the meadow.

"Looks like everybody's here," Bubba said with a grin.

"It's time to party-hardy," Billy agreed.

"Come on, Lucy. Let's kick some little green ass."

Lucy remained in the truck as Bubba and Billy retrieved the cooler and proceeded to do the man handshake with their buds. Only Brandon came over to introduce himself. Sized like a linebacker, with skin darker than the night, his voice was southern and soft. He shook Lucy's hand gently as if he might break it, then backed away into the group of boys, leaving her to look out over the canyon.

A shiver crept down her spine. It wasn't from the temperature which had dropped to a tolerable eighty-five. What had her nerves tingling was the knowledge that they had gathered like kids waiting for a drive-in feature to start. She alone realized if they saw anything, it was likely to be a real life thriller.

CHAPTER TWENTY

Billy popped open another Coors and smiled over at Lucy. "You can't be nursing the same beer."

"Same one." She held it up to prove she still had it.

"I thought you wanted to get away. Loosen up a little. Have some fun." He scooted closer, wrapped an arm around her.

Lucy had known this was coming. Bubba sat further up in the truck bed with a black girl he stopped fondling long enough to introduce as Jaz. Last time she'd dared to turn around, Jaz had lost her shirt and seemed well on her way to getting rid of the rest of her clothing. Lucy hoped for both of their sakes the UFOs or UAVs or whatever the hell flew through the night sky showed up soon. If not, this truck would start rocking. Then she'd have to go for a walk. No way she wanted to witness Bubba getting lucky. For one thing, it was making Billy too frisky.

"Lucy, I want a kiss."

She managed to squirm out of Billy's embrace, but he seemed to think persistence won the prize—or, in this case, at least a squeeze.

"Hell, I know you're out of my league, Lucy. But it wouldn't hurt to let a guy cop a feel."

"I'm getting restless, Billy. I need to walk around."

"I can help, if you're getting restless. Come back here." Billy lunged for her, and nearly fell off when she jumped off the tailgate and out of his reach. She caught him in time, helped him to sit back up.

"Wow, Lucy. You're strong for a little gal. I reckon that's how you managed to kick Colton's ass. You embarrassed the hell out of him. I'd steer clear of Colton if I was you." Billy finished off his beer and threw it into the cooler at the front of the truck bed.

Lucy shook her head and turned away from the truck. When she did, Billy reached out and grabbed her arm. He moved faster than she'd have thought possible given his state of inebriation—which either meant he was faking how drunk he was, or he could move quickly when he really wanted to.

"Stay here. You smell nice. Did I mention that before?"

"Yeah. I think you did." Lucy pulled away but stayed beside the truck. "You have any water in the cooler?"

"Who puts water in a cooler? Damn. I need another beer."

"More alcohol is what you don't need."

"You're wrong about that, little Lucy. Bubba, throw me another beer."

"Send Lucy for it, Billy. I'm busy."

"Yeah. You and Lucy come join us back here." Jaz giggled.

"See? They want us to join them. I won't bite. I promise."

Billy made another lucky grab in the dark and caught Lucy with both hands. She would have no problem outmaneuvering him, but the trick would be to do it without breaking any of his bones or calling any attention to them. So far the atmosphere had been light and festive. The last thing she needed to do was draw attention to herself, but Billy outweighed her more than two to one.

He lifted her back into the truck like she was a doll. She had an instant to decide whether to make a scene or play along. He'd had one beer at ET's, and two since they'd parked. Three beers in four hours. Her mind did the math. His blood alcohol level might not be past the legal limit, but he was undoubtedly closing in on a good buzz.

Pulling her up and past the tailgate, he lowered his voice. "Let's go to the back for a few minutes. Then, if you don't like it, we'll go." He left one hand on her arm, but had grasped her breast with his other.

This was her chance and she hated doing it. She felt guilty of taking down a giant panda bear, but she also didn't want to be mauled by said panda. Raising her arm in the dark, she pulled her knee back as far as she could and prepared to ram it into his balls at the same time her hand would come down on his shoulder blade.

Before she could follow through, everyone started shouting at once. It took a good five seconds for her to realize it had nothing to do with her or the blows she'd intended for Billy.

"They're here! To the west."

"Oh my god. They're bigger than the other ones."

"No. They're the same."

"Billy, grab the shotguns." Bubba had stood up in the back of the truck and was pulling on his clothes.

Billy jumped off her and stumbled to the front of the truck.

"I can't find my clothes." Jaz sounded frantic, as if being abducted half-naked was the worst thing she could imagine.

Lucy helped search the truck bed, locating the girl's shirt behind the beer cooler, and waited for her to put it on. As Jaz shifted toward her, something in her posture caught Lucy's attention. She was beautiful. Her lovely chocolate skin melded with the surrounding night. Hair braided with beads at the scalp fell smoothly to her shoulders.

Jaz shivered as she dressed. "I saw an *X-Files'* episode where the aliens caught these kids necking and implanted them with alien sperm instead of human sperm."

"Probably won't happen tonight."

"I guess you're right." Jaz didn't sound comforted as she hurried to join the others. They had gathered at the edge of the cliff. Most of the guys had shotguns or rifles, and Lucy was surprised to see many had attached night scopes.

Brandon had been right to have the group gather at Long Canyon. He'd parked with his truck facing the edge of the drop-off. After turning on the lights, he climbed into the back, crouched behind the window and rested the barrel of his rifle against the cab's roof. Within seconds, five others had joined him.

Billy stood on one side, with his weapon resting on the side-view mirror; Bubba took the same position on the opposite side. Starlight and a slip of a new moon provided enough light to make out their silhouettes.

"Hold your fire until they're closer."

Lucy nearly jumped out of her skin when Colton spoke directly behind her. Turning around, she felt, more than saw, his eyes bore into her, then he pushed past.

"The bastards came within a thousand yards last night. Not that we stand much chance of penetrating even if we do manage to hit one."

"Oh, we'll hit one," Brandon muttered. "Come a little closer to Papa."

The girls had huddled in a group a few feet from the truck. The boys had taken up positions around it. Lucy stood in a no man's land between the two with Colton. Three bright lights flew toward them. They darted in a random pattern, but continued to come closer to the top of Long Canyon. It seemed the collective curiosity of the group had drawn them there.

Lucy couldn't have pinpointed the exact time it took for them to arrive. One moment, everyone had their hands in the air, pointing and watching in amazement. Then, abruptly, the three lights had lined up in front of them like a sixty-eight Buick with one too many headlights. The night became day, and

Lucy fought the urge to cover her eyes. If light could be invasive, this was, and the idea crossed her mind that she had been violated somehow. They had seen not just the group, their guns and clothing, and Lucy, in particular. They had peered inside her.

"Not yet, boys." Colton kept his voice low, as if he expected whoever, or whatever, lurked in the flying objects to be able to understand.

As suddenly as they had appeared, the lights retreated. They were plunged again into darkness. The headlights from the truck only revealed the drop-off. Blinking, they scanned the emptiness, wondering what had happened, or if they had imagined it.

Silence and confusion fell on the group like a blanket. Even the desert animals had lost their voices. The truckload of guys continued to clutch their rifles. The girls remained bunched together, afraid they might be beamed up. Lucy had inched toward Colton. He still stared into the stars, as if none of this had surprised him.

Then the lights flared on again.

This time they were even more blinding, brighter than any lights could be. Every one of them was completely exposed. Colton reached for his rifle, went down on one knee, and raised it up, but it must be impossible to see where he was aiming. Firing would be like shooting into the sun. Heads jerked away as peoples' eyes teared. Time felt stretched, but when she thought back on it later, Lucy realized they'd stood frozen in the light only ten or fifteen seconds. Long enough to take pictures. Long enough to see and catalogue what they needed to know.

When darkness enveloped them again, the boys didn't wait for Colton's orders. The shooting filled the night with the sound and odor of a need to do something, anything. But the rounds simply dropped over the canyon's edge, hitting nothing. For there was nothing they could hit. Whatever had been in the sky had disappeared.

Thirty minutes later, Lucy was refusing to get into the truck when Colton walked up.

"Problem?"

"Hell yeah." Billy closed the beer cooler's lid and glared at Lucy in the light coming from the open door. "Everyone else is lined up and ready to go, but Lucy won't get in the damn truck."

"I'm not getting in, until he gives me the keys."

Colton peered into the cab where Bubba was leaning against the passenger door and snoring. "How much you had, Billy?"

"A few."

"Too damn much."

They answered at the same time, but Billy's words were slurred, and Lucy's weren't.

"Give her the keys."

Billy cursed, gave her the keys, and climbed in.

"He's not a bad kid," Colton said. "Just—well, a kid."

Lucy climbed into the truck, but she didn't start it. She didn't know what to think about having Colton come to her rescue. In fact, she'd been surprised about his whole demeanor during the last hour. He hadn't acted like the petulant boy who'd made a scene at the bar three nights ago.

"I owe you an apology about the other night."

She would have been tempted to brush it off, but he looked her in the eye when he said it, and he waited for her reply. It seemed to matter to him. She'd noticed he hadn't been drinking at all, at least not that she'd seen.

"It's okay, Colton. Everyone gets a second chance."

He smiled and ducked his head, and she realized he probably wasn't a bad guy. Then Dean's warning tickled her ear, which irrationally made her want to trust Colton all the more.

"I appreciate it."

"Tell me I don't have to drive down the way we came up."

"Those idiots bring you up the caliche road?"

"I'm sitting right here," Billy mumbled, though he didn't bother to raise his head from the back of the seat.

"Yeah. It wasn't exactly a smooth ride."

"There's a good farm road down. Follow the group. I'll be right behind you."

"Thanks."

"Not a problem. I was a little surprised to see you out here without Dean."

Lucy thought to defend herself, but settled on a shrug. She started the truck, waited for Colton to walk away. When he didn't, she decided to risk asking him. "How did you know what they would do?"

"Brandon and I drove up here two nights ago. They did the same exact thing. The bastards didn't show last night, but some of the guys spotted them at Felix Canyon. Their pattern has been the same every time."

"What do you think they are?"

Colton laughed. "Me? I'm not the UFO expert, Lucy. That would be you." He smiled for the first time, slapped the truck's side, and walked away.

The drive down was dark, but the road was good, like Colton had promised. Billy fell asleep long before they reached the county road. Good to his word, Colton followed her down, flashing his lights once when she turned off toward E.T.'s. Instead of driving on to Sally's, Lucy woke up Billy and Bubba and insisted on taking them home.

"I'll leave the truck at E.T.'s and the keys with Sally, when I go in at noon." It wasn't the best situation, but she refused to be responsible for them driving into a post or killing someone two blocks from their house.

They grumbled, as she knew they would, but both were too tired to offer much resistance. Billy didn't apologize for making a move on her, but then she doubted he remembered anything before the shooting began.

She parked the truck in front of E.T.'s, refusing to look at the boardwalk, afraid of seeing the blood-splashed boards. Something lurked at the edge of her vision, and she didn't know if she could face it tonight.

It was now four in the morning, that notorious middle of the night when she often did her best work, but tonight she felt fuzzy. She started the short walk home, hoping the night air would clear her head.

Of course, she'd known what the UAVs were the minute she'd seen them—and not only because of their speed and hovering ability. When they'd reversed directions, there'd been a brief moment when she'd caught them silhouetted against the night sky. It hadn't been long, but it had been enough. She knew their model type and could send the information to Commander Martin immediately.

But there was something else . . .

She walked to the end of Main and stopped to study the Hondo River. Her eyes adjusted enough to make out reflections of starlight twinkling on the water's surface. She considered those thousands of pinpoints of light, and she suddenly knew without a doubt what the terrorists were doing. The answer came to her in brazen certainty.

She grabbed her ribs, unable to breathe. Panic seized her so fiercely, she sank to her knees—right there on the corner. She put her head to the ground, forced deep breaths into her lungs, and tried to push the knowledge away. She could be wrong. Maybe they didn't have the capability yet, or perhaps she and Dean could stop them. If they could tell Commander Martin in time . . .

Only she knew, as surely as she knew the boardwalk behind her would be stained with blood, the planes she saw tonight would deliver their payload over the citizens of Roswell. It wasn't a vision now. The facts had come together like pieces of a lab experiment—data that couldn't be disputed anymore than tomorrow's sunrise could be denied. Knowledge tore at her heart, until she felt compelled to rub at the pain in her chest, as if that could end it. But she knew she couldn't erase the panic rising within her.

There was nothing she and Dean could do to stop the terrorists, the method of delivery, or the bio-agent that would soon rain from the sky above them.

CHAPTER TWENTY-ONE

Dean heard the soft fall of footsteps when he should have heard the crunch of tires. The hour—four-thirty in the morning—did nothing to improve his disposition. Leaving his makeshift post, he circled around the parking area leading to their rooms. Spying Lucy, he holstered his Glock and came up silently behind her—though apparently not silently enough. She had her weapon pulled and rammed into his stomach before he could identify himself.

"You're going to shoot me?"

"Damn it, Dreiser."

The meager parking lot lights allowed him to make out the fire in her eyes, note the quick rise and fall of her chest. Turning away she stepped back into the shadows. He followed, giving her space and time to bring her adrenaline down. After several deep breaths, she reached down and replaced the weapon in her ankle holster. When she still didn't turn around, he slipped behind her, closed the space between them.

He knew he shouldn't touch her. They hadn't really spoken, hadn't touched since the fight over Jerry, but her shoulders were drawn up and tense. Alone and forlorn, she stood in the deep darkness before dawn, so close the smallness of her hit him as hard as the feel of her firearm in his stomach. The top of her head didn't even reach his chin. Putting his hands on her arms and bringing his lips down to her hair, he inhaled the clean scent of her, felt her muscles tremble ever so slightly.

God, he didn't ever want to let her go. Holding her in the darkness, all of life came back in its vibrant heart-stopping color.

She relaxed into his hands for a moment, then pulled away.

"I'm sorry I scared you."

Instead of answering, she searched his face in the starlight. "We need to talk."

"Why were you walking?"

"The boys were too drunk to drive."

"So, you had to walk?" Dean didn't know where Bubba and Billy lived, but he could wake up Eaton and find out.

"Easy there, Dreiser." Lucy reached up and touched his face with both hands. "I played designated driver and dropped the boys off at their house. Their truck is parked at the bar."

"What's wrong?" He again felt a twisting in his gut, afraid to hear the words she would say next and knowing no way to stop them.

"Not here." She kissed him once, ran her fingers through the hair that curled at his collar. It scared him more than anything she'd done so far. All of the anger from the last three days had completely left her. It had been replaced by resignation and sadness. It filled him with a dread unlike anything he could fathom. If Lucy had decided things had gone horribly bad, and she was the optimist, they were in deep shit, indeed.

Once in her room, Lucy booted up the laptop and retrieved a bottle of water while they waited on it. She gave Dean the modified version of her ride up to Long Canyon. The last thing she needed was Bubba and Billy maimed. If Dean ever saw the road they'd used, the boys would have their licenses permanently revoked.

Pulling up the UAV files she'd studied, she selected two and split the window screen, so they were displayed side by side.

"They're using a hybrid of the RQ-E Dark Star and the RQ-7 Shadow."

"How can you be sure?" Dean glanced at Lucy, then back at the screen.

"I saw it."

"Did it land in front of you?"

"It didn't land. It hovered for approximately two minutes, then turned and left."

"And, in the darkness, you could identify the model?"

Lucy pulled up a chair beside Dean's and manipulated the images on the screen, so they could view a side display of the robotic planes. "They had bright lights on most of the time while they hovered, so I couldn't see them. When they turned to go, though, I had a clear view. See the lattice fins on the Shadow? They're shaped like paddles and very distinctive. Now, look at the Dark Star. There's no mistaking this design, although I'd estimate the size at approximately fifty percent larger."

"There have been rumors the Dark Star became a black project." Dean leaned back and glared at the screen. "Supposedly production terminated in 1999, but I've never seen any proof. All right. So you think these two designs have been combined into one new super UAV, and the bad guys have some. Why this particular combination of vehicles for this terrorist attack?"

Lucy leaned forward, her dark hair cascading over her shoulders. She stared at the floor, not to find the answers, but to find the courage to utter them.

Dean reached forward and tucked her hair behind her ear, cupped her neck. "This has spooked you. Tell me, and we'll find a way to stop the bastards."

Somehow his touch had brought her strength. She pointed at the monitor. "The Dark Star is fully autonomous, which is one point in their favor. Even if we catch them, their attack will go off as planned. Secondly, by design, this model incorporates high altitude endurance and stealth technology."

"Catching the planes will be damn near impossible," Dean said, beginning to understand. "Because we built them to be undetectable."

"The Shadow launches from a rail, which could have been what the military truck was pulling. What Jerry couldn't see. It has a digitally stabilized electro-optical/infrared camera."

"EO/IR video in real time."

"Which explains how they followed him for two days."

"Wait," Dean said. "The endurance of a Shadow is only eight hours. Another reason Jerry's story doesn't line up, and don't get pissed at me for pointing it out."

Lucy smiled at him, wishing with all her heart he had found a fault line in her reasoning. "We're not talking about a Shadow though. We're talking about a hybrid. The Dark Star had an endurance of twelve hours, seven years ago."

Dean studied her. The pieces were coming together, but they weren't all there yet. She'd know when they were, because he would look as hopeless as she felt.

He shook his head, ran his hands over his face. "What am I missing?"

"The Shadow can carry a payload. Up to twenty pounds."

Dean felt as if Lucy had pulled the trigger. It didn't take long for the full weight of her words to sink in.

"Maybe you're wrong." He knew she wasn't, but he needed to believe she might be.

She didn't argue with him, but she didn't offer any false hope either.

"Shit. We'd never know when it happened would we?"

"The weapon itself is microscopic. We'd know as the casualties started adding up—"

"Which would create mass panic."

"Or there would be an increase in flu-like symptoms and then deaths." Lucy met his gaze now, held it until he reached for her hand.

"Or there might be more UFO sightings."

"Yeah." She continued to stare at him with those bottomless brown eyes.

"And people go up there like lambs to the slaughter." Dean closed his eyes, as the last piece fell into place.

She came to him then and curled up on his lap. He held her close, needing to know they at least had each other. For the moment, it helped to revel in the touch and presence of each other.

Dean knew then they might never agree on the methods of this business—Lucy would always want to trust someone. It would be her blind spot, the one thing that could get her killed, and it was where he needed to cover her. He would have never put this puzzle together in a split second of new moonlight. The head cradled against his shoulder held a brain that functioned on a different level than his, and he'd do well to recognize he needed her as much as she needed him. The thought humbled him, and Dean wasn't used to being humbled.

Lucy pulled away, stood and stretched. He heard the shower running, looked in surprise at the window and saw the darkness receding from the sky. Why didn't the light bring him any comfort? He sat contemplating their next move, watching the day push back the night.

If the terrorists held to their original timeline, they had four days to stop them, maybe seven. And what terrorist had ever been known to keep his word? More than likely, the first deadline they'd given was a red herring. The real attack could be any day, any moment. It could have already taken place.

"Do we send all of this to Martin?" She stood in the doorway to the bathroom, wearing only a t-shirt, all the energy drained out of her.

"No. We can't trust any of our communication channels at this point."

"We could ask for a meeting."

"Yeah, we could."

She pulled back the sheets on the bed. Running a hand over them, she stared up at Dean, as if unsure what she should do next.

"Lie down," he said.

She curled into the sheets, one hand tucked under the pillow, eyes still wide open.

When she finally lifted her gaze to his, he read her trust there. Somehow she believed he would know what to do.

He sat beside her on the bed, touched her face. Thought again of life in color.

"Do you ever wonder why?"

"It doesn't matter why," he said. She struggled to keep her brown eyes open. He bent over her, kissed each eyelid shut. "You can't stop the bastards if you don't sleep."

"What about you?"

"I'll join you soon."

"Promise?"

"Yeah. I promise."

He had one ace in the hole. If he planned to use it, now was the time.

He kept the phone in the inside pocket of his leather jacket, because the jacket stayed with him at all times. Walking down to the river, he glanced at his watch, though he knew Aiden wouldn't give a thought to the time. Five-thirty wasn't too early to wake up an old friend, especially if it meant saving lives.

They'd bought the phones after Operation Dambusters. Their

unit had been compromised then, too. Dean had been the one to figure it out, and he'd only been able to get word to Aiden through Madison's personal phone. That day they realized the need for a backup plan. One even USCIS didn't know about. They'd purchased two prepaid phones after Aiden and Madison made it off Mt. Gould. After they'd killed three terrorists. After the bastards had killed thousands in Virginia. All the rules had changed that fateful day, and they'd changed with it.

Dean hated to bring Aiden into this, but knew he had no choice. He leaned against a tree. As a light breeze stirred the leaves, he punched in the number he'd memorized three years ago—the one he'd hoped he'd never need to use. Aiden remained the one person on this chunk of rock he knew couldn't, wouldn't be compromised. Dean stared out over the Hondo River, then he pushed talk.

The phone rang twice. The voice that answered should have been muffled with sleep, but somehow wasn't. "You never write. You never stop by."

"And you damn sure never send flowers." Dean felt the weight of their friendship cover him like a cloak. He might not have superpowers, but he felt stronger.

"Long time, man."

"Too damn long. You're alone?"

"Negative. Most beautiful female in the world is curled beside me. She sends her love."

"We can assume she's not compromised." Dean no longer saw the Hondo or the New Mexico desert. He saw Madison and her laughing eyes.

"Affirmative."

"You're in the mansion?"

"Looking out on the river, as we speak. What's up, Falcon?"

"I've got more than six hybrid UAVs carrying biologicals. My partner identified them as a cross between the RQ-E Dark Star and the RQ-7 Shadow."

"Both are still in production, but I have no knowledge of a crossbreed program."

"Well, they're zipping over the night skies of Roswell. Forecast says they'll spread out over six other major metros in the next fourteen days."

"How many vics have they shown you?"

"I've seen three."

"How badly has your unit been compromised?"

"We were ambushed five nights ago, at a rendezvous with Martin."

Silence filled the line as the gravity of the situation sank in for both of them. Neither Aiden nor Dean had thought himself James Bond, and Roswell was not a movie set in Hollywood. But if they didn't stop this, then who would?

"Burn the phone, and pick up a new one. I'll do the same and send the number to pcip 4.13.87.56. Give me twenty-four hours, and I'll either be there or have you some solid information."

"Copy that." Dean hesitated before clicking off. "I'm sorry to bring you into this."

Dean had seldom heard anger in Aiden's voice, but a touch crept into his response. "These bastards deserve the two of us. We knew something big would come after Virginia."

They both waited, not willing to sever the connection while their memories sifted through the images. "If it weren't for you, she wouldn't be lying beside me today. Hell, I wouldn't even be alive. Those twelve boys you saved—most of them have graduated. So, don't insult me by apologizing. It's an honor to serve with you."

A silence settled over the line as the space between Montana and New Mexico shortened until it almost ceased to exist. "Besides, I've been on a leash too long. It's about time I get to kick some ass. Now, watch your back, and take care of the girl."

Before Dean could ask how he knew about Lucy, the line disconnected, and he was left looking out over a beautiful, ordinary sunrise.

Chapter Twenty-Two

Lucy woke snuggled safely in Dean's arms, afternoon sunlight streaming through the window. As she stared at the shaft of light, she tried to block the truths of the night before a little longer, but even Dean's arms couldn't maintain an illusion of safety. As the facts of their mission tumbled one by one into her consciousness, her heart rate accelerated, and every muscle tensed, until she'd broken out in a cold sweat.

Dean stroked her arm, whispered in her ear. "Breathe, Doc. Try to relax."

"I thought you were asleep."

"I was, until you transformed into a crouching tiger."

She tried to laugh, but it sounded more like a sob, so she bit it back. This would be a long day if she didn't get control in the first three minutes.

"Missions overwhelm you sometimes. Every agent has felt that way."

Lucy twisted so that she was facing him but still didn't look up. Instead she concentrated on the stitches in his arm that she needed to remove, traced them with her finger. "Even the Falcon?"

Dean's laughter felt like a balm to her soul, easing her tension ever so slightly. If he could laugh in the face of death, she could at least stop crouching. "Someone ratted me out."

"You do have a reputation."

"Yes, Doc Brown. Even the Falcon has his moments of

panic." He gently touched her lips, tugged her chin so she pulled her gaze from his arm to his eyes.

His gaze was as steady and calm as his voice. His blue eyes reminded her of the sea after a storm—quiet, clean, a haven. They might not hold all the answers, but they didn't hide anything either. She burrowed deeper into his arms, the embrace of a man she knew she could trust. Someone who would have her back through this day and through tomorrow. It would be enough to get her out of bed. Or to keep her in bed, come to think of it.

"Too bad we can't stay here, Sleeping Beauty."

"You're becoming a mind reader."

"Not too hard to do when your hand starts straying, Doc."

He kissed her then, and she let herself forget, for a moment, that they needed to accomplish the impossible today. The love they made was tender and filled with a peace not present in the world outside their room.

Afterwards, as she burrowed in the cocoon inside his arms, she found the strength to utter the words that tore at her throat. "What if this was the last time? What if this is all we get?"

Dean traced his hand down the length of her long, dark hair. Everything he did to her had its own soothing rhythm.

"I know you're not afraid of dying, Lucy. I saw you at Bitter Lake. You stood up in the line of fire. You never blinked."

"I'm fine on the battlefield. I know a lot of people worry about women, but our training takes like any agent's."

When Dean didn't speak, she added, "I did what needed to be done."

"Not everyone does."

Lucy considered that for a moment and shrugged.

"You work with scarier shit in your lab than most agents deal with in a lifetime."

"A calculated risk which you accept in order to do your job."

Dean's laughter welled up and spilled over. "Ebola, Marburg, Smallpox? You call those calculated risks? Give me bullets. I can see them coming, or at least I hear them the moment a shot is fired. Whoever saw or heard a fucking virus?"

Lucy tried to answer, needed to explain what she felt, but she wasn't any good at this. She'd managed to avoid caring for too many years. She flipped over on her back and stared at the ceiling.

Dean raised up on his good arm, gently cupped her face, and waited for her to meet his gaze. When she did, she was surprised to see tears in the Falcon's eyes.

"I know, Lucy. I'm scared, too." He drew a shaky breath. "Shit. I could afford to be brave before. It wasn't courage as much as recklessness. I didn't have any reason to be careful, anyone who cared if I came home. Now I do, and I'm scared every bit as much as you are."

He leaned forward, kissed her again, kissed her softer than a hummingbird drinks from a flower. When he pulled back, he didn't have answers, but he did have a smile for her. "We'll find a way through this, Doc. We have to."

Lucy nodded and wiped at the tears she hadn't let fall. "So it's you and me against the world."

Dean winked, slapped her butt, and headed for the shower.

Walking into E.T.'s, they did their best to play it cool. Which took bravado considering the number of cars outside—too damn many for three in the afternoon on a Wednesday. Sally still used an old-fashioned punch clock, located in the stock room. You didn't get paid, until you clocked in. They made it as far as the bar.

People packed the area, and not a single one held a pool cue. They lined the walls, leaned against the tables, even sat on the juke box. Everyone talked at once, and most held a beer.

Without exception, each person glanced every few seconds toward the map on the wall. It didn't take long for Dean to figure out why. The question remained who had done it, and what it meant.

"Weird, right?" Nadine passed by with a tray of burgers and stared at the map.

All eyes shifted to the map every few moments, as if it might do another trick. And for good reason. Someone had repositioned all the pins—every last one of them.

Lucy walked through the crowd, directly to the wall, and squinted up at Chaves County. Colton, of all people, stepped up beside her.

Dean turned toward Paul who stood behind the bar. "You've been busy."

"Damn straight. Haven't seen this much business since the *X-Files* movie came out in ninety-eight."

"You opened today?"

"Yup."

"The map looked that way when you got here?"

"Hell, Dean. You know I don't pay any attention to the damn thing. Didn't notice anything else out of the ordinary, though."

"All the doors were locked?"

Paul stopped pulling the Bud draft and gave Dean a quizzical look. " 'Course they were locked, son. You locked them. You closed last night."

Dean met Paul's eyes. His training told him to trust no one, but his instinct told him Paul was solid. If he needed a local man, the sixty-eight-year-old would have his back. Understanding passed between them, confirmation that they were in deep shit.

"I'll clock in and be right back to help you." Dean headed to the storeroom, noting Lucy still had her head bent close to Colton, struggling to hear him above the crowd.

186

He had donned his apron and circled back, when Lucy ran into him.

"Not here," he warned.

"Where?"

He pulled her around to the back of the storeroom, where the sound of the machinery churned. If someone had placed bugs there, they wouldn't operate well with the interference.

"The pins on the map have been regrouped into three main areas," she said. "Cornucopia, Monument, and Felix."

"At opposite ends of the county."

"And all are canyons, where the UAVs can fly over, drop their payload, then drop out of sight."

"Shit."

"Every kid out there is planning on going tonight."

Dean knew their situation would deteriorate, but he didn't realize it would blow up within six hours.

"We have to stop them." Lucy's fingers dug into his arms.

"Easy, Doc." He peeled her fingers away from his stitches. "I don't know how to stop them, but we'll think of something. We need to go back in there and work our shift. We have to maintain our cover."

"We can't allow those boys to go to the canyons. They will become infected and could become carriers. There's a ninety percent chance the payload is contagious."

"I understand the situation."

"Then, we have to do something."

"What do you want to do, stand on the bar and make an announcement?"

"I don't care if we have to arrest every person out there. We have to stop them."

"*We* don't have the authority to arrest them. And what good would it do anyway?"

"It would keep them alive." Lucy's dark eyes snapped, daring him, begging him, to do something.

"This is a test site. When no one shows up, they'll move to a bigger site to release. Is that what you want? You want them to go to Albuquerque? Because we have a chance to stop them here, if we play this right. But not if we blow our cover."

She continued to glare at him, but she stopped talking, which Dean considered a good thing with women in general and an exceptional thing with Lucy.

"Can you think of a reason to leave early?" he asked.

"I can throw up on command."

Dean was pulling the prepaid phone from his pocket, but he stopped short to stare at her in the storeroom's dim light. "What did you say?"

"It's a skill I learned in college. Best cure for a hangover. Where'd you get the phone?"

"A gift from an old friend. I placed one call on it earlier today. You do your, uh, thing in about an hour. Go back to our room and call the one number on here. When the person answers tell them they never send flowers. Give them the locations, say it will be tonight, then disconnect."

"They never send flowers?"

"It's a code."

"We can trust this person?" Lucy took the phone and pushed it in the back pocket of her jeans.

"I'm glad you're starting to think like me, and the answer is yes. He's the only person I'm sure we can trust. I'd do it myself, but I don't know how to throw up on command. I'm not sure I want to learn, either. Plus, I need to stay here and catch the bastard who's messing with my map."

"You think he's still around?"

"Yeah. I do."

Lucy frowned, stepped away, then stopped. Strolling back to Dean, she reached up, put her lips to his. Kissed him long and deeply, pressing her body to his. Without another word, she turned and walked away.

Damn, but he had fallen into deep waters. Watching her go, he realized how bottomless they were, because he could hear the gurgling. He pushed the thought away and went to work. He had a fucking terrorist to catch.

With the size of the crowd, he didn't have a chance to speak to her again for the next hour. He knew when she'd made her move, though. The unmistakable sound of retching was followed by chairs scraping the floor. A palatable silence fell over the bar, until Sally's no-nonsense voice pierced it. "Show's over folks. I know you've seen the flu before. Nadine, you want to come clean this up. Lucy, for heaven's sake, *go.*"

Their plan almost fell apart when Sally wanted Dean to drive her home.

"I'd rather walk," Lucy pleaded.

"You threw up on not one, but two, of my customers," Sally said. "I'm not letting you walk home. Dreiser, take her now and get back here."

"If I have to ride in a car, I know I'll be sick again."

Lucy's face went so white as she said it, even Dean thought she'd hurl again. He found himself wishing he had a secret signal to tell her to back off the drama. If the girl lost any more liquid, she'd faint dead away before she could make the call. Sally had so many customers, she didn't have time to argue. With a wave of her hand, she sent Lucy on her way as she barked at Nadine to get a mop and told Dean to get the unlucky customers a free round.

Lucy stepped out into the afternoon air and drew a deep breath. Heat slammed into her like a fist. Pulling bottled water from her bag, she swished some in her mouth, then spit it out into the nearest potted plant.

Making her way down Main, she glanced back to see if Sally had stuck her gray head out the front door to watch her. The woman had a maternal streak she did her best to hide.

Coming to the end of the boardwalk, Lucy made a left and picked up her pace. Sunset would be in three hours, full darkness another hour after that. Four hours until the UAVs flew over. What could the person she was calling do in such a short amount of time? When she reached Josephine's, she veered down toward the river. Dean had told her to call from the room, but how could she know they weren't bugged? Dean swept them every night, but open spaces were still the least vulnerable to eavesdropping devices.

Besides, sitting underneath the tree calmed her. She pulled out the phone and keyed up the menu. Only one number had been called, with no name beside it. She didn't recognize the area code.

Pushing talk she waited.

On the second ring, a male voice answered. "Still no letters."

"And you never send flowers." Lucy waited, wondering if he would hang up.

The silence stretched so long, she checked the display to see if he'd disconnected.

"Well, a man would be foolish not to send flowers to you."

Lucy wanted to weep. She wanted to reach through the phone and drag the man on the other end back to Roswell. She didn't want to be in this alone, anymore. Dean looked exhausted. She was frightened. This person still had a sense of humor. She planned to never hang up.

"You still there, sweetheart?"

"Yeah, I'm here."

"Tough op."

"Yeah."

"You have information for me?"

"Three locations. Tonight. Cornucopia Canyon, Monument Canyon, and Felix Canyon. The locals think it's a divide and conquer game."

"Copy that. We'll see what we can do from the bat cave."

"Thank you."

Lucy knew she should hang up. Dean had told her to give the three locations and disconnect. No doubt, some protocol existed for limiting the amount of seconds on covert phone calls. She hadn't realized how isolated they had become in one week. She hadn't understood how much they needed reinforcements on their team. She didn't even know who this was, but it was someone Dean trusted. What else did she need to know?

"By the way, nice catch on the hybrids. I confirmed UAVs with those specifications have existed for the past twelve months and are deployed in your area."

Lucy fought the lump in her throat, tried to think of something to say.

"Take care of the old guy for me."

She gripped the phone, listened to the static of dead air. Pushing *end*, she slipped the phone back into her pocket, and felt a shiver slide down the back of her neck. She acknowledged what a part of her mind had recognized several seconds ago.

She wasn't alone. Someone was watching.

CHAPTER TWENTY-THREE

Lucy resisted the urge to turn around. She had no doubt someone crouched behind the scrub brush at six o'clock. She'd heard a very slight rustling as she'd ended her conversation with Dean's friend.

Should she draw her weapon?

Dean's words to maintain their cover at all costs rang in her ears. Surely, she could make an exception to defend herself.

The nearly imperceptible sound came again, and every hair on Lucy's arms bristled. She reached down to rub her ankle and gripped her weapon. Drawing a deep breath, she prepared to flip onto her stomach and roll left—behind the tree.

Jerry's voice sounded, low, but unmistakable. "Don't shoot me, Lucy."

She released the hold on her weapon and rubbed her leg, as if she hadn't even thought of riddling him with bullets. "What the hell are you talking about, Jerry?"

He emerged from the scrub brush and dropped beside her in one fluid movement. The man could move with incredible stealth. How *had* his training returned so quickly? Looking into his haunted eyes, she felt a tug on her heart. She didn't want to doubt he was a veteran-turned-cook, caught up in heartbreaking circumstances. Didn't want to, but did.

He leaned against the tree.

A human chameleon, he faded into the bark. No one would see him unless they stumbled over him. The color of his clothes, the shade of his skin and hair—it all melded into the grass and the trees.

"What gave me away?"

Lucy shrugged, continued searching his face for some sign of where he'd been, and what he'd been doing.

"You have good instincts—or you really aren't just a waitress."

"Don't start that again, Jerry."

"I have some buddies who are still in the military."

Lucy didn't know what to say, so she didn't say anything.

"They ran a background check on Dreiser."

Lucy remained silent, but she did meet his gaze.

"Do you want to know what they found?"

"I'm not taking him home to meet my mama, Jerry. I don't need to know what you found."

"They found nothing. He has no background. How many people have no history at all? No credit history, employment history, no driver's license. How is that possible? Unless you're a spook. Unless you're not who you say you are."

"Maybe you should get some rest, Jerry."

"What would they find on you, Lucy?"

She refused to look away, didn't blink.

"How did you know I was following you?"

"My *abuela* says I have the second sight."

Lucy thought he might laugh, but he nodded. "Our grand-mothers know us best."

"Why did you follow me, Jerry?"

"I needed to talk to you. Without Dreiser."

"Dean's a good man."

"Maybe. He's not sure what side I'm on."

"And how do I know?"

"You have the sight, remember?"

As Lucy watched him, Jerry's shoulders slumped. His hard expression melted. The anger that had propelled him for the last six days abandoned him. It could have been an act, but Lucy didn't think so. She might not have been an agent as long as Dean, but she'd been a woman for twenty-eight years. She knew a broken man when she saw one.

As if it hadn't happened, Jerry drew himself back up, put the mask firmly in place. "What happened at the bar?"

"You know about the map?"

"The one with the UFO sightings?" Jerry spat the word UFO, as if it offended him.

She nodded. "The boys go out hunting for them every night. The map notes all the sightings in Chaves County. There's not an inch of the map without a pin in it. Every night they go."

"Boys around here have more pistons than brains."

Lucy smiled, but it hurt her to do so. "Today, when Paul opened the bar, someone had repositioned all the pins."

Jerry clenched his hands, and Lucy again realized he outsized her by over a hundred pounds. She didn't feel intimidated, figured she could take him down in a pinch. Size could be a hindrance as well as a help. But she knew Jerry would exact his revenge eventually, and she couldn't help but pity the guy who happened to be in his way.

"Tell me the new locations."

"Go to the bar. Look for yourself." Lucy wanted to lie in the grass and sleep for hours. She wanted to say the right words.

"You don't make this easy. You know it?"

"And you shouldn't do this alone."

"Who's baiting the boys?"

Lucy didn't answer.

"Why?"

Lucy picked up a blade of grass and split it with her nails.

"Who do you and Dean work for?"

"We work for Sally. You do too, so why don't you come back?" Lucy picked up another piece of grass, proceeded to shred it.

When Jerry didn't answer, she glanced up at him.

"In the last six days, I've managed to accept Angie's death. I've even come to terms with the fact we're at war—a war Angie stumbled into. She became a casualty of something she didn't realize was going on. None of us did." Jerry's eyes scanned the river's banks. "It would help if I knew who you and Dreiser work for."

"We work for Sally." Lucy's voice didn't sound like her own. She wouldn't have believed herself. "We stumbled into this just like you did."

Glancing to see if Jerry could have possibly bought her explanation, she saw the hunted look return. "I saw a lot of disbelief overseas. People not realizing the battle had begun until they were already losing it, not adapting fast enough."

He stood, towered over her. Lucy resisted the urge to stand, too. The agitation she'd seen in him three days before had vanished, but not the intensity. The doctor in her wanted to check his vitals, bring him in for a workup.

"You can't avenge Angie's death alone. Go talk to Eaton, like Dean said. What do you think you can accomplish running around in the desert?" she asked.

"More than I can standing behind a fucking grill."

"Promise me, you won't go out there tonight." Now, she did stand, touched his arm. He winced, and she realized he'd already given himself to the mission. Jerry didn't fear dying. She'd bet he'd even welcome death, joining Angie. But her touch had made him uneasy. Her touch had reminded him of life.

He pulled away, stepped back.

"Promise me," she said.

"I can't promise that. What are the UAVs doing here?"

Lucy shook her head, whispered, "I'm a waitress, remember?"

"Yeah. But I also remember folks aren't what they seem. Especially in Roswell."

At six o'clock, Dean glanced up to see Sheriff Eaton standing at the bar. He was surprised to find the man was a welcome sight. He hadn't decided what side, if any, Eaton stood on—but at this point any semblance of law and order would be a step in the right direction.

"Coffee, Sheriff?"

"Yeah. I could use a cup." Eaton stared at the crowd which hadn't thinned at all around the wall map. "Who put the damn map up in the first place?"

Dean poured strong, black coffee into a mug. "I thought it would settle them down. I didn't know they'd view it as a treasure map."

"Outsiders. You underestimated their attraction to trouble."

"I suppose I did." Dean wanted to broach the subject of keeping the boys away from the canyons, but he needed to do it casually. Since the Sheriff didn't seem inclined to arrest him today, and Paul was busy filling orders for the girls—now might be his best chance.

But before he could open his mouth, Sally eased onto a stool beside Eaton.

"Paul, I'll pay you double to man the grill for twenty minutes." She took her cigarettes out and twirled them on the counter once, twice, three times.

"You sick, Sally?" Eaton put his coffee down. Sally never paid anyone double for anything.

"Sick and tired of cooking. Could you put an APB out on my cook?"

"Still no sign of Jerry?"

"Nope. I'd fire his ass, if I didn't need him, and if I didn't hate cooking."

Paul didn't wait around to discuss terms. As he slipped from the bar to the grill, Dean set another coffee in front of Sally.

She nodded her thanks, then motioned for him to listen in. Turning to Eaton she asked, "You here because of the map?"

"Can't a sheriff stop by the local bar just because he wants a cup of coffee?"

Sally doctored her coffee. Dean watched the boys continue to mill around the pool table, waiting for dusk and danger and the things they thought they could conquer.

Eaton sighed, drank again from the coffee, then got down to business, "Sally filled me in on the strange business with your map."

"Odd happenings," Dean agreed, "But it isn't my map."

"Did you open today?" Eaton asked.

"No," Dean said. "Paul did."

"So, maybe one of the boys played a prank."

"Maybe."

"But only you, Paul, and Sally have a key."

"Right."

"And the map had been changed when Paul got here."

"So he told me."

Eaton drank his coffee, as he stared at the map. When he turned back around, he met Dean's eyes dead on. "So what's the point?"

Dean didn't offer an answer, since a bartender shouldn't have one. Instead he cleaned his bar top and waited.

He glanced up in surprise when the answer came from Sally. "There is no point. You know that, Theodore."

The sheriff winced when she used his name, but didn't interrupt. Everyone knew to stay quiet when Sally gathered speed, and she was accelerating.

"We've both lived here long enough to recognize a prank. There are no fucking UFOs." Stopping the pack of cigarettes in mid-spin, she pulled one out and lit it in one fluid motion.

Dean had the ashtray on the counter before she'd put the lighter back in her pocket.

"So, why the map?" Eaton asked.

Sally shrugged and blew out smoke. "When Dean put it up, I thought it might be good for business. It was. Still is, to a point. But those boys aren't drinking, as much as they're seeing who can piss the farthest. I'd rather they get out of my bar to do it."

"Then take the map down," Eaton suggested.

"Sure. I've thought of that, being pretty bright myself. But did you see the crowd of people you had to wade through to get in here? Every one of them asked about the map as they came in. No. I don't want to take it down until the pins are gone, every fucking one of them. And by gone I mean no more sightings."

Eaton studied the map, the boys, and finally Dean. "Sally knows you and I have had our differences, Dreiser. But the last thing I need is a panic in Roswell. You run a clean bar, and you seem to have your finger on the pulse of things. The boys respect you. What are you hearing? Do they really think something's out there?"

Dean's number one priority had not changed. He needed to maintain their cover. He had sent the encrypted message with a photo of the map to Martin directly. He couldn't contact him again and risk breaking their cover—especially with no new information. They realized a mole threatened to undermine their organization, he had stitches in his arm to prove it. Aiden was the only agent he knew without a doubt could not be compromised. If Lucy had managed to contact him, he would set up roadblocks to the canyons. What more could the Sheriff do to help those boys?

Looking Eaton in the eye, he allowed himself to pause a second longer than was natural, then refilled his coffee and shrugged. "I better restock this cooler. Dinner crowd will be here soon."

As he headed for the storeroom, he spotted Bubba with a nice looking, well toned black woman, who outclassed Bubba by a mile. He didn't recall ever seeing her in the bar before. Before he could give the two another thought, Nadine told him to hurry with the case of beer he was retrieving. Soon the stools around the bar filled up with the dinner rush.

Next chance he had to look up, Bubba and his newfound friend were gone. In fact, the whole group Bubba and Billy hung out with were gone. Gone in search of adventure. Drawn by the points on the map. Growing up in Roswell had put a heavy expectation on their idea of once in a lifetime experiences, and they didn't mean to let this one pass them by.

Dean glanced at Sally and saw she was studying the map from the grill. Something like regret crossed her face.

Could Sally be involved?

Or perhaps the hours and stakes were taking their toll on him, for as quickly as he'd seen the look it vanished. Sally's expression was once again annoyed and disgruntled as she scowled at her waitresses and yelled, "Order's up."

Chapter Twenty-Four

Dean stepped into the alley. Throwing a sack of beer bottles into the trash bin, he made enough noise to stir up more than a few rats. On edge, at the skitter of gravel, instincts took over, and he reached for his weapon.

"Keep it in the holster, Dreiser." Lucy's soft, sweet voice sent shivers down his spine—her voice and the thought he might have shot her.

"Hell, woman. I thought you were a rat."

"Worked with them before, but I've never been mistaken for one." Lucy leaned toward him in the darkness, cupped his face and kissed him on the lips. When she would have stepped away, he put his hands on her hips, tugged her in closer.

She cocked her head. "Don't you need to get back?"

"Guess I do." But instead of leaving, he nuzzled her neck. Damn. He was acting like a hormone-afflicted teen instead of a federal agent. Why did he fear this might be his last chance to kiss her? His only moment to hold her? He'd been in tight spots before, so why did he feel the brush of the net settling over them with no escape route in sight? They could walk to the end of the alley, get in the truck, and drive away right now. Couldn't they?

"Did you make the call?" He pulled away far enough to study her in the darkness.

"Yeah."

"So it's settled."

"Pretty much." Her hand trailed down his body.

This time when she stepped back, he didn't stop her. Sally would be wondering where he was, and he didn't trust Sally. He didn't trust anyone but Lucy, possibly Paul in a pinch. Sally had him worried, more, he realized, since he'd seen that look of regret on her face.

"Good. I'll meet you at the room in about an hour."

"I might not be back in an hour." Lucy's voice was low, resolute.

"Back from where?"

"Aiden called. He could only set up two roadblocks without tipping our hand and calling out the National Guard. He and Martin agreed the terrorists would only change their target if they see Guard troops moving in."

"Lucy—"

"I'm driving to the third access point."

"The hell you are. I've got the keys."

Lucy held up her hand. The truck keys glinted in the moonlight. "Sorry, Dreiser."

"Son of a bitch." He stepped toward her, she backed away, and he halted. Even chasing her down the alley, which he had a mind to do, likely wouldn't help. She was more nimble than a cat. She'd proven that firsthand in bed.

"Listen to me, Lucy. You can't—"

"Aiden agreed. Call him when you get off."

She tossed the phone. He twisted to catch it. When he turned back, she was gone. Her pitch had been wild on purpose. He resisted the urge to punch the wall. Calming himself with several deep breaths, he yanked open the alley door to E.T.'s. As it closed behind him, he heard his old truck crank down Main and into the night.

Lucy hated having to steal Dean's key, but she didn't let her conscience bother her long. As for the plan she and Aiden had hatched—well, no one would call it a great plan, but it beat none at all. Too bad it involved blowing up Dean's truck. Her conscience did twinge some over that. She hoped Dean would forgive her. It was the one distraction large enough to draw the UFO hunters away from the edge of Felix Canyon, provided she timed it exactly right.

She drove south out of Roswell, praying Roswell's finest were patrolling elsewhere as her speed topped eighty-five. She knew she could talk any of his deputies out of a ticket. Eaton, however, would be a problem. By the time she reached State Highway Thirteen, her hands were sweating, but her resolve hadn't weakened. There were so many ways this could go wrong. The statistical odds of it working couldn't be higher than—

The county road sign indicating her turn-off stopped her mind from working out the statistical chances she had of success. She drove past it and turned left as Aiden had instructed. It didn't matter what their odds of success were—she and Aiden had decided this was their *only* chance to save the people at Felix Canyon from the bio-agent about to be released. Dean would agree too, once Aiden made him see reason.

Dean. Her insides went warm. How had she managed to fall in love with that man? She'd sworn a week ago it wouldn't happen, that she'd guard against his hangdog look and his badass smile. But she hadn't been prepared for the way the man poured his heart and soul into his job. And into her. How could she resist someone who cared so passionately? She couldn't—anymore than she could resist her own need to give every ounce of herself to what she believed in.

Her *madre* was right about love, as she was right about most things. It was more powerful than the passion of the flamenco and the thrill of the tango. No single dance could portray it, and no person could resist its seductive allure. Love was the call of life, the whisper of destiny. Lucy rolled down her window and fought the panic rising in her chest.

Driving the last few miles to the canyon's top, it seemed she'd been gifted with more than sight. She could hear life, in all its pulsing melody, calling to her.

She drove deeper into the blackness, off the county road and across the canyon shelf. She checked her GPS every few miles, but never more than every fifteen seconds, as Aiden had instructed. She realized she could be driving toward her death. She told herself she was ready.

Fresh images of Dean collided with bittersweet ones of Marcos. He had recovered so much in the last year, but her brother would never be the young man who had so confidently shipped off. Superimposed over both of those were memories of her mother, spinning majestically to the Dances of *Granados*.

When the truck's wheels again hit pavement, she shifted down into second and put the images behind her.

The shortcut across the canyon's top should put her only a few minutes behind the UFO hunters. She buoyed herself for the job ahead. This was what she'd trained for. If she remained focused, she could save people from the fate her brother had suffered. It was all she had asked of God that stormy night seven years ago when she had wept by Marcos' bed. Tonight, she would be given her *opportunidad* to save innocents caught in the battle, and she would not waste it.

She checked her position one last time, then parked on the side of the road beneath some scrub trees. She hiked the short, easy distance to the canyon top, but her heart skipped and threatened to stop when she saw the cars and trucks parked there. These were not the beer-drinking throng she'd envisioned.

Instead, they belonged to the senior citizens of Roswell, who'd congregated in lawn chairs. Ice chests rested beside them. She'd seen most of them at E.T.'s over the last week. One couple she'd even vomited on earlier that evening.

"Shit." Lucy backed away.

There was no reason to change her plan. She'd go back to the truck, move it to the middle of the road, and set it on fire. Then, pretend to be hurt. When the old timers saw the explosion, they'd come to her rescue and take her to Roswell. The hitch in the plan was whether they would all take her to Roswell. She hoped their morbid curiosity would trump the UFOs they were suddenly curious about—curious, when any other night they'd be home watching television. Lucy wanted to blare her horn in frustration.

Then again, given the slight breeze and the slope of the hillside, perhaps moving them off the canyon top would be protection enough. If she made the explosion large, timed it perfectly, and if they came to see what had caused the fire, she could at least minimize the dosage they received.

Moving back down toward Dean's truck, she opened the door in the darkness. As she climbed in, she glimpsed, from the corner of her eye, a shadow. She hesitated briefly, but it was one second too long.

Long enough for Jerry to whisper, "Sorry, Lucy."

The blow, when it came, was swift and accurate. And then darkness completely engulfed her.

Dean had thought Aiden's plan was for Lucy to drive to the Canyon, talk the gawkers into returning, and get out of there well before the UAVs put in an appearance.

Then he finally contacted Aiden and learned what she intended to do.

"She could be killed up there, Aiden." His anger was so intense, he feared he'd crush the phone in his hand.

"Calm down, Falcon. She's a bright girl. We went through this from every possible angle. She has a window of fifteen minutes to get out of there."

"A hell of a lot can happen in fifteen minutes." Dean fought to lower his voice. The alley appeared empty, but he was too worked up to be sure.

"She knew the risk when she signed up, same as you and me."

Dean slammed his fist into the trash dumpster. The pain was sharp, radiating up his arm, but it released enough of his pressure that he could speak.

"What coordinates did you give her?"

Aiden relayed the numbers. "I'm not trusting anyone on this, Dean. That doesn't leave us a lot of options, but it's the way you want it. Am I right?"

"Yeah. You're right."

Dean disconnected the call and went in search of Paul.

Thirty minutes later Dean leaned forward and tapped Paul on the shoulder. A nod told him the old bartender had spotted the truck, too. Even before he'd stopped the Harley, Dean had hopped off the back and jerked open the door.

Dean's heart slammed into his throat when he saw Lucy slumped behind the wheel.

"Is she okay?"

"She's breathing, but unconscious." Dean pulled Lucy up, held her face in his hands, and willed her eyes to open. "Come on, Lucy, girl. Wake up for me."

"I don't have cell service. Want me to ride back down for help?" Paul's voice was concerned but calm, which could pretty much describe his every reaction since Dean had found him and told him he needed a lift to Felix Canyon.

"There's a bottle of water and some clean rags under the seat. Dampen one, would you?"

Dean had the cloth on Lucy's face within a minute. As soon

as the coolness touched her skin, she came around. One look at Dean's face, and she struggled to crawl across him, out of the truck.

"Hang on, beautiful. You have quite a bump on the back of your head. Take it easy a minute."

"Damn, Jerry. I'll kill him next time I see him."

Dean met Paul's eyes.

"Jerry did this to you? You're sure?" Dean asked.

"I'm sure. I'd gone to the top to—"

"Paul gave me a ride up when I didn't hear from you." Dean waited for the words to sink in.

Lucy turned her head. Paul gave a little wave.

"Hey, Luce."

"Hey, Paul."

"Dean said you might need a little help."

"I guess I did."

The three of them waited in the silence. Dean thinking of what he could and couldn't say.

The silence lasted, but the darkness didn't.

Lights began to fill the night sky, like a dozen search lights set on a random pattern.

"Dean." Lucy struggled to climb over Dean and out the door. "We have to get up there."

"Get in the truck, Paul. Shut the door. Shut it *now*." Dean forced Lucy back between them. Slammed his door shut, checked the window and vents. He noted in some part of his mind that Paul was doing the same without his having said a word.

They sandwiched Lucy between them, and Dean hoped the truck would be airtight enough to protect them against whatever the bastards released. Facing front, all three watched in the rear view mirror, as if turning to look would make them more vulnerable. Lights lit up the sky behind them, first three dots randomly darting like fireflies, then coming together in a choreographed dance of death.

Lucy's eyes met Dean's in the mirror, pleaded. But they both knew there was nothing they could do.

The brilliance of the lights blinked out.

Darkness enveloped them.

Then a low whine sounded, starting deep in the night. It crescendoed to an earsplitting pitch.

"Get down!" Dean shoved Lucy's head between her knees.

The world exploded in light. Invisible death rained down on them. The cab shook.

And as quickly as it had begun, it ended.

Silence fell.

Night sounds once more blanketed the truck—an owl hooting, a slight breeze stirring the leaves, then, distantly, the murmur of voices.

"What the hell was that?" Paul's voice shook. He pulled out a handkerchief and wiped at the sweat running down his face.

Lucy's eyes were wide, her posture stiff, but she no longer tried to get out.

"Exact time?" Dean had both hands on Lucy's head, was again probing the bump where Jerry had clocked her.

Paul pushed his watch light. "It's twelve thirty-eight. Sounded like a rocket propelled grenade. Saw a few of those in Nam. You think that's what it was, Dean?"

"Yeah." Dean drummed his fingers on the truck's wheel. "Short-range, portable. Best guess—"

"Stinger." Paul grimaced. "Nasty mother fuckers."

Dean was impressed at the man's knowledge, but not surprised. Little could shock him anymore. Ex-military men often remained current on technology, maneuvers, what was in and around their town. At the exact moment the bio-agent had been released from the UAV, someone had taken it out the plane with a stinger missile. Shoulder-launched, it would have been a difficult shot. Dean only knew of one person in Roswell with that sort of military experience—Jerry Caswell. "Might have been a Stinger. Question is—"

"How the hell did Jerry get his hands on one?" Paul ran his hand over his bald head.

"We don't know Jerry did that," Dean pointed out.

"The man was here. He attacked Lucy, then there's an explosion."

Dean remained silent. He didn't doubt Paul could help them, and they sorely needed help. But he still didn't know if he could completely trust the man sitting on the other side of Lucy.

Hell, his policy had always been to trust no one.

Dean squirmed in his seat. "I think he lost a screw when Angie died," Paul continued. "I know he loved her, but this—"

Lucy reached to rub the knot on the back of her head. "There's no accounting for what a desperate man can do, and Jerry's desperate right now."

"Last I checked a FIM-92 Stinger with an infrared scope ran over thirty-five grand. Not to mention they're illegal." Dean checked the rearview mirror again. "You can't walk into your local pawn shop and pick one up."

"The better question is what the hell did he hit with it?" Paul looked from Lucy to Dean.

"At this point, I think you're better off not knowing."

"What the hell is that supposed to mean?" When neither Lucy or Dean answered, Paul once more wiped his face with his handkerchief, then stuck the cloth back in his pocket.

Dean glanced again in the mirror as lights splayed across the cab. The line of UFO watchers had begun winding their way down from the top of Felix Canyon, blaring their horns, talking excitedly to one another.

Lucy noticed that, in every car, at least one person chattered into their cell phone.

In the far distance, she could hear emergency sirens, but, of course, when they arrived there would be nothing to investigate—what little bits of the UAV remained would have been blasted to the canyon bottom.

Lucy leaned toward Dean and whispered one final attempt. "We can't let them go back into Roswell. They've been exposed."

"Sweetheart, there isn't a thing in the world we can do to stop them."

The long line of cars made its way past them, unaware of what they had witnessed—or what they were carrying back. They had more than a story to tell of unexplainable lights in the night, midnight explosions, and unfathomable mysteries.

Dean wondered if it would be their last drive beneath the new moon, or for that matter, their last Wednesday evening on Earth.

CHAPTER TWENTY-FIVE

"Explain what happened to my plane."

His eyes held an impenetrable coldness. It caused a shiver to rise beneath the pit of the woman's stomach and wind slowly through her, depriving her lungs and mind of the oxygen she needed in order to breath. The oxygen deprivation did nothing to loosen the words which refused to come. Something had come undone inside her when she'd murdered Brent Johnson. She wasn't ready to succumb to it yet, but she would soon. She understood she would soon.

She'd crossed a line and knew there would be no turning back. Her soul was lost. Which was why she could look this man she feared so straight in the eyes—in spite of the uncurling she could feel in her chest.

She clenched her teeth against the shivering.

Forced a deep breath into her lungs.

And responded with equal coldness.

"All planes had released their payloads. They were leaving, so recordings show only a blurred and partial version of the event. Computer analysis filled in the blank spots. They indicated, with a ninety-five percent certainty, someone disabled the UAV with an FIM-92 Stinger."

He said nothing, but he waited.

She said nothing, not caring if he decided to kill her now or postpone it until this accursed business had wound its way to the end.

"I'm curious, given your considerable military experience as well as your personal knowledge of the residents of Roswell, what you make of this." He didn't move, revealed no emotion at all.

Yet, she had the distinct feeling her next words would decide someone's fate. His anger always lay just below the surface, ready to strike like a viper.

"A military-sanctioned attack would have struck all three. More to the point, they would have struck before the UAVs dropped their payload."

"Go on."

"Therefore it wasn't sanctioned. It was the work of a wild-card."

"Jerry Caswell."

"He has the military background to operate the machinery, has proven himself adept at adjusting to whatever we throw at him, and he has motive."

Silence again filled the office as he considered her explanation. Instead of looking through her, as her husband so often did—as most people did—his eyes seemed to bore into her very soul. The fact she had nothing left to hide kept her from flinching.

"Have we identified the agents in Roswell yet?"

"Possibly one, a black woman named Jazmine. Do you want her terminated?"

"Not yet. We know Martin has more than one agent there. She will lead us to others. Watch her, until we can take care of them all, but be sure it happens before the next phase."

She gave a single nod and turned to go. When she reached the door to the outer room, she waited. He didn't have to call out to stop her. She knew he hadn't finished yet by the way his unspoken words hung in the air.

"The sickness will start now. The first deaths within twelve hours. I want hourly reports."

She forced her hand to reach for the doorknob, opened the door, and stepped out into the hell she had helped create.

CHAPTER TWENTY-SIX

Lucy woke to sunshine streaming through the window in Dean's room. It spilled over the sandy hair tumbling across Dean's forehead. As he always did after every time they'd made love, he'd slung a protective arm over her. As if, even in his dreams, he could shield her from dangers both seen and unseen.

He would try. She knew he would try.

The lines around his eyes smoothed when he slept, and he looked his age—only thirty-five. Studying him in the morning light, she could better see the man minus the job. Unable to resist, she raised her fingertips to his face, ran her hand down his jaw line.

She knew the exact moment when the details of their mission seeped into his consciousness. He aged five years, then tried to hide his worry. Opening his eyes, he claimed her hand with his own, pulled it to his lips.

"Morning, beautiful." He nuzzled his way down her arm until he reached her breasts.

Running her fingers through his hair, then down his arm, she stopped to check the skin around his stitches. "We need to take these out this morning."

He pulled her nipple into his mouth.

She drew in a sharp breath of pain and ecstasy. "Dreiser, did you hear me?"

He ran his tongue around her nipple. "Uh huh." Then he

213

reached between her legs and began slowly, carefully preparing her.

Lucy took hold of his erection with both hands, and soon he was the one groaning. "You sure you heard me?"

"Yeah, Doc. I heard you."

She pushed him onto his back, sat on top, and lowered herself onto his erection in one fluid motion. She leaned toward him, her black hair falling forward over her breasts. Dean's hands went up, searching for her breasts, touching her hair, pulling her down, but she refused to come closer. Instead, she sat up straight, head back, eyes closed, so she could forget this place and today's danger. She lost herself in the feel of sunshine on her skin, Dean's hands running over her like fingers playing a five-string guitar, and the rhythm of their need. Each time he drove deep, she would rise off him while forcing his hips down on the bed with her small brown hands.

"You're killing me here, Doc."

"Is that your professional opinion?"

He might have aged on this job, but it hadn't slowed him down. Dean flipped her, pinning her on the mattress. She could no more have stopped the laughter that spilled out than she could have stopped the sun from rising. She wished she could. Then, she could hold onto this moment, and, oh, how she would like to hold onto it.

"I think it's time I give you my professional opinion, Dr. Brown."

Lucy thought she was ready, thought she knew him now. So, he surprised her when he tenderly, but completely, filled her. Grasping his hips, she pulled him further inside her until they became one. Sometime during their orgasm, her tears began. She wouldn't have been aware of them, if Dean hadn't been holding her, rocking her.

Promising everything would be all right, and that he

understood. "I know, Luce. I know."

"I'm sorry. I didn't want our last time to be sad."

"This isn't our last time."

She didn't argue with him, but she knew differently. She couldn't deny the sight when it overwhelmed all of her senses. She couldn't explain it, either. So she did what her *abuela* had counseled her to do so long ago—she accepted it.

This *would* be their last time together in this place, and possibly ever. She wasn't sure about that, couldn't see past the grief that threatened to overwhelm her. For in the hours ahead, she could see only darkness and death. With Dean's arms around her, Lucy allowed the tears to fall and then dry as she remembered every word of her promise to Marcos, "What you have suffered won't be in vain. I'll dedicate myself to saving as many as I can from the pain you've endured, even if it means I give my life." It was a lofty promise for a college junior to make, but it wasn't a vow she had made lightly.

As she and Dean rose and prepared for the aftermath of the attack at Felix Canyon—and it could have been nothing else— Lucy swore to herself the time of tears was past. The time for retribution had begun.

Dean studied the glucose machine and grimaced.

"Do not tell me you're going to be a baby about this." Lucy continued removing the stitches from his right arm, pausing long enough to give him an exasperated look.

"But we checked last night."

"And we're checking again today. Now, put your finger on the damn machine."

"Anyone ever suggest you need work on your bedside manner, Doc?"

"You're the first. All my other patients loved me."

"All your other patients were rats."

"I see the similarity."

Dean swore her grin grew wicked as she snipped out the last stitch, then slapped disinfectant on his arm.

"Son of a bitch. That hurts."

"Exactly. Pricking your finger is pancakes after this, so go on and get it over with. I don't have all morning, and you have things to do. Don't you?" She tapped her foot impatiently, eyebrows raised.

"I like you better when you're naked," Dean muttered, but he stuck his finger in the machine. He'd always hated needles, even small ones. Several agents over the years had fallen prey to drug problems. The thought made his stomach clench. Needles gave him a stomach ache. A gun he could handle—nice big bullets. Keep the damn needles away from him.

The machine popped him, and he scowled at his doctor. "You have a Band-Aid for this?"

"Hold this gauze on it ten seconds. You'll be fine. Now, open wide."

"Well, hell. Don't put that thing in my mouth again."

"Now."

Her temper flared, and he opened his mouth. She swabbed between his top gum and teeth. Shaking his head, he went straight to the bathroom and spit, then brushed his teeth again. When she'd done it last night, he'd felt like he had little cotton strings in his mouth for an hour. Even the shot of whiskey hadn't helped.

He paused in gargling for good measure and called out. "Explain to me why you're doing this again. You told me we were clean last night. Are you worried the virus might not show up immediately?"

When she didn't answer, he capped the mouthwash, hung up the towel, and walked back out to the room. The night before, arriving shocked and exhausted from Felix Canyon, they'd

216

moved the table from her room to his. He'd pushed the desk from his room under the window, and hers now intersected it forming an L. No surprise that most of her suitcase had been filled with scientific equipment—an electron microscope, DNA scanner, even a few test tubes and flasks. The space more and more resembled a small laboratory.

Lucy bent over the tables, samples lined up, computer set at the end. If she'd heard his question, she showed no intention of answering it.

She had pulled on a pair of blue jeans and a clean t-shirt, socks, but no shoes. She looked like a college student, not the military's preeminent doctor in molecular biology. Walking behind her, he put his hands on her shoulders. When she stopped fussing with the equipment, he gently turned her around.

"I need to know what you're thinking. Could we be infected?"

She glanced up at him, met his gaze—her eyes pools of promise he could lose himself in. "No, not really. I know we don't *have* the virus, or we would be dead. Dead or at least symptomatic."

She spoke calmly, clinically. The crying woman he'd held an hour ago was gone now. Dr. Lucinda Brown stood before him once more.

"We tested clean last night?" Dean knew the answer, but wanted to hear it again.

"Correct. Even if they've entered another phase of their production and slowed the growth of the virus down, we would at least register a low grade fever, increased respirations, dilated pupils, a change in our mucus lining, something."

"So why are you testing us again?"

"I'm worried we might be carriers. If what they released over Felix was an agent designed to make everyone there a carrier—"

"Those people would become the hosts."

"We would too, if we were exposed. I'm not sure the truck's airtight seal protected us, or if the concentration would have been diminished sufficiently so as to be harmless by the time it reached us."

"How long will it take you to run these tests?"

Lucy motioned toward the samples and laptop. "Last night, I checked against ricin, because of the paralysis, and the top five biologicals."

"Which are?"

"Smallpox, Plague, Ebola, Viral Hemorrhagic Fever, and Tularemia."

Dean looked into the eyes of this lovely woman and shuddered at the thought of her working with such tools of death. The fact that he willingly strapped on a gun each day and walked outside, risked taking a bullet seemed like child's play.

"How will your tests be different today?"

"I'll broaden the scanner's parameters. I want to check for the viruses that to our knowledge have not reached weaponized grade form yet."

"But perhaps they have."

"Perhaps."

Lucy reached into her pack, pulled out a portable glucose monitor, smaller than a contact lens case. "Carry this with you. If you encounter anyone with symptoms, or any deceased, I need a sample."

Dean slipped the case into the front right pocket of his jeans.

"There are twenty strips with sterilized containers. Once you take the sample, put the strip into the container and seal it. As long as it remains unopened, the sample's integrity will remain intact."

Dean nodded, and winced when she handed him a small baggie with five swabs and five vials.

"I realize this will be a harder sample to get, but it could be critical. Swab between the top cheek and gum, then stick the sample into the vial—cotton swab down—and break the handle off. When it breaks off, the vial seals."

Dean put the baggie in his shirt pocket.

"And here are a few sets of gloves."

"Shit, Lucy. Why don't you send me in an ambulance?"

"Remember how I showed you to take them off? Always strip them off by grasping the part near your wrist, then pulling the glove into itself."

Dean took the gloves, put them in his jeans' pocket, and looked around for his ball cap. Lucy continued to demonstrate the proper way to remove contaminated gloves—a process she had shown him at least three times last night. He spotted his cap, plucked it off the bed and set it on his head.

When he glanced back at Lucy, she was still demonstrating. He grabbed her hands, stilling them, and pulled her into his arms. "I'll go see Colton. My shift starts at eleven. If I don't stop by here before heading to E.T.'s you know the old folks are doing fine."

Lucy's head tilted, terrier-style. "Why Colton?"

"Something's been bothering me. Do you remember seeing an African-American woman, mid- to late-twenties, well-toned, hanging out with Bubba? She seems way too classy for him." Dean snuggled her neck, breathed in the scent of her.

"Jazmine."

"Is that what you're wearing? It's nice."

"No. Her name is Jazmine."

Dean stopped mid-kiss and pulled back so he could look his woman in the eye. "You know her?"

"I met her the night I went with Bubba and Billy to the overlook. Now that you mention it, I thought she seemed out of place too. Do you think Martin sent her?"

"Maybe. It's time to find her and confirm. Bubba would be

the best way to do that, but he works out at his daddy's farm. I'll never be able to find him before my shift starts. I thought Colton might be a good place to get some answers—since those two share a brain." With one hand he caressed her neck, then raised her chin, memorized her face. The words passed unspoken between them and said what needed to be shared. He kissed her once more, and then he was gone.

At nine-thirty Dean pulled into the parking lot of Great Southwest Aviation. It had been a simple matter to find out where Colton worked. The hardest part had been waiting for Eaton to leave. Once he'd seen him walk into E.T.'s for breakfast, Dean had slipped into the sheriff's office. Fortunately, Alice was the dispatcher on duty, since fortyish women tended to be his best bet.

He'd told her Colton had left his license at the bar. If she knew where Colton worked, he'd be happy to take it to him. A little smile, a touch on her arm, and he didn't even hesitate when she suggested he join them at George's bar on Friday. Of course, he also pictured Lucy slapping him on the back of the head. It made him smile even bigger, which Alice might have misinterpreted.

Fifteen minutes later, he pulled into Great Southwest Aviation. Colton had been on his radar since day one. The fact he worked for Roswell's sole full-service aviation facility didn't surprise him a bit.

CHAPTER TWENTY-SEVEN

"Can I help you, sir?"

Dean thought it must be his lucky day. He didn't have a deadly virus—so far—and both of his contacts had been female. Blond, and no older than twenty, the girl behind the counter gave him a once over. Her dazzling smile revealed perfect, pearly whites.

"I hope so." Dean offered his own lazy grin. "I'm looking for Colton Reid."

The perfect smile faltered, but she recovered. "Colton doesn't work on the sales floor. Is there something I can help you with?"

"I wish." Dean picked up a brochure, glanced through it, and put it in his back pocket. "I don't need a Cessna today, though. I'm the bartender at E.T.'s, and Colton left his license there last night. I was driving by, so I thought I'd drop it off."

"Oh. That would explain why I haven't met you. I'm Jessica." She offered a brightly manicured hand over the counter, a hand impossibly young and adorned with a variety of rings and bracelets. "I don't turn twenty-one for another two months. I would have come in, anyway, if I'd known someone was bartending besides Paul."

Dean laughed. "Ah, come on. Paul's a nice guy."

"Nice, but at least eighty."

Dean pulled off his cap, then set it back on his head.

"Colton's out back. You can go through those double doors onto the tarmac, then around to the right. He's supposed to be washing the planes in the third hanger."

"Thanks. I appreciate it. If I need a plane, you'll be the first person I call."

"And if I need a drink, you'll be the first person I'll call."

"After you're twenty-one."

Jessica stuck out her lower lip, but gave him a friendly wave as he stepped into the morning heat.

Dean assessed the facility as he hiked toward the third hanger. Great Southwest seemed to do a fair amount of business, judging by the five hangers and general size of the operation. This morning, things were quiet. A pilot and ground-man performed a preflight check on a Cessna 340 outside the second hanger. The doors to the fourth and fifth hangers were closed. According to the brochure, you could rent space to store your private plane in either of the last hangers.

The third hanger housed the rental planes. As Dean approached it, he could see Colton cleaning the windows on a Piper Warrior.

"Nice aircraft. Ever get a chance to fly it?"

Colton spun around, nearly falling off the ladder. When he saw Dean, his frown changed to a pronounced scowl.

"What do you want, Dreiser?"

"Maybe I want to rent a plane."

"Go talk to Jessica, then, and leave me the hell alone."

"I always wondered if your mood improved in the morning. Sure enough, it doesn't."

Colton climbed down the ladder and started to roll it off. Dean stopped him with a hand on his arm.

"Don't fucking touch me."

"Easy, Colton. I'm looking for a woman. I thought you might be able to help."

"Last I checked, you have a woman."

"Is that what you're mad about? Lucy?"

The two stood eye-to-eye, and Dean waited to see if the boy would throw the punch he'd held for a month. He didn't know how he'd managed to get under the kid's skin like a burr under a saddle, but he had. They should probably slug it out and get it over with.

"Lucy's all right. I don't know what she sees in your sorry ass."

"That makes two of us."

Colton rolled his eyes, but his expression eased. He went to a small cooler, pulled out a bottle of water, and took a long drink. "Why do you always piss me off, Dreiser?"

"I have a bad feeling it's because we're a lot alike." When the anger flashed back in Colton's eyes, Dean held up his hands, palms out, in what he hoped the kid would take as a peace gesture. "I don't like it anymore than you do. I'm just calling it like I see it."

"I need to go to the office. You want to walk with me, tell me what woman you're looking for, it's your business."

"She was with Bubba last night, and up at Long Canyon the night Lucy rode out with him and Billy."

"There were a lot of women in both places."

"This one is black, nice-looking, athletic."

"I know who you mean."

"She have a name?"

They'd covered half the distance from the hanger to the office. The tarmac stretched in front of them, empty except for the waves of heat rising off it. The Cessna 340 had lifted off and was now a silver dot in the clear morning sky. Dean scanned the area for the ground-man, but couldn't spot him.

"Everyone has a name, Dean. Why the sudden interest? Ask Bubba. And why do you need to know it at ten in the morning?"

At the runway's far north end, another ground-man came

out and stood with two directional wands, prepared to direct an incoming plane.

"She asked me something at the bar last night. She's embarrassed and doesn't want Bubba to know. I lost the paper with her number, and now I can't look it up because I don't even know her name. Now, stop busting my ass and tell me if you know who she is, and how I can get in touch with her."

Colton hesitated, then focused on the south end of the runway. A tiny bright spot had appeared in the sky.

"Yeah, I know who she is. I don't have a number, but her name is Jazmine—"

Colton stopped as a bloodcurdling scream pierced the morning air. It had come from the office.

"Jessica?" Colton asked.

They took off running. Entering through the double doors, they found Jessica backed up against the counter, hands over her face, still screaming. A man about sixty years old sprawled on the floor in front of the counter. He looked alive, but barely.

Although he wasn't moving, his eyes were frozen in an expression of agony. An expression Dean had seen once before. As they watched, the skin around his face sloughed off. Blood seeped onto the floor.

Jessica's screams dissolved to sobs. She threw herself into Dean's arms.

Colton stood frozen just inside the door. His eyes begged Dean to wake him from this nightmare.

"Who is he?" Dean led Jessica over to Colton.

She gripped Colton's arms and continued sobbing into his shirt.

"Simon Gordon. He's our sales manager. At least, I think it's Simon."

At the sound of Simon's name, Jessica's sobs broke again into hysterical screams.

"Get her out of here. Call 911. I'll stay with him." Dean nodded toward the double doors and saw a Cessna approaching for a landing, then veer off its course.

Colton backed up to push the doors open at the exact moment the plane skidded off the airstrip's far side.

As they watched in disbelief, it crashed into the maintenance building, turning both into one indistinguishable ball of flame.

The windows in the office rattled.

Colton froze once again, obviously torn between choosing the fiery hell outside and the bloodbath on the floor.

In his arms, Jessica fainted.

Chapter Twenty-Eight

"Carry her out the front doors." Dean positioned himself beside Simon's torso, but safely away from the pool of blood still expanding out from the man's head. He didn't think Simon would live longer than ten more minutes, and he needed to get Lucy's samples. "Keep her away from any glass and wait for the paramedics."

Colton nodded and picked Jessica up as if she weighed no more than a bag of cattle feed.

"Colton."

He'd pushed the door open, allowing in fresh air mixed with the unmistakable odor of burning diesel. Dean heard the sound of approaching sirens. They would deal with the blaze first, but he still had four, five minutes at the most before someone entered the office.

"Any idea who was flying the plane?"

"Yeah. Hugh. Hugh Comps. He comes in every morning this time."

"How old was he?"

Colton's eyes shifted to the dying man on the floor, then back to Dean's. "Old. Old as Simon."

"Okay. Get her out of here. Stay with her."

Dean slipped the gloves on as soon as Colton stumbled out of sight. Pulling the glucose monitor out of his pocket, he picked up Simon's hand. It appeared normal—showed no symptom of the agony the man was enduring. The sound of running feet on the tarmac snapped Dean back to his gruesome task.

"I think you can hear me, Simon. I'm a federal agent, and I wish I could do something to help you." He paused, forced himself to look into the old man's eyes. No skin remained on his face—only tissue, lips, and cartilage. The ligaments and eye sockets were plainly visible around Simon's eyeballs, which had frozen in place. Yet there still seemed to be consciousness in the gaze that stared back at him. "I will find the bastards responsible for this, Simon. I swear upon my life, I will. But right now I need to take some samples."

Dean wasn't aware of the tears slipping down his face, until he saw them drip onto Simon's wrist. Taking the blood sample from the man's hand, he placed the strip into the sterilized baggie. Then he removed the swab and a vial from his shirt pocket. He stayed near, but continued to avoid disturbing the circle of blood that still spread—more blood than he would have thought possible. More blood than bullets would have caused.

He still needed the saliva swab.

"I'm sorry, Simon." He whispered the words like a prayer, as he reached for the man's upper lip. When it came off in his hand, he dropped it, stood and jumped back. Stumbling to the counter, he fought the nausea, choked it down, refused to let it overwhelm him.

Flashing lights passed by the windows in a blur, speeding to the runway's edge, to the fire and the death waiting there. Dean reached for the comfort of his Glock, but it was no consolation. Pulling in a deep breath, he forced himself to return to Simon, to offer the man the dignity of not dying alone.

When he knelt beside Simon again, reached for the wrinkled hand and felt for a pulse, he realized he was too late.

He wanted to close the man's eyes, but that was impossible. Instead he breathed in and out—trying to bring his heart rate down to a normal zone—and focused on stripping off the plastic gloves the way Lucy had taught. Suddenly Dr. Kowlson's voice filled his mind, reminding him the area would remain a hot zone for some time.

Now Roswell was a hot zone and getting hotter by the minute.

He was stuffing the gloves back into his pocket when the main door burst open.

Eaton took a look at Dreiser, then jerked his gaze to the man on the floor. Any remaining doubts Dean had about the sheriff disappeared. Some things could not be faked—the look of pure horror on Eaton's face was one of them.

"My god. Is that—? It can't be. Tell me it's not . . ."

"Colton said it was Simon, the sales manager."

Eaton nodded and spun away, a hand over his mouth. Dean said nothing, knew he needed to give the man a minute.

Two deputies burst through the door, nearly colliding with their commanding officer. Their eyes flitted from Eaton, to Dean, to the body. The younger backed out. Dean heard him losing his breakfast. The second deputy stood there, speechless.

Eaton spoke to him. "You and Tommy secure this building. I don't want anyone else inside except the ME. I do not want any reporters near this." His voice shook with emotion. He paced the room. "I'll be damned if the last image Simon's wife sees of him is that."

Dean wasn't too worried about Simon's wife. In all likelihood, she'd also been at the top of Felix Canyon and had suffered the same fate. It was something Eaton would realize in another hour when the calls started. For the moment, Dean needed to give his statement, and get the one sample in his pocket back to Lucy.

"I can't begin to imagine why you're here, Dreiser. Tell me what you saw, and make it quick. That's one hell of a mess out there."

They both turned to look out the windows, where firefighters had managed to put out most of the fire. Additional emergency personnel were setting up a secure perimeter around the crash site.

"I came to see Colton. We were walking back from Hanger Three when we heard Jessica scream. We ran in and saw Simon on the floor."

"And he looked like-like he does now?"

Dean hesitated. How much should he tell? "Not at first. He was lying on his back, and he didn't seem able to move. I'm not sure he was conscious."

"Thank God."

"Then the bleeding started."

"What the hell happened to his skin?"

Dean didn't offer an answer, didn't think Eaton expected one.

"Colton and Jessica left?"

"She became hysterical. I told him to take her outside, which is when the plane crashed."

"What are the odds both things would happen at once?"

Dean shrugged and said nothing.

"I don't much believe in coincidences."

Dean met the man's gaze. He waited to see what Eaton would put together.

"Colton can confirm your story?"

"Yes, sir."

"And Jessica?"

"When she comes around. She fainted. Colton's with her now."

Eaton considered his words, sized up the scene and Dean in a way that spoke of years of experience—though none with tragedies such as this. "A long time ago I learned to go with my gut instinct. Right now, my gut is telling me you know something about this—something you can't—or won't—tell me."

Dean didn't confirm or deny what Eaton had said.

"My instinct is also telling me you're on the right side of this. Soon as I get the idea you're not, I'll put a bullet in you faster than fire ate that plane."

Dean didn't defend himself, didn't move, didn't blink. Eaton's ball.

"Simon was a good man." Eaton's voice wavered.

Dean didn't know what to say, so he nodded. "Damn."

Eaton's radio squeaked, and the sound filled the room like a coyote howl in the middle of the night. "Eaton here."

"This is Alice. We have an emergency at the golf course."

"What the hell do you think we have here, Alice?"

"I'm not sure, because no one's reported in. But if you have less than ten dead, I'd say what's at the golf course is worse."

Lucy glanced up from her laptop when Dean arrived. Like the first time she'd seen him, she thought of the burned-out cops from her father's district. Unlike the first time, it hurt her heart to see age and despair etched on his face.

"What happened?"

Dean sank into the chair, put his head back, and allowed himself to surrender for the moment. "My shift starts in fifteen, assuming there's anyone left to order drinks."

Lucy retrieved a soda from their small refrigerator, popped it open for him. "Drink this. It'll help."

He opened his eyes when she placed it in his hands. "Doctor's orders?"

"Yes. Doctor's orders."

She could tell the drink revived him. His color improved, and he managed to sit up a little straighter. Lucy sat down on the bed—close enough so their knees touched.

"Tell me. I haven't heard anything on the news."

Instead of answering, Dean walked over to the old television set. He imagined Josephine considered replacing televisions a ten- to twenty-year obligation, and then only if an electrical danger existed. Flipping through the news channels, he came up with two Hollywood celebrities and one stock analyst. Pushing mute, he sat back down, and finished the soda.

"You can be late," Lucy said. "Tell me everything."

"Short version?" He seemed to brace himself, his eyes going distant.

She felt her mind slip back into analytical mode, where it had been all morning until he'd walked into the room. The events he described were horrific, but she focused on biological details. She needed to identify the virulent strain based on the information he could give her.

As his recital continued, his breathing grew faster. Sometimes, he avoided her eyes, as if embarrassed by his emotions, but he gave her a detailed description of both the victim's last minutes and his own reaction.

Lucy fought the urge to grab her laptop and start taking notes. She focused instead on seeing what Dean had seen. When he stopped and stared down at his hands, she reached for them and covered them with her own.

"Watching someone die like you did, it's very different from killing someone with a gun or even coming across a victim who has already died in such a horrible way."

Dean nodded, met her gaze.

"Do you remember when you confronted me? The day we first met in Albuquerque?"

Dean had the grace to look embarrassed. "How could I forget?"

"You were right. I wasn't ready to shoot and kill someone, didn't realize the constant pressure of having people trying to erase me like a bad equation on a blackboard." Her voice quivered, but she pressed on. "Being undercover has been more pressure than I could have imagined."

"Lucy, I judged you wrong. You have turned all aces."

"I'm saying you were right that I wasn't ready for the field. Cut yourself some slack. You have not been trained to handle a level five biocontainment lab, let alone one breached in the real world. This kind of death, the kind of microscopic hell I deal with daily—whether it's unleashed on a rat or on a man—is a terror you must be trained to deal with. It's an abyss I have stared into since . . ."

Dean waited for her to finish, but she shook her head and started again.

"For a long time now. It takes some getting used to."

Dean knew it wasn't what she had started to say, but he let it go. "You'll run the sample?"

"Yes. Ours came up with nothing again, which is good. From what you described, they've settled on the timeframe we had predicted—ten to eleven minutes. Maybe I'll get a match, or a partial match, from this on what they're using."

"Lucy, when Dr. Kowlson and I saw the first victim, we wore biohazard suits with an elaborate air filtration system. When you and I saw Angie, you insisted we wear scrubs, including masks. What if I exposed myself to Simon? Could I give it to you?"

Lucy handed him his cap and keys. "What have you been preaching at me since this started? Our number one priority is to maintain our cover."

"Well, number one would be to catch the fucking terrorists. We can't catch them if we're dead."

"True. But we'll look pretty conspicuous if we're the only ones walking around town with biohazard suits on, or even filter masks."

When he didn't return her smile, she reached up and kissed

his lips. "I don't think it's contagious. If it is, we're all dead anyway. Now, go to work. I only have three hours until my shift starts, and I have a lot to do here. Shoo."

At her playful choice of words, they couldn't help smiling. Dean left for his shift, and Lucy returned to her lab. Knowledge awaited her. She had to know what these bastards were playing with, what they'd chosen as their instrument of death. They might not have the vaccine in their arsenal to stop them, but Mama had always said, know your enemy. As she thought of Dean and Marcos, and an old fella named Simon, Lucy vowed to know all she could about the enemy in Roswell.

Lucy woke to the ringing of her alarm, and although she punched the damn button on the clock, it refused to stop beeping. She finally realized it wasn't the clock, but her laptop.

Sitting bolt upright, she stared at the screen.

Two matches found.

She bent closer, stared at the message, but still didn't push the button.

Pulling in a deep breath she gathered her courage. *"Dios estar con nosotros."* A premonition told her if God wasn't with them, they wouldn't stand a chance.

She pushed the button and read the analysis for Simon's blood sample.

BT agent found. H1N1—93.2%. Ricin—6.8%.

Lucy didn't move, didn't breathe, didn't even touch her keyboard. She stared at the screen waiting for it to correct itself.

The program had malfunctioned. It was the only explanation. The sample Dean had given her did not contain ricin. She knew, because she had manually checked for it. Ricin had been on her priority list of agents to test for since Dean had described the first victim, specifically the girl's paralysis. Ricin caused paralysis, as well as a quick and painful death.

"No bleeding though," she mumbled, moving down the table to her microscope. "Ricin doesn't cause bleeding."

Slipping Simon's blood sample back under the lens, she pressed her eye to the scope, daring it to reveal what it hadn't before.

Ricin's protein chains appeared as two distinctive threads of ribbon. The A chains spiraled and looped as if they belonged beside a bow on a birthday package. The B chains were more elongated. A first-year intern could pick them out.

None showed in Simon's blood.

Yet, the computer analysis had found it, as well as influenza.

Lucy stood up, feeling old and tired and—yes—burned out. She splashed cold water over her eyes and cheeks, grabbed a towel, and stared at the stranger in the mirror as she blotted her face. "Influenza causes massive hemorrhaging. Ricin is a poor weapon because it degrades too easily. What if they slotted the ricin inside the influenza? They swapped out the RNA which makes it infectious. Now they have the perfect killing machine, and control the when and where. What if they have one containing the infectious component as well as the ricin?"

The world tilted, and Lucy let the towel fall. No longer able to face the person in the mirror, or the truth of what she knew, she sat down on the tile floor. Its coldness did little to slow the spinning in her mind.

Ricin was extremely toxic, twelve thousand times more poisonous than rattlesnake venom. But they had vaccines for ricin. What they didn't have vaccines for—what no one had vaccines for—was influenza. From the RNA viruses of the family Orthomyxoviridae, it was the wildfire societies had feared for generations.

It killed forty to fifty million people in Spain from 1918–1919. In 1957, the smaller Asian outbreak only claimed a few million lives. As did the 1968 Hong Kong Flu.

Of course they dealt with its cousin worldwide every year. People accepted the flu as they accepted the common cold. This time, the common cold held the kiss of death.

Lucy leaned over until her forehead pressed against the side of the tub. She needed to run a few tests, confirming what she knew. Then she would call Aiden, who could transfer the information to Commander Martin. After that, she had to tell Dean. Maybe he would have some idea how to fight the worst biological nightmare she could imagine.

CHAPTER TWENTY-NINE

Dean didn't realize he'd been holding his breath until he saw Lucy walk in the front door of E.T.'s. He expelled it in one relieved exhale.

"Come in late again, don't bother coming in at all." Sally deposited two plates of burger specials on the grill's window ledge and barked, "Order up!"

Lucy didn't argue. She tied on her apron, picked up her pad, and started taking orders. By sheer luck, her first table included several early drinkers. She circled back to the bar in three minutes.

"Dean, I need to talk to you."

"Yeah, well I need to talk to you, too, but the boss is watching."

"I know what it is."

Dean's hands froze at her words. He didn't realize he'd left the Bud Light tap running until Paul reached over and pushed it back.

"Seems like the world has ended today," Paul said. "But I doubt Sally will go for pouring beer on the floor."

Dean nodded his thanks. Set the beer on Lucy's tray before he dropped it.

"Hey, Paul."

"Hey, Lucy."

The three of them stood looking at each other until Sally yelled, "Order up!" once again, puncturing the stillness. Only three in the afternoon, and E.T.'s was full: packed with bewildered people who had no idea what to say in the face of such tragedy.

Bubba and Billy came out of the bathroom. Bubba's arm was slung around Billy. Both were red-eyed, which wasn't unusual. Normally, it was from hangovers. Today, though, both of them had been crying. Billy made it as far as the bar, then toppled onto a stool. Bubba slid in beside him. Dean sent Paul a look.

Paul set two glasses of ice water in front of the boys.

"My grandpa turned sixty-two this summer, Paul. Sixty-two ain't so old. You're older than sixty-two." Billy didn't seem to notice the river of tears running down his cheeks.

Paul nodded, but offered no answers. Answers were at a premium today in Roswell.

"Why won't they let us see him?" Billy peered into his water, then at Bubba. "Where did they take him? He felt fine when he left for his tee time. Then Ma gets a call saying he's dead."

Bubba grabbed his drink, downed the whole thing in one gulp, even though it was only water.

"Eaton wouldn't let anyone follow the ambulances. I got there while they were still loading the damn bodies. He had his fucking bullhorn out. He even pointed his weapon at me." Billy's hand fisted.

Dean pulled Paul to the back as Lucy walked up with another order. "Maybe we should call Billy's dad."

"Died in a factory accident, five-six years ago. It's just him and his mother now."

They all studied Billy. A big boy, Dean had heard him bragging about playing defensive tackle in high school. Like most boys out of high school, he'd probably added a good forty pounds, but the beer hadn't softened him yet. Add the tragedy of the last four hours, and you had a ticking bomb.

"Easy, Billy. Take a deep breath." Paul's voice was softer than the bar top's mahogany shine.

"I went by the morgue and the hospital. He's not there. They can't take him away and not tell us where he is. It's not right."

Bubba exploded before Billy did. "I have my gun in the truck. I say we go down there to the morgue, or the hospital, or wherever they keep d-d-dead people and demand some answers." He waved his arms around wildly. "They can't stop us. Let them try to stop us."

Dean and Paul exchanged looks. Paul reached for the Maker's Mark.

"Boys, why don't I get you a drink? On me."

"I don't want a drink. I want to see my grandpa." Billy rose, fury and grief reddening his face.

Lucy slapped her order pad on the counter and stepped between the boys. "Where is your mother?"

"What?"

"Where is your mother? You're a man, Billy, not a boy."

Billy stared at her, as if she spoke another language. Bubba took a step back; Lucy took a step forward.

"Do you think it's your time to grieve? It's not. Maybe tonight will be. Maybe tomorrow. Right now you should be with your *madre* and your *familia*. You're the man of the family now, Billy, whether you like it or not. You go home, and you take care of your mother."

Lucy whirled on Bubba. "And you—" she had to look up to glare into his eyes, but Dean knew from experience height or size wouldn't slow her down—"you are supposed to be his *compadre*. Yet, what do you think up? Getting a gun and landing him in jail. How will that help him? Take him home now. Sit with his family. Be the friend he needs. Any punk on the street can carry a gun. It takes a man with *cojones* to stay with a family when death passes over."

She waited, scowling at them as they inched away, stopping

only once to look back.

After they'd left, she snagged Nadine. "Honey, would you take this to table six for me?"

"Sure thing, Lucy." Nadine shouldered her tray and ambled off.

When Lucy turned toward him, Dean knew his turn had come.

"Stockroom. Now." She stormed off.

Dean raised his hands in surrender. "Guess I'm taking a break, Paul."

"I've got the bar covered. Don't stand near any knives."

Dean took off to the stockroom, but didn't immediately see Lucy.

One bulb hung from the ceiling near the door. Lucy waited in the far corner, pacing back and forth. The light barely reached her, but what little pierced the gloom allowed him to see the fear behind the bravado she'd shown with Billy.

He'd barely rounded the corner when she grabbed him by the shirt collar and pulled him close.

"The computer identified the BT agent."

"Huh?"

"Bioterrorism agent."

"That's good. Right?"

"Not exactly. It's ricin."

He reached out, brushed her hair behind her ear. "It's bad news, but we have a vaccine for ricin. We'll contact Martin. He can—"

"No, he can't. He can't do anything."

Dean felt sweat break out down his back at the certainty in her voice.

"It's not just ricin. It's also influenza. Type A influenza, H1N1 subtype."

Dean waited for her to say more. She didn't.

"I don't understand. How can it be both?"

"They've found a way to combine the two."

"You lost me. Back up a minute. Influenza. That's just the flu, right?"

"No, Dean. Listen. Influenza—Spanish influenza."

"How would they get their hands on a strain of the Spanish flu?"

"It doesn't matter how. Let Martin figure out how. I put a call through to Aiden. What matters is it's not infectious—not yet. At least what they released at Felix Canyon isn't."

"Influenza is always contagious."

"This one isn't."

"That's a positive thing." Dean felt light-headed, wondered if the virus had begun to crawl through his system.

"Maybe." Lucy pressed her forehead against the coolness of the freezer door. "Maybe not. They slotted in the ricin protein."

"What does that mean? Slots are what you play in Vegas. What does it have to do with BTs?"

Lucy banged her fists lightly against the freezer.

Dean stepped around a stack of cased beer. "I need to understand, Luce. I have to grasp what we're up against."

He didn't need to remind her that in the last six hours, at least twelve people had died. Tonight, the bastards could release more . . . But more of what? He angled closer, touched her. When she looked up, he understood something of the depth of her frustration. The look on her face told him she grasped the nature of the storm that threatened to overwhelm them, but she couldn't explain it to him.

Lucy yanked open the freezer door. "Think of this freezer as a single particle of influenza virus. It contains eight pieces of RNA, which encodes ten proteins. Somehow, they took out one of the proteins—possibly the infectious protein." She grabbed Dean's hand, pushed him into the freezer. "You're part of the influenza, one of the ten proteins. I'm ricin—one of the most venomous substances on Earth."

She stood across the doorway from him, staring at him with those bottomless brown eyes.

"Poison. Got it."

"If I can manipulate the protein strains, I can remove one part—maybe the infectious part. I have more control. In its place I slot in the ricin."

She took his arms again, waltzed him around so he stood outside the freezer and she stood inside.

"Now death occurs in eleven minutes instead of three days." Her voice had dropped to a whisper.

"And you control the *when* and the *who*." As understanding washed over him, he wished he could go back into the freezer.

"Exactly. You don't die immediately, as with ricin. You contract the disease, like you would with the flu. But, I set the time for the ricin to release—maybe twelve hours later. Once it releases, you die in eleven minutes, the same way you would with any exposure to ricin. It begins a chain reaction in the lungs, works up the throat, causes paralysis, then reacts with the sinus cavities on its way to the brain. The skin on the face sloughs away and massive hemorrhaging occurs as the patient dies." Her face had lost all color. "Since I've delayed the actual kill time, I can demand a ransom, if I want to. Or I can issue a bulletin to tell you when and where the deaths will occur."

"Magnifying the terror." Dean understood the extent of what Lucy was describing at the exact moment he heard approaching footsteps, steps quickly followed by the smell of cigarette smoke.

Slamming shut the freezer, Dean bent and picked up a case of beer from the stack against the wall. He almost collided with Sally as she came around the corner.

"Sally."

"Dreiser."

He stepped aside as she continued toward the freezer. "Have you seen Lucy?"

"I hope she's on the floor. She came in thirty minutes late. She better be on the floor."

"Okay." Dean switched the case to his other shoulder and started out of the stockroom.

"You know something I don't?" Sally stopped with her hand on the freezer door.

Dean hesitated, as if he couldn't decide whether he should spill the beans or not.

"Out with it, Dreiser. Lucy can't be in any worse trouble than she's already in for showing up late. It's not like I can fire anyone the way people are dropping like flies around here." Sally studied him through her cigarette smoke.

"It's nothing. She had a confrontation with Billy and Bubba, then she stormed out into the alley. I guess she needed to cool off."

"Well, fuck. Like I don't have enough to handle with Jerry still MIA." Sally dropped the cigarette on the floor and ground it out. "I'll find her. With all the shit going on around here, she needs to get her butt back to work. It'd help if you'd back me up."

Sally started back toward the bar, but stopped to holler back. "I'd forget my head if it weren't on my neck. Grab another bag of hamburger patties, would ya?"

"Got it, boss."

Dean waited a good ten seconds before he opened the freezer door, long enough to be sure Sally was gone. Most women would have cooled off in ten seconds. It was after all freezing in there, but then most women didn't have Lucy's temper.

"Why the hell did you shut the door?"

"Not so loud." Dean checked over his shoulder. "I heard Sally headed this way. I didn't want us to get caught."

"So you thought you'd freeze me instead?"

"There's something about Sally that isn't sitting right with me. I'd rather she didn't catch us talking bio-agents. You have to admit it would look suspicious if she found us back here."

"And it wouldn't look odd if she found me frozen in the freezer?"

Lucy slugged his shoulder as she pushed by him. For a girl—a small, geeky girl if he was truthful—she packed a good punch. He needed to find out how many brothers she had. First they'd take care of this biological shit, then he needed to find out how many brothers she had.

He wished his worries could be limited to a girlfriend's father who was a Boston cop and some brothers he needed to square it with before he could . . . before he could what?

It wasn't until he'd retraced his steps to the bar that Dean realized he had been thinking about Lucy in terms of after the op was over. If it ended without their deaths. Shit.

The Falcon settle down? Wouldn't Aiden laugh at the thought, as would his family. He'd never even come close. The idea confused him nearly as much as this op. But life without Lucy? He couldn't imagine it.

Fuck. He didn't need this kind of complication in his life right now.

He needed to get through this mission and then go somewhere and get his head on straight. What did he have to offer a woman? What kind of life could he give her? But what else did he know how to do?

No, he did not need a woman in his life, and, God knew, a woman did not need him. He was in no condition to emotionally support anyone. While he'd been alone, everything had felt frozen inside. Lucy had stirred up feelings, dreams he didn't realize he had. Dreams he didn't know how to handle.

The girl could pack a punch though.

As he filled orders, his despair changed to a senseless kind of optimism. He didn't know what their future together held, but Lucinda Brown would have a future.

Suddenly he realized maintaining their cover wasn't his highest priority—surviving was.

They would make it through if he had to duct tape a biohazard suit to her body.

Which was the last coherent thought he had before the screaming started.

CHAPTER THIRTY

Lucy walked out of the ladies' room and bumped right into her boss.

"Hell of a long break."

"Sorry. Feel free to dock me."

"I will." Sally didn't move so she could pass. "I don't know what happened with Bubba and Billy, but I need you to work. Folks are wound a bit tight, if you haven't noticed. We need to serve them and move them out. I don't want frustration brewing trouble."

"Got it."

Sally stepped aside, and Lucy brushed by her. The dining room had filled up even more. Most Thursdays, workers would be clocking out at five, deciding between supper at home or a night out. Lucy had the feeling most people had knocked off early today. Maybe some hadn't gone to work at all.

It seemed they were waiting for the other shoe to drop, and didn't want to be alone when it did.

Tonight, all the televisions throughout the place were tuned to local and national news.

The ticker at the bottom of the screen finally ignited the powder keg.

"What the fuck?" Jason Farmer, a quiet machinist of thirty knocked his chair over as he rose to his feet. "Did you see that?"

"See what, honey?" His wife, normally as sweet as the syrup Sally served over the breakfast biscuits, sounded as if she'd been crying all day. Looking dumbfounded, she stared at her husband as he stormed across the bar and halted in front of a television.

By now everyone in the bar had paused to watch the drama.

"Watch this." He wrenched his eyes from the screen for a moment. His face had paled with shock, and his voice grew louder with each word. "You won't fucking believe this. It's right after the line about stocks taking a dip. It said Roswell—"

They all watched in stunned silence. Paul un-muted the sound, and they heard two smiling newscasters discuss a woman's miraculous survival after nineteen hours at sea—an inset picture showed the woman being airlifted out of the ocean waters near Maui. Then the ticker passed the stock update and suddenly no one in E.T.'s heard the rest of the story about the woman's rescue.

The ticker proclaimed, "The Center for Disease Control issued a warning to the people in the City of Roswell, New Mexico to stay indoors tonight and every night until further notice. County health officials have confirmed at least a dozen bats have tested positive for rabies. Several local residents have been bitten in recent days and are being given the rabies vaccination. They are expected to make a full recovery. On the west coast . . ."

Paul muted the sound. For a few heartbeats, silence reigned. When Farmer whirled back around, Lucy barely recognized him. She had served the man at least three times a week in the past ten days, but the person staring at the crowd was a stranger to her. "Bats? They want us to believe we've been attacked by bats?"

On the heel of Farmer's words, Colton stepped forward. Lucy wondered how long he'd been listening. She'd been watching for him, but hadn't seen him come in.

He tried twice to speak, succeeded the third time. "What

happened at Great Southwest this morning wasn't bats. Simon Gordon sure as hell didn't die from a bat bite, and Hugh's plane didn't go down because of a bat, either."

No one in the bar moved. Again an eerie silence washed over them. No clinking utensils, no crying babies, not even a ringing cell phone. Lucy wondered where Sally had gone, but she didn't turn around to look. They all seemed frozen in place. Then one by one, people stood, as if ready to testify in some long ago revival service.

A young man near the back spoke first. "My uncle didn't get bitten on the golf course by a bat. He was putting on the seventh hole. Collapsed and died. He felt fine when he left the house this morning, and he got a clean bill of health from Doc Mason last week." The man started to sit down, then added as an afterthought "And why can't we see him? They won't even tell us where they took him. My aunt's going nuts."

A woman two tables over gave him a sympathetic nod. "I know what you mean. My sister-in-law's mother was watching her soap operas. No bat came in her house and bit her." Tears streamed down the woman's face, but she didn't stop. "I'll tell you what else. A bat doesn't leave that much blood. We scrubbed for hours." She studied her hands, shook her head, and sat down.

A shiver travelled down Lucy's spine when she recognized Nadine's voice coming from a table behind her—sweet Nadine, who she'd known less than two weeks. But she'd worked with her every day. Like the rest of Roswell's residents she did not deserve this heartache. Lucy forced herself to meet Nadine's gaze.

"My neighbor crashed his car into his house. He hasn't had a single wreck in the three years we've lived there. Why would he crash into his own house? He was such a sweet old guy—like a grandpa to my niece and nephew." Nadine's voice tremored.

247

The tray would have fallen if Dean hadn't eased it out of her hands. When she started sobbing he pulled her to him, led her over to the bar and helped her onto a stool.

One by one they all focused again on the television ticker. The Roswell alert scrolled by once more.

Lucy looked at Dean, but he shook his head. She read him clearly; he wanted her to stay out of it. Could the false news be Aiden's way of keeping people off the street at night? Aiden or Commander Martin trying to prevent panic? Or, did the terrorists have people in the national media? Had they managed to shut down the story? She didn't doubt their reach.

"I haven't seen any fucking bats." Farmer strode back to his table, pulled out his wallet, and dropped a twenty dollar bill on the table.

"Are we leaving, honey?" His wife grabbed keys, cell phone, her purse.

"Yeah. We're leaving. I think it's time we go to the hospital and demand some answers."

"I tried." Colton said. "They won't tell you anything, not even next-of-kin. Unless you're believing bogus heart attack stories."

"Yeah? Well, Roswell just became one big family. We're all next next-of-kin, and we're not settling for any more faked stories." Farmer paced from one table to the next, and as he did some people rose to join him.

"We'll go with you, Jason."

"Hell, yeah. If we're infested with rabid bats, I want to see one of those suckers."

They dropped cash on tables, pushed back chairs, knocking some over. As they stormed out, Lucy went back to her work, not knowing what else to do.

Passing Dean, she paused to whisper. "Shouldn't we do something?"

"Let them go. If they're in the hospital, they're at least off the street."

When she glanced over at the map, she saw the reason Dean didn't want anyone on the streets of Roswell. Intent on the television screens, it seemed nobody had noticed that all the pins had been removed from the canyons and placed along the streets of Roswell. No one cared about UFO sightings given the current tragic turn of events.

"Don't you think you should take that damn thing down?" Lucy asked.

"Why? Someone here is leaving a message. Pissing in our back yard is the way Martin put it. They're bold bastards, and I'm going to catch them."

Dean knew Farmer and the others would be back sooner, rather than later. When they reappeared, things were likely to explode. The question was whether he could or should do anything about it. His objective remained to stop the terrorists. If all the residents of Roswell decided to walk out in the middle of Main and gaze up at UFOs, who was he to stop them?

But as he served the regulars who'd stuck behind—people he'd been serving for over a month now—a picture surfaced in his mind. It was the image of a little boy, playing with a toy truck in the dirt outside a station in Corona, New Mexico. A little boy he had vowed to protect.

The ricin-slotted influenza didn't discriminate between big boys and little ones.

He set another drink on the bar, glanced at the clock and saw the hands slip toward eight-thirty.

"Thanks for staying past your shift, Paul."

"Not a problem. Home isn't where I want to be tonight." Paul hesitated, as if he wanted to say something else.

Before he could, Farmer walked back in, followed by the

group that had left with him. Billy and Bubba had joined them. Bubba nodded at Dean, then at Lucy. Billy stared down at his feet.

Sally peered out through the cook's window, then bolted from behind the grill to face Farmer head on. "Jason, I don't need any trouble in here."

"Do you think you can avoid this trouble? It's too big for that, Sally."

Sally motioned at Emily, who stood behind the counter.

"You wanting Emily to bring you that shotgun?" Farmer strode over, reached behind the counter, and pulled the gun out himself. He handed it to her. "You're my godmother, for God's sake. You gonna shoot me? Is that what we've come to?"

"I want you and your little group to walk back out of here like you walked in. Let these people eat and go home. They've had enough trouble today."

"You think so? Like we've had trouble? You're not forgetting our family was touched by this. Are you? You have talked to Katie and Carol, right? You've tried to see Ben? Because you can't. Are you telling me you believe bats killed him?"

When Sally didn't answer, he turned back to the people in the restaurant.

Everyone had stopped to watch the exchange.

"Most of you were here earlier. You know we went to the hospital. Tried to get the truth."

He looked around, forced eye contact with as many as would dare to meet his gaze. By now the men and women he'd picked up along the way filled the entry way of E.T.'s.

Dean wondered how they'd fit in, and what they would do with them when they did.

"What we got were more lies. They knew nothing about a rabies alert. No county officials. No doctors who had treated anyone with a bat bite—and none that wanted to talk."

"Though a revolver persuaded them some," Bubba murmured.

"It did manage to bring out the head of the hospital. It also brought out Eaton who threatened to throw us in jail."

"He would have too." Colton pushed through the crowd. "You could tell he wanted to, but not for his normal reasons."

"What do you mean, son?" John Curry, the principal of the high school, stood.

"Eaton got a mother hen look on his face," Colton said. "The one you used to get, Mr. Curry. If he'd had enough cars to load us in—"

"And enough men," Farmer added.

"Yeah. Apparently Roswell's finest are stretched pretty thin." Colton ran his hand over his face. "I think he would have taken us in so he could have kept us from getting hurt. From what, I have no idea. I didn't see any damn bats. I know it doesn't sound like Eaton, but nothing makes sense tonight."

"So you didn't learn anything." Curry sat back down, reached out and placed his hand over his wife's.

"We did learn one thing." Farmer looked to Colton, who nodded.

Farmer's wife began softly sobbing. Jason Farmer took off his ball cap, twisted it in his hands, then cleared his throat and pushed to the center of the room. "We checked around. Started asking questions and comparing stories. We think, actually, we're sure, that since last night, thirty-four people in Roswell have died."

CHAPTER THIRTY-ONE

Everyone started talking at once, and Dean felt the itchy need to reach for his weapon. He fought the urge and won.

Sally's voice rose above the others. "Everyone quiet down. Jason, what the hell are you talking about? That's impossible." Her eyes begged him to take it back. She had been grasping the shotgun, but now she lowered it, muzzle pointed at the ground, as if she didn't quite trust herself with it anymore.

"We thought so too. Tell them, Colton."

Colton's eyes again sought Dean's. Much of the bravado had left the boy. He no longer swaggered, and his words often came out as questions instead of definitive statements. More than anything else, his perpetual look of anger was replaced by grief— the scowl set into a firm line as if by clenching his jaw he could grasp hold of his emotions. Dean had the oddest sensation of looking in a mirror at a younger version of himself.

"Nine died at the airport—the sales manager, two in the plane, six in the maintenance building." Colton hesitated. "Another twelve died at the golf course."

"Alice said ten." Dean broke his silence. Everyone in the room shifted in their chairs to peer at him.

"Maybe, but I talked to a caddy. He said they'd locked down the clubhouse while he ran in from the course. He saw the ambulances roll up, saw them bring out the body bags. He had a first row seat, and he counted twelve."

"Who was this?" Curry asked.

"Alex. Alex George."

Curry nodded, as if Alex's word was good enough for him.

"There's more. Two others confirmed the number, but made us promise not to use their names."

"Why the hell not?" A trucker at the bar shouted the question. He came through town once a week. Usually had a meal, one beer, and drove on. Tonight, he'd stayed.

"Good question. People are scared. Don't want their names on the news. There's all sorts of talk about everything from an alien attack to a foreign invasion. They'd only agree to talk if we promised their names wouldn't be mentioned, and I gave my word. Most headed on home to lock themselves in for the night. Said we'd all be smart to do the same thing."

"I'll be damned if I'm locking myself in my house," Bubba muttered.

Several people seated at nearby tables nodded in agreement.

"This is a tragedy for sure." John Curry pulled a handkerchief out of his pocket, wiped at the sweat pouring down his face. He folded the handkerchief and put it back in his pocket. "I never taught math, but I think we're only up to twenty-one."

"Right." Colton pulled a piece of paper out of his jean's pocket and stared at it. Slowly he read it aloud. "Mike's uncle was part of the twelve at the golf course plus nine at the airport. Then there was Donna's mother and Nadine's neighbor, Mr. Anderson. Four from the Villa Del Rey Retirement Community. Mr. and Mrs. Cooks out on the loop. Rev. Banks and his sister, old Miss Winters. And finally Coach Johnson and his wife and sister."

Colton's voice had grown smaller as he spoke. When he finished, he continued to look at the list, as if staring at it might change the words written there. Finally, he stuck it back in his pocket.

Dean tried to make eye contact with Lucy, to warn her to

step away from the middle of the group. He knew what would happen next because he'd seen it in every town he'd witnessed tragedy. Shock came first. It always came first, and it played vividly now across the faces of the customers in front of him.

One or two stared down at their plates. Others peered around, as though trying to find something to settle their eyes on, anything that made sense. A few made the sign of the cross or turned to hug the person beside them.

Shock was a universal reaction.

In all the battlefields Dean had fought upon, it always came first. And it never lasted long.

Anger exploded from the trucker like oil from a well-placed drill. "Who the hell is killing the old folks? What kind of town are you all running here anyway?" He stood and made to pay his bill, but his hands shook too badly to pull the bills from his wallet.

"I don't like what you're insinuating, Frank." Bubba shouldered his way across the room until he stood in front of the trucker. "You saying someone in here had something to do with these people dying?"

Dean knew from the way Bubba's arm flexed he wanted to slug somebody and anyone would do, even an old man who occasionally passed through.

"I don't know *who* is doing it. I'm just pointing out that all those people ya'll called out was old," Frank muttered.

"They were old." Sally pushed between the two, shotgun still clutched in her hands. "So what? It's some kind of weird coincidence."

"So what? So, next you'll say the bats only bite old people." Jason sneered.

"Shut the fuck up, Jason." Sally's words were a screech, and no one could mistake the threat behind them.

Colton stepped closer to Lucy, as he pulled his pistol from

his waistband.

Dean had two ways to get Lucy out of there. He could jump the bar and tackle Colton, but Paul blocked his path. Or he could shoot him from where he stood. He reached for his weapon, when Colton held his pistol high over his head, palm out.

The room fell silent.

Sweat continued to trickle down Dean's back, but he released his grip on his weapon.

Outside the sun had nearly set, casting its final glow down the road.

"How many of you have a weapon?" Colton surveyed the crowd.

Over half raised their hands.

"One person knows what's going on, or at least a part of it." Colton hesitated, and Dean's heart stopped beating.

If Colton grabbed Lucy, Dean would kill him. The shot from where he stood would be clean.

"If we all go together, armed, Eaton will talk. He'd have to. We have a right to know."

Dean pulled in a deep breath, then held it when something cold and hard pressed into his back.

"Don't say a word, and don't reach for your piece." Paul spoke casually and quietly.

Nobody heard except him. Everyone had begun talking at once, discussing the merits of Colton's plan.

"We'll step out back. Just you and me. Clear?"

Dean nodded. He heard Paul click the safety off his weapon and knew the man wasn't bluffing. He tried to catch Lucy's eye as they turned to go, but neither she, nor anyone else, noticed as they stepped out the back door and into the shadows of the alley.

★ ★ ★ ★ ★

Lucy's attention was torn between Colton and what was happening in the street. The street finally won. As people in the
tavern began arguing over the merits of Colton's plan, Lucy slid
through the crowd unnoticed. She stepped out into the dying
sun and peered down the boardwalk.

Like their first morning in Roswell, she saw more than what
was there. The boardwalks were again deserted.

No people. No bats.

But she did see blood.

The sun's last rays pushed across the worn boards. Dust
covered the handrails and benches. Pickup trucks were pulled
to the curbs. Traffic lights hung over deserted streets, turning
from green to yellow to red.

And Lucy stood with her back against the plate glass window
of E.T.'s, trying to deny what she saw. She understood that to
reject the truth of her vision was to lose any chance of stopping
what would happen this night. Her *abuela* had often told her the
vision was a gift. As a young girl, she had laughed. As a teen,
she had cynically chosen not to believe. Then she became a
doctor, and put such foolishness behind her.

Tonight, though, she embraced her heritage—let it fold into
who she had become.

She stepped away from the wall, stooped, and traced the
patches of blood that were as yet unspilled. Shots would be
fired tonight. At least three would be injured, perhaps die, before
the stars came out. Then the UAVs would swoop over Roswell
to disperse their death, laden with their virus.

The equation finally balanced—what she saw with what she
knew. The influenza, ricin, bloodstains. Angela and UAVs.
Roswell had become a laboratory. Someone chronicled each
death, so others could analyze the data.

And someone inside prepared to pass on their plans to these

bastards. She would bet her life on it.

Lucy stood and gripped the handrail. She forced herself to watch the last of the dying light. Her faith had suffered much since Marcos had come home wounded. Watching the sun dip and darkness descend, she searched and found the small kernel of belief she had buried in her heart. Found it and offered it up.

"Dios estar con nosotros."

The prayer—simple, softly uttered, and desperate, had barely escaped her lips, when she heard the door behind her open.

She blinked, could hardly believe her eyes. Colton silhouetted against the lights of E.T.'s, his revolver firmly grasped in his hand and pointed directly at her.

Chapter Thirty-Two

"Use your left hand. Put your weapon on the ground. Real slow. Now push it away with your foot." Paul stood with his back to E.T.'s alley door.

Twilight quickly claimed the alley. The only light, near the street, hadn't come on yet. Dean couldn't make out Paul's expression in the nearly complete darkness, but he didn't care for his tone. He did as directed, pushing his gun toward the dumpster.

Paul stepped a little closer—not close enough for Dean to lunge for the weapon though.

"What the hell are you doing, Paul?"

"Asking some questions—questions I should have asked last night. How you answer them will decide whether I put a bullet in you or turn you over to the group back in there. The people Colton named are people I knew and respected. They didn't deserve to die like they did."

Dean lowered his hand, caught the faint glitter of light on Paul's revolver as he jerked it up. "Keep them high."

"Hell, Paul. Some things I can't tell you."

"I don't see as you have an option. Start with who you work for."

"I can't—"

"Leave out the alphabet soup. Give me a general idea."

Dean drew in a deep breath. He did not want to give up his cover. Then again, with things unraveling at the rate he suspected they were, his cover wouldn't matter much longer anyway. "I work for an agency within our government. We track and apprehend terrorists."

"Why are you in Roswell?"

"Four weeks ago we received information that there would be a widespread release of a biological agent over the U.S. A body dumped near here proved they had the technology to do what they claimed."

"What happened at Felix Canyon?"

"We suspect it was a test run."

"And Jerry?" Paul asked.

"He's been on a personal vendetta since someone murdered Angie. Jerry does not work for us."

"But Lucy does?"

Dean nodded.

"Makes sense. Maybe a little too much sense. Pretty convenient. Lucy looks kind of green to me, impressionable. How do I know you're not on the other side? You could be a mole they planted to use her."

Dean opened his mouth, then closed it. What could he say to defend himself? How could he convince this man? Paul represented all the disillusionment he'd been harboring in his own heart for the last five years. No doubt Paul had seen his share of betrayal while serving in Nam.

He'd never needed to prove his own loyalty. He'd always worked alone.

If Paul couldn't tell a traitor from a man willing to give his life for his country, well, hell. Things were worse than he'd thought.

Somewhere behind Paul, a weapon clicked. "He's not the mole, asshole. I am. Now drop the weapon, and move over beside him."

Dean knew from the way Paul went rigid that the gun's barrel was likely pointed at his head. He dropped his weapon, moved carefully with his hands raised.

Their attacker stepped into the last bit of light. Dean recognized her immediately. And he recognized the glint in her eyes. He'd seen it before, in other times on other faces. It meant they hadn't long to live.

Lucy studied Colton and wondered if she would have to kill him. Had he betrayed his town? Looking up at him, it didn't seem possible, but then tonight had been filled with the impossible.

"Hey, Lucy." He reached behind him, stuck the gun back in his waistband.

"Things calm down in there?" She tilted her head toward the bar.

Colton shrugged and leaned against the boardwalk railing next to her. As he stared out over the still empty street, his shoulders sagged. The gesture reminded her of how young he was.

"Shouting's mostly done, I guess. It's just a matter of who will go, and who will stay."

They watched the road for the space of a few heartbeats. No cars broke the silence. Roswell had rolled up and tucked itself in for the night.

"I want you to promise me something." Lucy waited until Colton's eyes met hers. "Promise me, whatever you do you won't be outside tonight. If Eaton gives you trouble, come back here and get inside. Or go to the hospital and stay there. Just don't, don't be out in the open. Promise."

Colton turned toward her. She had his complete attention now. He waited for more of an explanation.

"You don't realize it yet, but people follow you." Lucy stepped closer, put a hand on his chest. He could be on the wrong side, but she didn't think so. Something told her the sand had slipped almost completely through the glass. The time had come to trust her intuition. She might not get another chance to talk to Colton this way again. "They'll listen to you like they did in there. Lead them, Colton. Be sure no one stays outside tonight."

Colton glanced down at her hand, still resting near his heart, then back into her eyes.

"Do you promise?"

"But, I don't—"

"Do you promise?"

"Yeah. All right. I promise."

She felt a little of the weight lift off her shoulders. "Let's go in then. See how many are with you."

They stood shoulder-to-shoulder. Colton had just reached out to open the door to E.T.'s when they heard their names called. They spun to see someone step from the shadows at the end of the boardwalk.

Dean focused on Emily and wondered how he could have dismissed her all these weeks. He could see the bitterness in her eyes, even in the near darkness.

"Emily? What are you doing?" Paul kept his hands up, but he motioned at her semi-automatic weapon. "I think he's telling the truth. He's here to help."

"Depends what you consider helping, Paul." She motioned them toward the dumpster. "If you consider selling out our country to fucking foreign powers helping—okay. He's helping. I consider him a fucking traitor."

"And who do you work for, Emily? Domestic terrorists?" Dean resisted the urge to charge and break her neck with his bare hands. More than likely, she was an excellent marksman. "I guess you're a national hero for killing innocent people?"

"Don't get self-righteous with me, Dreiser. I'm sure you've

261

done your share of killing." She smiled, and Dean remembered how she had cried when Angie died. "Haven't we all? Two more won't weigh on my conscience, not that I plan on seeing the sunrise. Nor do I particularly want to."

Dean cringed to hear the resignation in her voice. The one thing worse than a lunatic with a gun was a lunatic who had nothing to lose.

Lucy and Colton stopped and waited for Jazmine.

"Trouble inside?" Jazmine joined them, but stayed well away from the light spilling on the boardwalk.

"Some. Colton is taking a group to Sheriff Eaton's. See if he can get more information on where they've taken the people who died." Lucy sized up the woman before her and wondered why she hadn't pegged her as an agent before. She had excellent poise, eyes that seemed to absorb everything, and not an ounce of body fat. She could get a job tomorrow in a James Bond flick.

"Lucy was just telling me I should try to stay, uh, inside." Colton looked from one woman to the other, as though sensing something he couldn't quite grasp.

"Lucy's right. In fact, skip the Sheriff's office. Everyone needs to stay inside until morning." Jazmine scanned the street, the sky, and E.T.'s patrons.

"Not going to happen," Colton said. "They're inside now deciding who's going and—"

"Check your phone." She glanced at him.

"Huh?"

"Both of you. Check your phones. You'll find they don't work. Nobody's cell phone works."

"Shit." Colton started punching buttons. "Damn cell service."

Lucy slipped hers back in her pocket. "Land lines, too?"

Jazmine nodded.

"I can't even get roaming. You can always get roaming, so the bastards can charge you double." Colton kept fiddling with his cell.

"You can put it up, Colton. It's not going to work. Not tonight anyway." Jazmine exchanged a pointed look with Lucy. "Where's Dreiser?"

"Wait a minute." Colton snapped his fingers. "I got it. Dreiser asked me about you this morning, before all the shit hit the fan. What is the connection between you three?"

Lucy opened her mouth, but Jazmine cut her off. She pointed down the street, south, out over the Hondo.

They blazed a long way off but were coming closer—lights in the sky. Lucy's mind flashed back on the pins in Dean's map, the pins lined down Main. Those lights were headed directly toward the center of Roswell.

"What about Joe?" Paul asked.

"What about him? If I could, I'd put him in the middle of the street when they fly over tonight. Let him get a good dose. But he's snuggled safely inside the house on his damn computer like every night. Too bad. Life isn't fucking fair. It never was. He can read about tomorrow's tragedy on the 'net."

"But, but you love Joe." Paul's voice shook and his arms trembled, but he stood firm beside Dean. His world might have tilted, but the man was trying valiantly to right it. "I saw you two just the other night."

"I'll tell you what you saw—what you wanted to see. Well, Joe and I haven't loved each other for some time. Not since my boy came home from Afghanistan in a box. Came home from another one of their fucking oil wars. Joe is so much less than a man, he makes me sick. I'd be happy to line him up with the two of you. Three bullets, twelve hours, and I can finish my job."

"They'll hear you inside," Dean reasoned.

"Above Colton's ruckus? They'll overlook me, like they always have. Same way both of you did."

Dean knew Lucy would notice he was missing, if he could stall a little longer. "How did you know to follow us out here?"

"I saw you leave at the same time. I see a lot, Dean. More than most people realize."

"People have underestimated you."

"Hell, yes, they have."

"So you came outside, then waited and listened."

"We knew USCIS had another man in Roswell."

"Who did you i.d. first?"

Emily laughed. The sad, broken sound echoed in the night. "You're not the one interrogating, Dreiser. But I'll play along since you'll be sucking dirt in another two minutes. Jazmine is the one we knew about. My men have picked her up by now. We didn't know about Lucy, but I heard you confirm as much to Paul. Thanks. She'll be a bonus my boss will be happy to hear about. Taking the little bitch down will be easy once I dispose of you two."

"Hell, killing us is one thing." Paul's voice had steadied. He had moved past disbelief, past fear, and stepped into the path of cold fury. "Killing thousands of people—that's insane."

"We are not killing thousands. Do I look insane? Don't believe everything he says."

"You think they won't use the infectious form?" Dean knew he'd found the weakness in her fortress when she blinked. "They planted it on Angie. Meant for it to infect Kowlson and everyone in the autopsy room. You haven't forgotten that, have you, Emily? Because that wasn't accidental. If they told you the infectious strain was only for specific targets, they lied."

"You think you know so much." The words seethed out of her like so many poisonous snakes. "The government we have now will never change and you both know it. Paul. You're a vet. You've been a pawn in their wars. If the event isn't big, it won't bring this government to their knees. Six large cities. Six surgical attacks, and then it's over. We'll rebuild with the pawns in charge. Finally a change, and a new government *by the people.*"

"I know you want to believe that." Dean's throat felt raw, as though he had screamed for hours, but his words were barely a whisper. "Lucy's a biomolecular scientist. They're using influenza and ricin. Tonight's the big test. Once unleashed, it will kill one third of the people in the United States—one hundred million people. And it won't stop there."

"Shut up."

"It'll go worldwide. Germs don't recognize borders. You're an intelligent woman. You must know that."

"Shut your fucking mouth." Her entire body trembled, and both her hands grasped the weapon.

"It will kill two billion people. A legacy of death to leave. Your organization might have immunized their people. Or maybe they're psychotic enough to want to kill everyone. They—"

"You stupid fuck. They *are* us!" Her scream sounded like a dying animal.

Paul lost control of his fury. He attacked her with the ferocity of a hurricane hitting a coast.

Emily's gun went off and found its target. Paul crumbled onto the alley's pavement.

Dean dropped and rolled.

His weapon still lay near the dumpster where he'd kicked it. He grabbed the gun, and came up shooting.

He fired off three rounds at Emily. She fled to the end of the alley and bolted around the corner. He glanced once at Paul's crumpled form, made his decision, and took off down the alley.

CHAPTER THIRTY-THREE

Lucy reeled toward the noise from the alley—a screech followed by four pops.

Fear coursed through her system.

Colton grasped the door knob and froze.

Lucy and Jazmine reached for their guns and dropped into a crouch.

Emily bolted around the corner at the far end of the boardwalk, her weapon drawn. She looked as if the hounds of hell were pursuing her. Firing off two rounds, she hit the one person still standing—Colton.

He sank to the ground as Lucy and Jazmine returned fire.

Four bullets brought her down.

Dean rounded the corner and Lucy holstered her piece, dropped onto the boardwalk beside Colton.

"Any others?" Jazmine remained in a shooting stance, her weapon still drawn.

"She's it, for now." Dean crouched beside Emily, checked for a pulse.

"She's dead," Lucy shouted. "I need help with Colton, or he's going to bleed out."

She didn't have to check Emily's pulse to know. She could tell from the amount of blood, as well as the unnatural angle of her body. As to why she had shot at them, Lucy realized those answers would have to wait.

Dean had covered the remaining few feet between them. He

knelt beside Lucy, yanked off his shirt when Lucy indicated she needed it.

"They're coming." Jazmine said. She nodded at the approaching lights. "We need to get inside now."

"We can't move him." Lucy knelt over Colton. She folded Dean's shirt, held it against the hole in Colton's chest. Blood seeped onto the boardwalk. "He won't make it if we move him."

"He won't make it if we don't," Jazmine said.

The patrons in E.T.'s had pressed their faces against the windows. Dean opened the door and called for Billy and Bubba.

"Everyone else get as far away from the windows as you can," Dean barked.

"Do like he says." Sally pushed her way forward. "The world is fucking falling apart, and you can't tell the good guys from the bad? Listen to Dean."

Sally's word, Colton's bleeding body, the UAV lights closing in, and Jasmine still holding her gun combined to convince people. Everyone began to clear a path.

"Bubba, help Jazmine and Lucy move Colton. Billy, get Emily."

Billy gawked at Emily's bullet-ridden body. He stopped short of the puddle of blood staining the boardwalk. "My god, Dean. She's dead. She's fucking riddled with bullets."

Dean pulled Billy in and pointed at the UAVs. "Those planes will be here in about twenty seconds, and they're not dropping care packages. So move her. Now."

Lucy had one last glimpse of Dean before he took off around the building. Watching him fly into the darkness, she realized there had only been two bodies bleeding on the boardwalk. She'd expected three.

How many minutes had passed since he'd left Paul in the alley—two, three, five? Dean couldn't remember. He needed to get Paul inside before the UAVs arrived. If he didn't, they'd both be dead.

In the faint glow from the street light, he could see Paul's still form.

Kneeling beside him, Dean wished he had time to tend the wound. With an unbound injury, moving the man might kill him. But leaving him would expose him to the UAVs, surely kill him.

He had no time to weigh his options.

Dean hoisted him in his arms, feeling Paul's blood soak onto his bare skin. Paul had saved his life by attacking Emily. Now, he would do his damndest to return the favor.

Still trying to save Colton, Lucy looked up when she heard Dean. Concern and relief washed over her face.

Jazmine helped him lower Paul to the floor. "He's been shot. I'm not sure where or how bad it is, but he's bleeding quite a bit."

"Let me look. I'm a field medic." Jazmine nudged him gently aside.

Dean checked the crowd. For the moment, their attention remained on the windows. Once the UAVs had passed, they'd have questions, lots of them.

He turned to Lucy. She shook her head. "He's lost too much blood. One bullet punctured a lung."

Jason Farmer's wife—Meg—was standing looking at them.

Dean walked over to her, touched the woman's arm. "Can you assist Lucy?"

"Yes." She swallowed, crossed her arms and hugged them to herself. "I can try."

"There's a medic kit inside the supply room, when you first walk in. First shelf on the right."

Meg nodded, took a few halting steps, then ran to the stock room.

Dean strode to the middle of the room, where most of the customers stood huddled in groups of twos and threes. Beyond the windows, the glow from the UAVs' lights had begun to penetrate the darkness in the streets.

He took a deep breath and plunged.

"There's no one in the planes. They're robotics containing poisonous gas. Everyone move toward the back, but give Lucy and Jazmine room to work. Women and children go to the stock room. Men with weapons, stay in this room, but away from the windows. Sally, make sure the air conditioner is off."

Everyone looked stunned, then Jason Farmer stepped forward, put his hand at the back of his waistband. "Why the hell should we believe you? Why should we do what you say?"

"Because it's my fucking bar, and I believe him." Sally appeared at Dean's side, shotgun at the ready.

Dean pushed the shotgun down. "Not good enough, Sally. Farmer's got a good question. You all *better* start questioning who you trust."

Silence filled the room as everyone pressed closer.

"Are you saying we can't trust each other?" Jason asked.

"I'm telling you to be careful. Because you've known someone a while doesn't mean you *know* them, and because someone's new in town doesn't mean you can't trust them."

"Why'd you shoot Emily?" Jason asked.

"We shot Emily because she shot Colton."

"I don't believe you," Nadine said. "Emily wouldn't—"

"It's true." John Rich's voice rose above the rumbling. "I was about to go outside and talk to Colton. I had a clear view of the end of the boardwalk. Emily fired first."

"Who are you then?" Jason stepped closer. "Who are you really?"

"Lucy, Jaz, and I work for the government. We came here to stop this, and we *will* stop it. But we need your help."

Jason shook his head, unconvinced.

Then the street outside of E.T.'s lit up like noon.

A gasp rumbled through the room as the planes bathed Main in an unnatural light.

It pierced through the bar's front windows, and people fell back, pushed against one another to avoid its reach.

The planes flew slowly. Silently. Deliberately.

The darkness left in their wake offered no comfort.

Everyone began talking at once, but no one questioned Dean's instructions. They gave him a wide berth as women and children stumbled toward the stock room. Men checked their weapons. Several people tried their cell phones, shaking their head in disbelief.

Dean motioned John and Jason over. "Check every room. Jason, take the south side. John, the north. If you see an open window, don't go inside the room. Shut the door. Block the air flow." He reached over the counter and grabbed a handful of towels. "Take these."

"One more thing." Dean grabbed two bundled sets of silverware. Shaking out the silver, he handed one linen napkin to each man. "Use these like face masks. I won't lie; they might not be enough, but they're better than nothing."

The men left. He glanced up as Sally came in.

"A/C is off," she said. She watched him checking his clip. "Bartender, huh?"

Dean tried to smile. It hurt, like new skin stretching around a recently-closed wound.

"Are these people safe in here?" Sally growled, clearly mad enough to kick some alien ass.

"I don't know. Maybe. Safer inside than out."

"They'll be back?"

Dean nodded. "Probably throughout most of the night. Try and catch anyone they missed."

"We need to get a doctor for Paul and Colton."

"Actually, we have one." He pointed at Lucy.

Sally did a double take when she saw Lucy's hands inside Colton's chest wound. Unconsciously, she reached for her pack of cigarettes and probably would have lit one up if Dean hadn't stopped her with a look.

Jazmine worked on Paul. Meg monitored Colton's vitals. From the women's expressions, Dean didn't have to be a doctor to realize Colton's situation was far worse than Paul's.

"What can I do?" He knelt by Colton.

"I stashed a surgical kit in the back of the store room."

"Why'd you do that, Luce?"

"The vision, the one I had the first day we came." A hardness came into her eyes. "Which doesn't mean I'm going to let them die. The kit is taped to the southeast corner of the freezer wall, two feet from the bottom."

"I'll get it." Sally slipped through Bubba and Billy, who were keeping a distance but unable to look away from their dying friend.

Dean pulled on gloves the way Lucy had taught him. "I can barely feel his pulse," Meg warned.

Sally returned with the surgical kit and knelt beside Colton.

"Glove up," Dean instructed. "Like this."

"Meg, put those masks on us." Lucy nodded toward the kit. "Colton has a collapsed lung and massive blood loss. Let's provide the most sterile environment we can."

Meg nodded, moving quickly from Lucy to Dean and finally to Sally.

"The bullet grazed Paul's side." Jazmine reported. "The dressings have stopped the bleeding. His pressure is good."

"Pulse?"

"Weak but steady. He's still unconscious."

"Check for evidence of a head trauma." Lucy eyeballed her

team. "Colton can't get enough oxygen because the bullet punctured his right lung. I need to insert a tube into his left lung to equalize the pressure."

Dean's mind flashed back to the morning in Albuquerque when he wanted to send her back to Virginia. Colton would be dead if he had.

"Dean, you need to put your hands where mine are so he doesn't bleed out. I haven't been able to tie off the damaged artery yet. Pinch and hold."

Dean looked into the brown eyes of the woman he loved. Then he placed his hands over hers—allowed her to put Colton's life into his hands.

"You okay, Dreiser?"

He nodded once.

"Sally, alcohol first, then chlorhexidine, the blade, and the tube—in that order. Meg, monitor his vitals. Ready?"

Everyone nodded, and no one breathed.

"Alcohol."

Colton didn't twitch when the cold swab touched his skin.

"Chlorhexidine."

Dean watched as Lucy wiped the skin again where she would make her incision. She worked without hesitation.

Light danced off the blade. Then, metal pierced skin. Dean was amazed the boy had so much blood left after all he'd spilled on the boardwalk. In the time it took the thought to cross his mind, Lucy had asked for and inserted the tube.

"Vitals are stabilizing," Meg said.

"Don't release the artery, Dean." Lucy turned to Sally. "I want to tape around the tube first. Then, I need to sew up the right side." They worked quietly, efficiently, with an economy of words and movement.

When Dean finally stood and stripped off his gloves, he felt as if he'd chased a perp across twelve city blocks. John Rich shoved a cup of coffee in one hand and a clean shirt in the other. "You look like you could use both of these."

"Yeah." He shook his head, trying to shake out the image of the interior of Colton's lung. The picture had been burned into his mind.

Sally joined them as he returned from the men's room. Cleaning Paul's blood off his skin had helped. He picked up the lukewarm coffee and downed it in one long pull.

"I should be pissed at you, Dreiser. Telling me Lucy's a college student, but hell—she looks like a college student. Guess she's not."

"No, she's not."

They watched Lucy move between Paul and Colton. Dean knew they'd been lucky tonight. Looking at the clock, he was shocked to see only an hour had passed since the shooting had begun. Ten—time for the evening news.

Jazmine joined them.

"How's Paul?" Dean asked

"Lucy says he'll make it. But, between a possible concussion and blood loss, she said he might not wake up for another hour or so."

"And Colton?" Jason Farmer asked.

"Still iffy." Jazmine pulled out her cell and tried it again. Shaking her head, she put it back.

Dean leaned over the bar, picked up the landline there. "These are out, too."

"Any idea what's wrong with the cell phones?" Jason asked.

Jazmine waited for Dean. When he nodded, she answered Jason's question.

"The communication towers are still standing, so they must have access to the control panels. They switched off service here. They want us isolated."

"The outage could work to our advantage." Dean sat down

on a bar stool. "We can't call out, but they can't listen in, either."

"What the hell are you talking about?" Sally's eyes narrowed.

"Nine-eleven legislation." John Rich said.

Dean scanned the bar. "There must be fifty or sixty people here. I wouldn't want to try and collect every cell phone. Usually someone holds out. Then, you have a mess on your hands."

"You lost me," Jason said.

"Cell phones are also listening devices. If they're on, they can be monitored by government satellites."

"Hang on. Stop. Time out." Jason held his hands up in a T as if he were calling a time out on a ball field. "First, are you saying the bad guys have access to government satellites? Second, why would they want to listen in on us?"

Dean glanced over at Emily, steeled himself for what he needed to do next. "If the bad guys—as you so aptly call them—have the ability to turn off our phones, control the news, and get hold of a few UAVs, chances are they do have access to government satellites. Why would they want to listen in on us?" Dean shrugged. "To know what we're up to."

"You lost me," Sally said. "I only got a damn cell phone this year, and I rarely get calls."

"But most people leave their cell phones on all the time."

Jason rubbed his forehead. "If it isn't open though—"

"Wrong. To speak to someone you hit the talk button—you request permission to connect to a cell tower. That can also be done remotely. Your service provider can turn on the microphone without your permission."

"No fucking way." Sally once again reached for her pack of smokes.

"It can be a good thing when a disgruntled worker shows up at his job with a rifle. He barricades himself inside without any real plan, just knows he's pissed."

Jazmine nodded. "I worked with a Hostage Rescue Team. We

had a similar situation twice. By manipulating the incoming signals to the cell tower, our techs were able to listen in to what was happening. We located the perp and were able to get everyone out safely, largely because we knew what was going on inside the building."

The people around Dean looked stunned, but suddenly relieved they had no phone access. "I think by morning your phones will work again. They're out tonight because the bastards didn't want anyone to interrupt their plans."

"What are their plans, Dean?" John asked.

"I know some, and I've guessed at more. But there's someone here who I think knew everything." He nodded towards Emily. "Even dead, she can tell us something. The dead always give up their secrets."

Grabbing a clean pair of gloves, he walked across the room to where Emily's body had begun to stiffen.

CHAPTER THIRTY-FOUR

Lucy watched Dean walk over to Emily. After pulling on gloves, he started sorting through her pockets. The act didn't bother her; in fact, she wondered why he had waited so long. But the gentleness he displayed tore at her heart.

Lucy squatted down beside him. "Paul will make it. I'm not sure about Colton, but I've done all I can."

Dean nodded, met her eyes, then continued turning out each pocket and feeling the lining of every seam. "Can you help me turn her? Slowly. She could be a kind of human booby-trap."

"Is that why you're handling her so gently? Because she would have just as soon shot you as Paul. In fact, she probably did aim at you." Lucy's anger filled her throat until it ached. She didn't want to be kneeling over this body, didn't want to be consumed with hate for this woman she had worked beside for over two weeks, but she was.

Dean stopped searching Emily's pockets and rocked back on his heels. Lucy felt as if his gaze could see into her soul, and she wondered why it bothered her. The man had seen her in his bed, had seen her naked and certainly more afraid than she was now. Why did she suddenly feel vulnerable? Why did she feel ashamed?

Dean glanced around. Although plenty of people were watching, none stood close enough to hear.

"There's no doubt Emily was involved, but I don't see how she would have had the resources or the expertise to pull it off alone. More than likely someone saw a weakness—or an old hurt—and took advantage of it."

Lucy considered what kind of past pain could drive a woman to sell out her friends, her town, even her country.

"She's responsible for what part she had in this, and I'm glad you and Jazmine brought her down," Dean said. "But she can't hurt anyone now, unless it's with a substance on her skin."

Lucy felt the tears slip—tears she'd held since the first gunshot had rang out. She turned so Dean wouldn't see, walked to the bar's counter and found a new pair of latex gloves. Who would have ever thought they'd need an entire box? Yet, it seemed they'd go through them before this night ended.

By the time she knelt beside Emily's body, Dean had emptied out the rest of her pockets. The contents made up a small pile.

"Turn her toward me."

When they did, gasses from her body escaped.

"Fucking health department would close me down for sure," Sally grumbled from the closest group. She handed Lucy a serving tray to hold the few things they'd found.

Dean had started at Emily's head and worked his way methodically down, checking her body. When he reached her back pocket, he pulled out a small GPS. "Looks like yours."

"Same model," Lucy said. "Top of the line. They just came out, and they're not cheap." She added it to the tray.

When Dean was convinced he'd find no other clues, he motioned to Bubba and Billy. They stepped closer, but Billy blanched, obviously afraid he would be asked to move the dead woman yet again.

"Get two of the tarps we use to cover the pool tables. They're under the bar top."

"Sure, Dean. No problem." Billy wiped his hands on his jeans.

Careful to stand as far from the body as possible, they helped cover Emily, then joined Jason and John near the bar. From there they could monitor the street and the storeroom.

"It's the best we can do for now," Dean said. "Moving her would raise the risk of contaminating two areas if she does have any biohazard residue on her. Eaton will need to call in a de-containment group tomorrow."

"I'm surprised Eaton hasn't shown up," Jason admitted.

"I'm sure he has his hands full at the hospital. Sally, it's up to you to explain all of this to the ME and Sheriff Eaton tomorrow."

Sally had broken down and lit a cigarette. She stubbed it out at the tone of Dean's voice. "Where the hell do you think you're going, Dreiser?"

"Depends on what Lucy finds on Emily's GPS."

Lucy had been thumbing through the system. "I think I found a map, but I'm not sure what the starting point is."

"You said it isn't safe to go out." Jason jerked his head toward the street.

"I think we need you here," John Rich added.

Dean picked up a set of keys from the tray. "Can you tell me where Emily lived, Sally?"

She twirled the pack of cigarettes once, twice, three times. Then rose and went to the map. She traced a route with her finger. "Last house on Mossman Road. Pretty desolate out there."

"Jazmine and I'll take my truck."

"No. Jazmine can stay here. I need to go with you." Lucy put the GPS and Emily's keys in her pockets.

Jazmine continued checking Paul's vitals. "You're lead on this, Dreiser. I'll go where you want me."

"Dean, I'm going." Lucy closed the surgical kit and handed it to Jazmine. "You know where this map leads, and you know I need to be there."

"Yeah. I know."

He pulled the prepaid phone out of his back pocket. "Jazmine, take this. There's one number in it. Try it every thirty minutes. When it's answered, apprise Aiden of our situation—he's the one agent I'm sure hasn't been compromised. Tell him everything you know. Local authorities are on a need to know basis. Clear?"

"Clear."

"Lucy, five minutes. Check on Colton and Paul and leave any final instructions. The UAVs have been passing every forty minutes, so we should be clear to make it to my truck. Meet me at the front door in five."

"You'd be better off taking the Harley."

They all pivoted to gawk at Paul. His eyes were open.

Lucy was beside him in seconds—checking his vitals, his pupils, his color.

"I'm old, but I'm not dead. You're a good doctor." He struggled to a sitting position.

Three people rushed forward to help him. Sally appeared with a glass of water. Billy offered him a shot of whiskey. When Paul wisely refused, Billy shrugged and swallowed it himself.

"Why should we take the bike?" Dean squatted at his side.

"The reconnaissance on the UAVs will have noted the license number of every vehicle parked on the streets." Paul coughed twice. "They won't have the license yet on the bike. It's parked inside the loading bay. Plus it's smaller and faster. Less heat signature. With any luck at all, they'll miss you."

Jazmine sat to the side, knees drawn up. "What he says makes sense, though a bike makes you vulnerable to the air."

Paul shook his head. "There's two helmets—one on the bike, another in my locker."

"We could wear masks under the helmets," Lucy suggested.

"Phase two is probably a hunt for specific targets. They're

looking for an agent, Dean—not a crusty old bartender. If they see the bike, they'll think it's me, taking one of the girls home."

"It's a good plan. Let's do it."

"Dean." Paul's voice wavered for the first time since he'd regained consciousness. "I owe you an apology. I'm sorry I doubted you. I'm sorry I got us into this."

"You were protecting the people you care about. Emily would have made her move tonight. You forced her into the alley." Dean looked around at the townsfolk he'd come to know so well in such a short time—people Emily might have killed if she'd confronted Jazmine in the bar. "You saved someone's life tonight, Paul. You took the bullet she would have put into me. No apology necessary."

"Keys are on the hook." Paul reached out his hand, and Dean grasped it. "Don't forget you have the late shift tomorrow. And take care of my doctor."

Lucy leaned forward and kissed Paul's weathered cheek. She wanted to promise him she would be back, but a shiver passed through her. Some part of her mind recognized she had not finished with death this night. Before she could utter a promise she might not be able to keep, she rose and followed Dean into the store room.

Dean wound his way through the women and children who had taken refuge in the back room. Most of the kids had managed to fall asleep. The women's eyes rose to meet his, and he did his best to return their looks with confidence. In truth, he thought they would be safe as long as they remained where they were. If the payload wasn't contagious.

Too damn many *ifs*. He dropped his eyes from the gaze of a mother holding two infants. If the bastards had switched to the infectious strain, one of the three would be dead within hours.

Dean increased his pace, snagging Paul's keys from the hook.

He was standing by the bike, checking his pockets for extra ammo when he heard footsteps.

Lucy arrived, a backpack slung over her shoulder.

"What's in the pack?"

"Supplies. Water, flashlight, extra batteries, medical kit. Two of the men donated their pistols."

"So, your average date stuff."

"Pretty much." She held out his mask. Her eyes locked with his, but the smile he loved trembled on her lips—trembled and faltered.

"You're doing great, Lucy." Instead of taking the mask, he took her in his arms. Sinking his hands into her hair, he let his thumbs trace the beautiful outline of her face. Breathing in the scent of her, he pulled her even closer and kissed her lips.

"Ick. I didn't know Captain America likes to kiss girls." The five year old stood practically pressed against their knees, looking up at them quizzically.

Lucy laughed and pulled back. The boy frowned at her, opened his mouth to protest more, but stopped when a sleepy redhead called him over.

Dean studied the loading bay. The southernmost end had large rolling doors. They could be raised for trucks to back in and unload their supplies. The Harley sat near the doors, as if waiting for its mission.

"Will the particles still be airborne?" Dean held his mask in one hand, his bike helmet in the other.

"No. They settle rapidly due to weight, which makes them good weapons. Instead of hanging in the air, they're inhaled quickly. As long as we don't fly under or in the path of a UAV, we'll be all right."

Dean nodded. "I'll drive with the lights off, until we're out of town. And keep to the side roads. The main streets may be empty, but the street lights are on. I want to draw as little attention as possible from any high-altitude reconnaissance craft."

"They'll also have heat-sensing equipment?"

"Yes, but they won't be able to distinguish us from the surrounding buildings and people. It'll be a problem once we're clear of town limits." Dean shrugged. "Nothing we can do about it."

Sally, Jason, and John entered the storeroom.

"Ready?" John asked.

Dean waited for Lucy's grim smile, then nodded. Lucy zipped up her jacket and shrugged into her backpack. He walked the bike around to the bay's door. Jason stood ready to open it.

"Keep your feet here." Dean pointed to the place for Lucy's feet, but she stopped him.

"I owned a Shadow my first four years of med school. Do you need me to drive?"

Jason chuckled, and Sally snorted.

"Why am I not surprised? Get on." Dean kissed her again, then donned his mask and helmet.

She did the same, wrapping her arms tightly around him.

"Godspeed," John said.

Jason opened the bay door, and Dean walked the bike out. Jason closed the door quickly. The darkness engulfed them, and Dean fought an urge to hold his breath. After coasting the bike to the street, he checked both ways.

Main remained deserted. Both Dean and Lucy looked up, but only stars shone overhead. They had offered their light for eons and would continue to do so, even when this nightmare was over.

Dean cranked the Harley and turned right.

CHAPTER THIRTY-FIVE

The ride out of town was uneventful. Whether everyone stayed inside because of the shock of the last twenty-four hours, or because they were suffering the effects of the weaponized virus, Dean couldn't guess. He didn't see any corpses to indicate more were dead or dying. With their headlights off and no traffic, they were making good time. Dean had dispensed with formalities like complete stops and merely slowed down at each intersection.

They saw the UAVs twice.

The first time Lucy touched his shoulder and pointed.

The UAV seemed larger at this vantage point than the glimpse he'd had from Felix Canyon. Larger and faster. A Volkswagen Beetle had pulled out from a convenience store and made it as far as the intersection when the UAV swooped down from above and hovered. The two vehicles remained there, as if suspended in time and space, then the UAV sped on.

The Beetle's driver had his arm slung out the window. When the UAV pulled off, he gave the UAV a middle-finger salute. The Beetle, which had to be a vintage sixty-five or older, seemed to agree. It shuttered once or twice, then caught in first gear and chugged off.

Dean realized with a jolt the driver would be dead within twenty-four hours. He felt Lucy's arms tighten around his waist, and he gunned the Harley.

The second time, they had just taken Buchanan Road and

entered the remote part of their route. The light from a million stars brightened the night, and a three quarter moon hung in the sky. Dean had finally switched on the headlight, afraid of killing them in a collision before a UAV had the chance.

When the second UAV appeared, Lucy's grasp on his waist tightened into a death grip.

He brought the bike to a halt, followed her gaze. Two UAVS streaked across the desert at full speed, perpendicular to where they sat. Dean understood the uselessness of trying to outrun something today's military had constructed. He knew their speed could top five hundred kilometers per hour. Fortunately, it didn't adjust course to their position.

Fifteen minutes later, they turned west onto Mossman. With no street lights, the road stretched before them, pitch black, the houses set well apart from each other. He felt like they were sitting ducks, their headlight a beacon.

A single light burned at the back of Emily's house.

Dean cut the engine, let the bike coast under the carport. By the time they'd made their way up the gravel path, Emily's husband had opened the front door. Joe didn't look surprised to see them, even though they hadn't removed their helmets.

Looking resigned, Joe motioned them in. He glanced up at the sky once before he shut the door.

Inside, Lucy lifted off her helmet; Dean did likewise. As he exchanged a few words with Joe, Lucy stared at the shrine on the living room wall, dominated by the portrait of a young staff sergeant.

"Did Emily tell you about Bodie?" Joe asked.

Lucy shook her head.

"Killed by a car bomb in Afghanistan, December of two-thousand-one."

Dean joined them at the wall of honor. "We didn't lose many

in the first three months. I'm sorry he was one."

"Twelve of them died." Joe stared at the portrait of his son with eyes that had moved past grief to a place Lucy somehow understood. "He served in the Third Battalion. They were advancing on Kandahar. The bomb took out Bodie and two others."

They gazed at the young man who would never return home.

"I realize it sounds inadequate, but I am sorry for your loss." Lucy reached out, touched Joe's arm.

"Thank you. Bodie knew the dangers when he went, but he loved the Army and his country."

An awkward silence fell. Studying Joe, Lucy wondered if perhaps he had caught the mutated disease, or maybe Emily had given him something else. The man appeared even more gaunt than when Lucy had last seen him at E.T.'s a week ago. As he stared first at her then Dean, she saw how sunken his eyes had become. She suspected he'd lost at least ten pounds in the last week.

"Joe, you look like you need to get off our feet." Dean nodded toward the couch.

Joe sat, and Lucy moved beside him. Dean pulled up the ottoman from the wing-back chair.

"I suppose this is about Emily. I knew someone would come eventually. Didn't expect you two, though. Expected the authorities."

Dean exchanged a look with Lucy. "We are the authorities."

"But you work at—"

"No time to explain it all now. Tell us about Emily."

Joe shrugged. And then he started talking.

"She went crazy at first when Bodie died, just crazy with grief. I didn't think it could get any worse those first few months. Emily used to be a good-looking woman—a kind woman. Bodie's death changed everything."

He met Lucy's eyes, then shifted his gaze to Dean. "She's dead. Isn't she?"

Dean nodded. "I'm sorry."

Joe stared down at the carpet. When he looked up, the shadows had deepened, but no tears tracked down his cheeks. "I figured as much, when I saw you ride up. I guess I knew."

"How did you know, Joe?"

He waited so long, Lucy thought he wouldn't answer. When he did, she had to lean in to catch all of his words. "After they came—they came all the way out here like you did. After they came to tell us Bodie had died, she screamed for three weeks solid. I don't mean crying or sobbing, I mean screams like a hurt animal will make. I thought I might lose my mind. The doctors tried to give her something to settle her down, but she wouldn't take it. They wanted to put her in the hospital. I thought if she stayed out here, maybe she'd find some peace. She always loved it out here."

Lucy went to the kitchen for a glass of water. He accepted it from her with shaking hands, drank half, then looked out the single window, out at the night sky.

"Then she stopped screaming. Only, she never recovered afterwards. She'd died with him. For a long while I told myself to give her time. One year became two, and what dreams had lived inside our marriage blew away. Like so many dried up tumbleweeds. It disintegrated into an empty, barren thing."

Lucy thought he might cry then, but he didn't.

"Paul said he saw you two just the other night." Dean leaned forward. "He said you seemed happy."

"Yeah." Joe tried to smile, failed. "We could fake it when we needed to. I don't know why we bothered."

"Did you suspect Emily might be involved in something illegal?"

"Yeah. Yeah, I did. I wasn't sure what to do about it. Didn't know who I could trust."

Lucy leaned forward. "Who you could trust with what, Joe?"

"With what I found. I'm a computer geek, remember? Emily became good at covering her trail. Once I knew to look for something though, she didn't stand a chance. I started compiling evidence. I didn't know who to give it to, and I wasn't sure if I was ready to testify in court against my wife. Even if she had tried to kill me."

"She tried to kill you?" Dean's voice cracked.

"Twice. Maybe I should show you what I've found."

"I think you should." Dean eyed the clock as it chimed eleven.

Lucy felt trapped inside the longest night of her life.

Joe led them into an office. It faced the rear of the house. The windows were draped with blackout curtains.

Joe whirled on them and asked, "How did Emily die?"

"I shot her." Lucy forced her eyes to meet his, didn't allow herself to look away.

Joe's shoulders slumped even more. He sat in front of the computer and entered a password. The computer sprang to life.

Pausing with his hands over the keyboard, he said, "I'm glad you did it, Lucy. I bought a gun, but I don't think I could have done it."

Then, he showed them what he had found.

An hour later, Dean gratefully accepted the coffee Lucy handed him. Joe had shown them everything he'd found. It was a lot. Dean knew they didn't have time to go through it all, so he'd judiciously chosen what they would have time to analyze. Lucy had taken the printouts and organized them into preliminary categories, taking notes as she went.

The coffee wasn't a luxury. The hour had slipped past midnight, and they'd had less than six hours sleep the night before. Their bodies had pumped out a lot of adrenaline over the last twelve hours. They were starting to drag. The caffeine would help. Dean surprised himself when he reached for one of the sandwiches. He couldn't believe he had an appetite, especially given what he'd just seen.

Joe refused the food, but accepted the coffee.

"Why have you stopped eating, Joe?"

He stared down at his hands.

"She's a doctor. It's hard to slip much past her."

Joe studied Lucy as he sipped his coffee. "Can't say I'm surprised."

"What gave me away?"

"Your hands. You don't have waitress hands. I noticed both times you waited on me at E.T.'s, the way you set down my plate, how precise you were. Do you realize you set the food down with the meat at six o'clock?"

"Seriously?" Dean reached for another sandwich.

"The meat belongs directly in front of you. Stop avoiding my questions. Why did you quit eating?"

Joe teetered, like a man on the edge of a very deep lake, then plunged in.

"The first time Emily tried to kill me was the night they came for her. She'd cooked, which I thought a little odd. When I got home from work, she insisted I go ahead and eat before everything got cold." He shook his head at the memory. "Two days before I had discovered she was deleting files, cleaning out caches, erasing anything traceable on the computer. When I asked her about it, she evaded. Things were tense between us. I couldn't stand the thought of eating in the dining room alone. So, I took my plate out onto the patio. She stood there watching me, smoking."

His hands began to shake. "I can't eat when I'm upset—acid reflux acts up. But I forced down a few bites, and she seemed satisfied. She went inside, and I fed the rest to Dakota, our Labrador."

Lucy glanced around for evidence of a dog.

"I went in and washed off my plate. She was waiting at the sink when I got there. Even asked me if I liked it. I said yeah, it tasted good. Thanked her for making dinner. Hell, part of me hoped maybe things were better. Maybe I was paranoid about the computer stuff. I'd worked a twelve-hour shift, so I told her I needed to go to bed. Told her I had a headache."

Joe stood up, started pacing. "She reached into the medicine cabinet and got me three Tylenol, but I saw her take three pills out of the Tylenol PM bottle."

"Tylenol PM contains Benadryl," Lucy said. "She probably put some sort of slow acting poison in your food. The Benadryl would have caused you to go to sleep—"

"And never wake up," Dean added.

"It also might have masked any toxicology results if an autopsy were done." Lucy looked at Joe apologetically.

"Emily kept insisting it was regular Tylenol. We argued about it. I'd taken my contacts out when I washed up, and I couldn't see the lettering on the side, but I could see the bottle's color which she'd shoved back into the cabinet. She got all puffed up, and I told her to just give me the damn pills."

"PM is usually a different color, as well."

"Yeah. I figured that out later. Honestly I don't usually take anything—just sleep it off."

"Did you take them?" Lucy reached for a sandwich, appalled by his story.

"Tucked them under my tongue and swallowed the whole damn glass of water. My heart was hammering. I just knew she was trying to kill me. As soon as she left, I spit them out, threw up all of the food, but I was careful to do it quietly—always flushing the toilet and running the water to cover any sounds.

Praying she didn't hear me. I went on to my bed—we'd had separate rooms for a couple of years—mine's at the front of the house. I lay there in the dark waiting, wondering what she would do next. Around three in the morning she made her move."

Joe sat down. Dean poured him more coffee from the pot.

"A car arrived at three." Joe took a deep drink of the coffee. "I went to the window. Saw her go out and talk to a man. He tied her hands. She let him. She just put her hands out and let him. Then, he blindfolded her. He helped her in the back seat and they drove off."

"How long were they gone?" Dean leaned forward, thinking of distance, thinking their home lay halfway between White Sands and Roswell.

"Two, maybe three hours. She came back before daylight. At first, I stayed at the window, too terrified to move, afraid they'd be right back. Then, I thought of Dakota. I ran out back, searched for him, kept calling. By the time I found him it was too late." The tears he hadn't shed for his wife came now. "We'd had him since Bodie started high school. I drove into the desert a ways and buried him. I didn't want her to see how he'd really died. The next day I told her coyotes had gotten him. He'd been known to spar with them before, to protect his territory. He was fearless."

"What kind of car did they drive, Joe?"

"A Land Rover. I couldn't see the color or the plates. They didn't turn on their lights until they were down the road a bit."

"Do you know what type of poison she'd used?" Dean asked.

Joe shook his head. "But I started eating out more."

Dean waited for Lucy to speak.

"It could have been several things," Lucy's voice softened. "She would have wanted something odorless and colorless, tasteless. Maybe arsenic or thallium. But why would she want to poison you, Joe? What threat were you to her?"

He straightened up, regained some of the poise he must have once possessed in full measure. "When you're married over twenty years, you know each other in ways it's hard to imagine. She knew I knew . . . something. Maybe she wanted me to die before this—" his hands reached out to all the papers on the table. "Before all this started. I'm not sure. After that night she tried to kill me, our marriage became an all-out war, one played like a game of chess. I no longer tried to hide my maneuvers. I took to locking my door at night, bought the gun, let her see me practicing with it. Maybe I could have killed her."

Joe's admission hung in the air between them.

"How did you find all of this if she deleted the files? How do we know she didn't plant it, expecting you to find it?"

"She covered her tracks well—deleting files as she went, then clearing out the recycle bins and internet caches. But nothing is ever completely deleted on a computer or a cell phone. The physical address is deleted, but the data still exists. I could retrieve her internet history, call up any messages she had received or sent, even view instant messages. Of course, she didn't use the computer much, but as you can see there are quite a few pieces here."

"Too many." Dean and Joe studied Lucy's neat stacks. "Any references to bio-agents?"

"No."

"Contaminants?"

"No."

"Viruses?"

"No. I don't even know what you're talking about."

Instead of explaining, Dean stood and paced around the table. "We know she didn't do this alone. Lucy and I have to find who controlled her, and we have to find them before sunrise. If we don't, the sweep occurring in Roswell tonight will expand. Then there will be no containing it."

CHAPTER THIRTY-SIX

Lucy pointed to the pile on the farthest side of the table.

"These are communications with other people in her organization." She noticed Joe pale as he picked up the stack and paged through it. He was holding up well, but how much shock could one man endure? "Our technicians will be able to track down the names and addresses, but I suspect they will all be dead ends."

Dean nodded. "The techs can do a lot, but anonymity is one wall that stops them every time. Continue."

"Content in this stack is useless to us, although it could be used to build a case in a court of law." She motioned to the next stack. "This contains more technical material. Something tells me she researched more than she needed to know here."

"What makes you think so?" Dean leaned forward, scanned the top sheet which had specifications for the RQ-7 Shadow unmanned aerial vehicle.

"First of all, she never refers in her communications to what she accessed. Secondly, there's a lot of it. Look at the size of this stack—it has to be four inches. Most soldiers go where they need to go, do what they're told to do."

Joe laughed—the broken, hollow sound felt like splinters against Lucy's heart. "That wasn't what Emily believed. Some of the interviews she gave after Bodie's funeral were pretty twisted."

Dean sat back and stared at Joe. "What interviews?"

"Remember this was 2001. Media followed every casualty of the war at first. Emily didn't handle it well. She was still grieving, questioning everything—and I do mean everything. She tried to place the blame for Bodie's death on his superiors. Some of that was printed in a few national magazines."

"That might have been when she caught the attention of some anti-government group. Do you remember any unusual phone calls or visits?"

"The phone rang so much, I took the damn thing out of the house," Joe admitted. "After that, we changed to an unlisted number. Someone else's son or daughter died and our thirty seconds of fame were over."

"Maybe. Or maybe some contact Emily made there reappeared in Roswell a few years later." Dean rubbed his face, then reached for more coffee. "What else, Lucy?"

She indicated the next stack. It, too, was large. "Flight patterns, aerials, maps, routes. I can't tell of what. No labels. Again, the techs will be able to identify some of it with landmarks, but it will take time."

"Something we don't have." Dean pointed to a single sheet sitting by itself. "I suppose this sheet is important."

Lucy picked it up, stared at it, and handed it over to him. "I don't know what this is. It doesn't make any sense at all, which is why I set it aside. Obviously it's encrypted—but why would she go to the trouble to encrypt it, then delete it? Seems redundant, not to mention it suggests a level of paranoia that isn't called for."

"Sort of like poisoning your husband," Joe said it softly, but his eyes were on the sheet. He angled his chair closer to Dean's.

"I've never been good at this shit," Dean admitted. "I'm a field rat. Damn. All right. So what we have is nothing—"

"Hang on." Joe grabbed a pencil, and began substituting letters over the numbers on the sheet.

"I'm sure it's a military encryption." Dean leaned forward hopefully nonetheless.

"Maybe it is, and maybe it isn't. Computer code is written in a basic binary—zeroes and ones. Emily wasn't good with numbers. She couldn't even keep the checking account balanced. She loved to do the puzzles in the Sunday paper though. I think she'd pick a common encryption system. Like possibly . . ." He finished substituting the last few letters for numbers and pushed the sheet toward Dean. "Morse code."

They all stared at the words Joe had penciled above the dots and dashes. As they read to the bottom of the page, a deadly silence fell over the room until Lucy was sure she could hear the beating of all their hearts. She started back at the top of the page and began reading again, thinking if she did, the words would mean something different than they had the first time.

Jaclynn Stone, Robert Thacker, August 1

Angela Brewer, August 2

David Johnson, August 5

Felix Canyon, August 9

Albuquerque, Dallas, Las Vegas, Mexico City, Montreal, Vancouver, August 11[*]

White Sands, Luke AFB, Hill AFB, USAF Academy, August 12[*]

For the space of another few heartbeats no one said a word as the list of targets, both past and present, stared up at them like epitaphs etched in marble.

Joe stood, nearly stumbled, as he pushed away from the table. Stuffing his shaking hands into his pockets, he fled from the room.

Lucy stared after him, wondering how he could endure the weight of even more pain. To live with a monster was one thing, to be threatened by one, another. But to be confronted with the scope of Emily's malevolence might push him beyond his ability to recover.

She moved next to Dean, who still stared at the paper. "Is it a mission list?"

He shook his head. "I'm not a homicide detective, but this looks like a kill list to me." He started at the top of the page, ran his finger down the list and stopped at Angie's name. "What do you notice is missing before Angie?"

"Commander Martin sent me the pictures of two victims."

"In addition to the hiker I saw at White Sands. And Martin mentioned a fourth—"

"An agent, which is how we knew a mole had infiltrated our unit." Lucy reached for her bottle of water. Suddenly she needed a drink badly.

"If Emily were listing everyone they had tested the bioweapon on then there would be at least four names before Angie's. Since there's only two here, I think this is a kill list."

"I don't know what that is, Dean."

"It's not something a terrorist would have, but it's something a killer sometimes needs in order to keep functioning emotionally." Dean picked up the piece of paper and surveyed the room one last time. "Pull together any extra supplies we might need. We're leaving in fifteen minutes."

"Where are we going?"

"I'm not sure yet, but I think there's something Joe isn't telling us." Dean pulled his Glock and chambered a round. "When he does, maybe we'll know where we need to go next."

Dean stepped out onto the patio. He didn't want to shoot Joe, but he was willing to be responsible for one more death if it meant saving tens of thousands. While torture wasn't his field of expertise, he was confident he could get the information he needed.

"She killed all of those people." It was an admission, torn from Joe's soul.

"Either directly or indirectly—yes. I believe so."

"Even Angie?"

"Yeah. Even Angie."

Whatever thin thread had held Joe's world together snapped then. Dean remained near the door as sobs racked the man—with his shoulders hunched forward and his head bowed, he was the picture of a broken man. Dean wanted to allow him time to grieve. Unfortunately, war seldom allowed for such luxuries.

He holstered the Glock and sat down next to Joe. "I think Angie's death was unplanned. She must have stumbled onto a meeting the night we went dancing. If Emily hadn't killed her, someone else would have."

Joe nodded, but still didn't look up.

"What haven't you told me, Joe? We don't have much time. Emily's list indicates the substance they're using—a bio-weapon—will be released over those cities in a few hours. If we have any chance of stopping it, I need to know what you know."

"I wish I'd killed her. I wish I'd reported my suspicions. I had no hard evidence, but maybe the authorities could have done something. Could have saved some of those people . . ."

"Whoever she worked for would have recruited someone else. I need to know *who* she worked for since Bodie's death. I need a name or a location."

Joe took a deep breath and peered out across the desert, out beyond Dakota's grave. "Four years ago, Emily said she needed to get away, spend some time alone. She claimed she was driving up to Santa Fe. I didn't buy it. We'd been sleeping in separate rooms, like I said before. I thought she might be sneaking off to see someone. Maybe I was past caring, but hell. It's a hard thing when you suspect your wife of adultery. Normally I wouldn't have done it."

"What did you do?"

"I bought a GPS tracking device and hid it in her car—top of the line, no expense spared. Geeks are very good at some things. I sat right there in the study and tracked her. She did go north, like she claimed, but she didn't go to Santa Fe. Instead she went to some little cabins in Taos. This package I bought with the system worked like Google Earth—but it provided live images. I could even make out the cabin number. Afterwards it was only a matter of hacking into the reservation system and getting a name on the reservation."

"You think you got a real name?"

"I know I did. Over the years I would check it again occasionally. She never went off over the weekend after that, so I'm not sure they were sleeping together. Maybe they had to meet in person once. But he's a real person all right. His name is Tony Goodwin. Major General Tony Goodwin."

"All right. It's a start. Once the phones and internet come back up we can do a search. Until then—"

"You don't have to wait to do a search. I know where he is."

Dean had started back into the house. He stopped halfway through the patio door, and somehow he knew the next words that were coming out of Joe's mouth.

"A year ago he transferred to White Sands. He's third in command now."

Lucy sat staring at Emily's handheld GPS. A single map blinked on the menu system for the unit. It had to be the key.

Dean and Joe walked back into the room, both talking at once. Joe's color had improved from ten minutes ago.

"We have a name, Lucy. And we have a location. We're headed to White Sands."

"Do you have a specific place in White Sands?"

297

Dean threw a scowl her way. "We'll figure the exact location out when we get there."

"Hell, Dean. It's only the largest military installation in the U.S. No worries."

"I know its size, Doc. I've been there, remember? So, the sooner we get started, the better."

Lucy watched him collect what supplies they'd taken out of their pack. Instead of helping, she studied the GPS. "Have you ever seen this, Joe?"

"No, why?"

"It was Emily's. It contained a single map. I think it must have been important. The trick is we don't know the starting point. In fact, the corresponding GPS coordinates have been erased. I don't know why she would do that." Lucy continued staring at the unit, then tilted her head and studied Joe. "You said before that Emily tried to kill you twice. When was the second time?"

"The night Angie died."

Both Lucy and Dean stared at him.

Joe held up his hands in a gesture of surrender. "You're thinking I should have called someone, should have turned her in then. I would have, but I didn't know Angie had died, didn't find out until the next day. Even after all this, I don't know . . ."

He reached for the wall, supported himself against it with one arm, held Dean off with the other. "Give me a minute. Emily loved Angie. I know that. She might not have cared about me, but she loved that girl. That night, I'd been up late, working on the computer. I heard her walk in, and I came out to get a drink from the kitchen. There was a butcher block of knives on the counter. She lunged for it. I think . . ." Joe stopped and wiped his hands on his pants. "I think she would have killed me that night if she had been faster. I tried to talk to her, but she left. Didn't come back again until the next night. I still can't believe . . ."

"Angie might have stumbled on something she shouldn't have." Dean said.

"I'm sorry, Joe." Lucy met his eyes for a moment, then went back to studying the GPS map.

Dean finished packing and picked up the sheet of paper again. Folding it carefully, he put it in his pocket. Lucy glanced at him, but still didn't move. Rolling his eyes, Dean stepped behind her.

"We need to go, Lucy. Now isn't the time to play with toys."

"This must have been important though. It was one of the few things Emily kept on her. There's not much in it except this map. It's easy to create one." She fiddled with it again, and the unit beeped.

"I've heard that beep before," Joe said.

"Why create a map, unless you think you can't find your way back somewhere?"

"Or if you're blindfolded the first time you go there." Joe backed up to the table, pressed his hands against it for support. "That's when I heard it. Before the car arrived the night they came for Emily. The night they blindfolded her and bound her hands."

"She knew they were meeting at a different place." Lucy said.

"And she wanted to know where." Dean set the pack down and frowned at the unit. "The map starts here, but where does it end?"

"It ends where Goodwin is." Joe motioned toward his computer. "The internet isn't working, but I've downloaded maps of all the surrounding areas. I use them for my consulting work." He pulled up a map of Chaves County, then keyed in a route from his address to White Sands.

"Hold the GPS next to the screen, Lucy." Dean said.

Lucy could feel his impatience. He wanted to get on the

Harley. She, too, could sense their time slipping away, but she knew they were close to something important.

Lucy zoomed out on the GPS, showing the entire map on the small screen. She held it up next to Joe's flat screen monitor. Joe's map ran from his house to the end of the White Sands' perimeter. Emily's went much deeper into the military installation. Otherwise, the two could have been identical.

"Looks like our search area just got a whole lot smaller," Dean said.

CHAPTER THIRTY-SEVEN

Joe followed Dean and Lucy out to the carport. "Are you sure there's nothing else I can do? I know I can't make up for all the damage Emily has done, but . . ." the words drifted away into the night.

Dean heard the desperation in Joe's voice. He'd tried again inside the house to tell him he wasn't responsible for Emily's actions, but the guilt the man bore weighed heavily on him. The guilt and the grief. Dean struggled with the decision he had to make.

Straddling the Harley, having Lucy climb on the bike behind him, fit her body next to his, he tried to imagine life without her. Tried and failed. They would need to deal with those questions at some point.

Looking at Joe, he attempted to measure the losses the man had endured against what he and Lucy risked losing this night—a life together they hadn't yet begun to experience. Joe's dream had died when his son came home in a coffin, and he'd been living the nightmare for years.

Reaching in his pocket, he pulled out the list. "You don't have to do this, Joe."

"I know."

"Get in your car and drive north. Don't use your lights until you're out of Chaves County. Try your cell phone intermittently. I've written a number at the top of the page. Keep trying that number—no other. Don't call the police. Don't call the feds. Don't call anyone but that number."

"All right."

"Tell the man who answers that the Falcon gave you the number. Read him the list. The list is the most important thing. He needs to alert the potential targets. Then give him Goodwin's name. Tell him Lucy and I have gone to White Sands. Describe as best you can the route we're taking."

"That's it?"

"That's it. After you deliver the message, come back home, and stay here. If you see a UAV, do not get out of your car or roll your windows down. Keep all your vents closed."

Joe nodded and put the paper in his pocket. When Dean reached out to shake his hand, he looked embarrassed, but he shook it.

"No heroics—what you're doing is sacrifice enough. This is not a suicide mission, Joe. Come back here and wait in case I need you for something else."

"All right." Joe stepped back, but not before Lucy reached out and hugged him. "You have the map to White Sands I printed you?"

"Got it."

"How will you get through their security?"

"We field rats have our ways." Dean smiled back at Lucy. "We clear about the GPS?"

"Keep it off until we near White Sands, then use it to monitor turns only."

"Five second bursts, maximum," Dean cautioned. "Goodwin's power grid will still be up, and he'll be tracking us."

Lucy nodded.

Then Dean started the Harley, Lucy slipped the GPS into her pocket, and they roared off into the night.

They sped through the blackness, headlight once again on. The moon had climbed higher, and the road remained deserted.

Glancing at his watch, Dean saw the time had slipped past one. He pushed the throttle. They needed to be on the base before the morning guards rotated. Time remained his biggest concern.

Until he checked his mirror and saw the UAV bearing down on them.

"Hold on," he shouted.

He pointed toward the mirror, and Lucy saw it, too. She leaned in closer.

There wasn't a chance they could outrun it, but he sure as hell would try. Pushing the Harley seemed to do no good. The UAV closed the gap in seconds. They both watched as it loomed in the mirror.

Dean considered evasive maneuvers, but he didn't want to drive the Harley across the desert floor in the dead of night. He had five more seconds to make up his mind, and then they would be crop dusted with the bioshit, rendering his decision moot.

The speedometer topped out, and Dean readied himself to brake. With any luck, the UAV would overshoot them. They rocketed past a field, then an abandoned gas station with a single street lamp still burning near its defunct sign. He recognized it as their only hope.

He began applying the brakes, careful not to send them into a spin. Never taking his eyes off the mirrors, he watched the UAV overtake, then speed past them. Just as they slowed enough to allow him to turn the bike around and head back toward the station, a terrific whine filled his ears. At first he thought it was in his head—something left over from the speed and the sudden stop.

Then Lucy screamed, "Go!"

A magnificent explosion filled the night sky as the UAV burst into flames. The Harley shot forward and the road lit up as if it were high noon. He could make out the stripes dividing the lane on the road and saw the hairs on the back of his knuckles. He gunned the Harley around to the station's back side.

By the time he'd cut the engine, darkness had once again claimed the night sky. They both sat there for a minute, and then Lucy swung off the bike, removed her helmet, and started walking toward the back door.

He had to jog to catch up with her. "Where are you going?"

She still had on the mask they'd worn under the bike helmets, but he had no problem understanding her. "To find Jerry."

And then she opened the door and stepped into the darkness.

At soon as Lucy stepped through the door, the scent of old auto parts and simpler times surrounded her. She'd grown up in the city but spent a month each summer with her aunt and uncle. Uncle Benny owned a small town filling station. She'd learned to run the register, pump gas, even change oil in the old model cars that frequented his place. The familiar odors reminded her again of the importance of what they were doing, for her family and for others.

It took several seconds for Lucy's eyes to adjust to the darkness inside. Then she saw him sitting with his back against the wall, underneath the window which had been shattered. Propped beside him was a FIM-92 Stinger portable surface-to-air missile. Pieces of shattered glass crunched under her feet. Crouching down beside him, she started to remove her mask. Jerry and Dean stopped her at the same time.

"Better not, Lucy." His voice was a whisper, but he offered her a ghost of a smile.

"How you doing, Jerry?" Lucy pulled on the gloves Dean slipped into her hands, then felt for Jerry's pulse. It was weak and thready. The cuts on his face were superficial. As far as she could tell, he hadn't lost much blood.

"I'm all right. Enjoyed blowing the bastard out of the sky."

"We owe you, man." Dean knelt at Jerry's other side. At Lucy's signal, he helped move the big guy. They laid him down in the center of the room. Dean pulled a flashlight from their pack and flipped it on. Their shadows leapt onto the station's wall.

Had it been six days since he'd appeared in their room looking for Angie? There was little left of him now, and Lucy didn't know if it was the grief eating away at him, being on the run, or something far worse.

"Sorry about Felix Canyon, Lucy. I couldn't let them get away with it. Guess I caught some of what came down there."

She loosened his shirt and listened to his chest with the stethoscope from her bag.

"They're operating from White Sands," Jerry said.

"We know. We're going in now," Dean assured him.

Jerry licked his lips, and Lucy reached for her water bottle. Holding his head up, they managed to get a little down his throat before he started coughing.

"There's a storage closet in the office. Under the bottom shelf you'll find a pack. It has a pair of magnetic displacer cutters."

"Where did you get them?"

"Inside. Guys on the inside. They're scared. They know someone's bad—" The coughing wracked his body and Lucy wondered if it started this way each time. "They don't know who to report it to. Don't know how high it goes. I tracked the UAVs to this side of the base. I wanted to go in, but their bio-shit caught up with me before I could. This was as far as I got."

"We'll take care of it," Dean promised.

Jerry shifted his eyes to Lucy, locked them on her. His hand grasped hers and she had the irrational urge to strip the glove off, to allow him to feel her skin against his as he died. "I knew you were on the right side, Lucy."

She noted the red tinge begin at the base of his throat and knew he had ten, or at the most eleven minutes.

"Don't cry, Lucy."

They were Jerry's last words. His hands went limp, but Lucy and Dean continued to hold them. They stayed with him as the horror Dean had seen before occurred again. There was no need for words. What could they have said? All they could offer him was the dignity of not dying alone. In the end, he bled out like all the others had. It took ten minutes and twenty-nine seconds.

Dean found an old jacket in the office. Watching him cover Jerry with it, Lucy felt herself begin to shake. She thought she had seen the worst that could happen to a man when her brother had come home, but this was worse than what Marcos had endured. She had seen a lot of death, dealt with terrible viruses for the past six years, but this was the first time she had stared into the face of hell.

Dean put his arms around her, helped her to the door of the station where she could feel the night air on her face. Then he went back into the office and found the cutters. He slipped them into the backpack with the rest of their gear.

"The sun will be up in another three hours. I know it's hard to leave him, but we're almost out of time here."

Lucy nodded, said a final prayer for the dead, and followed Dean out into the night.

CHAPTER THIRTY-EIGHT

Lucy followed Dean back out to the Harley, climbed on behind him, donned her helmet, and gave him a thumbs-up when he asked if she was ready. But as they sped off toward White Sands, his question echoed in her mind. Was she ready? Had she ever been ready?

Blessed with an exceptional mind and good looks, she realized life had been easy up to this point. Had she chosen any other field, it would have been a breeze. What had happened to Marcos had changed everything. What was happening with Dean was changing it again.

She wasn't supposed to fall in love right now. She wasn't supposed to care so much about the man she now clung to as they sped through the desert night. Yet, she did. Watching Jerry die had acted like a lens, bringing much of her life into focus. They might not survive this evening. Many hadn't.

If they did live to see tomorrow though, she would be foolish to walk away from a once in a lifetime love because he happened to be a stubborn, burned-out, older *gringo*. So what if he was exactly the kind of man she had vowed never to love? They had known each other less than a month. The statistical odds of their relationship succeeding were slim. Almost as slim as the odds of their living to see the sun rise.

She glanced again at the GPS map, then tugged on Dean's left arm. He slowed the Harley, and pulled off the road. The map showed six more turns. They'd made it through four when they came to the perimeter fence.

It stood ten feet high. Electricity surged through it.

Dean pulled the cutters out of their pack along with a small pouch. "The power grid shows up on their control panel. Any disruption will show the exact location, and those lights at the top will come on. If we didn't get fried—which we would—the guards would be here in a matter of minutes."

"You're not making me feel any better about this, Dreiser."

From the pouch, Dean removed what looked like clothespins. He clipped them to wires five feet up, then shifted down two feet and clipped along the same wires again.

"You rerouted the circuit," Lucy said.

Dean gave her the wolfish grin she had come to love. "We'll know if it doesn't work on the first cut. The lights will come on. Either way, we go through. Agreed?"

"Of course."

He took out the cutters.

"They look like gardening shears," Lucy said softly.

"We're damn lucky Jerry was able to snag a pair." Dean snipped quickly.

Knowing there would be no going back, they left the Harley. It was too conspicuous to take through.

"Any idea how far we have to go?" Dean asked. He'd taken the pack from her, and they were moving on a southwest heading. With any luck the patrols wouldn't find the cut wires until dawn.

"No more than two miles."

"We're a long way from central headquarters."

"Is this near the first victim?"

"No. Remember it's the largest military installation in the U.S." He mimicked her tone exactly, and he also managed to sidestep her swing.

"We got lucky on the map and on finding Jerry."

"Yeah. We would have found a way in though. We had to." Dean reached for her hand and held it until they came in sight of the facility.

One guard manned the post outside. They dropped to the ground in the darkness and pulled out their binoculars.

"Looks like a concrete bunker."

"Most bio facilities are constructed of cement block." Lucy looked for windows and found none. "If this base were attacked, no one wants the bugs to get out."

"We don't have bioweapons programs," Dean reminded her.

"This could be left over from when we did."

"There's one camera on this side, sweeping east to west," Dean said. "And we'll need that guard's card to get in."

"I could ask nicely."

"Or I could shoot him."

"He could be a good guy."

"Could be, but it's doubtful since he's posted here." They remained on their stomachs for another ten minutes, watching for activity. There wasn't any, and it soon became obvious the guard was bored and less than alert. Dean motioned for Lucy to slide back down the small hill they lay crouched against.

Unzipping their pack, he pulled out a rifle with a night scope and assembled it. Then he inserted two tranquilizer darts. He handed the rifle to Lucy.

"Give me three minutes to circle behind him, then use them both," he said. "Wait until the camera has panned away to shoot. It's on a two-minute sweep. Stay clear of the lens when you come down."

She thought he would leave, but he touched her face, whispered, "I love you, Lucy."

Before she could answer, he was gone, melting into the night faster than the falcon name he had earned.

She began counting, crawled back up the hill at two minutes, positioned herself, and had the guard in her scope at two forty-five.

Praying Dean hadn't encountered any problems, she checked the camera, then fired at exactly three minutes. The dart found its mark. Before the guard hit the ground, she fired again. She watched through the scope as Dean appeared at the exact spot the man had fallen. He dragged the body into the shadows.

Lucy broke down the rifle, placed it into the pack, and pulled out her pistol. Then, she hurried to join Dean.

Dean confirmed both of Lucy's shots were direct hits. Private Wilson would be out for at least six hours. If they weren't back outside by then, it wouldn't matter. Reaching around the man's neck, he removed his keycard. By the time he shouldered Wilson's rifle and pocketed his extra ammo, then made his way to the door, Lucy was standing underneath the camera.

Both had their weapons drawn. There was still no sign of additional guards, but since there had been a guard posted outside there would be men posted inside as well. Dean held the guard's card up to the scanner. Lucy waited and opened the door on his signal. He went in first. The blast of air conditioning was a shock after the hours they had spent in the desert night.

Bright fluorescent lighting revealed a long corridor of closed doors. The entire layout resembled a cross between a military facility and a research laboratory. Dean pointed to monitors at each intersection of halls. They had no difficulty telling which way to go. They followed the biocontainment warning symbols through Zones One, Two, and Three. As they approached Zone Four, Lucy looked longingly at the scrubs, but Dean shook his head. They didn't have time.

In front of them a pair of double doors displayed a warning. Dean didn't need to read the words. The biohazard symbol was the same one Lucy had pointed out to him in Roswell's morgue.

In case visitors were slow learners, someone had placed a radiation symbol below on the opposite door. If the bugs didn't get you, the radiation would. Shit. Why couldn't he be up against good old-fashioned bullets?

They slipped through the double doors like sand slides through an hour glass. A control booth stood three hundred feet due north. In it were three men, watching a replay of a baseball game, volume set low. They were not wearing scrubs or masks, which Dean took as a very good sign. He handed Lucy Wilson's rifle and gave her the extra ammunition. He motioned for her to hold her current position, while he circled around from the east hall.

Four in the morning was the perfect time for an attack. The guards would be tired and pissed for having pulled late night duty. Dean crawled to within twenty feet and heard every word.

"I'll be glad to get out of this shit hole."

"Be grateful you're in here and not in Roswell."

"Fuck, yeah. Nobody's out looking at little green men now."

"Nobody's left."

They all laughed, though uncomfortably so, as if they might be caught and have to explain what they found so funny.

One of the guards leaned forward and stared at the outside monitor, then turned the sound on the baseball game even lower.

"Where the hell did Wilson go?"

"He came in for a leak about two minutes ago."

"Why can't he go outside like everyone else?"

"Go and check on him. Tell him to get the hell back outside."

The control booth was well-lit.

Dean crouched in the darkness of the east corridor. From their conversation, Dean surmised the last speaker was the ranking officer, which was all he needed to know.

The first guard was pushing back from the television to go

and find Wilson when Dean's bullets slammed into him. He never knew what hit him.

The second guard swiveled toward the sound, then he too went down.

The officer reached for his weapon.

"Put your hands in the air," Dean shouted. Adrenaline pumped through his veins, and his ears rang from the four shots he had fired.

The major froze.

"There's a rifle on you." The click of Lucy's weapon sounded. "Keep your hands in the air."

Dean stepped into the control booth, over the guards' bodies. He relieved the man of his weapon, then searched for his backup weapon. When he'd found and discarded it, he motioned for him to turn and walk toward the south side of the booth.

"Keep walking until you hit the wall. One wrong move and I've ordered my man to shoot."

The major nodded once. Dean holstered his weapon and took a pair of plastic ties from his pocket. The guard didn't argue as Dean tied his hands behind his back, but he did glance at the monitor twice. The time on the monitor said four-fifteen.

"What time are you supposed to call in?"

When the guard didn't answer, Dean turned him around to stare him in the eyes. "I will kill you. You will only be alive as long as you're useful. What time are you supposed to call in?"

"Four-twenty."

"Who usually does it?"

"Dominique. You killed him."

"What is your name?"

"Major Quinn."

"All right, Quinn. You'll call tonight." Dean jerked the man back to the north counter. Pushed him over to the desk, next to the television where the game played on. He picked up the handset. "What's the number?"

"One-one-three."

"If they come in here, you die first. I'll personally make sure of it, if it's the last thing I do. Understand?"

"Yes."

Dean waited until the clock said four twenty, then dialed the extension. He held the phone up so Quinn could speak.

"This is Quinn, with the four-twenty check from the southwest quadrant." His eyes darted around as he spoke. Tiny beads of sweat dripped from his face down on to the papers stacked neatly on the counter. "Yes. Everything's fine. Dominique's in the john. His wife made green tamales again. He's been in there most the night."

Dean could hear a voice and some laughter on the other end. If it was a code, it was a very good one.

"No, we're fine. We'll see you at five-thirty then."

Quinn nodded, and Dean replaced the handset. Motioning Quinn back toward the north wall, Dean brought his fingers to his lips and whistled once. Time to bring Lucy in and let her take a look at what waited beyond the north wall of the control room.

CHAPTER THIRTY-NINE

Lucy entered the control booth, stepping over the bodies of the dead guards. Some part of her brain heard the crunch of shattered glass as her boots crossed the littered floor, just as a part of her mind noticed the shock on Dean's prisoner's face. No doubt he was surprised to see a female sharpshooter. Well, fuck him. She'd had about enough of the chauvinist crap.

Lucy noticed these things, sensed Dean watching her. But she saw all of it peripherally. Ninety-five percent of her attention was focused due north.

"Is that what I think it is?" Dean asked.

"Yeah." Lucy felt beads of sweat form under her hair, down the small of her back, between her breasts. "I need to get in there. How long do we have?"

"Replacements will be here in one hour."

"Then find a way to secure this facility. Keep everyone else out."

"Impossible," Quinn said.

Lucy looked directly at him for the first time. Sewn over the pocket of his uniform were his commendations as well as his name—Quinn. Dean had placed him in an office chair, with his arms looped over the back and bound together. She thought she'd faced evil once tonight—when Emily had torn around the corner of the boardwalk, guns blazing. Emily's hatred paled in comparison to Quinn's. Yet, this man didn't scare her a fraction as much as what lay beyond the wall of the control room.

"Why is it impossible?" Lucy now saw Dean had also bound his legs together. "Which part?"

"All of it." He choked on the words. "You will not stop us. You are foolish to try. Why don't you run like the rodents you are—"

Dean hit him across the side of his face with the butt of the rifle he'd taken from Lucy, the rifle Private Wilson had held thirty minutes before.

"Save the commentary. You remain alive as long as you help us."

"I will never help you."

Dean pulled his Glock out of his holster and pressed it to the man's temple.

Lucy didn't flinch. "What part is impossible?"

Quinn licked his lips. Blood ran from his eye and lip. Lucy had no urge to bandage either. This bastard was willing to kill thousands, perhaps millions.

"Last time, Major Quinn," she spoke softly. "I need in the biocontainment lab, and I need to keep everyone else out. Why is it impossible?"

"It is a Zone Five. Without training you would be dead in minutes."

"My death wouldn't bother you a bit. Can you get me in?"

"No."

"Wrong answer, Major." Dean had eased his weapon away from Quinn's head. At the word *no,* he raised it to the man's temple again.

"You must pass through the ocular scan." Sweat ran down Quinn's left eye as steadily as blood dripped from his right.

"Then you better hope your eye fits the scan." Dean produced a knife from his vest, cut the ties holding Quinn's legs, and pushed him toward the lab's door.

"Are you suiting up first?" Dean moved between Lucy and Quinn.

A door to the right had the word *showers* on it. Lucy knew the room would contain biohazard suits and respirators. "There's no time," she said, echoing his earlier statement.

He nodded once. "Let's see if there's any reason for you to keep breathing, Quinn."

The scanner was located to the right of the door. Quinn placed his eye against it and they all waited. The monitor light continued to glow red. A message running across the display blinked, "Access denied."

"Wrong answer," Dean said, reaching for his weapon.

Lucy wondered if he would shoot Quinn or try and shoot through the glass. She considered warning him neither would do any good. The glass was required to be bullet proof. As far as Quinn, if his eye didn't work, shooting him wouldn't help.

"Don't shoot," Quinn screamed. "I think it's the sweat. It's the sweat. Just wipe away the sweat, and let me try again."

Dean glanced at Lucy.

"It could interfere with the integrity."

Dean stepped over one of the dead guards, ripped off part of his shirt. Moving back to Quinn, he wiped around his eye. "Last try, Quinn."

The major nodded and stepped toward the scanner. After three seconds, the light changed to green and the display read, "Access granted."

Lucy walked up three steps into the small decontamination room, then continued into the main lab. Lucy stepped into it.

Dean blocked the path of the steel door, unwilling to let it close behind her. "Can we talk to her from the control booth?"

"Yes, there is direct communication between the two."

Lucy stared at Dean, tried to silently say everything she

hadn't. Then the door swung shut, and with a hiss the airlock sealed.

She wrenched her eyes away from where he had been and went to work.

The lab was state of the art. She'd never envisioned less. She also hadn't expected them to keep so much of their weapon cache in one place.

She found the comm unit and switched it on. "It looks like the bulk of their weaponized grade virus is here. It's been attached to trigger mechanisms. They must have been waiting to load it into the UAVs. I'll try and separate the vials from the triggers."

"Why would they keep so much in one place?" Dean asked. He'd retied Quinn's legs to the feet of the chair.

She peered down into the booth, noting the facility's design as she began to work. The lab itself sat one foot higher than the rest of the floor. The design would accommodate special cooling machines and backup generators positioned beneath the floor. The overhead exhaust fans had automatically switched on as soon as she stepped into the room. Her ears were still adjusting to the negative pressure of the lab, but it gave her some measure of peace—especially given the fact she hadn't taken time to put on a suit. Negative pressure meant there were vents and filters actively working. It also meant any microbes inside couldn't escape out—unless the bombs exploded.

"And why didn't they have more than three men guarding it?" Lucy asked. She set the tools she would need in front of her. Not believing her eyes, trying not to panic, she counted the vials in front of her again.

"Time to talk, Quinn."

"You'll kill me anyway. Why should I tell you anything?"

"You're a smart guy. Probably why you made Major. I'll tell you what. If you talk, I'll let you choose. I can kill you, I can guarantee you a military court-martial, or I can return you to your commanding officer."

Lucy glanced up and saw Quinn's face pale at the prospect.

"Why aren't there more guards?"

"It would have drawn attention to this portion of the facility. Plus, we had no need for more guards. We couldn't be breeched."

"Really? Did you hear that Agent Brown? They couldn't be breeched."

"Excellent. It's good to know we're very safe here."

"A little short sighted of Goodwin," Dean said.

"You—"

"Yeah, we know his name. Langley should know it by now as well. Why is there so much weaponized virus in one place?"

"I don't know."

Lucy jumped when the pistol went off, nearly dropping the viral glass she had separated from its detonator. "Warn me before you use your firearm, Dreiser."

"Son of a bitch! You shot my foot! I can't believe you shot my foot!"

"I will shoot parts of you more critical than your foot if you don't start talking. We do not have much time. Do not mistake this for an interrogation. Do you see a fucking lawyer present? Now answer my fucking question. Why is there so much virus here?"

"We risked less chance of being discovered if we stored all the weaponized grade here. This lab is no longer used officially, so it has minimal security attached to it. Also, we could run the UAVs here without anyone seeing them. This is a very remote part of the Missile Range." Quinn continued to sob and curse after he finished talking.

Lucy glanced down into the room and saw a bright red puddle of blood on the floor around his foot. On the other hand, his eye seemed to have dried up. Perhaps he only talked if it was flowing. Then she chanced to look at the clock and understood why Dean's voice had gained even more urgency. The hands pointed at five o'clock straight up. The new guards would be here in thirty minutes.

"How do we seal them out, Quinn? Think hard and you might live a little longer. Maybe you'll even see prison."

"I told you. It's impossible."

"It's not impossible." Dean glanced again at the monitors.

"Dean, I need at least three hours."

"You heard the Doctor. She needs three hours."

"You can disable the card reader," Quinn admitted. "But Goodwin will know we have been attacked and open the doors via the satellite. He will also call for backup."

"Goodwin is coming at five-thirty?" Dean smiled up at Lucy. "Best news I've heard in the last hour."

Lucy raised an eyebrow, but didn't look up from the viral glass she held in her hands. Hard to imagine an object the size of a silver dollar held enough bacteria to kill thousands. Walking to an electron microscope, she slipped the glass vial underneath it and looked into the eyepiece. Etched across the edge of the glass were the code letters for the weapon—RSF32. Lucy wanted to sit down. She had been right. Guessing something in the safety of Dean's room was one thing, holding it in her hand, something else entirely.

Ricin embedded inside Spanish Flu. Thirty-two could indicate the strain or the potency, any number of things.

Removing the glass from the microscope she set it aside and picked up the next weapon. Twenty-seven to go, and the first one had taken her eight minutes to disassemble. She needed more than three hours, or she'd have to get faster.

"You sound like you have a plan, Dreiser."

"Damn straight. We let them walk right in here. And my man

Quinn will help us. Won't you, Major?"

Dean waited again in the darkness of the east corridor. He had wrapped Quinn's foot enough to slow the bleeding, then untied the bastard. He could do nothing to reduce the swelling on the right side of the man's face, but he'd been very specific with his instructions. Looking through the scope of Wilson's rifle, Dean could see Quinn following them to the letter.

He stood facing the lab where Lucy lay on the floor, out of sight, and waiting for Dean's all-clear signal. As the clock ticked from five twenty-eight to five twenty-nine, the comm unit came to life. Dean heard what he assumed was Goodwin's voice.

"Where the hell is Wilson?"

"He just stepped inside, General. He's still having, err, stomach problems."

"I'll kick his fucking ass, and he'll forget his stomach. Buzz me in."

Dean knew the real reason—Goodwin wouldn't want any record of his own ID card accessing this lab. Quinn glanced his way, then back toward the western hall. He drew himself up to proper attention.

Dean heard Goodwin and at least two others walking at a quick pace down the hall. He'd removed all weapons from Quinn's area so his primary threat came from the south. The difficult part would be taking Goodwin alive. He estimated he would have five seconds between the time he came through the double doors and when he saw the dead guards or Quinn's injuries. Five seconds was plenty of time, if he could get two clean shots. If Goodwin brought two other men and not a squad.

"The UAVs will be at the west dock in twenty minutes. Have Dominique and—"

Dean brought down the guard closest to him with a single shot.

Quinn began screaming, "He's in the east hall. He has a rifle."

The other guard with Goodwin spun around, began firing into the darkness of the east wing. The man provided an easy target since Goodwin had deserted him. Dean took him with a single shot, then held his fire, listening for any sign of Goodwin.

A single pop rang out, followed by silence.

Looking through his scope, Dean saw someone—presumably Goodwin—had put a bullet through Quinn's head.

He glanced toward Lucy to confirm she was still tucked safely beneath the lab counter. And saw Goodwin placing his eye to the ocular scan.

"Step back or I'll put a bullet where your cornea is." Dean's voice carried easily to the lab door.

"I have flooded the lab with biocontaminant. Anyone in there is dead or dying. Why don't you let me get them out?"

"Fuck you."

A metallic voice over the building's universal comm unit informed them "Emergency shutdown system has begun," and then all of the lights in the building went out. They were replaced by red pulsing strobes, an ear piercing alarm, and a countdown on every clock and computer screen in the building. It flashed two minutes, and then began its downward count.

In the second it took Dean to process what he was seeing, Goodwin slipped through the darkness and down the building's west wing. Dean ran down the hall, into the control room. He looked up and saw Lucy standing there—beautiful brown eyes staring down into his.

He could see a light mist swirling around her, and his heart broke in two. Goodwin hadn't been bluffing. What kind of bastard had a backup system to kill his own men with a deadly virus? That *was* what he had done—wasn't it? He'd killed Lucy as surely as if he'd shot her.

Dean glanced back down the west hall, calculated how much time he had, and knew he had to talk to her one last time. He started throwing switches in the control room. The countdown clock read one minute, fifty seconds. At the end of each of the three halls, steel doors lowered from the ceiling.

CHAPTER FORTY

Lucy stared at Dean through the thick bulletproof window. The timers on the monitors throughout the facility continued to countdown from two minutes, lights strobing as in some garish fire drill. Dean had, at least, found the button to silence the earsplitting alarm. Lucy glanced down at the bomb in her hands, then looked into Dean's eyes, and said the words which meant she would die alone.

"You need to go, Dean. I'm contaminated, and the lock behind you will seal in—"

Both let their gaze slide to the monitors, then back to each other.

"In ninety seconds."

"I'm not leaving you, Luce."

"Go, Dean."

Lucy forced her eyes back down, resumed working on the bomb, but not before Dean saw the edge of terror in her eyes.

"The hell I will."

When she glanced up the seconds had slipped past one minute. She made no attempt to wipe away the tears sliding down her cheeks.

"Don't do this. You can't save me." Her voice hesitated. When she continued, her words were a whisper. He pressed against the glass to better hear her, instinctively reached out his hand.

"Let me die, Dean. Knowing I saved you."

She dropped her eyes to his one last time. Held his until he knew she meant it.

The monitors slid past twenty seconds, and the steel doors inched toward the floor.

Without another word, Dean turned and fled.

Lucy forced her attention back to the bomb. Hopefully, Goodwin had flooded the lab with the same form he had dispersed over Felix Canyon. If so, the ricin would be embedded in the influenza, and she would have several hours before her coordination and mental faculties became impaired. Maybe. She'd taken a very concentrated hit. And, she didn't know what version they'd released.

Tears streamed down her face, clouding her vision and her hands trembled. She nearly dropped the glass vial she held. Cutting herself with it would put the ricin directly in her system, which would kill her in an instant.

She set the vial down and stepped away. Wrapped her arms around herself and backed up against the wall. Crouching down, she could no longer see the dead guards or Quinn's brains splattered over the control panel. She closed her eyes for a moment and blocked it out. She needed to remember something important—the reason she had come here. And the reason she had stayed.

Marcos' face came to her then. He was a taller, stronger version of herself. She would never see him again, but she could picture him for a moment, long enough to remember what she was dying for on this day. As she let her grief pour down her cheeks, the memories of her brother were replaced by more recent ones—the days and nights she had spent with Dean. He might live, if she managed to disarm all the bombs. And if she could dispose of the vials. She had twenty-six to go.

She didn't know how they had specifically modified the disease. They might have sped up its delivery system so it would kill quickly and indiscriminately. Or, they might have slowed down the incubation period so it would have a chance to contaminate a larger section of population.

Opening her eyes, she focused on the stack. If she had Dean to help her, she could have shown him how, in case she became too sick to continue. But she had sent Dean away. It had been the right thing to do, and she would not curse him for going. He couldn't have gotten in the room anyway, though knowing Dean, he would have tried to shoot his way in.

Lucy ducked her head, wiped her tears on her shoulder, then stood and walked back to the lab bench. She set to work separating the detonator from the small crystal vial which capsulated the agent. It was agonizing work. If she made a mistake with the bomb, she would explode the lab, an explosion big enough to release the agents into the air. Depending on prevailing winds and the agent's concentration, the explosion might kill everyone in Roswell, at White Sands Military Base, or possibly in Albuquerque or El Paso.

If she didn't activate the bomb, but accidentally broke the crystal, the lab would become hotter than it already was, and she might become too sick to deactivate the rest of the bombs. She had no doubt the bastards had a remote detonator set on the facility. It was imperative she disarm the bombs and destroy the vials before the detonators went off.

She forced her mind away from Dean, away from the fact she would never see her mother and daddy again. She focused on the job in front of her, until her world consisted of nothing except for the vial, the wires, and the tools in her hands.

Dean heard the doors shut behind him with a thud, separating him from Lucy, and prayed he'd made the right choice. Yes, Dean Dreiser, lapsed Presbyterian, prayed. He prayed with every ounce of his soul the bet he'd just made had saved Lucy's life, or would at least keep her from dying alone.

The area he had been in connected to the central air system, but it didn't connect to Lucy's lab. He was willing to bet no air vents went between the two rooms, which is why the bastards had been so confident about releasing their plague into the lab. There was no way to reach Lucy from the control room, except via the ocular scan—and a dead man's eye wouldn't do the trick.

How had they flooded Lucy's room with the damnable stuff? It had to have come through its separate air ventilation system. Dean now stood trapped in the building's outer ring. He couldn't get out because the concrete perimeter had sealed shut. He couldn't get into the control room because of the steel doors. He didn't want into the control room though. He wanted into the lab, and he was betting there was a way in through the cooling vents. You had to walk up to get into the lab.

He forced his mind to think logically as he ran through the building—the building now imprisoning him like a fortress. He had to find those vents, and then he had to fit into them.

He might not be able to save her, but he would be damned if he'd let her die alone.

As far as Goodwin, he wouldn't allow his mind to focus on the bastard right now. For one thing, he knew Aiden was out there—Aiden or Martin. For another thing, he had a bad feeling he hadn't seen the last of Major General Tony Goodwin. The weaponized virus was in the building, and he wanted it. He was waiting for them to die, which based on the way Goodwin had fled the building shouldn't take very long.

Lucy sat with her back against the wall, looking at the twenty-eight thin glass vials stacked one on top of another. All were separated from their detonators. They looked like slices of cucumbers her mother had once cut paper thin. As a child, she would hold them up to the light, marvel she could see through them, then sprinkle them with salt and pop them into her mouth.

Lucy let her tongue run over her lips, surprised at how swollen and cracked they felt. Her fever must have spiked over 103. The wall's coolness against her back felt divine, but she pushed herself away from its comfort. She hadn't finished her job yet.

She had to be sure this plague couldn't be released into the desert air. What if they had a remote detonator? For all she knew one of the bastards might still be alive. What if they came back after she died?

The best way to be sure would be to break the vials herself now. A pre-emptive strike. She would be dead within another few hours, anyway.

She picked up half of the vials and carried them over to a sink with an exhaust fan. She would have liked to use a slotted incubation area with minimal space for her hands, but it wouldn't allow her enough room to use the hammer. She would have to be satisfied with the sink and the exhaust fan. It hardly mattered, since she had already been infected. The sink sat a few feet to the right of the counter she had been working on and faced the control room. She supposed the doctors had liked being able to look out at what happened below, or maybe the guards had wanted to be able to watch them.

Although it was a short distance, it felt much farther. She had to rest in between trips. The last thing she needed to do was drop one of the vials and have to crawl around on the floor looking for it. Something told her once she sank to the cool tiles, she'd never get back up again. Just the thought of lying on the shiny surface made her want to curl up in a ball and sleep forever.

Finally, she had transferred all of the vials to the sink. She stood at the far right edge of the window now and had a silly image of Martha Stewart cooking for her television viewers.

"No one here but me," she whispered. "No one alive anyway."

Steadying herself with one hand on the cool wall, she picked up the small lab hammer, tried again to find the courage to smash them. She closed her eyes, although she realized it was a very childish thing to do and, oh, how her fellow doctors at MIT would laugh if they could see the great Dr. Lucinda Brown with her eyes shut like a frightened girl. She was a frightened girl, though. A scared child about to release more biological germs than any terrorist had ever released.

Biting her lip, fighting the fever and chills that had plagued her for three hours now, she raised the lab instrument again—this time with both hands, squeezed her eyes tightly shut, ignored the roaring in her ears, and willed herself to bring it down.

Dean came to another Y in the air-conditioning ducts and fought the urge to bang his head against the wall. He'd probably sustained enough brain damage in the last three hours—no need to hurry things along. Each time he stopped to check his watch, he felt the panic in him rise like a noose tightening on his throat.

He could not have said what kept him going. Desperation possibly. Hope. Maybe a very small kernel of hope lay buried somewhere in his soul. For the life of him, he couldn't imagine why.

Trying to remember the maze he'd crawled through, he chose left and continued through the duct system. He barely fit into the narrow conduit, which only slowed the painstaking crawl he'd been on since shooting his way into the HVAC closet. He'd heard no sign of Goodwin, but he expected to very soon. He'd also heard nothing of Lucy.

Looking ahead, he saw the route he'd chosen had come to an end.

"Fuck."

Now he would either have to crawl backwards or figure out a way to turn around.

Turning around wasn't even a remote possibility. He rolled onto his back for a five second break—absolutely no more than five seconds—and saw the smidgeon of light above him.

Pulling out the power screwdriver he'd liberated from the utility closet, he set to work removing the panel.

He slipped through the floor vent in time to see Lucy raise a small hammer, hesitate, then steady herself by placing her hand against the wall. Her back faced him, but he could see how the last three hours had taken their toll. She resembled a rag doll, nearly all the life torn out of her.

He almost called her name, but she again raised the hammer. Fear seized him. If he called out she would bring the hammer down on the small stack of glass pieces—which he now realized were the vials of virus.

Something in the way she closed her eyes and bit her lip told him she didn't want to do this, shouldn't do this.

Dean stepped forward, seconds before metal met glass.

Chapter Forty-One

Lucy could practically hear the glass break. She knew her death would come more quickly—ten to eleven minutes to be exact. She almost welcomed it. Almost.

Dreams die hard, though.

Dreams of life. Dreams of surviving. Dreams of Dean. A part of her heart still cried, "What if—"

She jerked as cool hands pulled her hot ones back, away from the vials, away from death.

"No, Lucy."

She spun around, seeing, but not believing, and collapsed into Dean's arms.

Dean had never claimed to be a doctor, but even he knew when someone was dying—and Lucy was dying. Her fever had spiked so high her skin radiated heat. He wanted to crawl back through the shaft and look for ice. He wanted to do anything to ease her suffering, but fear paralyzed him. She'd be dead when he got back. So he held her and waited, and he prayed some more.

He must have slept, because it took him a full five seconds to realize the bundle of coals next to him was Lucy. She struggled in his arms, tried to speak.

"How long?"

Dean checked his watch. The digital display blinked one in the afternoon. He fought through the haze in his mind to recall the day.

"You've been out three hours, Sleeping Beauty." He combed the matted hair back from her forehead, pulled her more snugly into the crook of his arm. The bed he'd made for them in the room's back corner was hardly comfortable, but Lucy didn't seem to notice.

"How long?" she repeated.

"Since we killed the bastards?"

She nodded, eyes still closed.

"Over seven hours ago. Took me four hours to find the cooling unit and crawl through it."

Lucy made a feeble attempt to smile.

"Thought you left me."

"Not a chance, Doc."

For her answer, she squeezed his hand, her hot fingers branding his.

She slept again, and Dean checked his weapon. The dose must have been lethal for Goodwin to wait this long. Why hadn't Martin or Aiden shown up yet?

She woke twenty minutes later. She couldn't raise her head any longer, or squeeze his hand.

"You might be infected now," she whispered.

"Mama told me to be careful about the kind of woman I date."

Lucy tried to smile, but it brought on a fit of coughing which left her too weak to talk. When he thought she'd fallen asleep, she plucked at his arm. He moved his ear closer to her lips. Her voice was the barest whisper, something he might be imagining.

"There's a control panel on the inside of the door. Three chances, then you can't leave." She fought the urge to cough. "Emergency interior lock—code is 2727b."

"Our room numbers at Josephine's. I knew you loved it." He brought her hand to his lips, kissed her fingers. She never knew it, though. She'd slipped back into unconsciousness.

331

Dean had understood by coming back, he'd be infecting himself, but, hell—life without Lucy wasn't worth living, anyway. And, how would he have been able to live with himself, knowing he'd left her here to die alone? It hadn't even been an option.

Just like his father had told him all those years ago. "You do what you need to, son. Figure out the rest later."

Simple enough, Dean thought, as he let his eyes close. Exhaustion claimed him. He knew he'd have to sleep. Before he allowed himself to drift off, he checked the Glock again, chambered a round, and set it across his lap.

They'd have company soon. How he knew, he couldn't say. He'd left Emily's GPS gadget at the surface, left it on Wilson. Someone should have found him by now. Of course, both sides would be tracking it, so it was anyone's guess who would find them first. He knew Goodwin hadn't gone far. He remained somewhere close, waiting for the air to clear.

Seven hours should have been more than enough time to find them, so something else had happened to slow them down. Yes, the cavalry was late. Chances were high Dean would need the Glock.

Dean woke to tapping on the bulletproof glass. He couldn't tell who stood on the other side, since they wore full biohazard suits.

Dean gripped the Glock with one hand, checked Lucy's pulse with the other. It fluttered, thready and slow, but at least he could feel it. He didn't bother to stand. He didn't trust his legs to hold him. He could see the guards fine, which is why he had taken a position against the far back wall.

"Agent, I'm Special Agent Strickland. We need to get you out of there, but, first, you must put your weapon down and slide it across the room."

Dean counted five in the room. None were faces he recognized. Even if they were, he wouldn't trust them. Not after what they'd been through.

"No fucking way." Dean coughed into the back of his hand, ignored the blood he left there.

"You know the glass is bulletproof, son. Now, put the weapon down. We'll bypass the ocular scan and come in, but not until you slide your weapon across the floor."

"And you know the crystals in front of me contain ricin and influenza that had been loaded into twenty-eight fucking bombs. In case you've forgotten what you read in my file, I'm a damn good shot. One bullet through those crystals will release all of the virus, and I don't have a lot to lose here. This room would stay hot for how many years?"

"That would be a very stupid thing to do—"

"It would be more stupid to let someone like you get your hands on it."

Strickland—if that was his real name—marched to one of his goons and said something Dean couldn't make out. The goon started out of the room.

"He stays," Dean said.

The goon stopped in his tracks.

"Should I start to feel even fractionally worse than I do right now—if I even think you've flooded this room with gas—I break the vials. Do you understand?"

Strickland's face had colored from pale to crimson in a span of three seconds.

"What do you want? From the looks of you, we can wait an hour and you'll both be dead, but honestly there are places I need to be."

"Well, at least we've cut through the bullshit."

"You USCIS field boys are all assholes."

"Glad to uphold the reputation. One, I only release the

crystals to Commander Martin or Aiden Lewis. Two, the doc and I leave together and stay together."

"You'll be dead before I can get either of those men here."

"I guess you better hurry then, because I plan on using this weapon before I breathe my last."

Strickland appeared ready to come through the glass with a tank, but of course that would destroy the vials as well. There wasn't much he could do but wait for Dean to die, which could take hours. Instead, he spoke again to his goons, never breaking eye contact with Dean.

"Jones, Gallespie. Watch this agent and inform me if his condition worsens, or should he tragically draw his last breath while I'm out of the room." The two men assumed sentry position at both ends of the glass window, their eyes not quite meeting Dean's. With a smile, Special Agent Strickland left the room.

Dean let the Glock rest in his lap. It felt like it weighed at least forty pounds.

Touching Lucy, he could no longer tell where her heat ended and his began.

"Lucy," he whispered. "Sweet, sweet Lucy. Hang on, darling."

She never answered, but he thought he saw movement under her closed eyelids. He bent his head, kissed her there, willed her to hear him in her unconscious state.

"Just a little longer, sweetie."

Then he put his hand back on the Glock and waited.

Dean's watch told him he must have slept twenty minutes. Jones, or was it Gallespie, cleared his throat before asshole Strickland stormed back into the room. If Dean didn't know better, he'd swear the private did it purposely to wake him.

Dean put his finger on the Glock's trigger. He didn't doubt for a second Stickland would rather lose the vials than lose the turf war, but orders were orders. Strickland had received his.

Dean didn't care which agency had the vials, but he wasn't sure who he could trust at this point.

"Still alive, I see."

"Sorry to disappoint you."

Strickland stepped close to the glass, his voice a bare hiss. "We could have had medical help in there an hour ago. If she dies, it's on your conscience."

"Fuck you. She'll die anyway."

"We're on the same damn side."

"Prove it."

"Open your eyes. We're wearing the same uniform."

Dean tried to laugh, but it came out as a croak. "From what I can see, you have on a biohazard suit, and I don't. Those dead guys in the corner behind you—they have on U.S. military suits too, but they're the ones who did this to Lucy. Truth is I can't tell who the good guys are anymore. If I've offended you, I'm fucking sorry. But I'd rather offend someone than put this bomb from hell into the wrong hands."

Strickland's face flamed beet-red, and Dean thought maybe the oxygen processor in his suit had stopped working.

"You know what I think? I think you're full of shit. I think you're one of those guys who talks, but there's no way you'll risk her one chance to make it out of here alive. And, make no mistake, we are her one chance—even if it's one in a thousand. So let's see how big your balls are."

He reached for something below the level of the glass, brought up a walkie-talkie unit.

"I want the lab room flooded with sleeping gas at maximum levels, repeat I want it flooded with sleeping gas at maximum level."

Dean raised the Glock, though it made every muscle in his arm scream. "I'll give you one chance to rescind that order." He pulled the slide, forced his arm steady.

"Fuck you."

"No, Strickland, fuck you."

Dean sighted in the target.

At that moment, another voice sounded in his ears.

"Everyone stand down," Martin bellowed.

The soldiers lining the room immediately lowered their weapons.

Martin stormed down the center of the room, wearing his dress uniform—and no biohazard suit.

Dean felt relief wash over him.

He released the slide, let the weapon fall into his lap.

Martin peered through the glass, looked Dean straight into his eyes. "You all right, son?"

"Yes, sir."

"Lucy still alive?"

Dean nodded. The sudden lump in his throat kept him from answering.

"Those the crystals?"

Dean wiped the sweat off his forehead with the back of his arm, though it seemed to take the strength of giants to do so. "She disarmed all twenty-eight bombs before I could get inside to help her."

"You did well, Dean. We're releasing the lock on the door and coming in now."

"You can't."

Martin seemed surprised, but he waited.

Dean waited too, trying to remember. "Interior lock. Lucy found an interior lock."

One of the men at the back of the room swore. He wore a biohazard suit like all the rest, but there was something familiar about him. Dean tried to focus, tried to clear his vision.

"Who is that?" he asked.

"Who's who?"

"At the back, against the east wall."

When Martin pivoted to look, the man went rigid and Dean knew. The bastard had balls or else he was insane.

"He's our man, Commander." Dean could barely push the words out. "It's Goodwin. He's the one behind all of this."

Goodwin stepped up when Martin signaled him forward. He stood just inches away from Dean. Unfortunately they were separated by bulletproof glass. It didn't stop Dean from wanting to murder him.

"Your man has been under a lot of pressure, Commander Martin. Let me assure you, we will find all of the men responsible for this. I promise a full investigation—"

"*He* is the man responsible. He's the one Emily Middleton met with on at least three separate occasions. Her husband Joe has proof; he was supposed to contact you. He was supposed to call Aiden."

Martin shook his head, "I've received no communication from Aiden."

"Goodwin stood in this very room at five-thirty this morning. I watched him shoot his own man." Dean's voice shook with fatigue and anger. He would not watch this man walk away again.

"Sir, if you can't talk Dreiser down, maybe we should flood the room with the sleeping gas," Goodwin said.

"How did you know my name, bastard?"

Martin's shoulders tightened, and his hand went to his service revolver.

By the time he'd removed it, two guards had flanked Goodwin.

"You're under arrest, General Goodwin. These men will escort you out."

"Are you insane? You're taking the word of a field agent over me?"

Martin never flinched. "Take him."

When they had reached the door, Martin called to the men to stop. "Goodwin, I never told anyone Dean's last name. I'm curious as to how you knew it."

Goodwin didn't answer. Martin whirled to face him.

"Perhaps you intercepted a few communications. We knew someone was reading, and in some instances, diverting, my messages. Until today, we hadn't pinned down who. Moles always rat themselves out." He nodded for the men to continue, then shifted back to Dean.

"Thank you, sir."

"We knew the man was in this room. We were hoping you could provoke him into incriminating himself."

"I'm good at provoking people, sir."

"Yes, you are."

"I would have liked to shoot him."

"We needed him alive. He can and will tell us who else was involved." Martin pulled himself up to his full stature. "How about you open the door now. We'll care flight you both to Ala-mogordo."

Martin stepped closer to the glass, locked his gaze with Dean's. "And we'll make sure you share a room, but I need you to release the lock first."

Dean nodded, placed Lucy gently down on the makeshift bed, and pulled himself up. The door seemed a mile away. He stumbled toward it. The room tilted and swayed. He grasped at a rolling table to steady himself. It gave way, fell to the floor with a crash. He tripped, nearly went with it, grabbed on to a cabinet, and pulled himself back up.

"You're almost there, Falcon."

Dean heard again the voice of his father. "Do what you need to, son. Figure out the rest later." He reached the door, stared at the panel, and tried to remember what he needed to do. He should enter something, but what? He had been so focused on keeping people out, but there was a way to let people in. If he could just remember how.

He raised his hand to wipe the sweat from his eyes, and when he did he saw the numbers he'd written there—he didn't remember doing that. 2727b. Slowly, he entered them. The first time, he got them wrong.

Lucy's voice came back to him, whispered before she slipped into unconsciousness. "Three chances then you can't leave."

Drawing a deep breath that felt like shards of glass in his lungs, he tried again. This time, when he reached the end of the sequence, he saw the light turn from red to green.

Air hissed. The lock released and the door opened, but he never saw the personnel surge through. Unconsciousness reached out its arms and claimed him. He tumbled backwards into the comfortable, black abyss.

CHAPTER FORTY-TWO

Dean stood looking out over the Flathead Valley, Montana. He wanted to shut his eyes to the boldness of the leaves falling to the ground. The roar of the water rushing down Three Forks River did little to quiet the questions in his mind. He could just make out the brightness of the first snowfall on top of Big Mountain. It all threatened to overwhelm him.

Dean Dreiser had never considered himself a sentimental guy, but he'd been at Aiden's ranch for two weeks. He still couldn't take in the view without getting teary-eyed. The US-CIS docs said it was normal to be sensitive after a near-death experience. His mom said it was part of maturing. Personally, he thought it sucked. He felt raw all over. How did people get through each day this way? Might as well walk around without any skin on his bones.

Fortunately, Aiden interrupted his introspection. Analyzing his feelings resulted in more knots and no answers.

"You ready?" Aiden slapped him on the back, then reached out to rub Dean's bald head.

"Yeah, I guess so."

"Great." Aiden moved to go.

"But . . ."

Aiden stopped, turned back to his friend.

"It haunts me, Aiden. I let Goodwin walk away."

"You did the right thing, Dean."

"But what if—"

"You did the right thing. Your partner went down, you stayed with her. Goodwin is in prison awaiting trial. He'll face a court-martial before the year ends. He's given up over two dozen names—"

"Do we know who financed him yet?"

Aiden sat down beside him, stared out over the river, and seemed to weigh his words. "You know we don't. Martin would have called you first. We will, though. The man has been in solitary for five weeks. We have the best interrogators in the world working on him. We'll get the name."

"Why would he tell us?"

"We're offering him a deal—we get every ounce of information we want. In exchange we'll seek a life sentence instead of the death penalty."

"And we will get it." Dean thought of Lucy. The ache in his chest still burned.

"There's no doubt we'll get it." Aiden stood.

"I can't believe Goodwin thought he could get rich and run the new political party that would emerge."

"He had enough evidence stored away to keep all the new power players in line—if in fact the two parties folded. Their research told them that would happen if the attacks succeeded. He's slowly telling us where he stored the encrypted files. As far as the money, we've already confirmed over twenty million dollars in various Swiss accounts."

Dean stood, thinking of the money, the power, and what they had all sacrificed. Thinking of the choices he'd made and wondering again if he'd made the right ones. "What if he'd gotten away?"

Aiden stepped closer.

They had worked together on too many ops, taken a bullet for each other more than once. Dean could trust whatever words came out of his mouth.

"He didn't, and I would tell you if you'd fucked up. You didn't."

"Right. You would."

"Everyone's in place."

Dean nodded. Everyone consisted of less than twenty people, which was the way Lucy had wanted it.

"Sunset's in fifteen minutes. We're cutting it a little close."

Dean felt the familiar lump in his throat and pushed it back down. Sunrise would have been one thing, but sunset? He could still hear her laughing voice, "Dean, all good things begin at sunset—it's like God's blessing on tomorrow, stars to wish on, you and me making love under a blanket."

He stumbled on the steps, and Aiden caught his arm. They locked eyes, and the fact his best friend didn't ask, didn't need to ask, spoke volumes of the way they knew each other and the trust they shared.

"Let's do this," Dean said.

Folding chairs were arranged around Aiden and Madison's patio, pointed where everyone could watch the sun set over the Rocky Mountains. On this evening, like many others, the sight was a wonder to behold.

Dean barely noticed the sunset.

He made his way to the front, where his father clasped his shoulder. No words passed between the two men. His mother and dad had alternated time spent beside his bed at the hospital on Hoffman Air Force Base for three weeks. They'd been through hell together. Tonight, they would close the book on this chapter in Dean's life.

Dean fumbled in the pocket of his suit for the paper where he'd written what he wanted to say. Then he remembered he'd never been able to write the words. God, how he'd tried. When it came to Lucy, what could he say? How would he manage to even speak?

The preacher stood, nodded at Dean, and a cellist—a single damn cellist played softly. Dean would have rented an entire symphony orchestra, but in this, too, Lucy was to have her way. There had been moments of lucidity in the hospital room they'd shared, and she'd been quite clear about what she wanted. "One cellist, Dean," she'd said with a smile playing across those lips he longed to kiss again. "Each time they draw their bow across the strings, it's as if my heart is being pulled."

Dean felt as if his heart would burst, but Commander Martin chose just that moment to catch his eye. Dean realized he was still a government agent. He drew a deep breath into the scarred tissues that would have to pass for his lungs and stepped next to the preacher, turned to face the crowd. He had no idea what he'd say, but it didn't matter. One look at Lucy and all thoughts tended to fly from his head anyway.

She rolled out onto the patio as all the guests stood, and Dean felt again as if he'd been punched in the gut. How was it they'd been given another chance? What sort of charmed life did this woman live? And how lucky was he to be marrying the woman of his dreams?

If Roswell had taught Lucy anything, it was life was short and never to be taken for granted. She studied Dean, standing at the end of the patio and knew she could walk those few steps. The doctors had told her to wait until spring, but she needed to be married to this man today. And, she would rather not do it in a wheelchair.

Smiling at her father, she reached up for his arm.

Her legs trembled, and she stumbled, nearly fell.

Her father caught her, steadied her, whispered in her ear, *"Es bien. Le tengo, Lucinda."*

He had been there for her the past months—both her parents had and were there for her still.

343

Tears pooled in Lucy's eyes as Madison hurried closer to her side, steadying her.

Together, the three of them covered the short distance down the aisle, and she finally raised her gaze to Dean's.

Emotion swelled in her heart for this man—pride, passion, need. All the nightmares paled when she considered even one night in his arms.

When her father placed her hand into Dean's, she knew she'd finally come home.

Though she did have to stifle a giggle at the sight of his bald head. It was one thing she hadn't quite gotten used to. Of course she had one to match, both compliments of RSF32. Hair would grow back. She felt the final rays of the setting sun on her forehead as Dean lifted her veil, and thanked God they had both lived to see this day.

"Are you okay?" He whispered.

"I am happier than I have ever been."

Leaning heavily against Dean, she turned with him to face the preacher, and he began to speak. Lucy barely noticed, she was so entranced by the sight of the sun dropping beneath mountain peaks, a cello's soft whisper of love, and God's promise of tomorrow—at least one more tomorrow.

The preacher asked, "Dean, do you have a ring?"

Dean fumbled in his pocket, then pulled out a simple gold band.

"Lucy, sweet, sweet Lucy." Tears slipped down his face, tears he didn't bother to wipe away.

Looking in this man's eyes was like drinking from a cool mountain stream. Blue eyes locked on brown ones, and it was like the first time when she'd met him in the Albuquerque airport. She knew now she'd loved him from that moment, and she'd go on loving him until the stars slipping into the night sky over his very broad shoulders ceased to shine.

"With this ring, I thee wed." Dean slid the ring on her finger, then leaned forward and kissed her, tentatively, carefully, as if she might break. Then they lost themselves in the kiss, as they so often did these days, and they didn't remember where they were until the applause and the laughter broke the moment.

Which was fine. There would be other such moments. Dean's hand over hers, Lucy promised the rest of their lives would be filled with many more.

As the ceremony ended and the reception began, they were surrounded by her family and Dean's, by the few friends they'd invited up to this sanctuary in the mountains. Lucy thought about the many times she'd been warned about love, about how risky it was. Hell, life itself was a risk. Every time you drew in a deep breath, you were taking a risk.

She spotted her brother Marcos. He looked better—physically and emotionally—than he had in years. The bio-agent he'd been exposed to had left its scars to be sure, but he'd overcome. They were a family of overcomers.

Standing beside Aiden, Marcos laughed at one of Dean's stupid jokes. Marcos understood and accepted the risks they all willingly took. This month, he'd decided to go back on active duty—as an instructor. Her parents joined Marcos, pulled Dean into a hug.

Lucy watched the scene play out and found tears again clogging her throat. She might have even succumbed to them, but she was interrupted by Madison, and her nine-month-old son, Dayton.

Madison had pushed the wheelchair closer. Lucy sank into it gratefully. She reached out to play with Dayton's toes, thankful for the distraction.

"Can you believe I let Aiden name this child?"

Lucy nodded, wiped at the tears threatening to fall. "The things we do for love."

"Half the people we meet think he's named after a race. Actually he's named after a town in Wyoming, which I'm not sure is any better. Fortunately, I get to name the girls."

Lucy raised an eyebrow. "You're planning on several?"

"I've learned not to plan when it comes to Aiden."

"Right. Wise woman." They looked toward their men—both tall, rugged, scarred by the sacrifices they'd made.

Madison reached over and took Lucy's hand, brought it to her lap and held it there with Dayton.

"You're a beautiful bride, Lucy."

Lucy touched her head and laughed. "You should have known me when I had hair."

"I will," Madison said. "I'm glad to have you here at all—hair or no hair. I know Dean and Aiden are too. We all are."

Lucy nodded. "I've told myself a thousand times what a miracle it is. Everyone in the military is given a full barrage of vaccinations. Then when you enter the bioweapons program, you're given an even more intensive course of inoculations. But to have been exposed to the lethal doses within that lab . . ."

"Do the doctor's have any explanation?" Madison pulled Dayton's toes from his mouth.

"As far as the ricin, the inoculation I had was perfectly adequate. But we haven't developed a good vaccination for the Spanish influenza yet. They think it might have been something in my family's heritage that managed to combat that version of the Spanish flu." Lucy smiled at this last part. It did seem somewhat ironic.

"So, I suppose they'll study you now?"

"I've promised blood samples as long as they need them. In exchange for my choice of partners."

Madison and Lucy laughed until Dayton decided he wanted in on the joke.

"Push me over to Dean?" Lucy asked.

"Sure thing. If you don't mind holding this guy." Madison knelt down to tuck a blanket across Lucy's lap before placing Dayton there. As she looked into her eyes, she asked the question that had been on all of their minds. "What about Dean, Lucy? How did he survive the exposure?"

"The version they planned on using in the UAVs depended on direct skin contact or inhalation as it fell from the air. What Goodwin dispersed into the room had settled by the time Dean arrived, but taking care of me must have exposed him to residual amounts. I don't understand it. He would have been inoculated for ricin, and five percent of the population is naturally immune to influenza. Or perhaps it was a miracle? He risked his life coming back for me."

Madison leaned forward and kissed her on the cheek. "Sweetheart, he would have been taking as big a risk trying to live without you."

Madison stood and pushed Lucy's chair toward Dean.

And Lucy realized they would all continue to take the risks they needed to take, pay the price required of them. They would do it for the people they cared about. So Dayton, and any other children coming into this circle, could grow up in the country they loved.

Living without love was something she wasn't courageous enough to do. The cost of love? It had always been, would continue to be, high. Gazing across into Dean's eyes, she'd wager love was worth any cost. She'd take that bet to Vegas. Or to a château in Canada, which, at this moment, sounded like a much better destination.

ABOUT THE AUTHOR

Drue Allen holds a BA and MA degree in English. She lives in the Texas hill country with her husband, cats, and a rather large herd of deer. *The Cost of Love* is her debut novel. For more information, visit www.drueallen.com.

ML

3/10